263830

DATE DUE

Magic & Malice

OTHER BOOKS BY PATRICIA C. WREDE

The Seven Towers
Sorcery and Cecelia (with Caroline Stevermer)
Snow White and Rose Red
Book of Enchantments

THE LYRA BOOKS
Shadow Magic
Daughter of Witches
The Harp of Imach Thyssel
Caught in Crystal
The Raven Ring
Shadows Over Lyra

THE CHRONICLES OF THE ENCHANTED FOREST
Dealing with Dragons
Searching for Dragons
Calling on Dragons
Talking to Dragons

MAGIC & MALICE

Mairelon the Magician
Magician's Ward

PATRICIA C. WREDE

FANTASY

MAIRELON THE MAGICIAN Copyright © 1991 by Patricia C. Wrede
    Publishing History: Tor Hardcover June 1991
MAGICIAN'S WARD Copyright © 1997 by Patricia C. Wrede
    Publishing History: Tor Hardcover December 1997

Published by arrangement with:
Tor Books
Tom Doherty Associates
175 Fifth Avenue
New York, NY 10010

Tor® is a registered trademark of Tom Doherty Associates, Inc.

Visit our website at *http://www.sfbc.com*
Visit Tor's website at *http://www.tor.com*

ISBN 1-56865-684-X

Contents

MAIRELON
THE
MAGICIAN

one

Kim walked slowly through the crowd, slipping in and out of the traffic almost without thinking. She enjoyed the noise and bustle common to all the London markets, but Hungerford was her favorite. Though it was small by comparison to Covent Garden or Leadenhall, it was very busy. Carts stood hub-to-hub along the sides of the street, leaving only narrow aisles for the customers. The more fortunate among the sellers had permanent stalls; others displayed their shoes or brooms or baskets on bare strips of pavement. Still others walked through the crowd with baskets of turnips, apples, parsnips, onions, or cress, crying their wares in unmusical voices.

Kim let the flow of traffic carry her closer to the market's most recent addition, eyeing it with a mingling of curiosity and professional appraisal. It was a wagon painted in sun-bleached yellow and gold, its tall red wheels half hidden by the stalls on either side. Two large doors made up the end of the wagon that faced the street, and they were fastened with a rusty padlock. The doors carried a rough painting of a man in a black top hat, with a string of incomprehensible but decorative letters just below him.

The wagoneer had bagged one of the best spots in the market, right between Jamie the Tailor and Red Sal's fish stand. Kim frowned. Sal was a good sort, but she wouldn't take kindly to having Kim lighten a wagon next to her. Even if "lightening" wasn't exactly what Kim planned to do. Jamie was more irritable but not so noticing. Kim's frown deepened. She wondered, not for the first time, whether she'd been wise to take this job. Toffs were trouble, no two ways, and a toff knowing enough to find Kim in the back streets of London . . .

Firmly Kim brought her mind back to the business at hand. The wagon was close enough to Red Sal's to have scraped the paint off the side of the stall, had there been any paint to scrape. Small as she was, Kim would never be able to squeeze through. She'd have to go in past Jamie's, then, and time things so he was busy with a customer. She looked at the wagon with misgiving.

A man came around the corner of the wagon and began undoing the latches at the rear. He was tall and thin and everything about him seemed to droop, from his baggy trousers to his sloping shoulders to the brim of his slouch hat. Even his mustache drooped, and as he worked he chewed absently first on one end and then the other.

The doors swung open, and Kim blinked in surprise. The entire rear end of the wagon was occupied by a tiny stage. A faded red curtain separated the back of the stage from the wagon's interior. Kim forgot her eventual goal and slid closer, fascinated. The droopy man swung a small ladder down at the right side of the stage and latched it in place, then climbed onto the stage itself. He vanished behind the curtain, only to reappear a moment later carrying a table, which he set carefully in the middle of the stage. Then he began hanging lanterns on either side.

A crowd began to collect around the end of the wagon, drawn by the curious spectacle of something being set up in the market in complete silence. Some of the bystanders offered comments as the lanterns were hung and lit—"Waste o' good oil, that," and "Bit crooked, ain't she?" The droopy man chewed on his mustache, but gave no sign that he had heard.

He finished his work and disappeared once more behind the curtain. For a long moment there was no further activity, and the small crowd murmured in disappointment. Before they could begin to drift away, there was a loud crash, and a thick cloud of white smoke enveloped the stage.

"Come one, come all!" called a ringing voice from the center of the smoke. "Prepare to be amazed and astonished by the one, the only— Mairelon the Magician!"

With the last words, the smoke dissipated. In the center of the stage stood a man. His hair was dark above a rounded face, and he had a small, neat mustache but no beard. He wore a black opera cape and a top hat, which made it difficult to assess his height; Kim judged him middling tall. His right hand held a silver-headed walking stick. "Another toff!" Kim thought with disgust. She did not for a moment believe that he was a real magician; if he were, he would never waste his time working the market. Still, she felt a twinge of uneasiness.

The man held his pose for a moment, then threw back his cape. "I am Mairelon the Magician!" he announced. "Lend me your attention and I will show you wonders. The knowledge of the East and the West is mine, and the secrets of the mysterious cults of Africa and India! Behold!"

Mairelon pulled a silk handkerchief from his pocket and displayed both sides. "A perfectly ordinary handkerchief—as ordinary, that is, as the finest silk may be. Stuff of such worth should be kept close." The crowd chuckled as he stuffed it into his closed fist and it vanished.

"Dear me, I seem to have lost it in spite of my efforts," the magician went on, opening his fist. "Now, where . . . ah!"

He reached down toward a pretty muffin-maid standing in front of the stage and pulled the handkerchief out of her bonnet. A string of colored scarves came with it, knotted end-to-end. Mairelon frowned. "Now, what am I to do with all of these?" he mused. Carefully he folded them into a compact ball and wrapped the ball in the white handkerchief. When he shook it out, the scarves were gone.

The flow of chatter continued as Mairelon borrowed a penny from a man in the crowd and made it pass through his handkerchief, then vanish and reappear. He pulled an egg from behind another man's ear, broke it into his hat, then reached into the hat and removed a live dove. He covered it briefly with his cloak, then drew the cloak aside to reveal a large wicker cage with the dove inside. He placed cage and dove on the floor of the stage and gestured with his walking stick, and they vanished in a puff of smoke and flame. He showed the crowd a shallow bowl and had one of the barrow boys fill it with water, then dropped a sheet of paper in and pulled out ten tiny Chinese lanterns made of folded paper.

Kim watched the show with unabashed enjoyment. Near the end, the droopy man reappeared, carrying an ancient tambourine. As Mairelon finished his performance, his companion circulated among the crowd, collecting pennies and shillings from the onlookers.

Reluctantly Kim pulled her mind away from the fascinating sight of Mairelon the Magician juggling eggs that, as they passed between his agile fingers, changed from white to red to blue to yellow in rapid succession. This was the first time both men had been outside at once, and she had to know how long the wagon would be empty.

She started singing "Darlin' Jenny" in her head to mark the time, and scowled in irritation. Her dislike for this job was growing stronger

every minute. Nicking a purse or pocket watch from the swells in the
High Street had never bothered her, but she'd always hated working the
markets. Hungerford was the nearest she'd had to a home since old
Mother Tibb dangled from the nubbing cheat, and even if all she had to
do this time was a bit of snooping, it felt the same as nabbing a haddock
from Red Sal's stand when her back was turned. Kim contemplated conveniently forgetting to return to the public house where the toff had
arranged to meet her, but the memory of the pound notes the stranger
had offered held her like an iron chain.

Five pounds was a fortune by Kim's standards; she could eat well
and sleep dry for months and still have enough left to replace the ragged
jacket and boy's breeches she wore. If she played her cards right, she
might even get out of the streets for good. It was time and past that she
did so, she was, she thought, nearing seventeen, and her long-delayed
growth was finally arriving. She wouldn't be able to play the boy much
longer. A chill ran down her spine, and she pushed the thought, and the
darker knowledge of the inevitable consequences that would follow the
end of her masquerade, resolutely from her mind. Mairelon the Magician
was, for the moment at least, of far greater importance than her own
uncertain future.

Mairelon finished his show in a flurry of flashing knives and whirling
scarves, and bowed deeply. "Thank you for your attention—and for your
gracious contributions." He waved at the tambourine his dour assistant
carried, and the crowd chuckled. "That concludes this performance, but
soon Mairelon the Magician will return to perform even more wondrous
feats for your delight and astonishment! Until then, my friends!" In a
second puff of smoke and flame, the magician vanished.

Kim stopped midway through the eighth verse of "Darlin' Jenny"
and slipped away as the crowd began to disperse. She did not want Sal
or Jamie spotting her and remembering it later. Once she was safely away
from Mairelon's wagon, she breathed more easily. She couldn't do anything about the magician until the end of his next show. She had time,
now, to enjoy the market.

She stopped an ancient woman in a faded kerchief and exchanged
one of her carefully hoarded pennies for a bag of roasted chestnuts. She
ate them slowly as she walked, savoring the taste. The unaccustomed
warmth in her stomach made her feel more cheerful, though she still
wasn't too keen on the idea of mucking about in Mairelon's wagon. For
one thing, she didn't like the look of the skinny toff who'd hired her.

Unconsciously she flexed her fingers, making the bag rustle. Five pounds would buy a lot more than chestnuts. The skinny toff hadn't asked her to nick anything, she reminded herself, just to look around and tell him what she saw and whether the magician kept a particular bowl in his wagon. The toff had claimed it was a bet. He might even be telling the truth; swells'd bet on anything.

She stepped aside to let an oyster-seller push his barrow past. It didn't feel right. The gentry cove had been too keen on her finding that bowl. He'd gotten positively excited when he started describing it—silver, he'd said, with a lot of carvings and patterns whose details Kim had seen no reason to bother remembering.

Kim frowned. Curiosity was her besetting weakness. And five pounds was five pounds. It wasn't as if she'd be doing any harm. She finished the last of the chestnuts and stuffed the bag into one of her many pockets, in case she found a use for it later. She'd do it just the way the toff had asked: go in, look around, and slip out. Mairelon would never know anyone had been there.

And if she did happen to find that bowl, maybe she'd see what was so special about it. But she wouldn't mention it to the skinny toff. She'd collect her money and leave. She might even come back and warn Mairelon about the swell that was showing so much interest. Market folk should stick together, after all. She smiled to herself; that'd serve the skinny toff a bit of his own soup! Whistling cheerfully, she strolled off to see if the puppet show was still stopping at the far end of the market.

Evening found her lurking near Mairelon's wagon once more. This time she stood in the shadows next to Jamie's stall, leaning on one of its support posts. As the crowd grew larger, she let herself be pushed back until the open rear door of the wagon, which formed one side of Mairelon's stage, all but hid the performance from her sight.

Mairelon was as good as his word. He did not, as far as Kim could tell, repeat any of the tricks he had used in his earlier performance. This time, he made three unbroken silver rings pass through each other, locking and interlocking them in intricate patterns. He bought an apple from a passing vendor and cut it open to reveal a shilling at its core. The apple seller was promptly surrounded by hopeful customers, but his remaining wares proved disappointingly ordinary.

Meanwhile, the magician went smoothly on with his act. He borrowed a hat from one of the men in the crowd, boiled an egg in it, and returned the hat to its owner unharmed. Then he brought out a pack of playing cards and ran through a series of increasingly elaborate tricks.

Kim was so enthralled by the show that she almost missed seeing a small door open near the front of the wagon. The jingling noise of the tambourine caught her attention at last. Hastily she mashed herself flat against the side of Jamie's stall, holding one ragged sleeve up to obscure her face. Mairelon's droopy henchman glanced in her direction as he passed, but his eyes moved on once her dirty and impecunious appearance sank in.

As soon as the man had been absorbed into the audience, Kim darted for the wagon door, hoping Mairelon's show and the growing shadows would keep her from being noticed. Her luck held; no shouts followed her down the narrow aisle, and when she reached it, the door was unlocked. Kim pushed it open and half jumped, half fell into the wagon's interior, the first chorus of "Darlin' Jenny" echoing through her mind.

She paused briefly to get her breath back and look around. Once again, she found herself staring in surprise. The wagon's interior was paneled in dark wood, polished to a high gloss. Rows of cupboards ran down one side, topped by a shelf of smooth grey tile. A long chest was built into the other wall, from the neat roll of blankets at one end, Kim guessed that it doubled as a bed. Presumably the droopy man slept on the floor, or perhaps under the wagon, for she saw no sign of a second bed.

A small lamp, which Kim decided had to be pewter because it could not possibly be silver, hung near the door. Its light threw back rich highlights from the walls and cupboard doors. A wool carpet, deep red with strange designs in black and cream, covered the floor. Kim had never been anywhere half so elegant in her entire life; even the back room of Gentleman Jerry's was nothing to it.

The faded curtain at the far end of the wagon swayed as Mairelon crossed his little stage. Kim came out of her daze as she realized that the curtain was all that separated her from discovery. She could hear the magician's patter quite clearly. He would be able to hear her just as easily, should she be clumsy or careless.

Kim glanced around the wagon again, painfully aware of the need for haste. She had wasted nearly a whole verse in her musing. The cupboards were the most likely place to start. She stepped forward, like a cat stalking a particularly suspicious mouse, and opened the first door.

The cupboard was filled with dishes. Three mismatched plates and a shallow ceramic soup bowl occupied the lowest shelf; a row of china teacups hung from hooks on the bottom of the shelf above. The upper part of the cupboard contained a neat stack of copper pans, iron pots, and assorted lids. Kim took long enough to make sure there was nothing hidden in or behind any of them, then went on. Her hasty search revealed nothing of any interest in the remaining cupboards, and she turned to the long chest.

The lid did not respond to her careful tug. Closer inspection revealed a hidden lock. Kim hesitated. She had nearly three full verses of "Darlin' Jenny" left, even if she allowed herself all of the last one as a safety margin. And the skinny toff would hardly be pleased if all she had to tell him was that Mairelon the Magician kept pots in his cupboards and his chest locked. Her lips tightened, and she reached into her pocket for the stiff bit of wire she always carried.

The lock was a good one, and the overhanging wood that concealed it made her work more difficult. Two more verses of "Darlin' Jenny" went by while she twisted the wire back and forth, coaxing the tumblers into position. She was about to abandon her efforts when she heard a faint click and the lid of the chest popped up a quarter of an inch.

Kim straightened in relief and pocketed the wire. She took hold of the chest's lid and lifted, forcing herself to move slowly in case the hinges squealed. Then she held it in position with one hand and bent over to peer inside.

Piles of brightly colored silks met her eyes. Beside them were slotted wooden boxes, a bundle of tiny Chinese lanterns, several mirrors, a glass tube with a painted paper cover, a top hat, and several decks of playing cards, all arranged neatly and precisely according to some order Kim could not fathom. A few she recognized as props from Mairelon's first show; none of them looked at all like the bowl the gentry cove had gone on about. As she started to close the lid, she saw a swatch of black velvet sticking out from under a stack of neatly folded silk handkerchiefs. One last try, she thought, and brushed the silks aside.

Her hand closed on something hard and heavy, wrapped in velvet. Then there was a violent, soundless explosion and Kim was flung backward against the cupboards on the other side of the wagon. Through a haze of violet light, she saw the lid of the trunk slowly close itself. Purple spots danced before her eyes, then spread out to cover her entire field of vision. Her last coherent thought, as the purple deepened into black unconsciousness, was an angry curse directed at the toff waiting for her in the public house. Five pounds wasn't anywhere near enough pay for snooping on a *real* magician.

two

Kim awoke all at once. She was propped against something hard, in a semi-sitting position, and she could feel cord around her wrists and ankles. She heard voices above her and forced herself to be still, feigning unconsciousness. This was not, apparently, expected; after a moment, she heard a worried voice say, " 'Adn't 'e oughter be waking?"

"He is awake," said the voice of Mairelon the Magician. "He's just pretending. Come on, child, you might as well admit it. You'll have to open your eyes sooner or later."

Kim sighed and capitulated. She gave a hasty look around as she opened her eyes, in the faint hope of discovering a way out of her predicament. She was propped against the row of cupboards; one of the doors was open, presumably jarred free when she had been thrown against them. The cord that tied her looked regrettably sturdy, and the knots were unfamiliar tangles. After one glance, she abandoned any thought of slipping free while her captors' attention was elsewhere.

"Quite so," said Mairelon.

Kim looked up. Mairelon was standing next to the chest, on the opposite side of the wagon. He had removed his cloak and hat; without them, he seemed both shorter and younger than he had appeared on stage. His expression held none of the anger and annoyance Kim expected; instead, there was a gleam of something very like interest or amusement. She began to hope she would come around from this, after all.

Beside Mairelon stood the droopy man. He, too, had removed his hat, and his grey and black hair was plastered flat against his head. He alternated sour glares at Kim with nervous looks directed at Mairelon, and he was chewing continuously on one end of his mustache.

Kim looked back at Mairelon. "Proper knowin' one, ain't you?" she said in her best boyish tone.

"As far as you are concerned, not nearly so knowing as I would like to be," Mairelon replied affably.

"You going to call the nabbing culls?"

"That depends on how much you are willing to tell me."

"I got no reason to keep quiet," Kim said frankly. If the toff who'd hired her had been more open, she might have felt some obligation to keep her mouth shut, but not even an out-and-outer would expect her to protect an employer who'd withheld crucial knowledge about a job. Especially when she hadn't been too keen on it in the first place.

"Then perhaps you would explain just what you were doing in my wagon," Mairelon said.

"Lookin' about," Kim said promptly.

The droopy man snorted through the damp ends of his mustache. "Stealing, more likely."

"Quiet, Hunch," Mairelon said. He looked from Kim to the open cupboard with a speculative gleam. "Just looking?"

"That's right," Kim said firmly. "Just lookin' about."

The magician's eyes narrowed, and Kim wondered whether her reply had been too forceful for the boy she was pretending to be. It was too late to change it now, though.

"That accounts for the cupboards, I think," Mairelon said after a moment. "How did you—"

"You don't never believe 'im, do you?" the droopy man demanded.

"Hunch! Refrain from interrupting, if you please."

"And let you get yourself in a mort o' trouble from believing things you 'adn't ought to?" Hunch said indignantly. "I won't never!"

Mairelon gave his henchman an exasperated look. "Then you can go outside until I'm done."

Hunch's face took on a grim expression. "Nay."

"It's that or be silent."

The two men's eyes locked briefly; Hunch's fell. "Aye, then, I'll 'old my peace."

"Good." Mairelon turned back to Kim, who had been watching this exchange with great interest. "As I was saying, I think you've explained the cupboards. The chest is another matter. How did you open it?"

"Picked the lock."

"I find that a little difficult to believe. It's not a simple mechanism."

"Didn't have to be," Kim said, allowing herself to bristle at the implied reflection on her skill.

Mairelon raised an eyebrow. "Well, we'll leave that for the moment. Just *why* were you, er, looking about in my wagon?"

"A gentry cove at the Dog and Bull said he'd pay five pounds to know what you had in here. Said he had a bet on it."

"Did he." Mairelon and Hunch exchanged glances.

"He thought he'd gammoned me proper," Kim said. She took a perverse pleasure in betraying the toff who'd gotten her into this. "But if it was just a bet, why'd he let me talk him up to five pounds? And why was he so nattered over that wicher-bubber?"

"Wicher-bubber?" Mairelon said, looking startled, and not altogether pleased. "You mean a silver bowl?"

"That's what I said. The toff wanted me to look for it."

"Did he ask you to steal it?" Mairelon demanded, his expression tense.

"No, but I ain't saying he wouldn't of been right pleased if I'd a nicked it for him."

"There!" Hunch said. "What was I telling you? 'E's a thief."

"Look, cully, if I was a sharper, would I be telling you straight out?" Kim said, exasperated. "All I said was, I'd keep an eye out for it, and that's truth!"

"So all you agreed to do was come in, look around, and let him know whether you saw this bowl?" Mairelon said.

"That's it," Kim said. Hunch snorted, and she glared at him. "There wouldn't be no harm done, after all; just lookin' about. But he ought to of said somethin' about you being a real magician with fancy locks and exploding chests."

"What did this toff of yours look like?"

"A real swell. Top hat, and gloves better'n the ones Jamie sells, and a silk cravat." Kim shook her head in wonder that was only partly simulated. "A top hat, at the Dog and Bull."

"What color was his hair?"

"Muddy. Thin, too."

"His hair or himself?"

"Both."

Mairelon nodded, as if he had expected that answer. "And did he give you something to make it easier for you to get in here? And into my chest?"

"No, and I wouldn't of took it if he'd offered. I ain't no flat."

"Then suppose you show me how you managed it," Mairelon said.

Kim nodded, and the magician reached for the rope that bound her hands. Hunch made a strangling noise. Mairelon paused and looked at him with an expression of innocent inquiry.

"You're never letting 'im go?" Hunch said, plainly appalled by the idea. "You got no idea what 'e's up to!"

"I think the two of us can handle her."

Hunch bit down hard on the right side of his mustache. " 'Er?"

"Oh, you didn't realize?" Mairelon said. He turned back to Kim while Hunch was still gaping mutely, and gave one of the loops of cord a sharp tug. The knot slid apart as though someone had greased the rope, leaving Kim's hands free. She blinked, then darted a hand forward and yanked on the cord that held her ankles.

Nothing happened. "There's a trick to it, of course," Mairelon said blandly. "I'll show you, if you like, when you've finished your own demonstration."

Kim looked up in disbelief. Mairelon was smiling in what appeared to be genuine amusement. "You will?"

"Yes. When you're finished," he added pointedly. Hunch scowled ferociously at his master's back, but did not dare voice any more criticism.

"All right, all right," Kim said. She reached into her pocket, pulled out the bit of wire, and set to work. She was fairly sure by this time that the magician would not turn her over to the constables, but instead of reassuring her, the knowledge made her even more uneasy. Why did he hesitate?

She watched Mairelon surreptitiously as she wiggled the wire. He didn't look particularly impressive, but he was no flat, that was certain. He was no ordinary street magician, either, not with the inside of his wagon done up like a gentry ken. Not to mention that thing in the chest that had blown Kim halfway across the room.

The memory slowed her fingers. True, she'd actually been poking around in the chest when the spell or whatever it was had gone off, but Mairelon could easily have changed it while she was unconscious. She had no desire to repeat the performance.

Hunch shifted impatiently. "She ain't going to get it, not with just that bit o' wire."

"Give over," Kim snarled, and twisted her wrist. Again she heard the faint click, and the lid of the chest rose fractionally. Kim lifted it open and looked triumphantly at Hunch.

"Impressive," Mairelon said. He looked at Kim thoughtfully, and the gleam of interest was back. "I didn't think anyone but old Schapp-Mussener himself could open that chest without the key."

"It's a knack," Kim said modestly.

"It's a talent, and a very impressive talent, too." The gleam became more pronounced. "I don't suppose—"

"Master Richard!" Hunch interrupted.

"Mmmm?"

"You ain't a-going to do nothing dreadful now, are you?" Hunch said in a severe tone.

"No, no, of course not," Mairelon said absently, still looking at Kim.

"Good," Hunch said, much relieved.

"I was just going to ask our guest here—what is your name, by the way?"

"Kim."

"Kim. I was just going to ask Kim here if she would like to come with us when we leave London."

Hunch bit both ends of his mustache at once. "You ain't never going to bring her along!"

"Why not?" Mairelon said in a reasonable tone. "It might be useful to have someone along who's familiar with . . . things. A lot has happened in the past four years."

"You want me to come with you, after I snuck in here and blew things around?" Kim said incredulously. "You're bosky!"

Hunch started to nod agreement, then caught himself and glared at Kim. "You can't do it, Master Richard! She's a thief!"

"I ain't!"

"Stop it, both of you." Mairelon's voice was firm. He looked at Hunch. "I don't think Kim is a thief, though it's plain that she's had some of the training. Not that it matters."

"It do too matter! What are you going to do with 'er?"

"She could help with the act," Mairelon said. "She seems a handy sort of person."

Hunch snorted. "Ain't that what you said about that Frog 'oo sherried off with ten guineas and your best coat?"

"Yes, well, he was a little too handy. I think Kim will do much better."

"At what?"

"She could make a very useful assistant eventually. Provided, of course, that she would be willing to come along?" Mairelon looked questioningly at Kim.

"You ain't gammoning me?" Kim said suspiciously.

"No."

The single word was more convincing than Mairelon's speeches had been, but Kim still hesitated. What did he expect to get out of hauling her along with him? From the luxurious interior of the wagon, it was plain that Mairelon could afford the company of the best of the fashionable impures, if what he wanted was a doxy. He had no reason to pick a grubby imitation boy out of the market instead. And he wasn't the sort who *preferred* boys; Kim had learned long ago to spot and avoid them. So what *did* he want?

"You ain't unfastened me yet," she pointed out at last.

"An oversight." Mairelon bent and tugged at the cord that fastened Kim's ankles. Again the rope slid apart, and Mairelon straightened with a flourish. "Now, what do you say?"

"You'd really show me how to do that?" Kim asked, her mind whirling. If she could learn a few of Mairelon's tricks, she might be able to get steady work at one of the Covent Garden theaters—real work, the sort that required more than a low-cut dress and a willingness to do whatever might be asked. She could earn enough to eat regular and sleep warm without looking over her shoulder for watchmen or constables or Bow Street Runners; she could stop being afraid of Dan Laverham and his like; she could—she forced herself to cut that train of thought short, before the hope grew too strong, and waited for Mairelon's answer.

"That and quite a bit more," Mairelon said. "How else could you be any help in the act?"

"She don't look like she'll be much 'elp anyways," Hunch muttered. "Nobody's a-going to pay to watch a grimy little thief."

"Call me that once more, cully, and—"

"Enough." Mairelon's voice was quiet, but Kim found herself swallowing her words faster than she ever had for Mother Tibb's angry screeching. "Stop provoking her, Hunch."

"If you can't see what's under your nose—"

"Oh, she doesn't look like much now, but I think you'll be surprised at how well she cleans up."

"I ain't said I'm coming with you yet!" Kim said crossly.

"And you haven't said you're not, either," Mairelon replied. "Come, now; make your decision. I have things to do if you aren't."

"Huh." Kim was unimpressed. "I ain't wishful to get into no trouble with the nabbing culls. What's your lay?"

Mairelon smiled. "I'm a traveling magician. I play the markets and fairs."

"Give over! I told you, I ain't no flat. Folks that can do real magic don't waste time flashing tricks at the markets. And you ain't got yourself no wagon done up like a gentry ken that way, neither."

"That's my affair. I'll give you my word that we're doing nothing illegal; if you've other questions, you'll have to wait for answers. After all, we don't know you very well yet."

"No, nor want to," Hunch said under his breath.

Kim frowned at him automatically, but her mind was busy elsewhere. She'd never get a chance like this again, she was certain. Risking Mairelon's unknown objectives was a small price to pay for the promise of a few days' worth of regular meals and a safe place to sleep, even without the promise of tutoring. Add in the possibility of learning something that would free her from the perilous hand-to-mouth world of the London slums and Mairelon's proposal was well-nigh irresistible, especially since she'd probably never find out what the magician was really doing or what was so important about that bowl if she didn't go along. And if she didn't like it, she could always tip them the double and come back to London. She'd be no worse off than she was now.

"Well?" Mairelon asked.

"All right, then," Kim said. "I'll do it."

Hunch groaned.

"Good!" Mairelon said, ignoring Hunch. "We'll see the tailor tomorrow about getting you some clothes. We won't be long in London, so I'm afraid there won't be many of them."

"Sounds bang-up to me," Kim said. It took most of her will to sound moderately pleased instead of all but stunned speechless. Clothes from a tailor? For her?

"She'll run off as soon as she's got everything she can off you," Hunch prophesied gloomily.

Kim started to protest, but Mairelon's voice overrode her. "Hunch, if you don't stop trying to pick out a quarrel with Kim, I shall be forced to leave you in London."

"You wouldn't never!" Hunch said.

"No?"

Hunch muttered something under his breath and stomped to the far end of the wagon. Mairelon looked after him and shook his head. "He'll come around, never fear. You've nothing to worry about."

"Ain't you forgetting something?" Kim said.

"What?"

"That skinny toff down at the Dog and Bull, that sent me in here lookin'. What're you going to do about *him*?"

"I think he ought to get what he's paying for," Mairelon said after due consideration. "Don't you agree?"

Kim thought of the underhanded way the skinny toff had held back information to keep the price down. "No."

"Yes, he certainly should," Mairelon said, as though he hadn't heard Kim. "I think you should go back to that place you mentioned—what was the name again?"

"The Dog and Bull."

"Of course. I think you should go back and collect your five pounds." He paused and smiled at Kim. "What do you say?"

three

Kim darted across a street directly in front of a hackney, causing the horses to shy. The driver's curses followed her as she slipped into the pedestrian traffic on the other side, but she paid no attention. She was late for her appointment, and she didn't know how long the skinny toff would wait.

Not that she was particularly anxious to see him again, five pounds or not. She still wasn't sure how she'd been talked into this. Maybe it was because Hunch had been so set against it; knowing how much he disliked the idea, she couldn't resist going ahead with it. Or maybe it was Mairelon's persuasiveness. The man made it all sound so *reasonable*, and he knew just how to appeal to Kim's curiosity.

That, of course, was the root of the problem. Kim dodged a lamp-lighter, ducking under the end of his ladder. Someday she was going to get into real trouble if she didn't stop poking her nose into things just to find out what they looked like.

Still castigating herself, Kim turned down the crooked lane that led to the Dog and Bull. Here the traffic was less, and she made better time. When she saw the cracked sign with its garish painting, she broke into a run, and a moment later she was inside. She stepped to one side of the door and paused, panting, to survey the room.

It was a moment before her eyes adjusted to the gloom. Though the single window was large, half or more of its panes had been broken and stuffed with paper, and those that remained were dark with dirt. What light there was came from the fire in the huge, blackened hearth, and it did not penetrate far into the smoke and steam that filled the air.

Three long, bare tables occupied the center of the room. The backless benches on either side were half full of large men in well-worn clothes. Most were hunched over mugs of beer; some were eating with single-minded intensity from an assortment of battered bowls. There was no sign of the toff anywhere.

Kim frowned. Had she missed him, then? There was no way of telling. She decided to take the chance that he, too, was late, and made her way to one of the tables. She squeezed herself into a corner where she could watch the door, ordered a half-pint of ale, and settled in to wait.

The procession of customers entering the room was not exactly encouraging. Most were working-class men identifiable by their clothes—carters, bricklayers, a butcher, one or two costermongers, a sawyer. A nondescript man in a shabby coat slouched in and crept to the far corner of the table as if he expected to be thrown out. Kim sipped at her ale, wondering unhappily whether she should risk attracting attention by asking questions.

The door opened again, and another collection of solid men in rough-spun wool and grimy linen entered. In their wake came a tall man made even taller by his top hat. He wore a voluminous cape that made it impossible to tell whether he was fat or slim, but the white-gloved hand pressing a handkerchief to his lips was impossible to mistake. Famble-cheats and a top hat, Kim thought disgustedly, in a place like this. He was the one she was waiting for, all right. She straightened, trying to look taller so that he would see her.

The toff surveyed the room disdainfully, then made his way among the tables and stopped beside Kim. "I trust your presence means you have succeeded, boy," he said.

"I done what you asked," Kim said.

"Good. I suggest we conduct the remainder of our business in one of the private rooms in back."

"You want everyone here knowin' you got business with me?" Kim asked without moving.

The toff's face darkened in anger, but after a moment he shook his head. "No, I suppose not."

"Then you'd better set down afore everyone here ends up lookin' at you," Kim advised.

The man's lips pressed together, but he recognized the wisdom of Kim's statement. He seated himself on the bench across from her, setting his hat carefully on the table. The publican, a fat man in a dirty apron,

came over at once, and the toff accepted, with some reluctance, a mug
of beer. As the publican left, the toff leaned forward. "You said you'd
done as I asked. You found the bowl, then? You have a list of what is in
Mairelon's wagon?"

"What would the likes of me be doing makin' lists?" Kim said sarcastically.

The man looked startled. "I had anticipated—"

"You wanted a list, you should of hired a schoolmaster," Kim informed him. "I can tell you what I saw in that magic-cove's wagon, but
that's all."

The man's eyes narrowed. "In that case, perhaps five pounds is more
than the information is worth to me."

"In that case, you ain't getting no information at all," Kim said,
mimicking his tone.

"Come, now, I think you are unreasonable. Shall we say, three
pounds?"

Kim spat. "I done what you said, and you never said nothing about
no list. Five pounds and that's flat."

"Oh, very well. Did you find the bowl?"

"I ain't saying nothin' until I get what you promised."

The toff argued, but Kim remained firm. Eventually he agreed, and
unwillingly counted out the five pounds in notes and coin. Kim made a
show of re-counting it, her fingers lingering over each coin in spite of
herself. She had never had so much money at once in all her life, and
every silver shilling and half crown meant another day or week of food
and possible safety. She stowed the money safely in the inner pockets of
her jacket, feeling highly pleased with both herself and Mairelon. If it
hadn't been for the magician's urging, she might have passed up an easy
mark.

"Satisfied?" the man said angrily. "All right, then, tell me what you
found."

Kim smiled inwardly and launched into a detailed and exhaustive
description of the interior of the magician's wagon. She noticed the anticipation on her listener's face when she talked of the pots and pans in
Mairelon's cupboard, and carefully saved the information that they were
all made of iron for the end of the sentence. She got a perverse satisfaction
out of seeing the flash of disappointment on the toff's face.

The man got more and more impatient as she went along. Finally
she mentioned the locked chest. The toff sat up. "Locked?"

"Yes." Kim paused. "But I got in."

The man leaned forward eagerly. "And?"

"It looked like that's where the cove kept his magics. There were a whole bunch of little paper lanterns, and a couple of them little wooden boxes, and a stack of silk—"

"Yes, yes, boy, but the bowl!"

"Bowl?" Kim said, feigning innocence.

"The silver bowl I described to you! Did you find it?"

"I didn't see nothin' like that in Mairelon's wagon," Kim said with perfect truth.

"What!" The toff's voice was loud enough to make heads turn all along the table. He controlled himself with effort, and when the other customers had turned away, he glared at Kim. "You said you'd do as I asked!"

"And so I have," Kim retorted, unperturbed. "Ain't nobody could of found somethin' that ain't never been there."

"Not there?" The man sounded stupefied.

"Use your head, cully," Kim advised. "If this Mairelon swell had something like that, I would of seen it, wouldn't I? And I ain't. So it ain't there."

"You're certain?"

Kim nodded.

The toff glared as though it were her fault. "Not there," he muttered. "All this time, wasted on the wrong man. Amelia will never let me hear the end of it. Merrill could be anywhere in England by now, anywhere!"

"That ain't my lookout," Kim pointed out. "You want to hear what else he had, or not?"

"And you," the toff went on in a venomous whisper, "you knew. That's why you made me give you your money in advance, isn't it? You little cheat!"

On the last word, he lunged across the table. The sudden movement took Kim completely by surprise. He would have had his hands at her throat if a grimy, disreputable-looking man had not half lurched, half fallen against the toff's back at that moment.

The unexpected shove knocked the toff heavily into the edge of the table, Kim heard his grunt of pain plainly. She stood and backed away a little, watching with interest. She recognized the grimy man now; he had come into the public house just before the toff's arrival.

The grimy man was the first to recover. "Sh-shorry, very shorry," he said. "The floor jusht, jusht shook me over, thash all." He waved a hand to demonstrate, and lost his balance again.

"Get away from me, you idiot!" the toff snarled.

"Right. Very shorry." The drunk made ineffectual apologetic motions in the toff's direction. Since he was still draped halfway over the toff's shoulder, this succeeded only in knocking over the almost untouched mug of beer in front of them. A wave of brown foam surged across the table, picking up dirt and grease as it went.

The toff made a valiant effort to spring back out of the way, but with the drunk still leaning helpfully across his shoulder, he didn't have a chance. The pool of cool, dirty beer swished into his lap, thoroughly drenching his previously immaculate attire. The taproom exploded in laughter.

The drunk began a tearful apology, which was more a lament for the wasted beer than anything else. Cursing, the toff shoved him aside. He began wiping vainly at his clothes with a pocket handkerchief while the publican escorted the drunk firmly to the door. Kim judged it a good moment for her own departure and slipped quietly out in the drunk's wake. Her last sight was of the toff, gingerly picking his dripping top hat out of the pool of beer.

Still chuckling, Kim paused in the lane outside. It was now fully dark, and a yellow fog was rising. Not the best time for running about the London streets, even for as ragged a waif as Kim looked. Still, she hadn't much choice. She swallowed hard, thinking of the coins in her pockets. If she lost them, she'd have nothing to fall back on if her arrangement with Mairelon fell apart. She started off, hugging the edge of the lane.

As she passed the corner of the Dog and Bull, a pair of dirty, beer-scented hands grabbed her. One clamped itself over her mouth; the other pinned her arms. Kim threw herself forward, but the man was too strong. She was dragged quickly and quietly into a filthy alley beside the public house.

She kicked backward, hard, and connected. The man made no sound, but his grip loosened, and Kim wrenched one arm free. She bit down on the hand covering her mouth and felt her captor jerk. Then she heard a whisper almost directly in her ear. "Kim! Stop it! It's Mairelon."

Without thinking, Kim struck at the voice with her free hand. Then the words penetrated, and she hesitated. She couldn't imagine what Mairelon might be doing in this part of town, but magicians were a queer lot, and she'd already decided that Mairelon was one of the queerest of them all. And who else would expect that name to have any weight with her?

"It really is me, unlikely as it seems," the whisper said. "If I let go, you won't make a sound until you're sure, will you? Nod if you agree."

Kim nodded, and the hands released their hold. She turned and found herself confronting the drunk who had caused so much trouble a few minutes before. He no longer seemed drunk in the least, though he still looked and smelled thoroughly unpleasant.

Kim took a step backward. The man raised a warning hand and she stopped, peering at him. He was the right height for Mairelon, but he had no mustache and his face was half hidden by a layer of greasy dirt. Then he grinned, and Kim's doubts vanished. Impossible as it seemed, this *was* Mairelon.

She smiled back and he doffed his grimy cap and bowed with a stage magician's flourish. She opened her mouth to ask what he was doing, and at once he held up a warning finger. She stepped closer, wondering even more what was behind his strange behavior.

The creak of the public house door swinging open filtered into the alley. Mairelon flattened himself into a niche along one wall and motioned to Kim to do the same. She complied, still puzzled. Then she heard the skinny toff's unmistakable whine.

"—don't expect such treatment! You haven't heard the end of this!"

"Mebbe," the gravelly voice of the publican said. "And mebbe not. Evenin'."

Kim heard the door shut, then the toff muttering curses under his breath. A moment later came the incongruous sound of a small silver bell, ringing.

A large shadow passed the mouth of the alley. "There you are, Stuggs!" the toff said pettishly. "Did you catch the boy?"

"I ain't seen 'im," said a deep, slow voice.

"Not seen him? But he left just a few minutes ago."

"I ain't seen 'im," the second voice reiterated patiently.

"You fool! He must have gone the other way."

"Couldn't 'ave. Street's blocked."

"Then he slipped by you in the dark. Idiot! Nothing has gone right tonight, simply nothing! We've spent five days tracing the wrong man, my clothes are ruined, and on top of everything else you let the boy escape!"

"I never seen 'im. If I'd seen 'im, I'd a catched 'im."

"Oh, well. Under the circumstances, it hardly matters. But if it *had* been Merrill's wagon, we would have needed the boy. You're lucky."

Something in the man's voice made Kim shrink back against the wall of the building, trying to become one with the bricks and half-timbering. Why were they so interested in her? Surely five pounds wasn't worth such trouble to a swell!

"You want I should look for 'im?" Stuggs's deep voice said, and Kim held her breath.

"Weren't you listening? There's no need, he didn't find anything. And I'm not going to stand here smelling like a brewery while you blunder about. Come on."

Footsteps clicked against the cobblestones, passing the end of the alley. Gradually they died away, but Kim did not move until she heard the distant rattle of carriage wheels. Then she looked across at Mairelon.

The magician motioned to her and started off, but instead of heading back out to the lane, he went farther into the alley. Kim followed with some trepidation. The cramped maze of garbage-strewn alleys that twisted through the spaces between the main streets was no place for anyone who didn't know where he was going.

Mairelon, however, chose his course without hesitation, and in a few minutes they emerged on a side street two blocks from the Dog and Bull. "You can talk now," he said.

four

Kim was silent for a moment, trying to decide what to ask first. "Why was that skinny toff so wishful to get his dabbers on me?" she said finally, starting with the question which was of the greatest personal interest.

"I rather think he was afraid you might come and tell me what he'd been doing," Mairelon replied.

Kim did a quick review of the conversation they'd overheard. "He thinks you're this Merrill cove?"

"Not any more," Mairelon said cheerfully. He tipped his cap to a heavily rouged, overblown woman in an exceedingly low-cut gown. She eyed his shabby raiment and wrinkled her nose, then hurried past in search of more promising customers.

"So that's why you was so set on me gammoning the cull I'd done what he wanted," Kim said. She looked at Mairelon thoughtfully. "Are you?"

"Am I what?"

"Are you Merrill?"

" 'What's in a name? that which we call a rose by any other name would smell as sweet.' "

"Huh?" Kim said, thoroughly confused.

"Not literary, I take it? No, of course not, you wouldn't be. We shall have to do something about that."

"About what?"

"Teaching you to read."

"Read?" Kim's eyes widened, and she stopped short. "Me?"

"Why not? It's bound to be useful. Come along; you don't want to spend the night standing in the street, do you?"

Kim nodded and started walking again. It was a moment before the novelty of the idea wore off and she realized that she had been very neatly distracted from her original question. She scowled and kicked a pebble. It skittered over the cobblestones and disappeared into the damp and foggy darkness in the middle of the street.

Mairelon looked across at her and raised an eyebrow. Kim's scowl deepened. "You knew all that was going to happen!" she said accusingly.

"Hardly. I was suspicious, that's all."

"Then what were you doin' down at the Dog and Bull?"

"I was looking out for you," Mairelon said promptly.

"I don't need no lookin' out for," Kim retorted. She was suddenly tired of all these swells talking her into things without telling her enough about them first. Of course, her own curiosity was at least as much to blame as Mairelon, but that only made her more irritable.

"I'm inclined to agree," Mairelon said. He raised his hand and touched his right eye gingerly. "I believe you blacked my eye with that last swing."

"Too bad," Kim said callously. "It wouldn't of happened if you'd of told me you'd be there."

"If I'd told you I was planning to follow you, you would have told me to be off about my own business," Mairelon pointed out. "Which, as things turned out, wouldn't have been at all wise, now, would it?"

"Huh." Kim couldn't contradict him, but she wasn't willing to admit it.

"Besides, it wouldn't have been at all the thing to have sent you off into trouble without warning you *and* without sending along anyone to help in case there was trouble."

"Then why didn't you warn me?"

"About what? I wasn't *sure* anything was going to happen. And would you have listened?"

"If you would of explained—" Kim started with some heat, then stopped, her brain working rapidly. Mairelon had caught her rifling his wagon; he would have had to be very stupid to give her any explanations without learning more about her first. And however careless he might seem, he was not stupid. The thought crossed her mind that he had been watching to see whether she would tell the skinny toff the whole truth about what she had found in his wagon.

Curiously, the idea that he had been testing her drained away most of her anger. Caution was a thing she understood; if she wanted Mairelon's trust, she would have to earn it. She wasn't about to admit she knew it, though. "You shouldn't of gone," she said grumpily.

Mairelon gave her a quizzical look. "I couldn't let you go alone, and there was no other choice. I simply couldn't send Hunch."

Kim stared at Mairelon. Then her mind brought up a picture of Hunch, drooping over the skinny toff's shoulder and chewing on his mustache while he tried to tip over a beer mug. It was too much for her sense of humor; she burst into laughter. "No, I guess you couldn't. I bet he didn't want you goin' off in them flash togs, neither."

"You're right about that," Mairelon replied cheerfully. He raised his hand to touch his eye again, and winced. "He's going to be simply delighted about this, I'm sure."

"Not hardly he won't."

"He'll say it's what I deserve for going off without him. He may, just possibly, be right," the magician added thoughtfully.

"You goin' to tell him how you got it?" Kim said.

Mairelon looked at her and blinked; then he grinned. "Oh, I see. I hadn't thought of that." The grin widened, giving him a strong resemblance to a mischievous small boy. "Well, such things happen quite frequently in taverns, particularly the less respectable ones. I don't think there'll be any need to go into details, do you?"

Kim shrugged, sternly suppressing a flicker of relief. "It don't matter to me."

"Quite so," Mairelon said gravely. They walked a block in silence, watching the heavy, wide-wheeled drays clatter by over the cobblestones. Then they turned a corner and the sights and sounds of the Hungerford market washed up to greet them.

To Kim's surprise, Mairelon did not go directly to his wagon. Instead, he led Kim around the fringe of the market to a cramped alley. He paused in the shadows, watching the lamplit shops. Though the twists of the buildings hid them from sight, Kim could hear the calls of the costermongers clearly. It was a good place to hide; Kim had used it herself a couple of times. She was surprised that Mairelon knew it.

Kim heard a scratching sound behind her and tensed. Mairelon smiled and turned, his shoulders brushing flakes of paint off the building on his right. A moment later, Hunch appeared from an even skinnier opening near the back of the alley.

"Well timed, Hunch!" Mairelon said in a low voice. "You brought everything?"

"Right 'ere," Hunch said, lifting a large canvas bag in one hand and scowling as if he wished he could disassociate himself from such undignified proceedings.

"Good!" Mairelon stripped off his cap and dropped it, then pulled off his tattered jacket. He wiped his face and hands on the shreds of lining, which seemed relatively clean, then dropped the jacket on top of the cap and begin pulling off his heavy workman's boots.

"Master Richard!" Hunch's voice was not loud, but it expressed volumes of scandalized disapproval.

Mairelon paused and looked up. "What is it?"

"You ain't never going to just—" Hunch stopped and looked at Kim. "Not with 'er standing there!"

"Oh, is that all that's bothering you?" Mairelon looked at Kim and grinned. "Turn your back, child; you're offending Hunch's proprieties."

Kim flushed, as much from surprise as embarrassment, and turned away. "I ain't no child," she muttered under her breath.

"Under the circumstances, that's so much the worse," Mairelon replied cheerfully.

Kim snorted. She could hear various scraping and rustling noises behind her, and Hunch muttering through his mustache. She frowned, certain that at least some of the mutterings were derogatory comments directed at her. She couldn't quite hear them, and after a moment she was glad. If she knew what Hunch was saying, she would have had to answer in kind, and she couldn't see arguing with someone while her back was turned. It was too much of a disadvantage.

The rustlings stopped, and Mairelon said, "There, that's better. You can turn around now."

Kim did, and blinked. Mairelon still smelled faintly of beer, but otherwise he was once more the well-dressed stage magician she had first seen. Top hat, cape, mustache—mustache? "How'd you do that?" Kim demanded.

"The mustache?" Mairelon said. "Spirit gum and horsehair. It isn't crooked, is it?"

"Not as I can see," Kim replied.

"Good! I was wondering; it's a bit tricky to do without a mirror. Still, it only has to last until we get back to the wagon."

"What about them things you was wearing?" Hunch demanded. "You 'adn't ought to be leaving them 'ere."

"No, I suppose not," Mairelon said, nudging the little pile of dirty, beer-scented clothing he had been wearing. He glanced at Hunch's face and turned to Kim. "Can you get rid of them?"

"I could pitch them in the river," Kim offered, eyeing the clothes almost as dubiously as Hunch.

"No, no, sell them somewhere or give them away. Preferably not in this market."

"Huh. You don't expect much," Kim muttered, but she picked up the clothes and wadded them into a compact bundle. The boots were in fairly good shape; she might actually be able to turn a few shillings on them.

"We'll see you at the wagon in an hour or so, then," Mairelon said. He smiled as he followed Hunch out the back of the alley.

Kim whistled softly through her teeth as she finished making up the bundle. The secondhand clothes dealers on Petticoat Lane ought to fit Mairelon's requirements. Tom Correy would be the best; he was sure to take the clothes in order to get the boots. He'd think Kim had stolen them, so he wouldn't pay much, but he wouldn't ask questions, either. It evened out.

She swung the bundle to her back and hesitated. Mairelon had sounded casual enough, but he'd nonetheless been taking fairly extreme precautions against being seen. Maybe she should do the same. She slipped easily through the crack at the back of the alley and worked her way among the courtyards to the street.

She was turning to head for Petticoat Lane when she remembered the money she'd collected in the Dog and Bull. Tom was a good fellow, but some of his customers weren't. She didn't want to lose her five pounds before she'd even gotten used to the idea of having them.

Changing direction, she circled the market until she came to the hidey-hole where she spent most of her nights. It was little more than a few rotting boards leaning against a tenement, but it provided privacy and a minimum of shelter. Kim wormed her way inside, then set about redistributing her newfound wealth. She buried a few shillings in the corner of the hidey-hole and slipped a few more into her shoes.

After some consideration, she tore a strip of cloth from the bottom of the shirt Mairelon had been wearing and bound the rest of the coins tightly around her bare waist. She pulled her own shirt down over the resulting lumpy wrap and belted her breeches. She studied the effect, then smiled and patted her belt with a sense of satisfaction. In the dark, and with her jacket over the top of everything, even old Mother Tibb would have been hard put to notice anything unusual.

She rebundled the clothes and set off. Near Holborn Hill she swung
herself onto the rear end of a farmer's wagon that was heading in the
right direction. She hunched down behind the hay, clinging to the back-
board and hoping she would not be noticed. Her luck held; not only did
the wagon continue east, but the driver did not see her until she jumped
off. She darted into the gloom, pursued by his angry cries. He'd settle
down once he realized that all she'd stolen was a ride.

Petticoat Lane was only a few minutes' walk. Tom's shop was closed,
but Kim had expected as much. She slid around to the rear of the building
and rapped at the weathered oak door. She had to repeat her knock before
a stocky, grizzled man opened the door and peered out at her. " 'Oo's
that?"

"Kim. I got somethin' for Tom."

"Ah. Inside, then." The man stepped back and Kim lifted her bundle ·
and followed him in.

The back room of Tom's secondhand shop was a mess, as usual.
Clothes were piled carelessly in every corner and stacked on top of the
single chair. Kim saw everything from a laborer's homespun smock to a
tattered but undeniably silk cravat.

Four men were seated on crates around the rickety table in the center
of the room. The tin cups and the reek of gin made it clear what they
had been doing before Kim's arrival; just at the moment they were staring
at her. Two of them were as unknown to Kim as the doorkeeper. The
third was Tom's brother-in-law Jack Stower, a dirty dish if Kim had ever
seen one. He'd never had much use for her, either.

The last person at the table was a grey-haired man with squinty eyes,
wearing a dark grey coat and a linen cravat. Kim stiffened. "Dan Laverham!" she blurted. What was that flash cull doing in Tom's back room?
For all he carried himself like Quality, he could call up half the canting
crew from Covent Garden to the Tower of London if he had a need for
them.

"Kim, dear boy, how good to see you," the grey-haired man replied.
His eyes raked her apparel, and she was suddenly very, very glad she had
hidden her money so carefully before setting out. Dan would think nothing of ordering his men to strip her of her hard-won gains, if he knew of
them.

"Been a long time," Kim offered, keeping her tone noncommittal.
Dan was a bad one to offend. He was smart and smooth, and he'd hold
on to a grudge until the moon turned blue. She suspected that he was

the one who'd turned stag and peached on Mother Tibb to the constables, though he was too clever to have acted openly.

"That it has," Dan said, leaning back on his crate as though he sat in a tall, straight-backed chair. "And to what do I owe the good fortune of your arrival?"

"Says 'e's got sommat for Tom," the doorkeeper said.

"Then, my dear, go and fetch him," Dan replied. The doorkeeper grunted and clumped up the stairs. Dan looked at Kim. "Do join us," he said, and waved at the table.

Kim shook her head. "I ain't got time," she lied.

Jack Stower shifted so that his crate creaked alarmingly. "Think you're too good to have a drop of Blue Ruin with your friends, eh?" he mumbled.

It was on the tip of Kim's tongue to retort that he, at least, was no friend of hers, but caution restrained her. Gin made Jack's uncertain temper positively explosive, and she doubted that the other men would intervene if Jack started something. She tried to make her voice placating as she said, "It ain't that. I got to meet a man down by the docks in less'n an hour, and I ain't going to finish with Tom in time as it is."

Jack started to reply angrily, but Dan put a hand on his arm and he subsided at once. "An appointment on the docks?" Dan said. "That's a bit out of your usual way, isn't it?"

Kim shrugged, wishing the doorkeeper would come back with Tom. "I go where the pay is."

"Not always, my dear, or you would have accepted my generous offer," Dan said, watching her with bright, penetrating eyes.

"I like bein' on my own," Kim said shortly. And she strongly disliked the idea of falling into Dan's clutches. He'd have her forking purses off the market crowds during the day without regard for her scruples, and once he discovered her sex she'd spend her nights in the stews. Kim had no illusions about that sort of life. Let alone she had no taste for it, she'd be lucky not to end swinging from the nubbing cheat as Mother Tibb had.

"Well, let it pass," Dan said, waving a hand. "But tell me, what has lured you to Tom Correy's establishment tonight?"

"Bilking old Tom out of a tog and kicks, I'd say," Jack muttered.

"Quietly, my dear." Dan's voice was velvet-smooth. Jack shot him a glance of mingled fear and resentment, but he did not speak again. Dan gave Kim a look of polite inquiry.

"I got business with Tom," Kim told him.

"Really." Dan's eyes shifted to the bundled clothes dangling from Kim's right hand, then back to her face. "Not back on the sharping lay by any chance, are you, dear boy?"

"No, nor I ain't goin' to be, neither."

"I can give you a better price than Tom, if you've any trinkets to dispose of," the man persisted.

Kim suppressed a scowl. Dan had been trying to get a handle on her for a long time. He was obviously hoping that greed would get the better of her sense. She shook her head. "I ain't got nothin' in your line, Dan."

"Pity. You're quite sure—"

The creaking of the stairs interrupted as Tom Correy came down them, followed closely by the doorkeeper. Tom scowled at the gin drinkers, but his face lit up when he saw Kim. "Kim, lad! Where've you been keeping yourself?"

"Around," Kim said with deliberate vagueness. She didn't grudge Tom the knowledge, but there were too many interested and not entirely friendly ears present to overhear.

"You come for another coat?"

"What'd I say?" Jack muttered.

"Quiet, you," Tom said without looking. "It's my shop and I'll run it my way, see? And the boy looks like he could do with a jacket."

"I ain't after one," Kim said hastily.

Jack snorted and gulped at his cup. Tom looked at her. "What, then?"

"I got some stuff for you to look at. Here." Kim crouched and undid the bundle.

"Where'd you come by this?" Tom said, studying the untidy pile with disfavor.

"Got it off a bingo-boy up by Spitalfields," Kim said glibly. "What'll you give me for 'em?"

Tom knelt and examined the clothes more closely. "They ain't much."

"Those're good boots," Kim pointed out quickly. "Some people would give three shillings just for the boots."

"Three shillings? You must think I'm as lushy as that lot," Tom said, waving towards the table. "I'll give you a bender for the whole pile."

"Sixpence ain't enough," Kim said stubbornly. "Two shillings nine-pence."

Dan and his cohorts soon lost interest in the bargaining and began a muttered conversation of their own, punctuated by frequent passage of the gin bottle. Kim watched them warily from the corner of her eye while she dickered. Jack was thoroughly castaway, and one or two of the others looked at least a little lushy. Dan, however, was being careful not to get the malt above water; though he passed the bottle and refilled cups with a comradely air, he himself drank little. And several times, Kim saw him watching her.

By the time she had finished her bargaining and collected one-and-sixpence from Tom, Kim was worried. She bade Tom a cordial goodbye and the drinkers a polite one, then stepped out into the cool, damp night. As the door closed behind her, she took a deep breath to clear the gin fumes from her head. The fog had thickened; the streetlamp by the shop-front was a dim smear of yellow light, blurred by the veil of moisture in the air.

Whistling softly, Kim started down Petticoat Lane. Half a block from Tom's, she cut sharply to the left. She hunted along the backs of the shops until she found one with a drainpipe she could climb, then shinnied up it. She crept to the front of the building and lay flat, peering down at the street.

A moment later a man came skulking down the street from the direction of Tom's shop. She couldn't make out his face in the foggy darkness, but his silhouette was stocky and he moved like the man who had been keeping the door for Dan and his friends. He hurried by, heading toward the docks.

Kim stayed where she was for a while, considering. Dan had sent the doorkeeper after her, but why? She could think of no answer. Finally she slid down the drainpipe and started back toward the City. Her mood was thoughtful, and she made sure she took a circuitous route. Whatever the reason for Dan's renewed interest in her, she was sure she wouldn't like it when she found out what it was. She was glad she'd accepted Mairelon's offer. With any luck at all, she'd be out of London long before Dan could find her.

five

It was near midnight when Kim arrived back at Mairelon's wagon and rapped softly at the door. To her surprise, it swung open instantly. Mairelon stood just inside, dressed in evening clothes fine enough for gentry. His right eye seemed puffy, but showed no signs of discoloration. Kim looked more closely and saw streaks of stage makeup, all but invisible in the dim light. "It's me," she said to cover her sudden, irrational feeling of guilt.

"Ah, Kim," Mairelon said with no perceptible change in his worried expression. "I'm glad you're back."

"Not so's you'd notice," Kim muttered as she entered the wagon. "I got rid of them flash togs, right enough."

"Good," Mairelon said absently, still frowning at the door.

Kim looked around for some hint as to the cause of Mairelon's abstraction. She saw no sign of the droopy assistant, and on impulse asked, "Where's Hunch?"

Mairelon picked up a top hat from the grey tile that topped the row of cabinets by the door. "I was just going to find that out."

"You mean he's run missing?"

"I sent him on an . . . errand. He should have been back an hour ago."

Kim sighed. "It's your lay. Where do we start lookin'?"

"We don't start anywhere. You're going to stay here and keep an eye on things, in case he gets back before I do."

"I ain't fond of sittin' and waitin'," Kim objected. "And if you're that nattered about it, maybe you ought to take along some help."

"I'm afraid you'd be rather out of place where I'm—" Mairelon broke off in mid-sentence, and his head turned toward the door. A moment later it swung open and Hunch climbed into the wagon. He looked at Mairelon, and a disapproving frown settled over his face. Mairelon grinned like a schoolboy caught in a prank and tossed his top hat back onto the shelf.

Hunch snorted. "You ain't queering me none, Master Richard. You was a-going to go looking for me."

"It seemed like a good idea."

"You 'adn't ought to of done it," Hunch said severely.

"Yes, well, I didn't. What took so long?"

Hunch looked at Mairelon sharply, but allowed himself to be drawn away from his scolding. "Couple of sharpers tried to follow me, and I 'ad to lose 'em afore I come back."

"What?" Mairelon looked up in the act of seating himself on top of the chest that had caused Kim so much trouble. "How many?"

"Two as I noticed."

"Anyone we know?"

Hunch shook his head. "I 'adn't seen neither of 'em afore."

"Mmm-hm. I suppose they could have been some of Shoreham's."

"That's as may be," Hunch said. He sounded both skeptical and disapproving. Mairelon looked up. Hunch gave a warning jerk of his head in Kim's direction.

"What? Oh, yes, of course," Mairelon said. "Did you get what you went for?"

"Aye."

"Well, let's have it, man!"

Hunch shot another look in Kim's direction, then reached stiffly into one of his pockets. He pulled out a folded paper sealed with a great blob of crimson wax and handed it to Mairelon.

Mairelon held it up to the light, edgewise. "The seal hasn't been tampered—oh, Lord."

"What is it?" Hunch said anxiously.

"Shoreham's done it again," Mairelon replied in annoyance. He turned slightly, so that his back was to Kim, and muttered something under his breath.

There was a bright flash of blue-white light that left Kim's eyes momentarily dazzled. When her sight cleared, Mairelon was squinting at a fine dust of ashes that drifted from the folded paper. "I do wish he'd stop using that Egyptian Light-Lock," he complained. "I never manage to get my eyes shut in time."

Hunch grunted. Kim realized that he had turned his head away before Mairelon broke the seal, and so escaped the temporary blindness. She glared first at him and then at Mairelon. One of them might have warned her what to expect.

Mairelon shook the letter open and began to read. A moment later he straightened with an exclamation. "Tomorrow!"

"What's that?" Hunch said.

"Shoreham wants us to meet him tomorrow evening." Mairelon looked up. "How long was this waiting?" he demanded, waving the note.

"Since yesterday. Where's 'e looking to be? Same place as last time?"

"Yes." Mairelon shook his head. "He's in a rush again. Blast the man!"

Hunch considered. "We'll 'ave to leave early," he said at last.

"I know," Mairelon said irritably.

"What about 'er?" Hunch said, jerking his head in Kim's direction.

"What?" Mairelon looked up from rereading the note. "Oh. You wouldn't mind leaving London a little earlier than we'd planned, would you?" he asked Kim.

"No," Kim said, remembering Dan Laverham and his unpleasant crew. She thought of mentioning them to Mairelon, but caution made her hold her tongue. If he knew about Dan, he might change his mind about letting Kim accompany him.

"That's settled, then," Mairelon said. He folded the note and tucked it in an inner pocket, then picked up his top hat. "I'll be back in an hour or so."

"You ain't never just leaving without telling me where you're off to!" Hunch sounded outraged.

Mairelon looked back over his shoulder and smiled angelically at Hunch. "Exactly," he said, and the door closed behind him.

Hunch glared at the door. After a moment, he transferred the glare to Kim. "And what's 'e want me to do with you?" he muttered.

"I'll just go doss under the wagon," Kim offered, sidling toward the door. She wanted to think about what she'd overheard, and she wanted to get away from Hunch. She also wanted to retrieve the shillings she'd left in her hidey-hole; she might need them once she left London.

"No, you ain't," Hunch said, leaning against the door. " 'E may be willing to let you go jauntering about, but I ain't 'aving you blabbing things all over London."

"What things?" Kim asked scornfully. "You ain't told me nothin', neither one of you."

"Hah." Hunch squinted at her, and his mustache seemed to droop even more. "You 'eard enough to make trouble. And don't gammon me you don't know it, neither."

"Maybe." Kim studied Hunch. She was rapidly acquiring a good deal of respect for him; despite his appearance, he was no fool. "But I ain't no troublemaker."

" 'Ow do I know that?"

"You've had time enough to ask questions about me all round Hungerford," Kim said shrewdly. "And if you ain't done it, I don't know a sharp from a Robin Redbreast."

Hunch did not reply. He also did not move away from the door.

Kim heaved an exaggerated sigh. "Well, I ain't goin' to stand here arguin' with you all night," she said. "And I ain't leavin' London half asleep, neither. If you ain't letting me out, I'll doss here."

She sat down on the chest with more confidence than she felt, remembering her previous experience. No explosions or purple sparks followed, so she swung her feet up and stretched out on top of it. It wasn't as comfortable as it might have been, but it wasn't cold and there weren't any rats looking to share it with her. It'd do.

She grinned at Hunch's fulminating expression and closed her eyes. He'd think she was shamming it, and he'd watch her closely to see that she had no chance to slip away. So she wouldn't sham. There was no point in wasting however much time Mairelon planned to take, and no reason not to take full advantage of a warm, dry, safe place to rest. She grinned again at the thought of Hunch's probable reaction, and let herself drop into sleep.

The wagon door opened, and Kim came awake all at once. She gave an instant's consideration to the possibility of pretending she was still asleep, in hopes of hearing something of interest, then rejected the idea. She'd do better to let them know she was awake, as a sort of expression of good faith. It wouldn't calm Hunch's suspicions, but at least it wouldn't raise any more of them. She opened her eyes and sat up.

Mairelon had just entered the wagon. He carried a large parcel under one arm and there was a worried crease across his forehead; aside from that, he looked like one of the grand swells Kim had occasionally seen going into the Drury Lane theater. He glanced from Hunch's dour face to hers. Kim grinned and stretched.

The worried crease vanished and the corners of Mairelon's eyes crinkled in amusement. "Wise of you to have gotten some sleep, Kim."

"I thought so," Kim said smugly.

Hunch snorted and rose stiffly to his feet. He had been sitting beside the door, Kim saw, presumably to block any attempt she might make to leave. "You're late," he said to Mairelon.

"Not as late as I might have been." The remaining traces of amusement disappeared from Mairelon's expression. "Are you ready to leave?"

"Now?" Kim said, startled. She glanced involuntarily at the tiny window in the top of the wagon's door. There was no sign of an approaching dawn.

"Now."

Hunch looked at Mairelon suspiciously. "There's three hours yet afore morning," he pointed out.

"Yes. And we should be at least two hours gone by then," Mairelon replied.

Hunch and Kim were both staring at him. "What 'ave you gone and done now?" Hunch demanded at last.

Mairelon's lips set in a grim line. Carefully, he put his parcel down on top of the cupboards. After a moment, he looked up. "I haven't 'gone and done' anything," he said. "Unfortunately, Andrew isn't likely to believe that."

"You never went off to Grosvenor Square!" Hunch gasped.

"Give me credit for some sense," Mairelon replied. "No, I met my esteemed brother outside Renée D'Auber's."

Kim's eyes widened. Everyone in London, from the Prince of Wales to the poorest mud-lark, knew of Mademoiselle Renée D'Auber. She was the only child of a French wizard who had fled his country during the Terror and an English Countess who had been generally considered to have married beneath her. Mademoiselle D'Auber had kept a foot in both worlds. She was welcomed by all but the most stiff-necked members of the *baut ton*. She kept a select salon attended by magicians, bluestockings, and intelligentsia, and she was rumored to be a dab hand at spell casting herself. There were also whispers that she was personally familiar with some of the less savory elements of London society. The upper classes considered her wild and not altogether respectable; the lower shook their heads in fascinated wonder at the strange ways of foreigners and gentry, and pronounced her too clever by half.

"You 'adn't ought to 'ave gone there," Hunch told Mairelon almost fiercely.

"Where else was I supposed to get willow root, black alder, vervain, and rue at this hour?" Mairelon retorted irritably.

"You ain't a-going to 'ave a chance to use them 'erbs much if word gets out you're in London."

"Renée wouldn't give me away. And how was I supposed to know Andrew would be there? He never used to like Renée. He shouldn't even be in town yet; the Season doesn't start for at least a month!" Mairelon ran a hand through his hair in a distracted manner.

Hunch opened his mouth, then closed it again. Kim thought he looked more worried and upset than angry, and she filed that away in her mind for later consideration. At last Hunch said, "I'll be getting the 'orses, then."

Kim glanced at Mairelon's face, then looked away. "I'll help," she said quickly as Hunch rose.

To her surprise, Hunch did not object. He simply looked at her and nodded. Kim blinked and followed him out of the wagon. They started toward the end of the market where horses could be stabled for a fee. As soon as they were well out of earshot of the wagon, Kim looked up and demanded, "What was that about?"

"It ain't your affair," Hunch growled repressively.

Kim was ready to argue, but Hunch's forbidding expression made it clear that she would get no further information from him. She resolved to question Mairelon himself as soon as she could find a good opportunity. She looked up. Hunch was chewing on his mustache again. Kim snorted quietly and turned her attention to considering what little she had learned.

Mairelon the Magician knew more than stage magic, that was plain enough. And she'd bet every farthing she was carrying that he was the "Merrill" that the skinny toff at the Dog and Bull was so anxious to find. Odds-on, Mairelon was gentry, too, or at least very well breeched. Ordinary market performers didn't have brothers who owned houses in Grosvenor Square.

Then there was the matter of the men who had tried to follow Hunch. He and Mairelon seemed to consider it more of a nuisance than a threat, which implied that they were used to dealing with such things. And Mairelon knew Renée D'Auber well enough to expect a welcome at her home.

The whole thing had a havey-cavey look about it. Frowning, Kim considered piking off with her five pounds and leaving Hunch to explain her absence to Mairelon. The trouble was, she didn't want to go. She liked Mairelon. Furthermore, she trusted him. Whatever it was that he was involved in, she was certain he hadn't lied when he'd told her it wasn't illegal.

It might be dangerous, though. Kim's frown deepened. She didn't know anything about magic, but she'd been involved in smoky dealings before. Mairelon might be able to use her help. She blinked, surprised by the strength of her desire to go along with the magician, then pressed her lips together, determined to be objective. She shouldn't be staying with a couple of culls on a queer lay without a good reason. She'd had more than her share of close calls already. Her luck wouldn't last forever.

For a moment, she wavered; then she remembered Dan Laverham. With a feeling of relief, Kim stopped trying to convince herself that she ought to abandon Mairelon. She had to get away from Dan Laverham, and that meant getting out of London. That was a good enough reason for anything! Besides, if she sherried off now, she'd never find out what was really going on. Kim grinned to herself and hurried to catch up with Hunch.

six

They were on their way out of London within the hour. Hunch drove from a tiny ledge on the front of the wagon, while Kim rode inside with Mairelon. She would rather have been outside with Hunch, despite his suspicions, for she disliked the closed-in feeling of the darkened wagon. Mairelon's assurance that it was only until they were out of London, and her own thoughts of Dan Laverham, were all that stifled her objections. Kim was not anxious to be seen by anyone who might take word back to that slimy character, small though the chance might be.

The jolting of the wagon made her queasy at first, but the feeling passed quickly. Mairelon watched her closely. "All right now?" he said after a time.

"Right enough." Kim peered at him. "You couldn't do somethin' to make a bit of light in here, could you?"

Mairelon laughed. "I'm afraid you'll have to get used to the dark. No wagoneer would keep a lamp lit while the wagon's moving, not even on the best road in England." The wagon jounced across a rut and Mairelon grimaced. "Which this manifestly is not."

Kim hadn't been thinking of a lamp, but she let it pass. Mairelon's point was clear enough: a lighted wagon would attract attention. She stared at the window with some disquiet. She had no idea where they were going, she realized, or even which direction. Well, they hadn't crossed the river, so they weren't headed south, but that still left a lot of possibilities. Suddenly she grinned. If she didn't know where she was going, Laverham certainly wouldn't!

"Not going to sleep, I take it?" Mairelon said.

The wagon hit a bump that nearly threw Kim off the chest. "Ain't nobody could sleep through that," she said scornfully when she was secure once more.

"Sorry," Mairelon said. "This wagon wasn't built to be ridden in."

"I never would of guessed," Kim said sarcastically.

Mairelon laughed again. "I suppose that it *is* a bit obvious. If you aren't going to sleep, why don't we start on your lessons?"

"Lessons? You mean, reading and magic?"

"Eventually, yes. But you can't read if you can't see, and the same thing applies to the kind of magic I'll be teaching you. We'll start on those later, after it gets light."

Kim frowned. "How much you plannin' on teachin' me?"

"If you're going to be of any real help with the show, there are a number of things you'll need to know besides stage magic," Mairelon said dryly.

"What things?"

"The way you talk, for one." Mairelon looked at her and hurried on before she could reply. "You see, people expect a performer to sound like a Duchess. You don't, of course, but I think that with a little training you could."

"Hunch don't talk like a gentry cove," Kim pointed out, nettled.

"He doesn't assist me on stage, either."

"Huh." Kim considered. She hadn't known any truly successful actresses, but she'd seen enough of the shows in Covent Gardens to know that what Mairelon said was true. On stage, at least, the better actresses aped the accents of nobility. The prospect of learning to do the same was not unappealing. "All right, then. What's first?"

Mairelon let out his breath as though he had been afraid she would think the suggestion insulting. "First, you stop using quite so much thieves' cant," he said briskly. "You'll have to practice all the time, until it seems natural."

"Practice *talkin'*? Just to sound flash? I—" Kim stopped. "Oh. That's what you meant, ain't it?"

"It's exactly what I meant," Mairelon said, and waited.

"Mmmm." This was going to be harder than she'd thought. "What else?"

She could hear the smile in Mairelon's voice as he went on with his instruction. There seemed to be an endless number of different things for Kim to remember to say, or not to say, or to say instead of something else. Mairelon was both patient and creative. He explained each of his directions carefully. He made up sample conversations and recited them in different styles, so that Kim could hear the difference between the speech of a London costermonger and that of a Sussex yeoman, a middle-class tradesman, or a north country Viscount. Then he had Kim imitate each of his voices, correcting her gently whenever she slipped.

It was an amusing way of passing the time; Kim didn't even notice when the interior of the wagon began to grow lighter. She was almost disappointed when, shortly after dawn, Hunch pulled into the yard of a coaching inn, temporarily ending the lesson.

While Hunch watered the horses, Mairelon produced the package he had brought back to the wagon the previous night. To Kim's surprise, it contained a boy's jacket, shirt, and breeches. They were nearly new, and much finer than the best clothing Kim had ever worn. "That's for me?" she said in disbelief.

"Of course," Mairelon replied. "It wouldn't fit me, or Hunch, either. I'd intended to get you a dress as well, but there wasn't time. We'll have to attend to that later."

Kim was reduced to near speechlessness. Mairelon waved away her attempts at thanking him and shooed her out into the inn's yard. There he insisted that Kim wash as much of herself as could be decently managed under the inn's pump. Hunch fussed with the horses and muttered into his mustache throughout the entire proceeding. Only then would Mairelon allow Kim to try on her new clothes.

Back inside the wagon, Kim shinned out of her own tattered clothing immediately and pulled on the garments Mairelon had brought her. The breeches were a little tight and the jacket was a little loose, but the clothes remained the best she had ever worn. She shrugged her shoulders, testing the movement of the jacket, then grinned and threw open the wagon door.

Mairelon was nowhere in sight, but Hunch was standing beside the steps. " 'Ere," he said, and handed her a chunk of fresh bread and a slice of cheese. "We ain't stopping long," he added in response to her look of surprise. "Eat while you can."

This was entirely in accord with Kim's philosophy, and she bit into the bread with great satisfaction. "Where's Mairelon?" she asked as she munched. She was disappointed that he had not stayed to see how she looked.

"There." Hunch jerked his head toward the stable, but did not elaborate.

Kim nodded, her mouth full, and sat down on the steps to finish her meal. Mairelon returned just as she swallowed the last of the bread and cheese. She scrambled to her feet so that he could get the full effect of her new finery, and he nodded thoughtfully.

"You make a very pretty boy," he said. "But I don't think you'll want to hike the roads in those. Try this."

Kim caught the bundle he tossed her and looked at him in bewilderment. "Hike?"

"I told you the wagon wasn't meant for riding in, remember? Unless we're in a hurry, we walk. It's less work for the horses."

Kim nodded and went back inside. The bundle was yet another set of clothes, plain and much-mended, but clean. They looked like farmers' wear; Mairelon must have gotten them from one of the stable hands. She frowned suddenly. She was glad she wouldn't have to wear the rags she'd had on earlier, but she was rapidly becoming uncomfortable with the number of things Mairelon was giving her. She didn't like owing him so much; it gave him a claim on her, and she still didn't know what he expected in return. Well, she hadn't asked him for any of it. It was his own lookout if she sherried off with everything. She shrugged and reached for the clothes.

When she emerged, she found that Mairelon had changed his full-dress London evening garb for something very like a laborer's smock. Kim had to suppress a laugh; in the patched, brown homespun he bore a strong resemblance to a not-very-reputable tinker's helper. As soon as he was ready, they left the yard. Hunch led the horses instead of driving from the van, and Mairelon and Kim walked along behind the wagon.

Mairelon showed Kim some of his simpler magic tricks as they walked. He claimed that doing them on the move was more difficult than working them on stage, and therefore it was good practice. Kim was particularly fascinated by the various ways of tying knots that slid apart like oiled snakes if the right loop were pulled. She made Mairelon show her how they were tied, going slowly through the process several times. Then she practiced until she could manage a creditable performance.

She was disappointed to find that Mairelon's tricks owed more to his deft fingers than to real magic. But she hadn't expected him to teach her any *real* magic, she told herself sternly. And the things he showed her were certainly fascinating. She swallowed her regrets and concentrated on making a half-crown appear to vanish from one hand and reappear in the other.

Her language lessons continued as well. Mairelon had a way of looking at her and raising his eyebrows whenever she used a cant phrase or misplaced a word. It was far more effective than the scoldings and blows Mother Tibb had dispensed whenever her students were slow; Kim found herself learning more quickly than she would have dreamed.

They were well out into the country now, and Kim found the open fields and hedges very strange after the close confines of the London streets. Near noon they stopped to let the horses rest and graze on the verge. Kim helped Hunch unharness them, then Mairelon called her over to begin her first lesson in reading. She spent most of the two-hour stop scowling ferociously at the little brown book of letters Mairelon had produced. She emerged with a profound respect for anyone who had mastered this difficult art, and an even more profound determination to join their number.

The afternoon was occupied by more lessons, but this time Mairelon was the pupil. He asked Kim to teach him how to pick locks. Relieved to find that there was something he didn't know how to do, Kim readily agreed. She scornfully rejected, however, the notion of beginning with the lock on the chest inside the wagon. "You ain't—you aren't goin' to get nowhere—anywhere?—if you start in on a fancy job like that one," she told him.

Mairelon accepted the rebuke and brought out a smaller padlock from somewhere in the depths of the wagon. "Do we need anything else?" he asked.

"You mean, special keys and such?"

Mairelon nodded apologetically. "I've heard that they're useful."

"Maybe, but I just use a bit of wire. If you lose a key, you got to get a new one, and that takes time. A bit of wire's always easy to come by."

Mairelon nodded. Kim spent much of the afternoon demonstrating the twists and pulls that Mother Tibb had shown her so long ago. She was not as patient a teacher as Mairelon had been, but her student had the benefit of years of experience with sleight of hand, and he learned very quickly. By the end of the afternoon, she was ready to let him try his hand at the rusty-looking lock that held the rear doors of the wagon.

"Tomorrow, perhaps," Mairelon said. "I think I've had enough for one day."

Kim rather agreed with him. She was tired and very dusty from the long trek in the wagon's wake, and her brain whirled in an attempt to assimilate all the new things she had learned. When they reached the edge of a little village and pulled off the road to make camp at last, her main emotion was relief.

Hunch tended the horses while Mairelon and Kim gathered wood.

When the fire was well started, Mairelon hung a pot above it on a wobbly tripod affair that he had cobbled together out of green branches and twine. Hunch went muttering through the grass and weeds along the road. He returned with several lanky plants, which he threw into the pot along with a little meat and some vegetables from the wagon. Kim was not sure whether it was Hunch's seasoning or the long walk, but the stew was the best she had ever tasted. There was plenty of it, too; Kim ate until she was stuffed, and there was still some left in the pot.

When the meal was over, Mairelon and Hunch began a low-voiced conversation on the other side of the fire. Kim quickly grew frustrated with her inability to hear what they were saying, and Hunch's occasional fierce glares made it quite clear that she had better not move any closer. Kim glared back at him, which accomplished nothing beyond providing her with some emotional satisfaction, then rose and wandered back to the wagon. She glanced at the rusty lock holding the rear doors, shook her head, and went on around to the steps.

Inside the wagon, she gave the chest a speculative look. She decided against it; Mairelon knew she could open it, and had undoubtedly taken precautions. *More* precautions, she amended, remembering the purple explosion that had thrown her across the wagon. Instead, she went to the rear of the van. She hadn't been able to investigate that area before, because Mairelon had been performing just outside, and she was curious about how the folding stage worked.

The curtain was heavier than its faded, threadbare appearance had led her to expect. She examined it more closely and found a series of lead weights sewn into the hem. Her surprise lasted only a moment. Mairelon wouldn't want a stray breeze to reveal the luxurious interior of his wagon while he was performing. Kim frowned, wondering why he hadn't put a folding panel behind the curtain for added security. She'd have to re-member to ask him later; she was certain he had some good reason. She lifted one end of the curtain and peered behind it.

There was a foot-wide space between the curtain and the back wall. Kim slipped into it and let the curtain fall shut behind her. A little light filtered in around the edges, providing a gloomy reddish illumination. As she waited for her eyes to adjust, Kim ran her fingertips lightly across the rear wall. There was no break in the surface; this must be the floor of the stage, then. She crouched to study the base of the wall. Yes, there were hinges, carefully sunk into notches in the wood. They hardly showed at all, and when the stage was lowered, they would lie flush with the floor, providing no inconvenient lumps for a performer to trip over.

She completed her inspection and straightened, just as the sound of hoofbeats came clearly from just outside. Old habits took over; Kim froze, half crouched behind the curtain. She heard a shout and the muffled sounds of conversation, but she paid little attention. She was too busy reminding herself that she was doing nothing the nabbing culls could nick her for. She hadn't nicked anything for nearly two years, not since she'd been on her own. She had just managed to convince herself that it would be perfectly safe to go outside and see what was happening when steps sounded on the stairs and she heard the wagon's door open.

"—and you can take a look at it," Mairelon's voice said.

"Well, that's good news," an unfamiliar voice replied. "What's this Hunch says about you picking up another stray?"

Curiosity kept Kim motionless. "I would hardly call Kim a stray," Mairelon said. "And Heaven only knows what would have happened to her if I'd left her in the streets of London."

"Um. Still trying to make up for Jamie? No, no, I shouldn't have mentioned it. But you're certain she has nothing to do with the robbery?"

"Quite sure. Now, Edward, do you want to look at the bowl or not?"

"Yes, of course; let's have it."

Sundry clicks and thumps followed, the sounds of Mairelon unlocking the chest and throwing back the lid. Then light flashed brightly around the edges of the curtain, and the strange voice exclaimed, "My word!"

"Impressive, isn't it?" Mairelon replied. "Will you take it with you?"

"Not unless you want me to. The consensus is that it may help you find the rest of the pieces, but it may also make things more dangerous for you."

"How?" Mairelon asked sharply.

"Magic cuts in both directions. If you can use the bowl to find the platter and the spheres, they can be used to find the bowl. And you."

"Of course. But I thought you had more in mind than that."

"Marchmont thinks someone at the Ministry has been talking too freely," Mairelon's companion said reluctantly. "It may be deliberate."

"I see. And there's still the little matter of finding out which one of our colleagues at the Royal College planned the theft in the first place, isn't there?"

"You've no proof that anyone—"

"Don't be a fool, Shoreham! Someone arranged things very cleverly to make it look as if I were the one behind that theft. Someone *very* well informed. It was sheerest luck that I ran into you that night, or you'd be as sure I'm guilty as the rest of them."

"All right, all right. But I still wish you'd let me clear your name."

"And give whoever it is a reason to try again? No, thank you. Besides, as long as no one knows who is really responsible, there will still be those who believe I was behind it."

"I should think the word of the Earl of Shoreham will be enough to put an end to such gossip," Shoreham said stiffly.

Kim swallowed an exclamation and pressed herself against the rear wall of the wagon, wishing fervently that she had come out from behind the curtain as soon as Mairelon opened the wagon door. Robbery and intrigue were things she emphatically did not want to get mixed up in, particularly if there were Earls involved, too. The gentry were even more trouble than toffs.

Mairelon's laugh had little humor to it. "Nothing stops gossip, Edward; you ought to know that."

"If you would just—"

"Let it lie, Edward. What else do you have to tell me? I assume you didn't come all this way just to look at the Saltash Bowl and warn me that someone in the Ministry is too free with information."

"You're still determined to go through with this?"

"Would I be here, like this, if I weren't?"

"Oh, very well, then. We've finally traced the platter."

"And?" Mairelon's tone was eager.

"It's in the hands of one of those new druid cults."

"Druid cults?"

"There's been a sort of half-baked revival going on for the past year or two. It's all very fashionable—mistletoe and white robes under the new moon, with little golden sickles for everyone." Lord Shoreham snorted. "Quackery, all of it; no science at all. It's the sort of thing that gives magicians a bad name."

"Then why did it take you this long to find the platter?"

"This group has one or two members who dabble a bit in real magic."

"I see."

"They call themselves Sons of the New Dawn, I believe," Lord Shoreham went on. "They're located in Essex, near Suffolk, at a place called Ranton Hill."

"I'm familiar with the area. Edward, if I'm going to Essex, why in Heaven's name have you dragged me a day's trip in the opposite direction?" Mairelon demanded.

"To try and keep unwelcome attention centered in this area. The platter's been there for at least two years; there's no reason to hurry."

"Mmmm. It'll take me at least two days to get there now—"

"Three," Lord Shoreham said blandly. "I'd rather you went around London instead of through it."

"If you insist."

"Under the circumstances, I most certainly do."

"Very well. Tell me about these druids, then."

Kim heard a sound like a sigh of resignation, then Lord Shoreham's voice said, "There are only about ten members, mostly young men in it for a lark. The three most likely to have the platter are Frederick Meredith, Robert Choiniet, and Jonathan Aberford. I've brought a list of the others."

There was a rustling noise as the paper changed hands. "That will do, I think," Mairelon said with some satisfaction. "I'll leave in the morning."

Lord Shoreham cleared his throat. "Ah, there is one other thing. How well do you know the Viscount Granleigh?"

"I don't believe we've met."

"And St. Clair?"

"The Baron and I . . . have met. Where is this leading, Edward?"

Shoreham sighed. "I wanted to know whether you were likely to meet anyone who would recognize you."

"Then why didn't you just ask?" Mairelon's tone was infuriating in its innocence.

"Richard! The Runners *are* still looking for you in connection with the original robbery, you know."

"It's half the reason I left England. I take it Granleigh and St. Clair are likely to be in Essex?"

"Possibly. Charles Bramingham is married to St. Clair's sister, and his son is St. Clair's heir. His wife is a bosom bow of Amelia Granleigh, the Viscountess, and is addicted to house parties. It's not beyond the bounds of probability that you'll run into them."

"I know. I've stayed at Bramingham Place a time or two. Don't go ruffling your feathers about it, it was years ago, and they're not likely to remember me. What is their connection with the Ministry?"

There was a moment's silence, then Lord Shoreham said ruefully, "Richard, you are uncanny. How did you know?"

"There must be at least a hundred people in London who might have recognized me, including my dear brother Andrew. You didn't ask me about any of them."

"Andrew's in London? You didn't see him, did you?"

"As a matter of fact, I did. Briefly. It needn't concern you."

"Nothing in this affair—"

"You're avoiding the subject, Edward. What's so special about Bramingham and the Granleighs?"

Lord Shoreham sighed again. "Stephen Granleigh is involved with the Ministry in a number of ways. Of necessity, he's familiar with the history of the Saltash Bowl. Has decided opinions on the subject, too."

"I see. And St. Clair?"

"Was elected to the College in your place."

"He must have been delighted." Mairelon's voice was utterly devoid of expression. "I must remember to congratulate him if I see him."

"Richard! Don't take foolish risks."

"Foolish? Never."

"I ought to take the bowl, after all, and let someone else recover the platter."

"You can have it if you like, but it won't keep me out of Essex."

"I was afraid of that. Richard, if the Runners catch you with the Saltash Bowl—

"The Runners have criminals enough to deal with in London. What would one of them be doing in Essex?"

"Quite possibly looking for you," Lord Shoreham replied dryly. "I told you someone's been talking too much."

"I'll take the chance."

"Very well. I hope your luck holds, Richard. And don't hesitate to call on me if something happens."

"You may be sure of it."

The wagon door opened, and Lord Shoreham's footsteps sounded on the steps. Kim heard Mairelon moving about the wagon, then a soft thump as the lid of the chest closed. She held her breath, waiting for him to leave and wondering how she was going to sneak out unseen. But Mairelon did not leave. Kim was just beginning to wonder whether she would have to stay where she was all night when Mairelon spoke.

"I think you had better come out now, Kim, and explain why you've been eavesdropping on my conversation."

seven

Kim swallowed hard and pushed the curtain aside. Mairelon was standing in the center of the wagon, watching her. His face was expressionless. Kim swallowed again and said nothing.

"You *do* have some explanation, I trust?" Mairelon said.

"I was just—it was an accident," Kim said lamely.

"I see. You just happened to hide behind the curtain at exactly the time Lord Shoreham was planning to arrive," Mairelon said with a cool politeness that was worse than sarcasm and far worse than open anger.

"Yes!" Kim said hotly. "You and Hunch didn't have no use for me outside, so I came in here to look at that stage you got in back. Which you got to get back of the curtain to do."

"The timing was remarkably convenient."

"You never said when that Shoreham cove was comin'," Kim said angrily. "So how would I of known when to hide? You ain't told me nothin', neither one of you."

"Why didn't you come out?"

"With the two of you talkin' about me? And after that . . ." Kim squirmed. "It wouldn't of looked right."

"Wouldn't *have*," Mairelon said, sounding as if his mind were on something else. "No, I suppose not."

"How did you know I was there?" Kim ventured. She had been half afraid Mairelon would throw her out at once, but it seemed she had been wrong. He wouldn't be correcting the way she spoke if he'd made up his mind to get rid of her.

"The end of the curtain was hanging oddly; I noticed it when I was

showing Shoreham the bowl. Then I remembered seeing you come
around this way and that you hadn't come back. Simple, really."

"So why didn't you say something right then?"

Mairelon looked uncomfortable. "I had my reasons."

"You didn't want the gentry cove to know I was there!" Kim said
triumphantly.

"Shoreham has a nasty temper at times. Besides, I prefer to deal with
you myself."

"So what are you goin' to do?"

"I don't know." Mairelon studied her. Kim stared back, trying to
gauge his temper. He looked tired, and Kim was suddenly sorry she had
added to his worries, however inadvertently. She pushed the thought
aside; she had worries of her own.

"I suppose I shall have to bring you along," Mairelon said at last.

"To Ranton Hill?"

"That far at least. Afterward—well, we'll see how things go."

"What if I ain't wishful to go?"

Mairelon's eyes narrowed. "I beg your pardon?"

"I said, what if I ain't wishful to go with you?" Kim repeated. She
chose her next words carefully, aware that she might be jeopardizing
whatever fragile trust in her Mairelon still retained. "You told me you
weren't doing nothin' the nabbing culls'd be . . . lookin' out for. But it
didn't sound that way when you were talkin' to the gentry cove."

"No, I suppose it didn't," Mairelon said, and some of the tension
went out of his shoulders. He looked at Kim and shook his head. "I wish
I knew whether you—" He stopped short and snapped his fingers. "Of
course!"

Kim stared in surprise as Mairelon turned and pulled open the wagon
door. "Hunch! Do you have any rosemary in that cache of herbs you cart
around all the time?"

Hunch's response was muffled, but a moment later Kim heard
Mairelon say, "Thank you. Kim will be with me; don't disturb us for an
hour or so. I'm going to need to concentrate."

"Master Richard!" Hunch's tone was horrified. "You ain't going to
. . . You wouldn't never . . ."

"There are days, Hunch, when you remind me forcibly of my excessively estimable brother," Mairelon said in a tone of mild irritation.
"Is it her virtue or mine that you're worrying about?"

"You ain't a-going to gammon me," Hunch said severely. "What are
you up to?"

"I'm going to take that suggestion you made just before Shoreham arrived, if you must know. I trust you don't expect me to do so outside the wagon, in full view of the road?"

Hunch snorted but did not answer. A moment later, Mairelon pulled his head and shoulders back into the wagon and closed the door. His right hand held a small packet, presumably the herbs he had gotten from Hunch. Kim eyed him warily. "What're you goin' to do?"

"Reassure myself," Mairelon said absently. He set the packet down on the counter, then crossed to the chest and opened it. He muttered a word and made a quick gesture with his left hand, hidden from Kim by his body. Then he withdrew the velvet-swathed bundle that had been Kim's downfall. He set it carefully on the counter and gently folded back the velvet.

Kim's eyes went wide as she stared at the heavy silver bowl nested in the ripples of black velvet. It was shallow and circular, like the soup bowls the gentry used, but more than twice as large. The rim was at least two inches wide and carved into intricate leaves, flowers, and vines. It shone softly in the lamplight.

Kim looked at Mairelon. "Is that the silver bowl you and the gentry cove were on about?"

"The Saltash Bowl. Yes." The magician opened a cupboard and removed several small jars. He measured carefully as he added portions of their contents to the bowl, then mixed them with a long wooden rod. Kim noticed that he was careful not to touch any part of the silver with his hands as he worked.

She started to ask another question, but thought better of interrupting him. She waited until he finished the mixing and laid aside the wooden rod. As he reached for Hunch's packet, she said, "You ain't explained nothin' about what you're doin'."

Mairelon paused in mid-reach and looked at her. "No, I haven't, have I?" He hesitated, studying her, then sighed. "I suppose you have a right to know what to expect. Very well, then. One of the uses of the Saltash Bowl is to compel people to speak truthfully."

"And you're goin' to use it on me?" Kim asked cautiously. It was not a welcome thought. There were any number of things she would rather not be forced to discuss truthfully: the uses to which she had put her expertise in lock picking, for instance. On the other hand, this was an opportunity to observe real magic at close hand, and she wasn't about to pass it up without a reason. Assuming, of course, that she had a choice.

"Not exactly. The magic of the Saltash Bowl can be used only under

very specific circumstances. More important, it can be used only when
the entire set is together."

"That platter the gentry cove was talkin' about?"

"Among other things. I cannot, therefore, use the bowl to force you
to be truthful. However, I believe I can cast a similar spell, using the bowl
as a focus, which will let me know whether or not you are telling the
truth."

"So if I don't say nothin', you can't tell what's true?" Kim said.
Mairelon's lips tightened, and she added hastily, "I'm just tryin' to understand. You ain't got no business knowin' everything about me."

"A reasonable objection," Mairelon said after a moment. "Very well.
The spell is just an indicator. If you don't say anything, it won't have
anything to work with, so it won't tell me anything."

Kim nodded. She understood the unspoken implication well enough.
Mairelon would be able to tell a good deal by which questions she chose
not to answer. "All right, then," she said. "I'm ready. What do I have to
do?"

"Just stand there, for the time being." Mairelon turned back to the
silver bowl. He smoothed a wrinkle from the velvet on which it rested
and laid a twist of straw beside it, not touching the silver. Then he opened
Hunch's packet and sniffed at it. He nodded in satisfaction, but to Kim's
surprise, he did not dump it into the bowl with the root of the herbs.
Instead, he set it down and reached for the lamp that hung beside the
door. He adjusted the wick, then did something to the hook that held
it. When he pulled on it, the lamp came away from the wall on a long,
flexible arm.

Mairelon positioned the lamp to hang a hand's breadth above the
center of the silver bowl. Then he looked at Kim. "If you have any other
questions, ask them now. From here on, any interruption could have . . .
unpleasant consequences."

"I understand." Every street waif in London had heard whispers of
the fate that came to anyone foolish enough to interrupt a true wizard in
the practice of his magic. Burning alive would be nothing to it. Kim
might have her doubts about some of the things she'd heard, but she
wasn't about to test them now.

Mairelon gave her a searching look, then nodded. He turned back
to face the bowl and took a deep breath. The lamp above the bowl threw
the magician's shadow against the opposite wall, large and dark, and made
a mask of his face. Kim shivered, then froze as Mairelon began to speak.

The language was unfamiliar to Kim, but every word seemed to hang in the air, clear and sharp as broken crystal. She could almost feel their edges, and she was afraid to move and jostle their invisible presence. She understood, now, where the saying had come from, "deadly as a wizard's words." She wondered how there could be room in the wagon for the solid sounds Mairelon was speaking.

The magician's hands moved suddenly, sliding with exquisite precision into a gap in the growing lattice of invisible, razor-edged words. One hand seized the packet of herbs Hunch had provided; the other lifted the twisted straw on the opposite side of the bowl. The straw touched the lamp's wick and burst into flame. Mairelon's voice rose to a shout, and herbs and burning straw dropped together into the silver bowl.

Smoke billowed out of the bowl, spreading a strong, sweet smell throughout the wagon. The lamp went out with the suddenness of a snuffed candle, and the silver bowl began to glow. Mairelon lowered his arms with a sigh and looked at Kim. "What is your name?" he said.

Kim hesitated. "Jenny Stower," she said deliberately.

The glow of the silver bowl dimmed to an angry red point. "Your name?" Mairelon repeated. "And the truth, this time."

"Kim."

The bowl flashed into silver light once more. Kim stared at it, awed and frightened. "Where did you first hear of me, and from whom?" Mairelon asked.

"At the Dog and Bull, the day afore I snuck into this wagon. A skinny toff offered to pay me if I'd find out what you had in here." The bowl remained silver, and Kim relaxed a little.

"What, exactly, did he tell you?"

Kim repeated the story she had told Mairelon at their first meeting. The bowl glowed a steady silver throughout the tale. Mairelon nodded when she finished, and made her repeat her reasons for eavesdropping on his conversation with Shoreham. Kim did the best she could, but the bowl's light faded slightly.

Mairelon frowned. "And were those your only reasons?"

Kim shifted uncomfortably. "Mostly."

"You'll have to do better than that," Mairelon said, watching her closely.

"All right! I was curious."

The silver light brightened. Mairelon's lips twitched. "Curious?"

"Why not?" Kim said indignantly. "Anyone as meets you can see you're a regular swell, and it queers me what your lay is. Bilking the culls in the markets ain't work for a gentry cove, and you ain't told me nothin'. I got reason for wonderin'."

Mairelon laughed. "I should have guessed. Well, I'll explain as soon as we're finished here. You've enough of the pieces to get us all into difficulty by accident if you aren't told the rest."

He asked Kim a few more offhand questions, but his suspicions seemed to be laid to rest. "That's all, I think," he said at last. He turned to the bowl and raised a hand, then paused and looked at Kim. "Why *did* you decide to leave London with us? Curiosity again?"

Kim swallowed. "Yes," she said, and the bowl flickered.

Mairelon looked from her face to the bowl and lowered his hand. "There is more, I think?"

"It ain't nothin' to do with you!"

The light held steady, and Mairelon nodded. "Perhaps it is not, now. However, we will be returning to London eventually, and I don't like the possibility of a nasty surprise waiting for me."

"He ain't waitin' for *you*," Kim muttered.

"Nevertheless, I should like to know who 'he' is, and why you considered it so important to remove yourself from his vicinity. Particularly if the reason is something that is likely to interest the constables."

"It ain't the nabbing culls I'm worried on," Kim said, scowling. "It's Laverham." She sighed. "I suppose now I got to tell you."

"Have to. I would appreciate it. Who is Laverham?"

Kim took a deep breath and began trying to explain her antipathy to Dan Laverham. Mairelon waved her to silence after a few sentences.

"I'll take your word for it that the man is unpleasant," the magician said. "But what set you off?"

"He was at Tom's shop, where I took those flash togs you asked me to get rid of. He asked a lot of questions, and one of his men tried to follow me when I left."

Mairelon frowned. "He had you followed? How far?"

"Half a block in the wrong direction; I tipped him the double right off."

"And you're sure it was you he was interested in?"

Kim shrugged. "What else? Laverham's been aching to get his fambles on me since before old Mother Tibb stuck her spoon in the wall."

"Who is Mother Tibb?" Mairelon asked.

"She raised me and some others," Kim said shortly. "She's dead." She didn't want to talk about Mother Tibb. Even after two years, talking brought back memories of the skinny old woman's terrified howls as the constables hauled her off to prison, and of the hangman's steady tread and the sickening thud as the trapdoors dropped away beneath the feet of his line of victims. Kim preferred to remember the dubious safety and fleeting camaraderie of the earlier years, when she thought of Mother Tibb at all.

"I'm sorry," Mairelon said gently. He paused. "About Laverham—" He made her describe her brief encounter in as much detail as she could remember. At last he paused and said, "All right, I'll agree that he seems to have been after you. But if anything else like that happens, or if you run into Laverham or any of his men again, tell me."

Kim nodded. Mairelon turned to the still-glowing silver bowl and moved both hands in a swift, complicated gesture above it. The light gathered around the rim of the bowl, as though something were sucking it upward. Then, with a faint popping noise, the lamp flared into life and the glow of the bowl vanished.

Mairelon smiled in satisfaction and began setting the wagon to rights. The extended lamp hook folded neatly and invisibly back into the wall beside the door, the ashes of the herbs were thrown outside, and the Saltash Bowl was wiped and wrapped in velvet once more. Kim watched for a few minutes in silence before reminding Mairelon that he had promised to explain to her what was really going on.

"So I did. The story really starts about fifteen years ago, when old Lord Saltash died. He left a rather large bequest to the Royal College of Wizards. You've heard of the Royal College, I trust?"

"As much as anybody."

"Mmmm. Well, Saltash fancied himself a magician, and he'd collected a tremendous number of odds and ends of things that he thought ought to be properly investigated. He dumped the lot on the College. Most of them turned out to be quite worthless, but—"

"That's why you called it the Saltash Bowl!" Kim said. "It was part of the rum cull's collection!"

"Yes, though I wouldn't call Saltash a rum cull. The bowl is only part of the grouping; there's a silver platter that matches it, and four carved balls of different sizes. Together, they're the key to a very interesting spell."

"Making people tell the truth," Kim said, nodding.

"I don't think you realize what that means," Mairelon said testily. "It's easy enough to bind someone *not* to do things, but a spell to force a person to *speak*, and to speak only the truth, without interfering with the ability to answer intelligently—well, it's remarkable. Most control spells are obvious; they make the people they're used on act like sleep-walkers. But the Saltash group—"

"All right!" Kim said hastily. "It's bang-up. What next?"

"The Royal College spent a good deal of time, here and there, trying to duplicate the spell on the grouping. No one ever succeeded, and the Saltash group became a curiosity. And then, four years ago, it was stolen."

Mairelon paused. "It was stolen," he repeated, "in such a way that it appeared that I was the thief."

"You were in the Royal College?" Kim asked.

Mairelon blinked, as if he had expected some other response. Then he smiled slightly. "Yes, I was. Under another name, you understand."

"Richard Merrill?"

"You *are* a shrewd one. Yes, that is my name."

"But you ain't the sharper who nicked the bowl."

"No. If I hadn't been lucky enough to run into Edward, though, I'd have no way of proving it. The evidence was overwhelming. Even my brother Andrew believed it."

Kim snorted. "He's a noodle, then."

Mairelon's face lost its set look, and he laughed. "A surprisingly apt description, I'm afraid."

"So why didn't this Edward cove tell anybody that you ain't the one who lifted them things?"

"Those things, Kim, not them things. At the time, it was . . . convenient to have an excuse for leaving the country quickly."

"How do you mean?" Kim asked suspiciously.

"I was spying on the French," Mairelon said baldly.

"Oh."

"And there was my pride, too. Hubris, the failing of the gods. I wanted to recover the stolen items myself, you see. I thought I'd find out who was behind the theft. Someone at the College was involved, I'm certain. I asked Edward to let me try."

"And that's how you got hold of that bowl?"

"It took me a year to track it down after the war ended. It was in a little town in Germany, property of the local Baron. He'd picked it up as a souvenir of England, and he was incredibly stubborn about selling it."

Kim thought back to the conversation she'd inadvertently overheard. "So now you're going to Ranton Hill to find the platter part. What about the rest of it?"

"I can use each piece to help find the others, and it gets easier the more pieces I have. With the bowl and the platter together, it won't be hard to locate the four spheres."

"What about—" Kim's question was interrupted by a peremptory knock at the door. Mairelon lifted an eyebrow in amusement and went to open it.

Hunch stood outside, his expression clearly disapproving. "You've 'ad your hour, Master Richard," he said. "And I'd like to know where 'Is Lordship's sending us off to this time."

"Essex," Mairelon said, and grinned. "Ranton Hill, to be precise. Did you have any other questions, Kim? Then, if you'll excuse us, we had better go and figure out what route will get us there with a minimum of delay. We can talk more in the morning."

eight

For the next five days, it rained. Torrential downpours alternated with misty drizzle or bone-chilling showers that made even the best roads treacherous going. The seldom-frequented lanes used by Mairelon's wagon became a sticky quagmire which plastered the horses and mired the wagon wheels. Despite Mairelon's best efforts, their progress slowed to a crawl.

None of them rode; the wagon alone was nearly too heavy for the horses to tow along the roads. Hunch and Mairelon took turns leading the horses, sliding and stumbling through cold, oozy mud that sucked at their feet and weighted down their boots in inch-thick layers. Even Kim sank ankle-deep unless she kept to the verge and slid on the slippery wet mats of last year's grass instead.

By the time they stopped to camp each night, they were all exhausted, but Mairelon insisted that Kim continue her lessons no matter how tired she was. It was easier to agree than argue, so Kim applied herself as best she could to arts such as reading and legerdemain which could not be conveniently practiced while marching through the rain. During the day, Mairelon continued her instruction in what Kim privately called "flash talk." When her voice grew hoarse, he let her stop and listen while he recited poetry or plays, or rendered the same speech over and over in a variety of styles and accents.

They slept in the wagon, though Hunch muttered balefully and chewed his mustache over the arrangement. Kim was not really sure whether he was fretting over Mairelon's morals or the spoons; by the end of the second day, she no longer cared. Sleeping in a place that was even approximately dry was far more important than Hunch's disapproval. Mairelon appeared as unaware of Hunch's glares as he seemed unconscious of any impropriety, though Kim did not for a minute believe that he was as oblivious as he looked.

On the sixth morning, Kim followed Hunch out of the wagon to find a steady, soaking rain falling from an endless sheet of clouds the color of lead. With a snort of disgust, she pulled the collar of her cloak tighter around her neck in a hopeless effort to keep the water out. The cloak was Mairelon's, and much worn, and she had had to tie it up with a length of rope at her waist to keep it from dragging in the mud. It made a bulky, awkward garment and she was positive that she would slip and end up covered in mud before the morning was over.

"Cheer up," Mairelon said as he passed her, heading for the horses. "It will stop before noon."

"Hah," Kim said. She took an injudicious look at the sky, which was still uniformly leaden, and water dripped down her neck. "Ow!" she said, and glared after Mairelon. "If you're so knowin', why ain't you put a stop to it afore now?"

"Haven't," Mairelon said absently. "Why *haven't* I put a stop to it before now."

"All right, why haven't you?" Kim said crossly.

"Because weather magic is tricky, time-consuming, costly, and extremely noticeable," Mairelon replied with commendable patience. "I can't afford the time or the energy, and I certainly can't afford to be noticed. Not until we've gotten our hands on the Saltash Platter, at least."

He continued on and Kim scowled after him. "What's the good of traveling with a wizard if you have to get wet in the rain like other people?" she muttered.

Low as her voice was, Hunch heard her. "You'd ought to be glad you wasn't left in London!"

"Why?" Kim demanded. "At least there I could keep dry. And I wouldn't have to worry about no nabbing culls, either."

"Any." Mairelon's voice came floating over the heads of the horses. "If the two of you have finished exchanging pleasantries, it's time we left. Rear doors, please; Hunch, take the right side, the wheel's sunk a little deeper there, I think."

Kim and Hunch took up positions on either side of the wagon. "Ready? Now," Mairelon called, and they pushed while he urged the horses forward. After a brief struggle, the wagon rolled forward and they were on the move again.

To Kim's disgust, the rain soon dwindled to a light drizzle. By noon it had stopped entirely, and Mairelon was wearing a smug expression. Kim was more than a little inclined to snarl at him, but in the past few days she had learned that snarling at Mairelon did little good. He simply smiled and corrected her grammar.

They stopped early that evening, for travel was still muddy and exhausting. Then, too, they were less than an hour's travel from Ranton Hill, even with the mud, and Mairelon had not yet decided whether he wanted the wagon to be much in evidence when they arrived. With that in mind, he had chosen a campsite where a small wood came down to meet one side of the road, so that the wagon could be drawn in among the trees.

Hunch built a large fire while Mairelon and Kim hauled pots and buckets of water from an irrigation ditch on the other side of the road. When they arrived back at the camp, they found that Hunch had already hung the dampest of the cloaks and bedding around the fire, blocking most of the heat. Hunch accepted the buckets with his most dour expression, and Kim and Mairelon retreated at once to the far side of the wagon.

"What's got into him?" Kim asked, settling herself onto the footboard at the front of the wagon.

"Hunch is merely expressing his desire to continue his own activities without distraction from the two of us," Mairelon explained, leaning against the wall next to Kim.

"Does that mean he's goin' to start dinner soon?" Kim asked hopefully.

"Not soon, I'm afraid. First he'll want to get as many things cleaned and thoroughly dried as he can. Resign yourself to scorched bedclothes tonight."

Kim made a scornful noise. "Hunch ain't got no sense. Dinner's more important than blankets."

"Don't try to convince him of that," Mairelon said, smiling. "You won't succeed, and there's nothing to be gained from trying. Though perhaps I shouldn't be the one to make that argument; it's my dignity Hunch is trying to defend, you know."

"Ho! Hunch, worryin' over your dignity? After he's been naggin' at you for two days for wearin' that cloak instead of the one with the patches?"

"Yes, well, Hunch gets these notions from time to time. Have you practiced that handkerchief trick you were having trouble with?"

"I ai—haven't had time," Kim said. "I can't do it at all on the move, and we only just got here."

"Then practice it now, before the light goes," Mairelon said, handing her a handkerchief.

Kim rolled her eyes and spread the handkerchief out on her lap. She flexed her cold fingers several times, trying to limber them up a little, then began carefully folding and rolling the linen square as Mairelon had taught her. She was only half finished when Mairelon's head turned and she heard him murmur, "Now, I wonder who that is?"

Kim looked up. Through the screen of trees she saw a coach-and-four making its slow, soggy way up the lane; the heads of two postillions were clearly visible above the coach's roof. Kim blinked in surprise. What was a bang-up turnout like that doing on a quiet farm lane? And where was it heading?

"Exactly what I would like to know," Mairelon said, and Kim realized that she had spoken aloud. Kim glanced at him and saw that he was frowning slightly. "And we're not going to find out sitting here."

Without waiting for Kim to respond, Mairelon pushed himself away from the wagon, pulled his shapeless, still-damp hat farther down on his head, and started briskly off into the trees in the same direction that the coach was traveling. Kim blinked, then dropped the handkerchief and scrambled after him.

The coach passed them a few minutes later. Screened by the small trees and untrimmed scrub along the edge of the woods, Mairelon and Kim studied it. Kim could hear loud female laughter from the carriage windows, but the curtains were drawn and she could not see who was inside. The driver and postillions were wrapped in driving cloaks against the damp, and their faces were impassive.

"Blast!" Mairelon said softly as the carriage lurched on by. "Can you keep up with it, Kim?"

"I don't know about that coach, but I can keep up with you right enough," Kim answered. "But shouldn't we go back and tell Hunch where we're goin'?"

"If we do that, we'll lose it," Mairelon said, ducking under a low-hanging branch. "You're right, though; Hunch should know. Why don't you—"

"I ain't goin' back now," Kim interrupted in as firm a tone as she could manage while trying to follow Mairelon's erratic path among the trees.

"All right," Mairelon said to her surprise. "But when Hunch finds out—look, they're turning off!"

The coach was indeed easing its way off of the lane and into the woods. From where Kim stood, it looked almost as if the coach were trying to force its way through the trees, but when she and Mairelon reached the spot a moment later, they found another lane leading into the woods.

"That driver is good," Mairelon commented, eyeing the trail. "This is hardly more than a deer path."

"You goin' to stand there jawing or get on after that coach?" Kim asked pointedly. "It's gettin' dark."

"So it is," Mairelon said. "Come along."

The trail wound through the trees almost as erratically as Mairelon had, and the curves hid the coach from sight. Fortunately the imprint of the wheels in the soft ground was easy to follow, and they made better time now that they did not have to worry about being seen. Even so, walking became more difficult as the light faded. Kim was about to suggest that they turn back before they lost their way completely when Mairelon stopped.

"Look there!" he said in a low voice, pointing.

Kim, who had been concentrating on following the coach tracks through the deepening gloom, looked up. Light danced among the trees. "Some cull's lit a fire on the hill, looks like."

"It does indeed," Mairelon said. "And I'll lay you odds that's where our coach is headed."

"Doesn't look like it to me," Kim said, though without a great deal of conviction. The trail they followed did not, at the moment, appear to head in the direction of the bonfire, but that did not mean it would not shift its bearing on the far side of the next bend.

"Let's find out, shall we?" Mairelon said with his most charming smile, and, turning, he headed for the bonfire.

After a moment's hesitation, Kim followed. Sticking with Mairelon was certainly safer than trying to continue after the coach alone and in the dark, and she was decidedly uninterested in going back to the camp and explaining all this to Hunch without Mairelon's support. Besides, she was at least as curious about the bonfire as she was about the coach and Mairelon's interest in it.

The fire was farther away than it looked; it took ten minutes of brisk walking to reach the foot of the short, steep hill with the fire on top. Kim was a little surprised at the way the hill poked up out of the flat ground, but she supposed that things were different in the country than in London. The hill was bare of trees except for a single large trunk at the top, clearly visible in the firelight, and the grassy slope had been recently scythed.

Several young men stood around the fire in the positions of people waiting for something and rather bored with doing so. One was staring down the far side of the hill; three others squatted over a game of dice, while two more watched and contributed unrequested advice; another drank surreptitiously from a pocket flask. Their voices carried clearly to the edge of the forest.

"Meredith's late again," the man with the flask commented.

"So's Robert," one of the others said. "Maybe they've got better things to do on a cold, damp night like this."

"What, in the country?" said the man next to him.

"No main," said one of the dicers. "Throw again."

"It's Robert's turn to bring the girls," a fifth man spoke up. "He'll probably come along with them."

"I told you he had something better to do!"

"Eight for a main," announced the second of the gamblers. "Shoot again."

"Robert's coach is just turning in at the lodge," said the man who was watching the far side of the hill. "He'll be here in a minute or two. I hope he has sense enough to leave the rest of his party there. We don't need any bits of muslin giggling over the ceremony."

"Good; that's everyone but Meredith," said the man with the flask. "We can start without him."

"Not tonight," the watcher said without turning.

"Burn it, Jon, are you going to make us stand here all night?" the man with the flask expostulated. "Meredith may not even come! He's missed meetings before."

"Two guineas on the fader's point," said one of the dicers coolly.

"If you don't like it, Austen, finish your flask and go," the watcher said. "But remember that you swore an oath—"

"I didn't know it was going to mean standing out in a cold wind in the middle of the night, scorching my boots at a great stupid fire while you prose on at me!" Austen said in tones of deep indignation.

"If your boots are scorching, you've only yourself to blame," said a cheerful voice, and a new figure climbed over the far edge of the hill and into the firelight. His arms were full of something that strongly resembled a very large bundle of laundry. "You don't see anyone else standing close enough to the fire for ashes to fall on his coat, do you?"

"Ashes!" Austen leaped backward, brushing at his cloak. He peered closely at his garments, then gave the newcomer a reproachful look. "Burn it, Robert, if that's your idea of a joke—"

"Don't get in a stew about it," Robert advised him. "Here, take your robe before I drop the lot of them in the mud."

This thinly veiled warning caught the attention of the rest of the group, and for the next few minutes they crowded around the newcomer, laughing and shoving and tugging at the bundle in his arms. Kim glanced at Mairelon, to see whether he had had his fill of watching this strange gathering. By now it was too dark to make out much of his expression, but he seemed to be concentrating closely on the hilltop group.

"Who are those coves?" Kim whispered.

Mairelon glanced down as if he had just remembered her presence. "A pack of imbeciles," he answered. "And if I'm not mistaken—ah, yes. See for yourself."

Kim looked back at the hilltop. About half of the men were pulling long, baggy, light-colored robes over their heads. "They look like Bedlamites to me," Kim muttered. "Who—"

"Ssh!" Mairelon said as the man called Jon said something to Robert that Kim did not catch.

"No, I didn't," Robert said, evidently answering Jon's question. "The girls and the robes were almost more than I could manage as it was. I left it with Meredith after the last meeting."

"And Meredith's still not here." Jon's voice sounded grim. "If he doesn't come, you're for it, Robert."

"How much longer are you planning to wait, Jon?" one of the white-robed men asked. "Have we got time for a few more throws?"

"Can't you think of anything but your dice?" Jon snarled.

The man gave a cheerful, unrepentant shrug. "Well, there's the doxies at the lodge, but I have the feeling you wouldn't like that much of a delay."

Some of the others laughed. Jon looked as if he were about to explode, but before he could deliver whatever rebuke he had in mind, Austen said, "There! Isn't that him?"

Heads turned, and someone said, "That's Freddy, all right. Nobody else sits a horse that badly; you can spot him even in the dark."

"Hurry it up, Meredith!" Austen shouted.

"Quiet, you fool!" Jon said, rounding on him. "Do you want to be heard from here to the village? Do you want people to come spying on our Sacred Rites?"

"Oh, really, Jon, don't get carried away," Robert said. "There's a dozen light-skirts in the lodge who can see us from the windows if they want to bother."

"They are here by our permission," Jon said loftily.

His dignified effect was spoiled by someone at the back of the group, who snickered and said audibly, "I should hope so!"

Jon glared around him, but could not locate the speaker. He turned away, and a moment later another figure came panting over the crest of the hill. Robert handed him the last of the robes, and he struggled into it hastily while the others pointed out the difficulties his tardiness had caused them.

"Didn't mean to be so late," said the newcomer in a muffled voice from halfway inside his robe. "I . . . had to make a stop on the way here."

"There will be time to hear your explanations later, Meredith," Jon said. "Now we must begin. To your places, gentlemen!"

The white-robed figures spread out in a circle around the fire and drew the hoods of their robes up over their heads. It made them look suddenly eerie, almost terrifying, and Kim shivered slightly. One of the anonymous figures raised his arms above his head, and Jon's voice cried loudly, "By the Sacred Oak, and Ash, and Thorn! By the Three Wise Birds and the Three Generous Kings! By the Ineffable Name Itself! The rites of the Sons of the New Dawn are now begun!"

nine

The white-robed figures lowered their heads and began a strange, droning chant.

Kim shuddered again as sonorous phrases drifted down the hill, and she jumped when Mairelon touched her arm.

"I'm going to see if I can get a little closer," Mairelon said, looking at her quizzically. "You can wait here, if you're feeling jumpy."

"Wait here, with them frog-makers up there mumblin' spells? Kim whispered indignantly. "What do you take me for?"

Mairelon snorted. "Spells? Don't be ridiculous. That's the most preposterous rigmarole I've ever had the misfortune to have to listen to. Don't let it worry you."

"Why not?"

"Because they're mixing magic at random, from the sound of it. Half of it's Welsh, half of it's Scottish, and half of it's cribbed from someone's classical education, with a few things that are entirely out of someone's imagination thrown in for good measure. They'll never get anywhere if that's the tack they're taking."

"That's too many halves," Kim said, frowning. "And whatever it is, it sounds pretty impressive to me." The words didn't have the crystalline quality of Mairelon's magic, but they had a portentous power of their own that was just as striking.

"That's because you've never read Homer in the original Greek," Mairelon said. His attention had returned to the hilltop, where the white robes were now marching solemnly around the fire. Kim reached for his arm, anticipating his next move, but she was an instant too late. Mairelon slipped out of the trees and started up the hill, crouching low to avoid the firelight. With a sigh and a string of mental curses, Kim followed.

To her relief, Mairelon did not try to sneak all the way up to the edge of the hilltop. He stopped about halfway up the slope, near enough to hear every word clearly but still well below the level where a casual glance might see a careless silhouette. Kim stopped beside him and flattened herself against the ground. Mairelon looked at her, then, with visible reluctance, did the same.

The cold and damp seemed to penetrate Kim's clothes almost instantly. She ignored the discomfort as best she could, knowing from years of Mother Tibb's somewhat irregular training that an unnecessary movement was likely to attract unwanted attention. Beside her, Mairelon lay just as motionless, and Kim tried to distract herself by wondering where he had learned the trick. Had someone told him about it when he went off to spy on the French, or had he figured it out for himself the hard way?

The chanting stopped at last, and Kim heard Jon's voice announce, "So is the beginning ended, and the Central Mysteries begun."

A murmur of agreement rose from the assembled figures. As the muttering died, Jon went on in a much brisker tone, "Tonight we are to dedicate the Sacred Dish, the first of the Four Holy Things. Austen, you're the Bearer; George, you and Quembly-Stark can do the Escorts, and Robert can act as—"

"Uh, Jonathan, I'm afraid there's a bit of a problem," someone put in tentatively.

"You forgot to bring the dish, didn't you?" Jon snapped. "Well, I'm not putting off the ceremony again just because you have a bad memory, Meredith. This time you can just ride home and bring it back."

"That'll take hours!" someone else objected. "Especially if he came on that broken-down nag of his; the creature can't move above a trot even with a good rider in the saddle."

"As long as we can wait down at the lodge instead of up here in the wind, who cares?" another of the men retorted.

"No reason to wait at all," Meredith said. Cautiously Kim raised her head. As she had expected, all eyes were on the bland and rather foolish-looking Meredith. "I can't get the thing, you see," Meredith explained. "So there's no point in my going back, and no reason to wait."

"Can't get it?" Jon's voice rose. He put back his hood and glared at Meredith. "What do you mean, you can't get it?"

"I just can't," Meredith answered with dogged stubbornness. "That's all, and there it is. No use going on at me about it; might as well finish up and go on down to the lodge."

"Explain this . . . this recalcitrance!" Jon commanded.

"Yes, Freddy, just why is it that you can't bring the dish out tonight?" Robert asked.

"If you must know, I haven't got it any more," Meredith said. "Now can we go down to the lodge and eat?"

Jon goggled at him, all but speechless with rage. "You haven't *got* it?"

"Got a problem with your ears, Jon?" Meredith asked with interest. "M'grandfather's been having a bit of trouble that way, but you expect it in a man his age."

"What have you done with the Sacred Dish?" Jon grated.

"Lost it in a card game," Meredith said. "Debt of honor; pay or play, you know. So it's gone."

"How *dared* you!" Jon shouted, waving his arms for emphasis. "That dish was ours, the property of the entire Order! How dared you even *think* to appropriate it for your own uses!"

"Actually it wasn't," Meredith said almost apologetically.

"Wasn't what, Freddy?" Robert asked.

"Wasn't the property of the Order. Bought it myself; never been paid. Logically the thing was mine. All quite in order." Freddy Meredith nodded, as if to emphasize the logic and propriety of his actions.

Jon turned a fascinating shade of purple and opened his mouth. "Freddy's got a point, Jon," Robert said hastily. "If he didn't use the Order's funds to buy it with—"

"What funds?" Austen put in. "This Order hasn't got any funds; nobody's paid their subscription fee in over six months. Including you, Jon."

"There, you see?" Freddy beamed.

"You idiot!" Jon said. "Do you know how long it took me to locate that platter? We must get it back!"

"It's quite all right, Jonathan," Robert said. "We'll just buy it back from whoever won it from Freddy. Who did win it, by the way? Not Lord North, I hope."

"No, no, I don't play at his table," Freddy assured him. "Been around long enough to know a flat from a leg, you know. No, I was playing whist with Henry."

"What does Henry Bramingham want with the silver dish of the Sons of the New Dawn?" someone asked.

The grass beside Kim quivered as Mairelon tensed, but she could not tell what had provoked the reaction from him. Surely it couldn't have taken him this long to guess that the "sacred dish" these culls were so nattered about was the Saltash Platter he was looking for?

"Only stake I had left by the end of the night was the platter," Meredith explained. "Henry cleaned me out. Last hand, that went, too."

"Who cares?" someone else said. "It's obvious that we're not going to dedicate the Sacred Dish tonight, so let's finish up here and get inside where it's warm."

This suggestion produced a round of enthusiastic cheers, and the entire group threw off their robes and started down the hill despite Jonathan's grumbles and the glowering looks he continued to throw at the oblivious Freddy Meredith. None of them bothered to check the far slope of the hill, so Mairelon and Kim escaped detection. Even so, Kim did not really relax until the last sounds of merriment were muffled by the solid closing of a door.

Kim sat up at last, feeling cold and stiff, and realized that Mairelon was still lying prone against the side of the hill. She crouched again hastily and hissed, "Somethin' wrong?"

"What?" said Mairelon in a normal tone. "No, nothing's wrong; I'm thinking, that's all."

"Think about gettin' us back to camp," Kim advised. "Or Hunch'll be comin' after us with a rope, like as not."

"Oh, Hunch won't start worrying until well after dark," Mairelon said, still without moving.

Kim looked at him with profound exasperation. "It *is* well after dark," she pointed out.

"Then we'd better get back to camp quickly, hadn't we?" Mairelon said. He pushed himself away from the hill with his hands, twisted sideways, and slid down the slope feet-first. Kim scrambled after him, muttering curses. She was beginning to understand how Hunch had acquired the habit.

Getting back to camp took nearly as long as Kim had expected. Mairelon got lost twice, forcing them to retrace their steps in the dark. Kim did not enjoy these detours. The noises of insects and the occasional rustling movement of small animals made her jump, where the calls of lamplighters and the rumble of the heavy drays would have been soothing. Stumbling over an uneven clump of grass and falling into a bush was somehow different, and more unpleasant, than tripping on a broken cobblestone and landing in a pile of litter. Even the darkness had a different quality, a clarity and depth that bore no resemblance to the foggy blackness of the back streets of London.

Hunch met them on the road. He was carrying a lantern and frowning heavily, and both ends of his mustache looked distinctly damp and ragged. "Master Richard!" he said in evident relief when Mairelon came close enough to be identifiable. "You ain't 'urt!"

"What? Of course not," Mairelon answered. "Why should I be?"

" 'Cause you 'adn't got no reason for a-goin' off and not tellin' me, if you ain't been 'urt," Hunch said, recovering rapidly. "Leastwise, I don't see as you did."

"That's because you don't know where we've been," Mairelon said in his most reasonable tone. "You really ought to have a little more faith in me, Hunch."

Hunch snorted expressively. "All right, where 'ave you been?"

"Finding things out," Mairelon said. "Among them, the reason why our friend Shoreham has such a low opinion of the Sons of the New Dawn. As well as a hint to the current owner of the Saltash Platter."

"And 'oo might that be?"

"According to the ersatz druids whose undeniably imaginative ceremony we observed this evening, Henry Bramingham. Not the best of news."

" 'Enry," Hunch said, frowning. "I ain't sure—"

"Later, Hunch, if you please. Later, and preferably warmer, drier, and much less hungry. I hope no one has stolen our dinner while you've been swanning about out here."

"You 'ad ought to be sent to bed without any," Hunch grumbled, "and that dratted girl, too."

"Really, Hunch!" Mairelon said in a shocked tone before Kim could do more than gasp in outrage. "And all this time I'd thought you were worried about the proprieties."

Hunch's tangled efforts to refute this deliberate misinterpretation lasted until they reached the wagon. Kim was sure that this was exactly what Mairelon had intended, and while she would normally have been annoyed at his high-handed method of taking over her battle, this time Kim was grateful. She was cold and tired, and her hands and face bore scratches that stung when she thought about them. She was in no condition for an argument with Hunch.

Dinner was waiting, and if the stew was thick enough to cut with a knife and the potatoes in it were so well cooked that they came apart at the touch of a spoon, Kim did not mind at all. Mairelon was either pickier or preoccupied; he settled himself on the bottom step of the wagon with a full dish and a spoon, but ate so slowly that Kim was halfway through her second bowl before he finished a quarter of his own.

When Kim paused long enough to notice this curious behavior, she glanced at Hunch. He was frowning and nibbling delicately on the left half of his mustache whenever he looked in Mairelon's direction. That was enough for Kim. She moved to a conveniently situated rock, rattled her spoon against the side of her dish, and when Mairelon glanced up, said, "What's got you so nattered, then?"

"Henry Bramingham," Mairelon said. He took a spoonful of stew and looked down at his bowl with a frown of annoyance. "It's gone cold."

"If you'd of eaten it right off, you wouldn't of noticed," Kim said without sympathy. "Who's this Bramingham cove?"

"Henry Bramingham is the son of Charles Bramingham and Harriet St. Clair Bramingham," Mairelon answered. Hunch made a strangled noise, and Mairelon looked up. "Yes, exactly."

"Exactly what?" Kim said, thoroughly exasperated.

"Exactly the problem," Mairelon said. "Harriet, you see, is the sister of Gregory St. Clair. And the Baron has, shall we say, very little liking for your obedient."

"'E's the one as called in the Runners," Hunch said darkly. "*And* gave 'em Master Richard's name."

"So we think," Mairelon said. "He's also something of a wizard, and well known for his interest in unusual magical objects. If young Henry turns the platter over to his uncle, and I can think of no reason why he shouldn't, our chances of recovering it are small."

"So?" Kim said. The two men looked at her, and she shrugged. "I don't see what's the good in your havin' this platter you're so set on. If the Robin Redbreasts catch you with it, they'll be sure you cracked the crib and took it. I thought that was what you didn't want happenin'."

"You're right, but unfortunately there's no other way of finding out who really took the Saltash Set in the first place," Mairelon said. "If we can get all the pieces together, Shoreham and I can use one of the Ribensian Arcana to locate the person who stole them; but it won't work unless we have everything."

Kim shrugged again. "It's your neck. Which direction are you goin' to stick it out in next?"

Mairelon grinned. "The inn at Ranton Hill, I think. I can pick up some gossip and get some idea of how things stand at the Braminghams', how recently Lord St. Clair has visited, that sort of thing."

"Not tonight," Hunch said firmly. "And this time you ain't a-going off alone, not if I 'ave to 'ide every pair of breeches you 'ave."

Mairelon looked startled, then thoughtful. "Yes, I think it will do very well," he said after a moment. "You can poke about in the stables and kitchens, Kim can sit in the public room, and I'll see what the news is in the private parlors. Someone's bound to know something, and this way we don't stand a ghost of a chance of missing it."

"Why're you so sure?" Kim asked.

"The country inn is the heart of every village, or at least its ears and tongue," Mairelon explained. "Think of it as a London public house, only more so."

"If you say so," Kim said dubiously. "Just what am I goin' to have to do?"

They spent the next hour or so discussing the exact methods each would use in their descent upon Ranton Hill's inn, what stories they would tell, and what clothes to wear to be convincing. Mairelon declared that he would pose as a fashionable Town buck, victim of a carriage accident while driving down to a friend's country house. Kim would be his Tiger, despite her protests that she knew nothing about horses and would be unable to convince anyone that she was what she pretended to be. Hunch was a groom who had been traveling with the baggage coach; he would lead the horses from the wagon, claiming that they belonged to the ostensibly demolished phaeton. Mairelon's confidence overrode his companions' misgivings, and by the time the fire began to die everything was settled.

ten

Ranton Hill consisted of three shopfronts, two houses, an inn, and a stable. The buildings looked to Kim as if they had huddled together for protection from the empty farmland all around them. Not that the land was, technically, empty, but some low stone walls, a few trees, and a couple of sheep did not go nearly far enough, in Kim's opinion, toward filling up the space.

In addition, the village was so quiet that as they approached along the rutted dirt road Kim began to wonder if it was peopled by ghosts. The sound of the wind, the squeak of the harness leather, and the crunching of their feet and the horses' hooves against the road were the only noises. She was a little reassured when a dog began to bark as they reached the first house, summoning a stable hand in a well-worn smock from the rear of the inn.

Mairelon gave the man an offhand nod and disappeared into the inn. Kim looked after him, shifting her weight from foot to foot while the stable hand and Hunch eyed each other measuringly.

"What happened?" the man said at last, making a gesture that included the horse, Kim, Hunch, and the vanished Mairelon.

" 'E tipped 'is phaeton over trying to feather a corner," Hunch said with fine contempt. "Leastwise, that's 'ow I make it. '*E* says a coach-and-four ran 'im off the road."

The stable hand spat. "Another one o' them wild uns. He stayin' the night?"

" 'Ow do I know?" Hunch said. "Even if 'e'd told me, 'e's just as likely to change 'is mind as not."

"That's the Quality for you," the stable hand said, and spat again. "Well, bring your horses around back; no reason they should suffer for their master's stupidity."

The man started walking as he spoke. Hunch tightened the makeshift leads attached to the horses' halters. The animals bobbed their heads, slightly out of sequence, and began to move. Kim shifted her weight again, wondering whether she should follow or wait and wishing Mairelon had told her a little more about the duties of a Tiger. She was just about to start after Hunch and the horses when Mairelon stuck his head out of the door of the inn.

"Kim! There you are. No need to stand about; the luggage won't be along for a couple of hours at least. Come inside and wait where it's warm."

Kim nodded, glad to have some direction at last. As she started into the inn, she noted that the village was showing a few signs of life at last: a large, round woman had emerged to sweep the step in front of the mercer's shop (and get a look at the new arrivals), an open carriage was descending a distant hill toward the town, and a second dog had joined the barking of the first, prompting a volley of curses from an unseen person on the second floor of the inn. The last thing Kim saw before the door of the inn closed behind her was a large jug hurtling out of the window in the general direction of the dogs. The crash was audible even after the door closed.

Mairelon was standing just inside the door, in a short hallway at the foot of a steep flight of stairs. Beside him, the innkeeper darted uncertain looks at the mud-splattered boots and breeches of his newest guest, clearly trying to decide whether this was truly one of the Quality or only some jumped-up Cit trying to pass himself off as gentry. Kim could almost sympathize. Mairelon's cape was well cut but, to her experienced eye, a little shabby and out of fashion, and the mud made it difficult to determine whether his boots were similarly well used. Had she been looking him over on the London streets, she would have given him a casual glance and gone on hunting for a better pigeon to pluck.

"Get yourself something to drink while you wait," Mairelon said, seemingly oblivious to the innkeeper's worried frown. He tossed Kim a coin that glittered silver in the air, and the innkeeper's expression lightened. Kim suppressed a smile and bobbed her head respectfully as Mairelon turned to the innkeeper. "Now, since we're agreed, I'll just go up and clean off a little of this dirt."

"Very good, Mr. de Mare," the innkeeper answered. "Your lad can go on in there; my wife will be glad to see to him. Now, if you'll just come this way . . ."

Mairelon followed him up the stairs without a backward glance, leaving a trail of damp and dirty footprints. Kim snorted softly. At least she would be able to find his room if she needed to. She looked down at the coin Mairelon had tossed her. It was a new shilling, more than enough for a pint of ale and perhaps a roll. She flipped it into the air, caught it, and went into the public room to listen to whatever local gossip there might be.

The room was nearly empty. Two weather-beaten men in farmers' smocks glanced up from their mugs as she entered, and a small, brown-haired man in the corner jumped nervously and then relaxed. Kim took a seat beside the door, where she could get a good look at everyone who might come in and still watch the rest of the big, square room. Once she was seated, she discovered that her view of the yard outside was limited to a slantwise glimpse of a corner, but she dismissed that limitation with a mental shrug. Nothing was perfect, and her job was to watch and listen to the coves inside, not the goings-on outdoors.

A large, grey-haired woman who was presumably the innkeeper's wife appeared a few moments later, carrying a tray of mugs. She replaced the farmers' drinks without comment, then looked over at the nervous man in the corner. He shook his head, then nodded and beckoned. "Make up your mind, Mr. Fenton," the woman said as she set a mug in front of him. "I haven't the time to be mucking about back and forth to the kitchen twelve times an hour, not for the likes of you."

"My money's as good as anyone's," the small man said. "And if you 'forget' to let me know when my . . . associate arrives, I'll see you regret it."

"Keep your hair on," the woman advised. "Nobody's come asking for you, not even Mr. Frederick. And what *he*'s thinking of, letting you off your work like this—"

The small man flushed. "I have my half-day free, the same as anyone."

"Only more often," the woman shot back, and the two farmers chuckled audibly. "I'm surprised he doesn't turn you off, but there, he's always been the sort to put up with more than he ought."

"Mr. Meredith is kind enough to give me an extra holiday occasionally," the small man said, and Kim thought he sounded even more nervous than before.

"Yes, because you ask him straight out! You're abusing Mr. Frederick's trust, you are, and you ought to be ashamed."

"That's 'Mr. Meredith,' to you," the small man said with an attempt at a haughty sneer.

"Ho! 'Mr. Meredith,' to me that's known him since he was a lad? Next thing you'll be telling me what to call my husband! Drink up and hold your peace, *Mister* Fenton, or we'll see, that's all."

With this obscure threat, the woman picked up her tray and sailed back toward the door. She stopped long enough to give Kim a mug of warm, dark ale and collect the shilling, but Fenton did not take the opportunity to renew hostilities. He seemed content to glower over the top of his mug, alternating between dark looks at the grey-haired woman and equally dark but more apprehensive glances in the direction of the window overlooking the yard.

The innkeeper's wife left, and the farmers continued to sit in companionable silence. For lack of anything better to do, Kim studied Fenton while she sipped her ale and waited for someone else to come in and start another conversation for her to listen to. He was brown-haired and thin-faced, and he had an indefinable air about him that marked him as London-bred. From the conversation she had overheard, Kim guessed that he was in service with Mr. Meredith. A footman, perhaps; he was too well dressed to be a groom or stable hand, and not well enough turned out for a butler or valet.

Kim had just reached this conclusion when the serving room door flew open to reveal a dark-haired young man in fashionable riding clothes. He surveyed the room with an air of brooding intensity, then strode to the corner table and flung his gloves down in front of Fenton. "You sent me a message," the young man said.

Kim choked and slopped ale over the side of her mug. She recognized the young man's voice instantly; it was Jon, the most zealous of the druids she and Mairelon had observed the previous evening.

"I don't know that I would put it that way, Mr. Aberford," Fenton said, giving a significant glance in the direction of the farmers. "Merely, there are some things I think you ought to know."

"If your intention is to sell me the information that your master doesn't have the object he was commissioned to bring me, your luck is out," Jon said with gloomy relish. "I already know."

Fenton's shoulders hunched together as if he were bracing himself for a blow. "How did you find out—"

"He told me himself, last night. Blithering idiot! What possessed him to play whist with Henry Bramingham, of all people?"

"Ah, I believe there was a wager involved," Fenton said. His shoulders relaxed, but he did not look at all happy.

"Well, he certainly didn't *give* Henry the Dish!" Jon snapped.

"Of course not, Mr. Aberford. I, ah, thought you ought to know, that's all. So if—" Fenton broke off in mid-sentence, looking out the window. He jumped to his feet, his face a pasty white color, and bolted for the door. Jon sat staring after him in simple astonishment, taken too much by surprise to remember any of his brooding airs.

Fenton reached the door just as it opened to admit an enormous man in ill-fitting new clothes. " 'Ere, now! Watch what you're about!" the man said in a deep, slow voice as Fenton skidded to a stop in front of him.

"Sorry!" Fenton gasped, then dodged under the big man's arm and vanished.

" 'E's in a bit of a rush, ain't 'e?" the big man commented to the room at large.

Kim rose quietly as the newcomer lumbered into the room and slipped out the still-open door of the serving room. There was no sign of Fenton in the hall, so she took a quick look out the front door to see if she could tell what had driven him to make such a dramatic exit.

The yard was full of activity. A landau had pulled up in front of the inn, its top open despite the cool weather. A handsome and vaguely familiar young man sat with his back to the coachman; facing him were an extremely elegant woman in her early forties and a stunningly beautiful blonde girl of perhaps seventeen. A second young man, whom Kim recognized at once as the bland and somewhat foolish Freddy Meredith from the druids' meeting, had pulled a large, placid bay horse to a halt at the edge of the innyard. He was sitting in the saddle as if stunned, gazing in admiration at the blonde. Standing next to him (or rather, next to his horse) was a shabby, sour-looking man, and Kim found herself first blinking, then squinting in surprise, and then sternly suppressing a strong impulse to take to her heels as rapidly and unceremoniously as Fenton had done.

Jack Stower! What was Jack Stower doing in Ranton Hill? Fortunately, his attention was fixed on the rider, and Kim had time to pull her head back into the inn. She shut the door far enough to hide her face and forced her frozen wits into motion. Dan Laverham *couldn't* have sent Jack after her; she hadn't known herself where she was going when she left London. Jack was on some other errand, then, and all she had to do was keep out of his way so that word of her presence in Ranton Hill wouldn't get back to Laverham. To do that, though, she needed to know what Jack was up to, so that she could avoid him. Hoping that no one would come into the hall to find her in so odd-looking a position, Kim opened the door a crack and peered out, listening with all her might.

"He's your man," Stower was insisting to Freddy Meredith.

Freddy did not appear to hear. "Bramingham!" he called with every appearance of delight. "Didn't expect to find you here."

The young man in the carriage twisted to look over his shoulder. "Freddy? Good Lord! I mean, what are you doing out at this hour?"

"Things," the rider said with a vague wave. He clucked to his horse, which ignored him. A faint frown creased his forehead, and he made a tentative movement with his heels. The bay bent its neck to eye its rider, then ambled over to the carriage, leaving Jack Stower standing with his fists clenched and a black expression on his face.

"Henry!" the elegant woman said in a peremptory voice as Freddy was performing this maneuver. "If you *must* stop to speak with your friend, at least send someone in to inquire about Jasper. At this rate, we shall never get to Swafflton."

"Yes, of course, Lady Granleigh." Henry nodded to the footman, who jumped from his perch at the rear of the landau and came over. "See if Mr. Marston is in, and have a note sent up to tell him we are here."

"Be better to go inside," Freddy advised from his perch on the horse. "Private parlor for the ladies. Much nicer than sitting out in the weather."

Kim missed Henry's reply, for she had to nip sideways and flatten herself against the wall to avoid the footman's entrance. He clumped past her without noticing, glanced around, then rang loudly for the innkeeper. Kim slipped back to the door and saw that Jack Stower had vanished. She heard the innkeeper's footsteps at the rear of the hall and made a quick decision. Better to have room to move than to be nabbed by Stower or the footman in the hallway. She slid out the door like a greased eel.

"Very well," the elegant woman was saying in a disapproving tone. "But I will have the proprieties observed. Present your friend to us, Henry."

"My pleasure, Lady Granleigh," Henry said in a harassed tone. "Lady Granleigh, Miss Thornley, this is Mr. Frederick Meredith. Freddy, Lady Granleigh, and her ward, Miss Marianne Thornley. They're down for one of Mother's house parties."

"A pleasure," Freddy said, bowing.

"Meredith," Lady Granleigh said pensively. "Are you by chance related to Lord Cecil Meredith?"

"M'uncle," Freddy answered. "Stood godfather to me, or so they tell me. I don't remember it, myself."

"Indeed." Lady Granleigh's manner thawed noticeably. "Lord Cecil is a dear friend of my husband's."

"What brings you ladies out in all this muck?" Freddy asked offhandedly, though his eyes had returned to the lovely blonde girl.

"Since it is not raining, Lady Granleigh and I thought we would drive to Swafflton to look at ribbons," the blonde girl replied in a low, musical voice. "Mr. Bramingham was kind enough to accompany us."

"This ain't one of the stops on the road to Swafflton," Freddy said in a knowledgeable tone. "Sure Bramingham gave the coachman the right direction?"

"Freddy!" Henry said. "Don't be ridiculous."

"We are here to meet my brother," Lady Granleigh said in an icy voice.

"Oh, that's all right, then," Freddy said. "Didn't know you had one."

Miss Thornley giggled. Her guardian gave her a quelling look. "Really, Mr. Meredith—"

The door of the inn flew open. "Meredith! I knew it was you," Jon Aberford said in threatening tones.

"Hullo, Jon," Freddy said mildly. "Bit of a surprise, meeting you here. I must say, I didn't expect it."

"I should think not! How do you dare show your face in public?"

"Because I ain't a Turk," Freddy replied in reasonable tones. "Why should I care who sees it? Perfectly good face; besides, it's the only one I've got."

"Don't play the fool!" Jon said. "Henry, do you know what this . . . this blithering idiot has done?"

"No, and I don't much care to," Henry answered frankly. "It's nothing to do with me."

"Henry, you will do me the favor of *not* presenting me to your unpleasant and most unmannerly acquaintance," Lady Granleigh put in. "I must have the lowest opinion of anyone who would enact a scene in so public an arena."

"Ah, but it does!" Jon said, ignoring Lady Granleigh's interjection. He gestured at Freddy. "This *traitor* lost the Sacred Dish to you at play. Will you return it?"

"Here, now!" Freddy said. "Got no reason to go calling names! Everything was quite in order; told you so last night."

"Sacred dish?" Henry said, bewildered. "What are you on about now, Jonathan? You don't mean that big silver platter, do you?"

"Platter?" Lady Granleigh said with unexpected interest.

"What have you done with it?" Jonathan demanded.

"If you *are* talking about the platter, I haven't done anything with it yet," Henry snapped in evident exasperation. "It's sitting in a display case in the library, and it will *stay* in the display case until Lord St. Clair arrives tomorrow. At which point I am going to present it to him for his collection."

"What, your uncle's coming?" Freddy said to Henry. "You didn't tell me."

"Why should I?" Henry retorted. "It's nothing to you."

"No reason to keep it a secret, is there?" Freddy answered. "And it's bound to be of interest. Why, m'mother will want to call if Lord St. Clair is staying with you."

"Be quiet, Freddy!" Jonathan said. "Henry, be reasonable. You can't just give away the Sacred Dish!"

"Don't see why not," Freddy said, giving the matter due consideration. "*He* isn't one of the Sons; the thing don't mean anything to him. Unless St. Clair don't arrive. Hard to give something to someone who ain't there."

"Come by Bramingham Place tomorrow at three and watch me," Henry invited Jonathan cordially.

"You don't know what you are doing," Jon said, suddenly calm.

"I know enough."

"Quite," said Freddy. He had one eye fixed on Miss Thornley, who was beginning to look distressed. "Here, Jon, be a good fellow and come away; you're upsetting the ladies."

"You haven't heard the last of this," Jon said. With a parting glower he turned and reentered the inn.

"If that isn't just like Jon!" Freddy said.

"I trust we have seen the last of him," Lady Granleigh said. "Henry, are you quite certain that man of yours isn't carousing inside instead of delivering your message? Jasper ought to have come out by now."

Henry pressed his lips together. "I'll go and see, if you like, Lady Granleigh."

"If you do that, we'll lose you, too," Lady Granleigh said. "Send that boy over there; he may as well be useful."

"Hi! You there!" Henry beckoned to Kim. "Pop inside and see what's holding up Mr. Marston; there's half a guinea in it for you."

"A shilling," Lady Granleigh said sharply. "No more than a shilling, and not until you come back. Really, Henry, you ought to know better."

Kim muttered something that would pass for "Yes, mum," and touched her hand to her cap. The respectful gesture might please the bracket-faced old cat, and it would screen Kim's face from unwanted notice. Reluctantly she turned and started for the inn.

Before she reached it, the door swung open and the footman emerged, followed by a tall man in a driving cape. Kim stepped aside without thinking, and froze as she got a good look at his face. It was the skinny toff from the Dog and Bull who had hired her to crack Mairelon's crib. Had all of London followed her to Ranton Hill?

"Amelia!" the toff said. "What d'you mean by arriving at dawn like this? I'd barely got my breakfast finished!"

"When we are in the country, we keep country hours, Jasper," Lady Granleigh replied. "I explained that to you yesterday; had I known you were going to be obstinate, I would have postponed our expedition until tomorrow. I am sure that Lord St. Clair would have been delighted to accompany us."

"Of course he would," Freddy said gallantly. "I mean to say, lovely ladies, pleasant company—anyone would be delighted."

Jasper Marston had by this time taken his place in the coach, and Lady Granleigh had had more than enough of Freddy, nephew of Lord Cecil Meredith or not. "It is high time we were going," she announced. "Good day, Mr. Meredith. Driver!"

The coachman nodded and slapped the reins lightly against the horses' backs. The team snorted and began to move; in another moment, the landau had pulled out of the inn's yard and was on its way east to Swafflton.

eleven

Kim drew a shaky breath as she watched the coach pull away, all too conscious that only good luck had kept Jasper Marston from noticing her. She wanted to run away, to hide, and she wished suddenly and passionately that she were back in London, where she might have had some chance of doing so. With both Jack Stower and the skinny toff in Ranton Hill, it was beginning to look very much as if staying in London would have been safer than leaving.

Freddy Meredith, who had also been watching the coach, chose this moment to turn and see Kim. "Hi, boy! Get someone out here to take this horse, will you?"

Glad of the excuse, Kim nodded and went inside. The innkeeper was coming out of the kitchen into the hallway, carrying a tray. "And where the devil have you been, boy?" he asked when he saw Kim.

"Man outside wants someone to take his horse," Kim informed him, ignoring his question.

The innkeeper rolled his eyes. "Quality! Well, I'll see to it. Your master wants you; third door on the right at the top of the stairs. Take this along with you."

The stairs were narrow and steep, and Kim had some difficulty in climbing them without dumping everything off the tray the innkeeper had handed her. She made it to the top at last, and stood balancing the tray against the railing while she caught her breath. Then she counted doors and kicked at the third one.

"Enter," Mairelon's voice called from inside the room.

"I can't," Kim called back crossly. "You'll have to open the door yourself."

She heard a scraping sound on the other side of the door, and then Mairelon opened it. "Kim! What are you doing with that?"

"The buffer downstairs said you ordered it," Kim replied, setting the tray on the table.

"And was too lazy to bring it up himself, hmm? Good Lord, you're white as a winding-sheet! Sit down, sit down, before you fall over." Mairelon took the tray from Kim's suddenly shaking hands and set it on the small table beside the window. Kim sank into the nearest chair. She was cold and her legs felt like jelly; she was too stunned even to think, though a corner of her mind marveled distantly at the strength of her reaction.

"Here," Mairelon said, pressing a glass into her hand. "Drink this. Will you be all right alone for a moment? I'm going to get Hunch."

Kim nodded, and Mairelon left. She took a deep breath, and the feeling of being far away from everything began to lessen. She sipped at the glass Mairelon had handed her, and coughed as a fiery liquid ran unexpectedly down her throat.

The door opened and Mairelon reentered the room. "Now, what's given you the wind up? Did your friend from the Dog and Bull see you?"

"I don't think so," Kim said. "But how did you know—"

"He's staying in the next room," Mairelon said. "I could hardly help noticing his presence, and I thought there was something familiar about his voice. So I contrived to get a look at him as he left. If it wasn't our skinny friend, what's upset you?"

"I ain't sure," Kim said. She was feeling more like herself, and her momentary weakness bothered her. "I ain't never done nothin' like that before, not even on my first crack lay."

"Really. And how long has it been since you did any house-breaking?" Mairelon asked.

"Couple years. Since old Mother Tibb died, anyways. After what happened to her, I lost the taste for it, sort of."

"What happened to her?" Mairelon said very softly.

"The nabbing culls got her. Most of the others, too. I was lucky I got away." She took a tiny sip from the glass and closed her eyes. "They got transported, mostly, but Mother Tibb swung because she ran things for the lot of us."

"I see."

"I shouldn't of gone to watch. It was stupid. And after that . . ."

"After that, you didn't feel as if you could go back to housebreaking."

Kim shrugged. "I never took to it much, not like some of the rest. Besides, it ain't a good lay for a loner, and I couldn't join up with one of the other gangs because—" She stopped short and shook her head. Why was she telling Mairelon all this?

"Because they'd have discovered that you were a girl," Mairelon finished quietly. He was looking at her with an odd expression that she didn't have the energy to figure out. "Was it so important to you, staying a boy?"

Kim nodded wearily. "You ain't never seen the stews in St. Giles, or you wouldn't need to ask. Mother Tibb kept me on a good three years longer than most, because I had a knack for locks, but that wouldn't of lasted much longer. Anybody else would of packed me off as soon as they found out I wasn't a boy."

Mairelon went still. "Drink your brandy," he said, and his voice was harsh.

The brandy wasn't so bad, now that Kim knew what to expect. It was a great deal better than the cheap gin she had sometimes bought in London. She sipped it slowly, and in a few minutes more her grim mood began to lift.

"I found out some things you ought to know," Kim said to end the long silence.

"Wait until Hunch gets here," Mairelon said. "No sense in going over everything twice."

Fortunately, Hunch was not long in appearing. He snorted through his mustache when he saw Kim, which did more to make her feel herself again than even the brandy.

"Sit down and stop grumphing, Hunch," Mairelon said. "I've taken separate rooms for tonight, but we can hardly talk through the wall, and Kim says she's found out something of interest."

"That's as may be," Hunch said darkly. "But she 'adn't ought to be 'ere, and neither should you. Someone's been asking questions down at the stable."

"But it's such an interesting place," Mairelon said, waving in a general way at the walls of the inn. "Really, Hunch, you have no idea how fascinating this inn is."

"Maybe not," Hunch said, "but I know when you're at one o' your queer starts, Master Richard. And you 'adn't ought to, not this time. Someone's looking for us."

"Oh, really, Hunch, how can you be sure of that?"

" 'Ow many people 'ave a yellow wagon with red wheels and a painting of a man in a top 'at on the back?" Hunch countered.

Mairelon frowned. "Someone's asking questions about the *wagon*?"
Hunch nodded. "It's us she's looking for, right enough."

"She?"

Kim thought that Hunch was enjoying the effect his news was
having, though his expression remained dour. "Aye. One of them grand
ladies, they said. Offered a meg to anyone as 'ad news of it, and a shilling
extra if she could be sure no one else 'ad the news afore 'er."

"What a good thing we left the wagon in the woods," Mairelon
commented. He moved to the window and stared down at the stable.

"That ain't all, neither," Hunch said. "There was a cove nosing
around, too, 'anging about in back of the inn and be'aving oddly. The
'ostler said 'is name was James Fenton."

"Fenton?" Kim said. "There was a Mr. Fenton in the taproom for a
while; he looked like a footman or somethin'. I think he works for that
Meredith cove, the one who had that platter and lost it playin' cards."

"Does he," Mairelon said thoughtfully. "I wonder. What was he
doing here, do you know?"

"He came to meet a Mr. Aberford," Kim said. "He wanted to sell
him the news about Meredith's losing the platter, only Aberford knew
already." Quickly she recounted the scene in the taproom. "When he
took off, I followed him, and then—" She hesitated.

"And then?" Mairelon prompted.

"I think maybe I ought to go back to London," Kim blurted, staring
down at her hands to avoid seeing Mairelon's or Hunch's expressions.
"I'm goin' to be trouble for you if I stay."

"I see," Mairelon said after a moment of silence that to Kim seemed
to go on forever. "Or rather, I don't see. Why don't you begin by telling
us exactly what happened, and then perhaps I will."

"It was Jack Stower," Kim said. "He's one of Laverham's boys. I told
you about Laverham."

"I remember."

"I swear I don't know how he followed me from London, I swear I
don't. He didn't see me, but if he's pokin' about, he'll find out I'm here
for sure, and—"

"Slow down and back up," Mairelon said. "Where and when did
you see Stower? In the hall? On the stairs?"

"Outside, talkin' to that Meredith cove," Kim answered. Reminded
of the task she had originally been set, she outlined the scene she had

witnessed in the innyard. "Bramingham said his uncle was comin' down tomorrow, and he was goin' to give the platter to him as soon as he got there," she finished. "The Meredith cull got Aberford inside, and then the toff from the Dog and Bull turned up. He's the Friday-faced mort's brother, name of Jasper Marston. They all drove off, and I came in."

Mairelon was staring into space with a heavy frown, looking as though he had not heard a word Kim had said for several minutes at least. "Stower, Laverham, Fenton," he murmured. "And a lady asking questions. A grand lady—Lady Granleigh, perhaps?"

"She acted grand enough," Kim said doubtfully.

"And her brother is the unpleasant but not altogether bright gentleman who arranged for my wagon to be broken into, thus beginning our acquaintance. And *he* obviously knows considerably more than he has any right to. Someone is playing a very deep game; I wonder whether it's him or her?"

"I don't see as it matters," Hunch said. " 'Ooever it is, we 'adn't ought to stay 'ere tonight."

"For once, Hunch, I believe you are right," Mairelon said. Hunch's jaw dropped. Mairelon did not notice; he was digging through the drawers in search of something. Not finding it, he went to the door of the room and opened it. "None of us will stay the night at the inn. Hi, landlord! Bring me up a pen and some paper."

"I thought you said we weren't stayin'," Kim said, bewildered.

"We are not staying the *night*. There is no reason not to stay the afternoon; it's a long drive to Swafflton, and the ladies will more than likely be shopping for hours. Besides—ah, thank you, landlord."

The innkeeper had arrived, carrying a scruffy-looking quill, an inkpot, and a sheet of paper. Mairelon took them with a charming smile and shut the door in his face. "Besides, I don't expect this to take long," he finished, setting the implements on the table.

"What are you goin' to do about Stower?" Kim asked as Mairelon made a face at the quill, dipped it in the inkpot, and began covering the paper with flowing, spidery letters.

"I am going to do nothing whatever, for the time being at least," Mairelon answered. He wrote another three lines and set the quill aside. "No sand? Our landlord seems singularly unprepared for Quality clientele; can it be that he seldom has any?" He picked the page up by one corner and waved it through the air to dry the ink.

"I'd better go back to London, then," Kim said.

"You will do no such thing. Hunch is the one who is going to

London. He'll be quite all right; this Laverham fellow isn't looking for him." He folded the note and handed it to Hunch, who scowled and chewed absently on one end of his mustache. "Hire a horse and change whenever you have to. I don't want any more time wasted. Give this to Shoreham and tell him what we've found out so far. I've asked him to learn what he can about Laverham, Marston, Stower, and Fenton; stay til he has an answer to send. He'll be quicker about it if he knows you're waiting."

Hunch's scowl lessened slightly during this speech, but his expression remained gloomy. "All right, Master Richard. But you ain't staying 'ere, are you?"

"After what I have heard, I have not the slightest intention of doing so," Mairelon said with evident sincerity.

Hunch chewed more vigorously, and his frown returned. "You ain't going to do nothing dreadful while I'm gone, are you?"

"That depends to some extent on how long you take, doesn't it?" Mairelon said, rising. "Come along, let's break it gently to the landlord that his newest guests are leaving already. I doubt that he'll be pleased."

The innkeeper was not nearly as unhappy about their abrupt departure as Mairelon had predicted, primarily because Mairelon informed him casually that he would, of course, pay for the rooms he had bespoken even though he would not remain to use them. He then hired a gig with which to drive to the next town and agreed to pay for the stabling of the horses until they could be sent for. A large purse changed hands; Kim had not known there was so much money in the wagon, and she wondered what else she had missed.

Three people were a tight fit in a gig, but they managed. Kim was almost grateful to be squashed between Hunch and Mairelon; they hid her very effectively from view on either side, and with her cap pulled low and her head tucked down she felt that Jack Stower was unlikely to recognize her, even if he should suddenly appear from around a corner.

Fortunately for Kim's peace of mind, Jack was nowhere to be seen, and once they were out of the village she relaxed a little. Mairelon was silent during the drive, staring out over the fields and hedges with an absent expression that made her think he was not really seeing any of them. Hunch chewed rhythmically on his mustache and scowled at the horse, casting intermittent glances in Mairelon's direction but saying nothing.

There was no one in sight when they reached the woods where they had left the wagon, for which Kim was grateful. She was tired of juggling roles; she did not want to have to think about whether she was supposed to be pretending to be a Tiger or a horseboy or a magician's assistant. She was tired of silent, empty spaces and the strange sounds and smells of the woods. She wanted London, and she realized that that, more than fear of what Jack Stower's presence might mean, was her real reason for suggesting she should go back.

She was still pondering this revelation as she stood beside Mairelon and watched Hunch drive briskly off. "Good," Mairelon murmured. "If he keeps up that pace, he'll be in London by tomorrow morning." He looked down at Kim. "Don't just stand there; come along. We have a great deal to do, and we had better get to it."

"I thought we were goin' to wait for Hunch to get back before we did anything," Kim said, all her homesickness swept away by a sudden wave of foreboding.

"Whatever gave you that idea?" Mairelon said in a tone of mild astonishment. "If we don't do anything, St. Clair will have the platter by tomorrow evening, and I can't have that. No, we're going to have a good meal and get a few things ready and then have a good nap, so that we'll be wide awake to burgle Bramingham Place at two this morning."

He turned and marched cheerfully toward the wagon, leaving Kim to stand staring after him openmouthed. She muttered a curse and plunged after him, already more than half resigned to the prospect. If Mairelon wanted to burgle Bramingham Place, burgle it he would, with or without her help. On the whole, she thought she would rather it be with, but she was not going to give up without an argument. Spluttering objections that she expected would be useless, she followed Mairelon into the wagon.

twelve

Bramingham Place was an enormous, rambling house that seemed to spread out in all directions. Mairelon, lurking with Kim behind an overgrown topiary duck while they waited for the last lights inside to be put out, explained in a whisper that building new wings had been a tradition in the Bramingham family for two centuries, hence the erratic sprawl. Kim wondered what they did with all the space. From the look of it, the house was larger than the entire village of Ranton Hill, and that was without considering the stables and gatehouse.

The last of the windows went dark, and Mairelon started forward with an exclamation of relief. Kim grabbed at his sleeve. "Give 'em time to fall asleep!" she hissed.

"It's all right; the library's at this end. They're far enough away that they won't hear a thing," Mairelon whispered back. "You did say Bramingham was keeping the Saltash Platter in the library?"

"That's what he told the druid cove, but what if he was gammoning him?"

"We won't know til we go find out, will we?" She could hear the smile in his voice, though it was too dark to see it clearly. "Shall we?"

Kim sighed. "How can you be so sure the library's at this end of the house?"

Even in the darkness she could see him stiffen. "I stayed with the Braminghams once, some years back," Mairelon said in a voice devoid of expression. "Just before the Saltash Set was stolen. I remember the visit . . . very well indeed."

"Oh." Kim searched for something to say, without success. She shrugged. "All right, then, let's bite the ken. But this is my lay, remember; don't go off on your own, or you'll muck up the whole thing."

"After you," Mairelon murmured, bowing. Kim shook her head, only half understanding, and slid through the night toward the house.

It was not, after all, much different from the jobs she had done so long ago in London. The house was bigger by far, but that was all. Mairelon pointed the way to a pair of long French doors near the room they wanted. Kim reached for the bit of wire hidden in her sleeve and opened the lock with a few deft twists of her wrist. They slipped inside, and Mairelon closed the doors softly behind them.

They were in a spacious sitting room. Kim could see the dim shapes of chairs and tiny tea tables scattered all around, deeper shades of darkness in the dark. Mairelon pointed toward a door in the opposite wall. Kim nodded and made a gesture which she hoped he would correctly interpret as a warning to be careful. Then she began picking her way across the room.

Three nerve-racking minutes later they reached the door. It was locked, but the mechanism was no more of a challenge than the one on the French doors had been. Kim had it open in a few seconds. On the other side was a hallway, thickly carpeted. Motioning Mairelon to keep to the center, Kim stepped cautiously into the hall.

The library was the second door on the left. It was unlocked, and Kim suppressed a snort of derision. That was gentry for you: they'd lock up half the doors and leave the rest wide open. They always picked the wrong half to lock, too. She pushed the door slowly inward, listening for creaking hinges. The door made no sound, and a moment later they were in the library with the door closed behind them.

"Well done!" Mairelon breathed in her ear, and she jumped. "You were particularly quick with that last door."

"Don't *do* that," she whispered back. "I was quick because it wasn't locked."

"Not locked?" Mairelon paused, and she could almost hear him thinking.

"Not locked," Kim repeated firmly. "And this ain't no time to chat. Find that thing you're lookin' for and let's get out of here."

"We'll never find it in the dark," Mairelon said. "A moment, please." He muttered a word.

A ball of cold, silver light the size of Kim's fist sprang into being just over Mairelon's head, casting threatening, sharp-edged shadows all around. Kim blinked, biting back a protest, and looked quickly about her. The library was a long room with bookcase-lined walls; its center was full of large chairs covered with needlework in bright colors that the silver light bleached to bearable pastels. A small table stood beside each chair on thin, fragile legs. Heavy curtains of a dark crimson shut out the light from the windows; unlike those in the sitting room, these came only to the bottom of the window. Below them, short bookcases alternated with glass boxes set on legs. Kim stared, then realized that these must be the "display cases" to which Henry Bramingham had referred.

Mairelon crossed to the windows and walked rapidly along them. He stopped a third of the way from the end and beckoned. "Here it is!" he whispered, and the strange silver light made an exultant mask of his face.

The Saltash Platter was a tray nearly two feet long, heavily ornamented around the edge with the same pattern of fruits and flowers and vines Kim had seen on the bowl in Mairelon's wagon. At either end a rope of vines twisted away from the edge and then back again, forming a handle. The silver shone brilliantly in the cold light, even through the glass of the display case. Kim looked at the case more closely. The top was hinged in back, and there was an unobtrusive gold lock at the front edge.

Kim pulled out her wire and paused, remembering what had happened when she tried to poke through Mairelon's chest. Of course, it wasn't the lock that had been enchanted, but still . . . She frowned and tugged at the lid, testing the strength of the lock.

It opened easily, cutting short Mairelon's impatient query. They looked at each other across the case, and Kim saw her own misgivings reflected in Mairelon's uneasy expression. "Magic?" she whispered.

"Possibly," Mairelon said softly. The sharp shadows magnified his frown. "If it is, touching the platter will set it off. Be quiet for a moment while I check."

He reached down, hands hovering just above the open case. The air grew heavy, and Kim held her breath, waiting for an explosion.

A soft crash sounded from the next room, and Mairelon jerked his hands away from the display case. He and Kim froze, and in the silence heard a well-muffled thud from the hall.

"We better get out of here!" Kim said, and started down the long room toward the door.

"Not that way; there's no time," Mairelon said, grabbing her arm. He gestured, and the light that hovered over his head shrank to a pinpoint; then he went swiftly to the bookshelf along the nearest wall. "Boccaccio, Boccaccio," he murmured. "Where—ah!"

Kim stared in astonishment as Mairelon reached out and tilted two books outward. She heard a small click, and then the sound of someone fumbling at the library door made her glance fearfully over her shoulder. The curtains were too short to hide behind. Perhaps if she curled up in a chair, she would be overlooked, but what about Mairelon? She turned back and almost forgot her fear in complete amazement.

"Inside, quickly!" Mairelon said. An entire section of the bookcase had swung outward, revealing a narrow, cupboard-like opening behind it. Kim pulled herself together and darted inside; Mairelon squeezed in after her, pulling the bookshelf to behind him. The silver light winked out.

Cracking a ken with a real magician certainly had advantages, Kim thought to herself as she wriggled into a more comfortable position. That book-achoo spell was one she'd have to be sure to learn. She felt Mairelon fumble at the wall and thought he was trying to latch the bookshelf in place. Then he breathed a nearly soundless sigh, and with a soft scraping a small panel slid aside, giving them a thin slot above a row of books through which to view the room they had just quitted with such haste.

Someone was moving slowly among the chairs, carrying a small dark-lantern that was three-quarters shuttered. The lantern beam swung toward them, and Kim wondered whether the bearer had heard Mairelon lower the panel. She heard a snort, and the contemptuous whisper "Mice!" and then the dark blob went on toward the display cases. The figure raised the dark-lantern and bent forward to peer through the glass, and for a moment his face was visible. Kim stiffened and stifled a gasp; it was Jack Stower again.

Mairelon put a warning hand on her shoulder. Angrily she shook it off. She wasn't such a flat as to make a noise that might reveal their presence, no matter how startled she was. Frowning, she watched Stower work his way slowly up the row of display cases toward the one that held the Saltash Platter.

Without warning, the library door swung wide. A pool of flickering amber light spilled through it, and an irritated masculine voice said, "Stuggs? Is that you? Confound it, where is the man?"

Jack Stower whirled, clutching his lantern, just as Jasper Marston, wearing a black and crimson brocade dressing gown and carrying a branch of candlesticks, strolled through the door. "Stuggs?" Marston said again, and then he saw Jack.

The two men stood staring at each other for a long moment; then a slow, deep voice from the hallway broke the stunned silence. "Right 'ere, gov'nor." An enormous figure loomed into view behind Marston. Stower cursed. He whirled and jerked the curtains from the nearest window aside, then yanked at the latch. The window did not budge.

Marston, shaking himself free of his paralysis at last, started forward (none too rapidly, Kim noted with scorn), brandishing the candlesticks like a weapon. "He's trying to steal the platter!" he cried. "Stop him, Stuggs!"

The figure in the hallway ran forward. He was unusually fast on his feet for a big man, but he had too much distance to cover and there were too many obstacles in the way. Stower, after one terrified look backward, hurled his dark-lantern through the stubborn window, snatched up the fallen curtains to keep from being slashed by the fragments of glass and broken window slats, and scrambled out, tipping over the nearest display case in his hurry.

Stuggs lunged after the fleeing Stower and grabbed his feet as the rest of him disappeared out the window. Kim heard a muffled howl of rage and fear, and Stower kicked backward. Stuggs lost his balance and crashed into another display case, his fingers still locked around one of Jack's boots, while the last of Jack Stower vanished.

Jasper picked his way across the broken glass to the window and squinted out it. Kim could hear distant noises; it sounded as if the commotion had roused the household, and somewhere a dog had begun to bark. Jasper did not seem aware of it. He turned and frowned at Stuggs. "He's gone! Why couldn't you hold him?"

" 'Is bootlace broke," Stuggs said mildly. "I got to 'and it to you, gov'nor, you 'ad it right about that there bowl being valuable. But you ought to 'ave told me there was other coves after it besides us."

"This is the platter, not the bowl, you idiot," Jasper Marston said. "But I suppose I should thank you for reminding me what we came for." He left the window and went straight to the display case containing the platter. He set the candlesticks down on the nearest table and beckoned to Stuggs. "Come here and open the lock; hurry, before someone else gets here."

As Kim had done, Stuggs tested the lid and made the same discovery. "It ain't locked."

"Not locked? That fellow we chased off must have opened it! We arrived just in time. Give it to me."

"No!" a familiar voice said in dramatic tones from the smashed window. Kim's eyes widened. What was the head of the druid group doing at Bramingham Place?

"What—" Marston turned his head and froze in mid-sentence.

Framed in the shattered glass and dangling splinters of the window were a man's head and shoulders. The man's eyes gleamed from the openings of a black mask, and a dark high-crowned hat covered his hair. His form was hidden beneath a driving cloak with several short capes, but the tone and timbre of his voice were unmistakable. "You are too late to further defile the Sacred Dish! Bring it to me, at once!"

Kim bit her lip to keep from laughing aloud. She should have guessed that Jonathan Aberford would be after the platter, the same as everyone else. This was becoming altogether too much like a Drury Lane comedy. Mairelon seemed to think so, too; she could feel him shaking in silent amusement. She hoped they would both be able to control themselves. It wouldn't be funny at all if they were caught.

"Now, look here—" Marston began.

Jonathan raised a hand, and Kim saw the glint of candlelight on metal. Her amusement died instantly. "Bring it to me!" Jonathan commanded.

"Put that down, you young chub," Stuggs said. "Pistols ain't a thing to go waving around like that."

"Bring me the dish!" Jonathan cried. "I won't have any more delay!" He waved his pistol again. "Bring—"

Abruptly the masked face vanished from the window. There was a crash and the almost simultaneous sound of a pistol shot. Stuggs cursed and ran to the window. A moment later he pulled his head back inside and shook it in wonder. "Silly chub was standing on a bucket, an' it tipped over," he said. "The pistol must 'ave gone off when 'e fell."

"Never mind!" Jasper said. "Help me hide this before someone else comes in."

"What's going on?" a voice boomed from the doorway. "Hi, Marston! Looks like you've had a bit of a turnup."

"I don't care what he's been having, Mr. Bramingham, I won't have him making such *dreadful* noises in my house," said a shrill female voice from farther along the hallway. "He's wakened all the guests *and* the servants, and I won't have it. Even if he *is* your brother, Amelia, dear."

"Too late," Stuggs said in a resigned tone as the occupants of Bramingham Place, in various states of déshabillé, began pouring into the library.

thirteen

The first person through the door was an older, heavier version of Henry Bramingham; Kim assumed he was the owner of the estate. Behind him came several other men in dressing gowns and a partially dressed footman carrying more candles. They were followed in turn by the ladies of the house, caps askew and clutching their dressing gowns about them, determined to miss nothing of whatever scandalous goings-on had been discovered.

Jasper dropped the platter onto the seat of a nearby sofa where it would be temporarily hidden by the back. "House-breakers, that's what happened, Bramingham," he said, waving at the broken window and the chaos of shattered glass and broken furniture below. "I, ah, came down for a book and interrupted them—"

"Housebreakers!" A plump, grey-haired woman wrapped in layers of ruffles stiffened indignantly. "At my house party! I won't have it, Mr. Bramingham!"

"Of course not, my dear," the heavy man said, patting her arm. "Good job, Marston; I see you've caught one." He eyed Stuggs's bulk with evident misgiving. "He looks a desperate rogue. Just hold him off a minute more, til Henry gets here with the shotgun."

"What? No, no, Bramingham, that's not a burglar," Jasper said, clearly taken aback. "That's my man, Stuggs."

"Jasper!" Lady Granleigh pushed her way to the front of the crowd and came toward him across the room, hands outstretched. "Dear boy, were you injured?" Her expression was at variance with her concerned

tone, and as she came nearer, Kim saw her soundlessly mouth the words
"Did you get it?"

"Yes," said Jasper. "I mean no, not at all. Ah, Amelia . . ." He gestured toward the sofa.

Amelia glanced down. She looked at Jasper and rolled her eyes heav-
enward. "The very thought of your ordeal makes me feel faint," she
declared, and sat down on top of the tray, spreading out her robe so that
it was completely hidden.

"Clever woman," Mairelon murmured. "Pity she's not on our side."

"Shh!" Kim hissed. "You want to get us caught?"

"Amelia, dear!" Mrs. Bramingham said, hurrying over.

"Faint? Lady Granleigh never faints!" a bluff voice said, and a
distinguished-looking man pushed his way through the crowd of servants
and visitors. He was fully dressed, which perhaps accounted for his tardiness, and there was mud on his boots. "I'm afraid they got away, Bramingham," he said. "That boy of yours is still chasing them, but I don't
see that he has much chance of catching up with them in the dark."

Mrs. Bramingham gave a faint, lady-like shriek. "Henry! My son is
out there with those villains? I won't have it! Bring him back at once,
Mr. Bramingham."

"Of course, my dear," Mr. Bramingham said, making not the
slightest move to do so. "Did you see them yourself, Lord Granleigh?"

"*Somebody* was running off through the woods," Lord Granleigh
replied. "I doubt that anyone got a good look at him, though. Now,
what's this about Lady Granleigh fainting? You're not ill, are you, my
dear?"

"I shall be quite all right in a moment," Lady Granleigh said, leaning
back against the cushions. She looked nervous, and Kim wondered
whether her husband knew that she and her brother were trying to steal
Henry's tray.

"I can carry you up to your room," Lord Granleigh offered, plainly
concerned.

"No, no, I shall do much better here," Lady Granleigh assured him.
"Perhaps if you sent Marianne to me . . ."

"Mademoiselle Marianne is in the saloon, having the hysterics."

Heads turned toward a lovely young woman standing in the doorway.
A lace cap lay like a snowflake on her auburn hair, and the pale green
wrap that covered her nightdress set off her slender figure better than a
ball gown. Kim felt Mairelon stiffen. "Renée?" he breathed in tones of
horrified disbelief.

"Me, I do not see that having the hysterics is of any use whatever, and I have a great wish to know whether we are to be murdered in our beds, so I have left her with her maid," the auburn vision went on. "I think that her maid is very nearly as silly as she is, so they will go on well together. What has happened?"

A confused babble of voices greeted this question. Lady Granleigh objected that her dear Marianne was not in the least silly; Mrs. Bramingham offered some complaint about her son; Jasper launched into a highly colored and very jumbled account of the way in which he had run the ruffians off; Mr. Bramingham made a series of vague and contradictory statements that seemed intended to be reassuring. The auburn-haired woman listened with an appearance of polite interest, though it was impossible to understand more than one word in six. Finally Mr. Bramingham put a stop to it.

"Enough!" he roared. "Miss D'Auber, I must apologize; it has been a very trying night."

So the auburn-haired woman was the infamous Renée D'Auber, whom Mairelon had gone to visit the night before they left London! Kim could not keep from glancing in the magician's direction, but it was too dark in the cupboard to make out his expression. Frowning a little, she returned to her contemplation of the scene in the library.

"It seems to me that of a certainty someone has been trying something tonight," Mademoiselle D'Auber said into the silence that followed Mr. Bramingham's bellow. "But I do not yet know what."

Mr. Bramingham attempted a gallant bow, the effect of which was somewhat spoiled by the belt of his dressing gown, which chose that moment to come undone and flap around his knees. "Nothing that need cause you concern, Miss D'Auber."

"Father!" Henry Bramingham burst into the room with a nod and a quick "Beg pardon" as he passed Renée D'Auber. His eyes were bright with excitement, and in one hand he held a dirt-covered pistol. Bits of earth and grass dropped from the pistol to the carpet as he waved it triumphantly before the eyes of the assembly. "We didn't catch him, but we found this on the South Walk."

"Henry!" shrieked his mother. "What do you mean by bringing that filthy object into the library?"

"I told you he had a gun!" Jasper said.

"Coo!" whispered one of the housemaids, who was standing wide-eyed in a corner, drinking in the uproar.

"Henry, you're upsetting the ladies," Mr. Bramingham said.

"I'm sorry; I didn't think." Henry looked down at the pistol as if he would have liked to hide it under his coat.

Mademoiselle D'Auber's eyebrows rose. "I see that Mademoiselle Marianne is perhaps not so foolish as I thought, unless your South Walk grows pistols, which is a thing unlikely. But do you say that this person has escaped?"

"Nothing to worry about, Miss D'Auber," Mr. Bramingham said. "If you'll just let us handle this—"

"But I do not see that you *are* handling it," Renée D'Auber pointed out. "And perhaps this villain has a second pistol and will come back to kill us all in our beds! I do not at all like this idea, me, and I will not spend another night in this house."

"Oh, *no*, Mademoiselle D'Auber, you mustn't leave!" Mrs. Bramingham turned in distress from her unwelcomed ministrations to Lady Granleigh. "Why, you've only just arrived!"

"I shall leave in the morning," Renée announced, and swept out of the room.

"There! See what you've done!" Mrs. Bramingham said crossly to Henry after a moment's silence.

"What I've done!" The look Henry gave his mother was full of righteous indignation. "I didn't break into the library and smash up the display cases. I didn't go dropping pistols in the South Walk. I suppose you'd rather I hadn't chased off the fellow who did!"

"I believe I am going to faint," Lady Granleigh announced loudly. The company turned to look at her and she sank back against the sofa, fanning herself with one hand. "If I could have a little *peace*," she said in failing tones, "I might be able to recover."

"Of course, Amelia, dear!" Mrs. Bramingham said. "Mr. Bramingham, take these people into the green saloon. I'll just get my hartshorn—"

"Alone," Lady Granleigh said with amazing firmness for a purported invalid.

"But, Lady Granleigh—" Mr. Bramingham began, frowning.

"Very well," Lady Granleigh sighed, cutting him off. "If you insist, I will allow Jasper to remain in case those villains reappear. But I must have *quiet*."

"But Mr. Marston was going to explain—"

Lady Granleigh raised a hand to her head. "Can it not wait?"

Mr. Bramingham blinked, then shook his head. "Yes, of course, Lady Granleigh, as you say. Come along, my dear. Henry, take that thing to the morning room; I'll come by in a minute or two. Come along, everyone, we must let Lady Granleigh recover."

Lord Granleigh gave his wife a penetrating look, but allowed himself to be shepherded out of the room along with the rest. Only Jasper and his "man" Stuggs remained behind. As the door closed behind the crowd, Lady Granleigh stood up briskly.

"Ah, Amelia, hadn't you better—I mean, what if someone comes back in and sees you?" Jasper stuttered. "You're supposed to be in a faint."

"I am not going to sit on that object for another instant," Lady Granleigh replied. "And if it had not been for your ineptitude, I would not have had to. What possessed you to rouse the household like this?"

"I didn't rouse the household, and if you'd listen for half a minute, you'd know it," Jasper said bitterly. "It was that Bedlamite in the domino with his pistol and his—"

"I am not interested in excuses," Lady Granleigh interrupted. "There will be time for that later. Right now we must decide what to do with this platter. We can't just carry it up to your room, you know. The halls are full of servants; it will be hours before things settle down."

"My room? Why my room? You're the one who was invited for the house party. You've got that hulking great wardrobe and at least two dressing tables to hide the thing in. I'm just an overnight guest; all I have is a shaving stand."

"You have neither a husband nor an abigail to pry into your things. I, on the other hand—"

"I should hope not!" Jasper said. Then he looked at his sister and snorted. "And if Stephen Granleigh has ever 'pried' in your things, I'll . . . I'll eat my cravat."

"If you dare to so much as hint any such thing about Stephen, I shall feed it to you myself," Lady Granleigh retorted. "Stephen is the soul of honor."

"Too honorable for his own good," Jasper muttered. His sister gave him a warning look, and he scowled. "Well, he is, and you know it, or why did you drag me into this mess in the first place? Granleigh stands to benefit as much as you do if he recovers the platter, but he wouldn't stand this havey-cavey nonsense for a minute." His expressive wave included the platter, the shattered window, the open display case, and his sister.

Lady Granleigh flushed. "That is not the point, and you are wasting time. What are we going to do with this platter?"

"Throw it out the window," Jasper said in a sulky tone.

"Don't be ridiculous, Jasper. There are still people combing the grounds in search of those housebreakers of yours; someone would be sure to find it before we could recover it."

"Why don't you 'ide it be'ind some of them books?" Stuggs suggested.

Lady Granleigh gave him a scornful look, but as no better idea was forthcoming, she and Jasper set to work removing books from one of the shelves. Unfortunately they did not think to check the platter against the size of the shelf before they did so, and when they tried to balance it on its edge against the wall, it proved too tall. They were forced to remove it and replace the books, reproaching each other viciously the entire time.

In the end, they hid the platter under the sofa cushions. Lady Granleigh was not altogether pleased with this solution, and warned Jasper several times that he must make certain to remove it before the maids came to straighten up.

"And on no account are you to allow Mr. Bramingham and the others to search this room," she added.

"How am I supposed to stop them?"

"I leave that to you. Now, I think it is time I recovered enough to return to my room. You may escort me. After that, I suggest you rejoin Mr. Bramingham and tell them your story. You, —she gave Stuggs a withering look—"had best stand guard outside the library door. It will look well, and that way we can be sure no one will come in and accidentally discover the platter before we have a chance to move it. Your arm, Jasper."

The three conspirators went slowly out of the library, Lady Granleigh clinging to her brother's arm as if she were about to collapse. The door closed behind them, and the room was empty at last.

Kim stirred, then poked Mairelon gently, somewhat surprised that he had not unlatched the bookcase door of their refuge. She felt him start at her touch. He let out a long breath and closed the little panel through which they had been looking. Kim felt him make a series of small movements, and then the bookcase swung wide.

Moonlight dribbled through the broken window, making Mairelon's magical light unnecessary. Kim darted out and began pulling cushions off the sofa. Mairelon pushed the bookcase back into place and followed, but more slowly. "Hurry up!" Kim whispered. "We ain't got much time."

"Yes," Mairelon said. "I know." He picked up the last of the cushions and threw it viciously to the floor. Kim winced, glad that it had landed on the carpet and not knocked anything over. Even a small noise was likely to attract attention, now that the house was alerted.

Mairelon reached down and curled his hands around the handles of the platter. A moment later, he let go and stood staring down at it, a grim expression on his face.

"Someone got here before us," he said in a low, tight voice. "This is a forgery."

"A forgery? You mean it ain't the right *one?*"

"Exactly." Mairelon turned away. "We had better be going."

Kim looked back at the platter and hesitated. "Are you sure? That's real silver, I'll go bail. And it looks a lot like that bowl of yours."

"The silver's real enough, and you're right about the pattern, but it's not the Saltash Platter," Mairelon replied. "It wouldn't fool any magician for an instant, once he got close enough to lay hands on the thing."

"All right, as long as you're sure." Kim went to the broken window and peered out. "Don't see nobody. Let's pike off."

"We can't do it fast enough to suit me," Mairelon murmured, and waved her on.

fourteen

Kim and Mairelon had no difficulty in evading the searchers who were still scattered here and there on the grounds of Bramingham Place. The servants were spread out and the lanterns they carried were visible for a long way, which made them easy enough to avoid, and there was plenty of cover among the hedges and trees of the sprawling gardens. Kim almost enjoyed dodging through the shrubbery and hiding in the formal borders.

The walk back to the wagon was long, cold, and silent. They kept to the roads, where the moonlight let them see to walk more easily. Mairelon seemed sunk in contemplation, and Kim was too tired to ask what he was thinking. When they reached the wagon at last it was nearly dawn. Kim fell into her makeshift bed at once, and was asleep before she had time to notice whether Mairelon was doing likewise.

She woke to full daylight and the sound of dishes rattling. "Hunch?" she said hazily, lifting her head to see over the mound of blankets she was huddled under.

"I'm afraid not," Mairelon's voice said from near the door of the wagon. "Hunch can't possibly be back before tonight, and I don't really expect him til tomorrow at the earliest. You'll have to put up with my cooking until then. Unless you have hidden skills?" he added hopefully.

"Gnngh," Kim said. She wormed one hand out from under the blankets and rubbed at her eyes. "No."

"Pity. You'd better come have breakfast before it gets cold."

Kim realized that she was hungry. Well, no wonder; she'd done a day's worth of walking since dinner last night, or at least it felt as if she had. She unwound herself reluctantly from the blankets and went out to correct the matter.

Mairelon was crouched over a smoky fire with a long stick in one hand. He was fishing for the handle of an iron pot that balanced precariously on top of two of the burning branches. "Just in time. Bring the plates over."

"I thought you said it would get cold," Kim said, picking up the plates. "Smells to me more like it's getting burned."

"Cold, burned, what's the difference? Ah!" Mairelon snagged the handle at last and lifted the pot out of the fire. He lowered it to the ground and picked up a spoon. "How much do you want?"

"How much is there?" Kim asked, eyeing the black pot dubiously.

"More than enough for two," Mairelon assured her. "I, ah, got a little carried away when I was adding things, I think. Here, take some. I'm afraid there isn't any bread. We'll just have to do without until tomorrow."

Kim frowned at the lumpy greyish blob on her plate, then shrugged. She had eaten worse-looking meals in her life, and the worst any of them had done was to give her a stomachache. Hunch's savory stews were spoiling her. She took a spoonful. It tasted burned.

Fortunately, Mairelon did not seem to expect her to give her opinion of his cooking. Kim ate slowly, sneaking glances at the magician when she thought he would not notice. He was unusually quiet, but perhaps that was just because Hunch was not there to glower and complain.

Mairelon caught her eye on her fourth or fifth glance. "Have I sprouted horns or a third eye, or is it just that I have charcoal smeared on my forehead?" he asked mildly.

"No," Kim said. Rather than try to explain, she asked, "How did you know that platter last night was sham?"

"Any magician would have. I thought I told you that."

"You said you knew. You didn't say how."

"Ah. Well, I knew because there wasn't any magic in it." Mairelon stared into the fire and swallowed another spoonful of his breakfast blob. "When a wizard puts magic into an object, it's generally because he wants the object to *do* something. That means the magic has to be . . . accessible, and if it's accessible it can be felt by other wizards. If the magic is destroyed or removed, it leaves traces, which can also be felt. The platter at Bramingham Place hadn't a farthing's worth of magic in it, and it never had."

Kim frowned. "But if any wizard who touched it would know it was a cheat, why would anyone bother makin' a sham platter?"

"A good question. Possibly the forger wasn't a magician, and didn't realize there would be any difficulty passing it off as the real thing. Or perhaps she only wanted to keep people from realizing it was missing right away. After all, she couldn't have known there'd be such a parade of burglars to blame it on."

"She?" Kim straightened, staring at Mairelon. "You know who put it there?"

"I think so." Mairelon poked at his breakfast. "Renée wasn't part of the parade, you see, and she has more than enough information to have had the platter copied. I can't think of any reason why she'd have come to one of Harriet Bramingham's house parties, either, except to steal the Saltash Platter. She hates house parties."

"Renée? You mean that French lady? I thought she was a friend of yours," Kim said cautiously.

Mairelon's laugh was without humor. "So did I. But she must have been planning this for a long time, certainly since before we left London. So why didn't she tell me?"

"Maybe that Earl cove told her not to," Kim ventured.

"Shoreham!" Mairelon frowned, considering. "I hardly think it's likely. He wouldn't have sent me here if he knew Renée was going to have a go at it."

"He might of—"

"Might *have.*"

Kim smothered a relieved sigh. If Mairelon was correcting her speech again, he must not be feeling quite so down-hearted. "He might have sent you anyway, if he wanted to get you out of London."

Mairelon looked up with an arrested expression. "Quite true. In fact, it would be just like Edward. I wonder . . ."

His voice trailed off and he stared at the air above the fire. After a moment, he shook himself. "Well, there's only one way to find out. Finish your breakfast, Kim. You'll want it."

"Why?" Kim said warily.

Mairelon gave her a winning smile. "You're going back to Bramingham Place, to take a message to Renée before she leaves."

"I'm *what?*"

"Well, I can't go. Gregory St. Clair is arriving today, and I don't dare chance his seeing me. Don't worry, you'll do fine."

Kim rolled her eyes and went back to eating. Burned and blobby or not, it was safer than talking to Mairelon.

Two days of relatively dry weather had done wonders for the roads, at least as far as travel on foot was concerned. Water still stood at the bottoms of the deepest ruts, and wagons and carriages continued to have a rough, sloppy time of traveling, but the edges of the lanes gave only a little under Kim's feet and no mud dragged at her boots to make walking a weary chore. If she had not been so worried about the task Mairelon had set her, she might even have enjoyed the walk.

"Message for Miss D'Auber, sir," she muttered under her breath. "The master said I was to give it only to her."

She frowned, wondering whether she sounded flash enough. Remembering the words wasn't hard, but the rhythms and the slightly different pronunciation Mairelon had insisted on were difficult indeed. And what if someone started asking her questions? She had some chance of getting the accent right for the sentences she'd practiced, but could she keep it up if she had to say anything else?

Firmly, Kim dismissed her doubts. She had agreed to run this rig, and fretting wouldn't make success any more likely than it already was. Practice, on the other hand . . . "Message for Miss D'Auber," Kim repeated in a low voice. "The master said I was to give it only to her. Message for Miss D'Auber."

So intent was she on her muttered repetitions that she did not hear the sounds of the approaching carriages until they were almost on her. A shout and the crack of a whip startled her into attention at last, and she glanced over her shoulder. Two high-perch phaetons were heading full tilt along the road, side by side. Their drivers crouched intently over their reins, shifting their weight automatically to compensate for the dangerous sway of their vehicles, oblivious to everything save their horses and each other. The one on the left pulled ahead, but his advantage was a matter of inches. The other driver's arm rose and fell, cracking his whip, and his horses leaped forward, bringing him even with the left-hand phaeton once more.

Kim dove for the ditch, praying that these Bedlamites wouldn't overturn or run off the road until they had gone safely past her. The thudding of the horses' hooves and the rumble of the carriage wheels grew louder, then passed by above her in a spray of water, mud, and flying gravel. As the sound began to fade, Kim looked up and saw the phaetons vanish around a curve in the road ahead, both of them still moving with furious speed.

She spat a curse after them as she picked herself up. Her left foot had landed in the muddy water at the bottom of the ditch, and some of it had gotten into her boot. The knees of her good breeches were wet and smeared with dirt and grass, and her hands were scratched and gritty. She cursed again and brushed herself off as best she could, then resumed walking, hoping darkly that something would teach those madmen a lesson. Maybe one of them would overturn his carriage and break a leg. Maybe both of them would.

As she drew near the curve, she heard shouts ahead. Prudently, she stepped off the road in case the phaetons were returning. The noises did not sound as if they were moving in her direction, but Kim took no chances. She trudged along the side of the ditch, sliding on the grass from time to time, until she rounded the curve and got a clear view of the road ahead. She stopped short.

Her wish had been granted: one of the phaetons had indeed overturned. It lay in a tangle of harness and broken wheels across the side of the road, while its owner, scowling ferociously and muddy to the eyebrows, tried to calm his frightened horses. On the opposite side of the road, a coach-and-four lay half in, half out of the ditch. A liveried postillion was tugging at the door of the coach, unconscious of the blood trickling down his face from a cut above his eye. His efforts only made the coach rock precariously. A second postillion was doing his best to control the four coach horses, which were plunging and rearing in a manner that threatened to reduce harness pole, coach, and all to splinters. The coachman lay motionless on the far side of the ditch, evidently thrown from his seat when the coach tipped over.

A little farther on, in the exact center of the road, the second phaeton had drawn to a halt. The driver was concentrating on his horses, and despite her poor opinion of his good sense, Kim had to acknowledge that he knew how to handle a team. Anyone who could come through such a tangle as this had been, at the speed he had been traveling, in a vehicle as notoriously unstable as a high-perch phaeton, without overturning his carriage or losing control of his horses . . . Kim could think of one, or perhaps two, hackney drivers in London who might manage such a feat if they were lucky. This gentleman did not appear to have turned a hair.

"Burn it, Robert!" The driver of the overturned phaeton backed up two hasty steps as one of the chestnut horses he was trying to calm half reared in the traces. "If either of them is hurt—"

"The master appears uninjured," the postillion at the carriage said, temporarily abandoning his pulling at the door to peer through the carriage window. "And I believe John Coachman is not seriously hurt."

"Not them, you imbecile, my chestnuts!" the infuriated driver cried. "Robert—"

"I would be happy to help you, George, but I can hardly leave my horses, can I?" Robert said, half turning without taking his attention from his restive greys. His voice and the outline of his face came together in Kim's mind, and she recognized him as one of the druids she and Mairelon had spied on. George's voice was familiar, too; he was probably another of them. Kim started to roll her eyes, only to be brought up short.

"Who, exactly, is responsible for this outrage?" said a cold, hard voice authoritatively.

Every drop of Kim's blood seemed to congeal into ice. She knew that voice; she had fled from London to get away from its owner. First Jack Stower, now Dan Laverham, she thought in despair. She would never get away from them. She wanted to dive for the ditch and the hedge beyond, but she could not make her muscles obey her. It was all she could do to force her head to turn in the direction of the speaker. When she did, she suffered a second shock.

The tall man who was in the act of climbing out of the ruined coach was not Dan Laverham. He had the same narrow jaw and sharp eyes as Dan, and the same long nose, but his dark hair had less grey in it. Under the superfine coat he wore, his shoulders were broader and more muscular than Dan's. He could have passed as Laverham's brother, if Laverham had had one who dressed like a toff, but he was *not* Dan Laverham. Relief made Kim's knees feel weak.

"Accident, not outrage," Robert said politely. "I am Robert Choiniet, and my friend with the unspeakable chestnuts is George Dashville."

"I take it you were racing on a public thoroughfare," the man from the coach snapped. "You should be horsewhipped for such carelessness."

"Possibly," Robert said with unimpaired calm. "I doubt that anyone will do so, however. May I take a message to someone for you, sir? I must go by Stavely Farm first, but after that I am at your disposal."

"Robert, you traitor!" George had finally succeeded in getting his animals under control, but his angry cry startled them into another round of sidling and head-tossing. "You can't mean to go back to Austen and claim you *won!*"

"Why not? Just because your driving was so bad that you overturned instead of merely losing by an inch or two?"

"Enough." The man from the coach spoke with a quiet deadliness. "I have no interest in your disagreements, and you will oblige me by saving them for another time and place." He turned to Robert Choiniet. "You will go by Bramingham Place and inform them that Lord St. Clair has met with an accident on the road. I trust you are capable of giving them sufficient directions. Beyond that, all I require of you is that you do not return."

"I understand perfectly, sir," Robert said coldly. "Give you good day."

He raised his hands a quarter of an inch. His horses sprang forward, eager to be away, and the phaeton swept off down the road. George Dashville stared after it, spluttering incoherently, while the Baron straightened his cravat and brushed at his coat and breeches. Kim shook herself out of her daze and eased herself farther down the slope of the ditch. A low stone wall ran along the far side; if she could get over it, she had a good chance of getting around the entire muddle of men and carriages without being seen.

Her luck held. The chestnut horses took exception to the Baron's abrupt movements, and George's efforts to keep them from bolting occupied both his attention and St. Clair's while Kim slid over the wall unnoticed. She bent over and crept along it, keeping her head low despite her curiosity. She didn't want St. Clair to catch her, even if he wasn't Dan Laverham. From the way Mairelon acted, St. Clair was as bad as Dan. She didn't straighten up until the Baron's caustic observations regarding George's horsemanship began to fade with distance.

fifteen

Kim's back was sore and stiff from her long, crouched-over walk to avoid Baron St. Clair, so she took things easier on the last mile to Bramingham Place. Once she reached the drive leading up to the house, she slowed even further. She enjoyed looking about at the bushes through which she and Mairelon had dodged the night before, though the manicured lawn and meticulous placement of the trees made her nervous. Besides, she was in no real hurry to complete her errand.

Slow as she went, the house drew inexorably nearer. Kim sighed and straightened her jacket. She had better get this over with before her nerve failed her. She went up to the door and knocked.

The door opened at once, and Kim thought she saw a faint, fleeting expression of surprise on the face of the butler who had opened the door. "Message for Miss D'Auber," Kim said, touching her cap respectfully.

"Very good." The butler held out his hand.

"The master said I was to give it only to her."

The butler's features stiffened into cold disapproval, but all he said was, "I will see that she is informed. Wait here."

The door closed, leaving Kim standing on the step outside. Kim frowned at it. She had a vague idea that there was something not quite right about the butler's action, but her knowledge of gentry kens was limited to the most likely location of the silver. She shrugged. Wait, the man had said; well, she would wait, then. She sat on the step and stared out across the drive.

Several minutes later, Kim heard the door behind her open. She could practically feel the butler's disapproving stare digging into her spine, and smiled to herself. She twisted her head and shoulders around without rising and looked up with an expression of hopeful inquiry.

"Miss D'Auber will see you," the butler said. His mouth was turned down at the corners and he was standing rigidly erect, as if to make up for Kim's informality.

"Good," Kim said cheerfully, and scrambled to her feet. "How soon will she get here?"

The butler winced. "She will see you in the green saloon. I would not presume to say how soon. This way."

Kim tried to suppress a grin as she followed the butler. She was only partially successful, but as the man's back was toward her it did not really matter. He led her down a short hall and showed her into a large room with pale green walls and spindly-legged chairs covered in green-and-gold-striped silk. There were two gilded pier tables between the windows, each with a large gold-rimmed mirror hanging on the wall above it, and at the far side of the room stood a small writing desk.

As the door clicked shut behind her, Kim eyed the chairs dubiously. They did not look as if they were meant to be sat on, but the two foot-stools did not look any sturdier and she couldn't sit on the pier tables. She finally settled herself on a footstool, reasoning that if it collapsed under her she would be closer to the floor. She had hardly sat down before the door latch clicked again, and Renée D'Auber walked into the room.

"I am Mademoiselle Renée D'Auber," she announced, frowning at Kim. "You have a message for me, yes?" Her auburn hair shone in the sunlight and her figured muslin morning dress was the height of elegance. Looking at her made Kim feel small and rumpled and unpleasantly aware of the dust and grass stains her clothes had acquired on her walk to Bramingham Place.

"Yes," Kim said shortly. She rose and reached into her jacket for the letter Mairelon had given her. As she did, she saw Renée's eyes widen.

"But what is this? You are a girl! Of what is it that Monsieur Merrill is thinking?"

"You ask him, if you want to know," Kim said. French or not, this woman was altogether too fly for comfort. Kim scowled and tapped Mairelon's letter with her forefinger. "And how'd you know this was from him?"

"It is of all things the most likely," Mademoiselle D'Auber replied. "Who else would know I was here? Also, I have been asking for him, and he would of course hear of it. It is unimportant. Give me the message."

Reluctantly Kim held the letter out to her. Mademoiselle D'Auber took it and tore it open at once without stopping to look at the seal. She turned away as she began reading; a moment later Kim heard a brief exclamation in what was presumably French. Kim had no idea what the words meant, but the tone in which they were spoken was one of surprise rather than anger or annoyance.

Renée D'Auber glanced over her shoulder at Kim, then returned to the letter, this time studying it with evident care. Kim wondered what Mairelon had said about her and what this Mademoiselle D'Auber thought of it. She shifted uncomfortably, wishing she could sit down again but not daring to do so for fear of offending Mademoiselle D'Auber.

Mademoiselle D'Auber finished reading and turned back to face Kim. "Of a certainty, this is not at all good," she said, waving the letter.

"That's what we thought," Kim said, emphasizing the "we" slightly.

"To find the real platter becomes a thing most necessary," the Frenchwoman went on as if she had not heard. "I do not at all see how we are to go about it."

"We?" Kim said.

"But of course! It is why I am here, to help."

Kim's frown returned. "Hold on! I thought you was the one that nicked the real platter. Mairelon said nobody else could of got to it before we did."

"Monsieur Merrill is not altogether right," Mademoiselle D'Auber replied. "I looked at Monsieur Bramingham's so-remarkable platter yesterday afternoon, yes, but at once I saw that it was only a copy. I thought, me, that Monsieur Merrill had been very clever, but now I find that it was not him at all, but someone else. It is most annoying. This business is not well arranged, I think."

"It ain't no fault of ours," Kim muttered.

Renée had crossed to the writing desk and did not hear. "I shall write something for you to carry back to Monsieur Merrill," she said, taking out a sheet of heavy, cream-colored paper. "And you must take his letter with you as well. I will allow Madame Bramingham to persuade me to stay here for another day or two." She made a face as she spoke, then shrugged and bent over the page.

"Why do you want me to take Mairelon's message away again?" Kim asked.

"But it would be most awkward if it were found!" Mademoiselle D'Auber said, writing busily. "Monsieur Bramingham would of a certainty call the Bow Street Runners. He has already spoken of it. It was very foolish of Monsieur Merrill to take the copy of the platter, I think."

So Mairelon's letter had not included all the details of the previous night's events! Kim considered the implications of that while Renée finished her letter, and she began to feel more cheerful. "Why did you come—"

"A moment." Mademoiselle D'Auber sanded her letter, then folded it neatly and sealed it with a blob of wax, muttering under her breath as she did. Her voice was too soft for Kim to hear what she was saying, but each word had a sharp, crystalline quality that distance and muttering could not disguise. Kim remembered the spell that Mairelon had cast to test her truthfulness, and backed up a pace.

Mademoiselle D'Auber finished and straightened up with a smothered sigh. She studied the paper for a moment, then turned and held it out to Kim along with Mairelon's unfolded letter. "Here; take this to Monsieur Merrill and tell him that I will be at the inn down in the village tomorrow morning at, oh, ten o'clock precisely."

Kim nodded and took the letters, doing her best to hide her reluctance. Renée D'Auber had put some sort of spell on that letter, Kim was sure of it. And she, Kim, was going to have to carry the thing all the way back to Ranton Hill at least, and maybe farther, if Mairelon had given up waiting at the inn and gone back to the wagon. Kim wasn't normally squeamish, not even about magic, but she didn't like not knowing what kind of spell she was carrying.

Mademoiselle D'Auber watched closely as Kim stowed the letters away beneath her jacket, which did nothing to improve the state of Kim's nerves. "There is one thing more," the Frenchwoman said. She fixed her eyes on Kim's face and said with great seriousness, "It is of all things the most important that Monsieur Merrill not leave before I see him. You understand? So if he thinks to go, you must try to stop him. I think he will listen."

"Be the first time, if he did," Kim said, shrugging. "I'll tell him, though."

"Good." Renée D'Auber gave Kim a long, measuring look, and Kim found herself wondering once again just what Mairelon had said about her in his letter. Then the Frenchwoman went to a long, embroidered bellpull and gave it a vigorous tug. A few moments later, the door opened and a footman stepped into the room. "Mademoiselle?"

"See this . . . boy out," Mademoiselle D'Auber said.

"Mademoiselle." The footman bowed. With a single, side-long look at the enigmatic Frenchwoman, Kim followed him out of the room and down the hall to the door of Bramingham Place.

When Kim arrived back at the inn late that afternoon, she found Mairelon in the public room playing cards with Freddy Meredith. They were the room's only occupants, and judging from the litter of coins near Mairelon's left elbow, they had been at it for some time. An empty wine bottle lay on the floor beside the table; a second bottle, barely a third full, stood next to the pile of coins that had been wagered on the current hand.

Kim paused in the doorway, wondering what the magician could want with a cloth-head like Meredith. Her eyes flicked from one to the other, and she frowned. Both men were impeccably turned out, from the stiff folds of their cravats to their gleaming Hessian boots; they looked the perfect picture of a pair of gentry. That, Kim realized, was what was bothering her. She had seen Mairelon in his gentry togs before, but she had never realized how well they suited him. No, not quite that, either. She had never realized how well the whole role suited him.

Still frowning, Kim stepped into the room. As she did, Meredith looked up and saw her. He blinked blearily in her direction. He was, Kim saw, more that a little bit on the go. "Who's this, Merrill?"

Mairelon turned. "Kim! What news?"

"Message for you, sir," Kim said, remembering just in time that she was still playing the part of an errand boy.

"Can it wait?"

Kim hesitated. What on earth was she supposed to say to that? "I think you should look at it, sir," she answered at last.

"Ah, well. Let's have it, then." Mairelon held out a hand expectantly.

Kim froze. "Uh—" She couldn't tell him straight out that Renée D'Auber had set a spell on the letter, not with Freddy Meredith sitting there, but she couldn't let him open it without warning him, either. "Sir, I, um—"

"Bailey didn't write it down? I see." Mairelon shoved his chair away from the table and rose, tossing his cards faceup as he did. Kim was relieved to see that there was nothing wrong with his balance or his speech; she had been afraid that he would be as bosky as his companion. "Sorry, Meredith, but duty calls."

Meredith muttered something and began gathering up the coins from the center of the table. Mairelon scooped his own winnings into his hand and thrust them into one of his pockets, then turned and followed Kim out of the room.

"That's a relief," he said as the door shut behind him. "I was wondering how to get out of there without winning too much from him. You caught on very quickly. Where's Renée's message?"

"Here." Kim took the sealed paper out of her jacket. "She put a spell on it."

"What? Nonsense! There's no reason for her to do that." Mairelon twitched the note out of Kim's hand and reached for the seal. He stopped, frowning, and set his forefinger gently against the dull red wax. "You're right, though," he said after a moment's concentration.

Kim let out her breath in a soundless sigh of relief. "Can you do anything about it?"

"Not here. We'll have to take it back to the wagon."

"You sure we should?"

Mairelon looked irritated. "There's no other way to find out what she's done. I'd also like to read whatever she's written; that *is* why you went to Bramingham Place, after all."

"I was just askin'."

Mairelon tucked the note into his breast pocket and started for the door. "There's no point in waiting. You can tell me what happened on the walk back. Come along."

Kim rolled her eyes, shook her head, and followed.

Between Kim's desire to include every detail of her journey to Bramingham Place and Mairelon's periodic interruptions, Kim's tale took up most of the walk to the wagon. Mairelon commended Kim for avoiding the Baron St. Clair and frowned over his strong resemblance to Dan Laverham, but Kim could see that he was not giving her his full attention. When she began to speak of Bramingham Place and Renée D'Auber, however, the magician's preoccupation vanished. Kim found this extremely annoying until she noticed Mairelon's right hand rise to touch his breast pocket from time to time. He was more worried about that spell than he wanted to let on.

As soon as they reached the wagon, Mairelon began rummaging in the large chest. Kim sat on the floor beside the door and hugged her knees, watching with great interest. She was cold, tired, and very hungry, but she did not mention it. She was, after all, used to being cold, tired, and hungry, and if she said anything, Mairelon might remember she was there and send her away while he read Renée's letter.

Mairelon laid a white silk scarf and a small crystal globe on the counter and closed the lid of the trunk. He turned and spread the scarf out, smoothing it carefully until not a wrinkle remained. He drew Renée D'Auber's letter from his pocket and set it in the exact center of the scarf, with the blob of sealing wax facing him. Then he lifted the crystal globe with the tips of his fingers and set it on top of the letter. It showed a strong tendency to roll off the lumpy surface of the wax, but he got it positioned at last.

Finally he was satisfied. He raised his hands slowly and extended them, cupping them around the precariously balanced globe without touching it. He bent his head and began to whisper. The words hissed and sizzled in the confined space of the wagon, rough and saw-edged. Kim held her breath.

Orange light flared from the crystal globe, and Renée D'Auber's voice filled the wagon. "My friend, there are things that you must know, and even this means of communication is not entirely safe. I will meet you two hours before the time I told your young companion, in the hollow below the oak hill southwest of Ranton Hill. Do not fail me in this."

Slowly the orange light faded. Mairelon stood motionless, staring down into the crystal, even after the last of the light was gone. Kim twisted to get a better look at his face and realized that he was not looking at the globe in front of him. His eyes were focused on empty air, and he was frowning.

Kim cleared her throat, then cleared it again. Mairelon did not respond. At last she said loudly, "Hey! Is that all?"

"What?" Mairelon said, then shook his head and turned to look reproachfully at Kim. "Don't ever interrupt a wizard in the middle of a spell, Kim. Magic requires a great deal of concentration, and breaking it can be very dangerous."

"I wasn't interrupting a spell," Kim said. "You were just thinkin', far as I could see."

Mairelon blinked and glanced at the crystal. Then he rolled it to one side and picked up Renée's letter. He stood staring at it for a moment, tapping it gently against his left hand, until Kim was afraid he was going to go back into a brown study. She tried to clear her throat again and started coughing in earnest as she inhaled something the wrong way.

This attracted Mairelon's full attention at last, though his first inclination was to proffer cups of water instead of explanations. As soon as Kim got her breath back, she pushed the cup away and demanded, "What was it that was takin' you such a lot of thinkin' on? You ain't goin' to meet that gentry mort like she says to, are you?"

"Meet Renée? Of course I'm going to," Mairelon said. He looked down at the note, which he had still not read, and his frown returned. "I was just wondering why she chose that particular place."

"What particular place?" Kim said, exasperated.

"The hollow by the oak hill where those ridiculous 'druids' had their ceremony the other night," Mairelon said. "Feeling more the thing? Good, because we're going to have a busy evening. I want to get a good look at that hollow while there's still light, and after that—well, we'll see. Come along." He was out the door of the wagon before Kim could respond.

"Hunch ain't goin' to like this," Kim muttered as she climbed to her feet.

"Isn't," Mairelon's voice corrected. A moment later his head reappeared in the open doorway. "And since Hunch isn't here, it doesn't matter. Bring the lamp and the little sack in the corner; I may want them." The head disappeared once more.

Kim rolled her eyes, picked up the lamp and the sack Mairelon had indicated, and started after him.

sixteen

For the rest of the afternoon, Kim and Mairelon tramped through the wood at the foot of the druids' hill, peering under bushes and up into trees. Kim had only the vaguest idea what they were looking for, but after several attempts to pry an explanation out of Mairelon she gave up and simply copied him. Half-remembered warnings about mantraps and poachers made her move warily, but she found nothing. Mairelon seemed to do no better than she had, but he was preoccupied on the walk back to the wagon, and Kim was positive he had noticed something she hadn't.

At Mairelon's insistence, Kim spent the evening working on her lessons. Her fingers were growing more used to the moves and twists that made coins seem to vanish from one hand and appear in the other, and she had mastered the art of tying knots that slid apart when the proper bit of rope was pulled, but she was not doing nearly so well at reading. She pored over the stubborn little black marks for hours, muttering to herself, while Mairelon prowled restlessly up and down the wagon. Once she ventured a question about his meeting with Renée, but he was so completely uninformative at such length that she did not try again.

Mairelon was up at dawn the next morning, blundering around the limited space inside the wagon in a way that made sleep impossible for anyone else. Kim tried muffling her head under the blanket, but it was no good. Finally she gave up and rose, yawning, to see whether breakfast was one of the things Mairelon had been getting ready during his annoying rambles.

It wasn't. Kim had to make the porridge herself, which did not improve her mood. Her irritation increased further when she noticed that

Mairelon had put on his flash togs, rather than his smock or stage clothes, to go to his meeting with Renée. He looked very well in them, which somehow annoyed Kim even more. To top things off, she didn't do much better with the porridge than Mairelon had the day before. "I'll be glad when Hunch gets back," she muttered as she spooned the lumpy grey mixture into her bowl.

"What? Not already!" Mairelon said. He glanced around hastily, then turned a reproachful expression on Kim. "Don't scare me like that."

Kim stared at him in complete bewilderment. "What're you talking about?"

"I thought you said that Hunch was back," Mairelon explained.

"No, I said I'd be glad when he was," Kim said. Then, in response to Mairelon's skeptical expression, she added, "So we can get some better grub."

"Oh." Mairelon looked thoughtful. "You have a point. Perhaps we should dine at the inn tonight if Hunch hasn't arrived by then. I rather hope he hasn't."

"Why? Hunch cooks better than that fat cove," Kim said.

"If Hunch gets here today, it'll be because he's in a hurry," Mairelon answered. "And he'll only hurry if he thinks Shoreham's information is important. I'd prefer not to have any startling news about any of the people connected with the Saltash Platter. Or its copy."

Kim mulled that over while she finished her porridge. She scraped the last few lumps from the sides of her bowl and surreptitiously shook them off her spoon and onto the ground beside the steps where she was sitting. She scowled down at the bowl, dropped her spoon into it with a muffled clink, and said, "We ought to leave if you want to be the first one at that hill."

"Yes," Mairelon said. "Thank you for reminding me." He rose and brushed at his pants, as if to dispose of nonexistent crumbs. "Practice that handkerchief trick while I'm gone; you still haven't got the last twist right."

"You ain't leavin' me here!" Kim said incredulously.

"I most certainly am," Mairelon replied. "When Renée says alone, she means alone. I shouldn't be long."

"You shouldn't be goin' at all," Kim told him. "And you particularly shouldn't be goin' alone. What if that druid cull shows up wavin' his pops, the way he did the other night?"

Mairelon looked amused. "Jonathan Aberford? I doubt that he's even out of bed at this hour, much less wandering about in the woods with a pistol."

"How do you know? He's dicked in the nob, if you ask me, and there ain't no knowing what notions a Bedlamite'll get."

"All the more reason for you to stay here," Mairelon said. To Kim's indignation, he still looked more diverted than concerned. "If he shows up, you can bar the wagon door. No more arguments, Kim, if you please. You're not coming, and that's that."

"It don't please me at all," Kim muttered, but she could see that Mairelon was determined, and she knew from experience that once he took a notion, he was stubborn as a costermonger defending his route through the market. She sat and glowered at him while he straightened his jacket and brushed his hat, but she did not make any further remarks until he had disappeared into the woods. Then she burst out, "Bubble-brained, pigheaded, sapskulled gull! Muttonheaded flat! Nod-cock. Goosecap. It'd serve him well enough if I up and followed him. Bufflehead. Shab—"

She stopped suddenly, staring at the place where Mairelon had vanished. She *could* follow him, as easy as not. She scrambled to her feet, then hesitated, considering. Mairelon was a wizard, and in spite of the abuse she had just been showering on him, Kim had to admit that he was sharp as two needles. That ginger-pated D'Auber mort was a wizard, too, and she had a powerful reputation. She was foreign into the bargain, and therefore unpredictable. What would they do if they caught Kim spying on them?

The thought gave Kim a moment's pause. Then she shrugged. She'd just have to make sure they didn't catch her, that was all. Stay hid and sherry off if they looked like suspecting anything. It was no different from being on the sharping lay in London. And if there *was* trouble, Mairelon would excuse her obstinacy in following him. Besides, given Mairelon's idea of "explanation," there was no other way she could be sure of finding out what happened at the meeting.

That decided her. She threw some dirt on the fire, kicked her bowl under the steps of the wagon, and started off. She did not take the same route as Mairelon had, but cut sideways up to the road. After all, she knew where he was going. There was no point in risking discovery by sticking too close.

The road was dry enough for comfortable walking, and there was no sign of approaching vehicles, but Kim, remembering her experience the day before, stuck to the far edge anyway. "What am I doing?" she asked herself as she trudged along. "Goin' off to spy on a couple of frog makers? I must be madder than *he* is!" But she continued walking in spite of her misgivings.

The sound of hooves and the rattle of a carriage brought Kim out of her reverie. Glancing up, she saw a landau coming briskly toward her from the direction of Ranton Hill. She sighed and angled down the verge, hoping that the driver would not pay any heed to a shabby boy heading into town. When she looked up again, the carriage had slowed and begun to turn down the lane that led to the druids' meeting place. It was close enough now to give Kim a clear view of the occupants, and she nearly choked trying to smother an exclamation. Lady Granleigh sat stiffly erect in the rear seat, while her brother Jasper made shift with his back to the horses. The driver was the heavyset Stuggs, and he was frowning in evident concentration as he tried to maneuver the landau around the corner.

"This is the outside of enough!" Lady Granleigh said in a carrying voice as the landau lurched forward. "On our return, you will drive, Jasper."

"Really, Amelia, I don't see why you think I'll do any better than Stuggs," Jasper replied. "I'm no Corinthian. You should have let me bring the coachman."

"You are, at least, a *gentleman*," Lady Granleigh said firmly. "And the fewer who are aware of this excursion, the better. Since you have seen fit to confide in this . . . person, we have no choice but to utilize his admittedly second-rate skills. And I must say, Jasper, that I think you could have found someone with more ability if you had only applied yourself properly."

The landau lurched again and rolled reluctantly into the lane, and Lady Granleigh's complaints were lost among the trees. Kim shook off her paralysis and sprinted forward. That skinny toff and his sister were trouble, whatever their lay was, but Kim was willing to bet sixpence that they'd be a particularly whacking great lot of trouble if they found Mairelon and Renée D'Auber at the druid hill. Fortunately, the lane was rough and curving, and with Stuggs driving they wouldn't make good time. Kim might, just possibly, get to the hill first with a warning if she ran.

She didn't manage it. The uneven ground, the constant need to dodge inconveniently placed trees, and the thin branches of the young trees and brush that whipped her face, all combined to slow her more than she would have believed. As she neared the hill, she heard voices ahead of her and cursed under her breath. In London she would have gotten there in plenty of time.

Kim slowed and began to pick her way with more care. It would do Mairelon no good at all if she made too much noise and Jasper or Stuggs discovered her. She reached the fringe of bushes below the hill and started working her way toward the voices. As she came around to the far side, she heard Jasper's voice with sudden clarity, saying, "—question is, who are *you?*"

"Tell him to come down here, where we can talk without shouting, Jasper," Lady Granleigh put in imperiously.

As Jasper repeated his sister's command, Kim stopped and peered through the bushes. Lady Granleigh and her brother were standing at the foot of the hill. Stuggs was a little behind them; beyond, the landau and horses were a sketchy outline between trees. The dark bulk of the druids' lodge was barely visible, though Kim knew from yesterday's explorations that it was only a few steps from the hill.

Mairelon was sitting on the ground halfway up the hill, careless of the damage his fine clothes must be suffering. His face was in shadow and Kim could not make out his expression, but his pose conveyed polite but bored attention.

"Well?" Jasper said when Mairelon did not reply. "Who are you?"

"No, no," Mairelon said. "I asked you first. I also, if you recall, asked how you found this place and what you intend to do here, and you haven't told me that, either."

"We might ask you the same thing," Jasper retorted.

"You might, but I don't recommend it," Mairelon said. "You'll get a reputation as a poor conversationalist if all you can do is repeat what other people say to you."

"This is absurd," Lady Granleigh said. "Tell us who you are and what you're doing here, or be off about your business. I haven't time to waste on this nonsense."

Mairelon rose to his feet and bowed. "It is impossible to refuse such a charming request. My name is de Mare, and I'm here by way of guarding the Sacred Hill."

Jasper and Lady Granleigh looked at each other. Behind them, Stuggs stiffened, and Kim saw his right hand rise toward his chest, as if to touch something underneath his coat for reassurance. Kim frowned. Mairelon had done a perfect imitation of Jonathan Aberford's tone, and both Jasper and his sister seemed to recognize the phrasing. Stuggs's reaction was more difficult to interpret, and more ominous.

"Well, you can go along now," Jasper told Mairelon grandly. "Jonathan Aberford said—"

"If I may speak with you a moment, Jasper," Lady Granleigh interrupted.

Jasper turned his head and glared at her.

"*Now*, Jasper," Lady Granleigh said with unruffled calm. Without waiting for him to respond, she turned and walked straight toward the bushes where Kim was hiding. Kim froze. She was certain she hadn't been seen yet, but if she tried to move now, Lady Granleigh would spot her for sure.

Lady Granleigh stopped a few steps short of the bush and tapped her foot impatiently as she waited for her brother to join her.

"What are you playing at, Amelia?" Jasper said irritably. "And what are we going to do now? Burn it, Miss Thornley never said anything about a guard!"

"Marianne is far too innocent to think of such a thing, and Frederick Meredith was clearly too shatter-brained to mention it," Lady Granleigh replied. "You should have talked to him yourself, Jasper, instead of leaving it to Marianne."

"That was your idea! You were the one who said Meredith would tell more to a pretty face. I never liked the idea of letting my fiancée empty the butter pot over that nodcock, and so I told you."

"Miss Thornley isn't your fiancée yet, Jasper, and you'd do well to remember that before you take that tone with me," Lady Granleigh said. "If you want my help in winning her—and her fortune—you will have to earn it. I must point out that so far you have been precious little help."

"How do you expect me to help when you ruin everything I try to do?" Jasper waved his arms indignantly. "I was about to get rid of that fellow so we could go ahead with your precious scheme, only you stopped me."

"You were about to make yet another muddle, you mean." Lady Granleigh shook her head. "Really, Jasper, sometimes I despair of your intelligence. Don't you see that Mr. de Mare's presence changes everything?"

"No, I do not," Jasper said. "If we could just persuade him to go away—"

"He would remember us, and when the platter was found, he would connect us with its reappearance. That could be very awkward for us."

"Well, what do you think we should do?" Jasper asked in a sullen tone.

"We shall give Mr. de Mare the platter," Lady Granleigh answered serenely.

"What?" Jasper all but shrieked the word, and both Mairelon and Stuggs turned interested eyes in his direction. Jasper scowled back at them and lowered his voice. "Amelia, have you gone mad?"

"Do you want to have Jonathan Aberford lurking about Bramingham Place for the remainder of our stay?"

"No, but—"

"Can you suggest some other way we might be rid of him?"

"We've already been over this, and you know I haven't. But you just told me a minute ago why we can't give this de Mare fellow the platter!"

"I explained why we cannot simply leave the platter here for Mr. Aberford and his friends to find, as we had originally planned," Lady Granleigh corrected him. "If you had been listening, or thinking, you would have understood. Presenting the package to Mr. de Mare is another matter entirely."

"I don't see how. He's bound to remember us, and you already said that that would be awkward."

Lady Granleigh sighed. "The platter is well wrapped, tied up, and addressed to Mr. Jonathan Aberford. If we tell Mr. de Mare that a young man, whom we took to be one of Henry Bramingham's friends, gave us the parcel in town and asked us to deliver it here, it will not matter whether he remembers us. Once they discover that the platter is a forgery, Mr. Aberford and his friends will look for the mysterious young man, if they look for anyone at all. You and I will be mere innocent go-betweens."

"And how are you going to explain it if anyone asks why Miss Thornley was prying into Meredith's business?"

"I shall say that she finds him interesting," Lady Granleigh replied. She frowned slightly. "I shall have to see that she continues to spend time in his company for the next day or two. After that, it will not be thought wonderful if she tires of him."

"Interested in *Meredith*?" Jasper snorted. "That won't fadge, Amelia. *Nobody* could be interested in that simpleton."

Lady Granleigh gave him a cold look. "Are you hinting that I will not be believed? I assure you, no one will think twice about it. Mr. Meredith is no more foolish than most young men, and Marianne is no less so than most girls, so it is quite plausible."

"Yes, but look here, Amelia, how am I supposed to pay court to Miss Thornley if you're forever telling her to talk with Meredith?" Jasper said hastily. "I don't like it."

"I did not ask you to like it," Lady Granleigh said. "I simply wish you to refrain from interfering. Keep quiet, and let me talk to Mr. de Mare."

"Amelia—" Jasper was too late; Lady Granleigh had turned and started back toward the hill as she finished her sentence. "Friday-faced harpy!" Jasper muttered, so low that Kim almost missed the words. He raked his fingers through his hair, patted his cravat, and smoothed the front of his coat, then started after his sister.

Lady Granleigh reached the foot of the hill and raised her chin to study Mairelon. "Mr. de Mare," she said as Jasper, still glowering in disapproval, joined her, "you have an honest face, and your reasons for being here interest me. Are you by some chance acquainted with Mr. Jonathan Aberford?"

"He is the leader of the Company that meets here," Mairelon said cautiously.

"Very good," Lady Granleigh said. "My brother and I are on our way to Swafflton. A young man in the village requested that we deliver a package to this place, and we agreed. The package is addressed to Mr. Aberford; presumably he will know what to do with it. I trust you can see that he receives it?"

"I am quite capable of doing so, madam," Mairelon replied.

"Then we will entrust the package to you. We have spent far too much time on this errand already. Stuggs!"

"Ma'am." The large man lowered his eyes as Lady Granleigh turned to face him, transforming his expression from one of intent interest into one of bored resentment.

"Fetch the parcel from the carriage at once, and give it to Mr. de Mare, with my compliments," Lady Granleigh commanded.

Kim frowned as she watched Stuggs nod and walk off. Unless she'd forgotten the difference between a sharper and a flat, there was something about that cove that didn't fit. He smelled of the back streets and rookeries of London, and gentry didn't hire servants there if they wanted to keep their silver. If only she could pike off to the Hungerford Market for a few hours and ask Red Sal or Tom Correy what they knew about Stuggs! One of them was bound to have heard something . . . Kim put the thought firmly aside; there was nothing to be gained by wishing for the impossible.

Stuggs returned, carrying a large brown package. He paused at the foot of the hill, but one glance at Lady Granleigh set him climbing. Mairelon waited where he was and accepted the package with a solemn half-bow. Kim, still watching Stuggs closely, saw a crease form between his eyebrows as he turned and came down the hill, and realized that Mairelon's bow had prevented Stuggs from getting a good look at his face.

Kim brooded over the possible implications while Lady Granleigh and Mairelon exchanged polite farewells. Jasper's concession to good manners took the form of a curt nod, which drew a glare from his sister and another half-bow from Mairelon. Lady Granleigh hesitated, looking as if she would have given her brother a rare trimming then and there, except that she would then have been guilty of even worse conduct than his. In the end, she turned and swept away without saying anything, but her lips were pressed together in a manner that boded ill for Jasper's peace during the coming carriage ride. Jasper followed, still scowling, and a moment later Kim heard the sounds of the coach departing.

seventeen

Kim let out a long breath as the noise of the carriage died away among the trees. She could hardly believe she had gone unnoticed.

"Well, well," Mairelon's voice said meditatively from the hillside. "How very interesting."

Kim jerked at the unexpected sound, and her arm grazed the bush in front of her. Mairelon's head snapped in the direction of the rustle. "Renée?" he called.

"No, it's me," Kim said, rising. She walked forward, brushing dead leaves from her coat.

"You were supposed to stay at the wagon," Mairelon said without heat.

"That's what you said," Kim agreed. "I never told you I would."

"True." Mairelon pursed his lips and gazed at Kim thoughtfully. "I can see I'll have to listen to you more carefully in the future. How long have you been here?"

"Since right after the bracket-faced gentry mort and her brother came," Kim answered. "I saw them on the road, but I couldn't hop it fast enough to get here first."

"You didn't by any chance see Mademoiselle D'Auber as well, did you?"

"No," Kim said with some satisfaction. "I didn't."

Mairelon eyed her sharply, then frowned. "It's not like Renée to be late." He tucked Lady Granleigh's parcel under his arm and pulled a watch from his pocket. As he glanced at it, his frown deepened. "Certainly not this late."

"Maybe she saw them two on their way here," Kim suggested, jerking a thumb in the direction Lady Granleigh's carriage had gone. There was no reason for Mairelon to get in a taking over Renée D'Auber. She was a wizard, after all; she could take care of herself.

Mairelon looked up, still frowning. "Yes, that would explain it," he said. "And it's 'those two,' not 'them two.' "

"Those two, then," Kim said, obscurely comforted by this offhanded correction. "What are you goin' to do with the platter?"

"Platter?" Mairelon's expression went blank; then his eyes followed Kim's pointing finger. "Oh, is that what's in this package? How convenient."

"It's the cheat they nicked from the library at Bramingham Place," Kim added. "I heard them talkin'."

"Indeed." Mairelon took the parcel out from under his arm and studied it. "Why would Lady Granleigh want to give the fake platter to Jonathan Aberford? And why deliver it here? He lives in the vicinity; his direction can't be particularly difficult to discover."

Kim shrugged. "They didn't say."

"Mmmm." Mairelon continued his examination of the parcel for a moment. Suddenly he flipped the package end for end, tucked it back under his arm, and started briskly down the hill. "Time to be going. It wouldn't do for someone to get into the wagon while we're away."

"Or catch us hangin' about here with that thing," Kim muttered, eyeing the package Mairelon was carrying. As he reached the base of the hill, she fell into step beside him and added in a louder voice, "There's somethin' smoky about that Stuggs cove, that drove the carriage."

"Do you think so? He's not the usual gentleman's gentleman, I'll admit, but then, Jasper Marston doesn't seem very good at being a usual sort of gentleman."

"I don't know what his lay is, but he's no flat, that's sure," Kim said positively. "He pokered up when you said your name was de Mare, and he was watchin' everything too close. And he wasn't keen to give you that package, no matter what the bracket-faced mort said."

"Wasn't he, now," Mairelon said. "How interesting. You know, Kim, this whole business is beginning to look extremely odd."

"*Beginnin'* to look odd?"

"Marston, who has no reason I can think of to even be aware of the existence of the Saltash Set, hires the unlikely Mr. Stuggs to run errands and you to find out whether I have the bowl. Not, mind you, to steal it, but only to discover whether the thing is hidden in one of my cupboards.

He and Lady Granleigh go to a great deal of trouble to steal a copy of the Saltash Platter from Bramingham Place, in spite of interruptions from several people who ought not to know anything about it, either. Then when they get it, they immediately set out to give it to Mr. Aberford, whom Marston, at least, must have recognized as one of the inept housebreakers."

"Maybe he didn't," Kim said. "And they've had the platter since night before last. That ain't givin' it back very immediately."

"Isn't," Mairelon corrected. "The real question is, why would Lady Granleigh want to turn the fake platter over to Aberford instead of giving it back to Henry Bramingham? Bramingham is, after all, the person from whom she stole it."

Kim shook her head. "There's no accountin' for gentry folk."

"Nonsense," Mairelon said firmly. "She must have had some reason. Your Mr. Stower is another puzzlement. I doubt that he is in league with Lady Granleigh, but given Marston's obvious penchant for unusual servants, I don't think we can rule out a connection there."

"He ain't my Mr. Stower," Kim said. "If he's anybody's, he's Dan Laverham's."

"So you've said. In which case, the question that leaps immediately to mind is, is Stower on his own in this or not? And either way, why is he, or Laverham, interested in the Saltash Set? And how did they find out about it?"

"The last part's easy," Kim said. "Laverham's got an eye for anything that'll bring in money, and London's full of coves as would put him in the way of nicking the platter just to get on his good side."

Mairelon gave her an indecipherable look. "Possibly Hunch will have more to say about it when he returns from London. Then there's Mr. Aberford, whose desire for the platter is the only one that appears simple and straightforward. I therefore distrust it on principle, particularly given Mr. Aberford's, ah, unorthodox attempts to retrieve the thing."

"You weren't above breakin' into that Bramingham cove's library yourself," Kim reminded him. "Unless that ain't—isn't—what you meant by 'unorthodox.'"

"*Everyone* broke into Bramingham's library," Mairelon said testily. "Including Renée. Everyone who was anywhere near Ranton Hill, that is. I suppose I should be glad St. Clair didn't arrive until a day later, or we might have seen him bumbling around with everyone else."

Kim suppressed a shiver. "I don't think so. He didn't look like no bumbler to me, and for sure he's no flat."

"Quite true," Mairelon said with another sidelong glance at Kim. "I stand corrected; I've been acquainted with St. Clair long enough to know better. He would undoubtedly—"

Mairelon broke off as they came within sight of the wagon. A curl of smoke was rising past the far side of the roof, and Mairelon looked reproachfully at Kim.

"I put the fire out before I left!" Kim protested. "I'm not sapskulled."

"Then it appears we have company," Mairelon said. His stride lengthened, and Kim had to skip twice to catch up. "Perhaps Renée has found us, after all."

Kim, who had been thinking of Jasper Marston and his sister, or the unpleasant Lord St. Clair, was surprised and not altogether pleased by this suggestion. She was even more surprised, but considerably relieved, when they came around the corner of the wagon and found Hunch feeding medium-sized sticks into a new fire. A placid-looking roan, presumably Hunch's means of transportation, was tied to the back of the wagon, chewing quietly on an invisible wisp of hay.

"Hunch!" Mairelon said, stopping short. "Well, that was always a possibility. You haven't seen Renée around anywhere, have you?"

"*If* you mean that Miss Doo-bear friend o' yours, no, I ain't," Hunch answered. "Nor I ain't likely to. She's in London, laid up with a chill."

"No, she isn't," Mairelon said, frowning. "She's a house-guest at one of Mrs. Bramingham's interminable parties. I've seen her myself. I wonder why she thought she had to pretend she was staying in London?"

"You've seen 'er?" Hunch frowned. "Now, 'ow would you 'ave done that when you was supposed to be a-staying 'ere out of trouble while I was gone?"

"These things happen," Mairelon said, waving a hand in airy dismissal.

"Don't you gammon me, Master Richard," Hunch said severely. "What 'ave you been up to now?"

"This and that," Mairelon answered. "What did Lord Shoreham have to say? Or did he send you off without any information? I hope not; I did tell you to wait."

" 'E 'ad a lot to say." Hunch's expression was grim, and he paused for a moment to chew on the right side of his mustache. "And I ain't repeating any of it til you tell me what you've been doing!"

"Oh, we've been keeping busy, haven't we, Kim?"

"Don't go draggin' me in!" Kim said quickly. "It ain't none of my lay."

Hunch scowled at Kim, then turned his attention back to Mairelon. "You 'adn't ought to—what 'ave you got there?"

Mairelon shifted the parcel under his arm and smiled. "This? I'm not sure. Kim says it's the Saltash Platter, but I haven't looked yet to see whether she's right."

"I never—" Kim gasped, only to be cut short by a look from Mairelon.

"Let's find out, shall we?" Mairelon said, holding the parcel out to Hunch.

Hunch tried to glare at Mairelon, but his eyes kept returning to the package. At last he took it. With a final glare and considerable muttering, he sat down on the step of the wagon and began undoing the knots. Kim realized suddenly that Hunch was just as curious about things as she was, and as little able to resist the opportunity to find something out.

The strings fell apart and Hunch unfolded the wrappings. A silver platter lay across his knees, shining even in the leaden sunlight that crept through the clouds. It was very like the one Kim had glimpsed at Bramingham Place, but she wouldn't have wagered a farthing one way or the other on this being the same article.

"Where did you come by this?" Hunch demanded suspiciously.

"One thing at a time, Hunch," Mairelon responded. "Let me have a look at it first."

"No, you don't," said a new voice as Mairelon reached for the platter.

The surly tone was unmistakably Jack Stower's, and Kim's stomach sank as her head swiveled in the direction of the voice. There was no chance that he wouldn't see her now. Then she got a good look at him, and froze where she stood.

Jack Stower was standing at the rear corner of the wagon beside the roan. He had a large sack strapped over one shoulder. In each hand he held a pistol, and his face wore a forbidding scowl. "I'll have that there wicher cheat, and no gammon," he snarled.

"Just so," said Mairelon without moving. "Do I bring it to you, or do you come and get it?"

"Put it on the ground, there," Stower said, gesturing with one of the pistols. "Then you and the turnip-pated cove get over by the fire. Hop it!"

With exaggerated care, Mairelon lifted the platter and set it in front of Stower. Then he backed away, his eyes fixed on Stower's face. "Hunch," he said without turning, and the dour servingman rose and joined him.

Stower stuck one of his pistols through his belt and swung the sack down from his shoulder. The coarse fabric stretched and shifted around something large and flat and rectangular as he lowered it to the ground. Kim stared at the sack in sudden wild surmise.

"Now you, boy," Stower said, taking the second pistol from his belt and aiming it at Mairelon and Hunch once more. "You take that wicher cheat and—Kim!"

"Surprise," Kim said sourly. "Long way from London, ain't it, Stower?"

Stower's face darkened. "I'll London you! You think you're going to nick a few of the yellow boys Laverham's offering, don't you? Well, you ain't getting nothing. This is my lay, see? How'd you get here ahead of me, anyways? You didn't follow the old cove from the inn. I'd a seen you."

"Just luck," Kim managed. She felt sick. After Stower's hints, Mairelon and Hunch would never trust her again.

"Sorry, Master Richard," Hunch said in tones of chagrin. "I thought as I 'ad shook 'em off the trail in London."

"But Mr. Stower wasn't in London," Mairelon said, and Kim nearly jumped when she felt the unmistakable crystalline quality of the words. Surely Mairelon couldn't mean to try a spell on a man holding two pistols at his head?

"He was in Ranton Hill," Mairelon went on, and the sharp edge of magic was clearer and more threatening than before. "He should still be in Ranton Hill. He should go back to Ranton Hill before something happens to him, *tzay min po, katzef!*"

Jack Stower's face contorted, as if in fear or pain. He gave a strangled cry and hurled one of his pistols at Mairelon. Instantly Hunch dove sideways, knocking Mairelon out of the way as Stower turned and plunged into the wood behind the wagon. Kim threw herself down as the pistol hit the ground and went off, sending a bullet whistling through the empty air where Mairelon's chest had been a moment before.

"The shotgun, Hunch," Mairelon said, panting slightly. "He's still got one pistol, and that spell was only a makeshift. It won't hold him long."

Hunch rolled to his feet and ran for the wagon without wasting time on words of acknowledgment. Kim picked herself up and followed, pausing just long enough to scoop up Jack's bag and the silver platter that lay beside it. Mairelon was the last one inside. He barred the door behind him, then reached up and pressed a knothole in the ceiling.

There was a barely audible click. Mairelon set his palms flat against the ceiling and pushed, and a two-foot section lifted up half an inch, then slid back out of the way. "The gun and a lift, Hunch, if you please," Mairelon said softly.

"You 'adn't ought to be doing this, Master Richard," Hunch grumbled, but he handed Mairelon the shotgun and knelt. Mairelon set a hand on the edge of the opening in the ceiling and a foot in Hunch's cupped hands, and a moment later slid noiselessly out onto the roof of the wagon.

Kim watched this performance with considerable admiration. The speed and smoothness with which it was done spoke of much practice, and she was impressed by the fore-thought that had designed the hidden panel in the ceiling. After a moment, it occurred to her to wonder just how often Mairelon and Hunch had had to make use of this particular device. It threw a whole new light on their possible doings in the past.

The minutes ticked slowly by. At last, Mairelon's head reappeared in the opening. "No sign of him," the magician said. "He's gone for now. Here." He handed the shotgun down to Hunch, then climbed down through the hole. "I'll have to see about setting up some wards; we can't have people popping in and waving pistols around whenever they feel like it. It's becoming altogether too popular a sport to ignore."

"Like that Aberford cove the other night," Kim said, nodding.

"And just what 'as that got to do with all this?" Hunch demanded. "What 'ave you been at while I've been gone, Master Richard?"

"Back to that again? Really, Hunch, I'm beginning to think you're prudish, and I see no reason for Kim and me to elaborate on our relationship merely to satisfy your vulgar curiosity. Particularly when we have more important things to do." Mairelon smiled beatifically at Hunch's outraged expression and waved toward the sack Kim was holding. "Just open that up, Kim, so we can see what our Mr. Stower has been hauling about the countryside."

Kim deposited the silver platter on the floor and began wrestling with the knots at the mouth of the sack. She got them loose at last and reached inside. A moment later she held up a large silver platter, to all appearances identical to the one on the floor.

"Well, well," said Mairelon. "What have we here?" He reached out and took the platter from Kim, and a frown creased his forehead.

"It looks like this other one," Kim said, nudging the first platter with her toe.

"That's exactly what it is," Mairelon said. "Exactly."

"What does that mean?" Hunch said in a resigned tone.

"It means that it's another fake," Mairelon replied.

eighteen

Hunch stared at the platter in Mairelon's hands. "*Another* fake?" he said at last. "You mean that one—" he nodded at the platter on the floor, "—ain't the Saltash Platter, *either*?"

"That is correct," Mairelon said. He turned the second copy over in his hands, studying it with a thoughtful expression. "Kim," he said suddenly, "bring it over here and hold it up so I can look at them both."

Kim did as she was instructed. Mairelon peered intently at a section of the platter he held, then turned to Kim's. After a moment, he returned to the first platter and repeated the process. There was a smear of dust above his left eyebrow, and Kim wondered how he could keep from noticing it, even if his reflection was blurred by the intricate patterns incised on the surface of the platters.

Finally Mairelon set his platter on the counter. With a relieved sigh, Kim did the same; Saltash Platter or not, all that silver was *heavy*. Mairelon stared absently down at them both.

"Well?" Hunch demanded.

"Two copies," Mairelon said, more as if he were thinking aloud than as if he were answering Hunch. "Two *identical* copies. Identical right down to the scuffs and scratches. Whoever made these wasn't working from a description or from drawings."

"Then he had the real one to copy?" Kim said tentatively.

"I would be willing to bet on it," Mairelon replied. "So if we find the silversmith, we'll find the Saltash Platter."

Hunch snorted. "Sounds to me as if you're back where you started, Master Richard."

"Not quite," Mairelon said, and smiled. "There's only one person in this area who's had the platter long enough to make copies. Freddy Meredith."

"*Meredith?*" Kim said incredulously. "You're bammin' me! That sapskull?"

"I'll admit it doesn't sound likely," Mairelon conceded. "But who else is there? Bramingham only had the platter for a day or so; he couldn't have gotten *one* copy made in that time, much less two. None of the other, er, interested parties has even been in Ranton Hill long enough, much less had the platter in his possession."

"What about that Aberford cove?" Kim objected.

"Well, yes, I suppose he ought to be considered a possibility," Mairelon said. "But I don't think he would have tried to burgle Bramingham Place the other night unless he thought the platter there was the real one."

"Burgle Bramingham Place?" Hunch said. His lips tightened, causing his mustache to wiggle alarmingly. "Master Richard—"

"Yes, I hadn't forgotten about you," Mairelon interrupted. He seated himself on top of the chest and looked at Hunch with an air of expectancy. "I assume Shoreham told you something worth hearing, or you wouldn't have come back so promptly. Let's have it."

Hunch rolled his eyes. Kim suppressed an impulse to grin, as much at Mairelon's tactics as Hunch's reaction. She wondered how long Mairelon would be able to keep from explaining to Hunch just what he had been doing in his henchman's absence. She sat down cross-legged on the floor and waited for Hunch to begin.

" 'Oo do you want to 'ear about first?" Hunch asked.

"Jack Stower, since he has intruded on us so recently."

" 'E's a nasty piece o' work," Hunch said. " 'E lives in St. Giles, far as anyone can tell, thieving and suchlike. Lord Shoreham says 'e ain't no different from most of the scum as follows 'is profession, and the most interesting thing about 'im is 'is master."

"Who is Dan Laverham," Mairelon said. "We'll have him next, but not before we're finished with Mr. Stower. Did Shoreham find out when Stower left London?"

" 'E left the day after we did," Hunch replied. "Lord Shoreham found someone 'oo was drinking Blue Ruin with 'im the night afore 'e left, and 'e says Stower was mumbling 'ints about some errand 'e was going to do for Mr. Laverham."

Mairelon looked interested. "Hints? What sort of hints?"

"Mysterious 'ints," Hunch said. "Lord Shoreham didn't say no more than that."

"How like him," Mairelon murmured. "Very well. What about Mr. Laverham?"

" 'E's a bit of a puzzle. 'E lives in the rookery, but 'e dresses and talks like one o' the *ton*. And 'e went to 'Arrow."

"Harrow!" Mairelon looked startled. "How did a boy from St. Giles get into a school like that? He *is* from St. Giles?"

"Far as Lord Shoreham knows," Hunch said, nodding. "As for 'Arrow, somebody paid 'is fees."

"He's probably the by-blow of someone with both a conscience and the money to indulge it, then," Mairelon said thoughtfully. "Unfortunately, the combination is not so unusual that it is instantly apparent who Laverham's presumed parent is."

"That's what Lord Shoreham thought," Hunch said. " 'E said 'e'd talk to some of 'is friends in the City and see if one of 'em could track the money, but it ain't much of a chance."

"I wonder how well Laverham did at Harrow? They're strong in Latin and Greek and wizardry, as I recall."

Kim chocked. "You mean Dan Laverham is a *wizard*?"

"If he was educated at Harrow, he ought to know the basics, at least," Mairelon replied. "Don't let it trouble you."

"Easy enough for you to say," Kim muttered. She didn't know what a first-class frog-maker could do to someone, but half-formed images of the horrible possibilities whirled through her mind. Their very vagueness made them worse than actual knowledge would have been.

"Anything else?" Mairelon asked, turning back to Hunch.

"Mr. Laverham 'as a name in some parts as the man to see if you want something done and you ain't fussy about 'ow. 'E ain't never been caught doing nothing wrong, though."

"That's Dan, all right," Kim said in an undertone.

"Yes, thanks to Kim, we probably have more information about Mr. Laverham's criminal activities than Shoreham does," Mairelon said. "Did he have anything to say about Marston or Fenton?"

"Mr. Jasper Marston is 'ead over ears in debt," Hunch told them. " 'E's supposed to be rusticating right now, to get away from 'is creditors."

"And Lady Granleigh has promised to assist him to a rich marriage if he helps her with whatever labyrinthine plans she has set in motion," Mairelon said.

Hunch looked startled. " 'Ow do you know that?"

"Kim overheard them talking," Mairelon said.

" 'E's Lady Granleigh's younger brother, and Lord Shoreham said 'e was a bit of a slow-top," Hunch resumed. "When 'e ain't wasting 'is money on cards and 'orses, 'e does what 'is sister tells 'im."

"That has become fairly evident. Shoreham didn't mention Marston's man, Stuggs, did he?"

"No."

"Ah, well. One can't have everything, and I didn't ask." Mairelon stared pensively at the window for a moment. Then he looked up and said, "I believe that leaves James Fenton."

Hunch grinned. The unaccustomed expression made him look positively fiendish, and Kim was completely taken aback by the change. Mairelon took one look and came to attention like a skilled sharper sighting a promising dupe.

"Fenton's the black sheep of 'is family," Hunch said, still with that disturbing grin. "They're mostly respectable tradesmen. 'E seemed clever, so they 'ad 'im put into service. 'E started off as a footman."

"Indeed." Mairelon's eyes narrowed. "And what house was he in service to?"

"Lord St. Clair's," Hunch said with great satisfaction.

"St. Clair!"

"*And* 'e was dismissed the day after the *Colony Queen* left the docks," Hunch added.

"Huh?" said Kim.

"The *Colony Queen* was the ship Hunch and I took when we, er, fled the country after the Saltash Set was stolen," Mairelon said. "So Fenton was dismissed right after the theft was blamed solidly on me, was he? I wonder if he knows something about it."

"Lord Shoreham thought 'e might," Hunch said. " 'E also thought you'd be interested in knowing that on the night the Saltash Set was stolen Fenton 'ad some unscheduled free time."

"Unscheduled? You mean he took French leave?"

"No, 'e 'ad Lord St. Clair's permission," Hunch said. " 'E just wasn't supposed to 'ave that night off, Lord Shoreham says."

"Well, if Shoreham says Fenton was supposed to be working that night, he's probably right," Mairelon said. "I don't know how he comes up with these things, but he hasn't been mistaken once in five years. What has Fenton been doing since he, er, left St. Clair?"

"Mucking about 'ere and there. 'E did a few jobs for some of them

'ousebreakers, but 'e ain't 'ad no honest work until six weeks ago, when
'e upped and 'ired on at Meredith's 'ouse."

"Six weeks," Mairelon said, frowning. "Time enough for him to find
out about the platter and notify St. Clair, if that was why he was here.
But if St. Clair let him go—"

"Couldn't it have been a blind?" Kim said. "That Lord St. Clair, he
sounds like a fly cove; maybe he didn't want any ties to a looby like
Fenton. If the two of them nabbed that silver stuff you're always on about,
then—"

Mairelon shook his head. "No, no, I can't believe St. Clair was involved in the original theft. He'd have to be completely lost to all sense
of honor."

"And I suppose he wasn't a Captain Sharp if all he did was peach
on you to the nabbing culls?" Kim said scornfully.

"It's not the same thing," Mairelon said.

"I don't see why not," Kim told him. "Anyway, lords aren't that
different from other folks. If they want somethin' bad enough, they'll try
to get it however they can, and never mind the right and wrong of it."

"What a remarkably cynical philosophy to find in one so young,"
Mairelon said, staring at Kim.

Kim shrugged, only half understanding. "I'm not that young; I'm
rising seventeen, I think. And I don't see what my age has to do with
how people are."

The muscles in Mairelon's jaw tensed, and for a moment he looked
positively angry. Then he said gently, "It's not a matter of how people
are, Kim; it has to do with how they ought to be. We'll discuss it some
other time, perhaps. Though I still don't think St. Clair had anything to
do with the theft, if only because he'd have kept the Saltash Set for himself
instead of splitting it up and selling it. He'd had his eye on it for years;
he wouldn't have given it up easily."

"Oh," Kim said, disappointed. "Then we still don't know who stole
it?"

"Don't look so cast down," Mairelon said. "We'll find out eventually.
Meanwhile, we have a few other things to take care of."

"What things?" Hunch asked, squinting suspiciously at his master.

"St. Clair is staying at Bramingham Place," Mairelon said. "So is
Renée D'Auber. And it is evidently no secret that the Saltash Platter—
or rather, an exceedingly good copy—was in Henry Bramingham's possession until the night before last. I doubt very much that all this is merely
a coincidence."

"So?"

"So I want to know how Shoreham's secret information on the whereabouts of the Saltash Platter managed to reach so many people in so short a time," Mairelon said. "Also, I'm worried about Renée. She was supposed to meet me at the druids' hill over an hour and a half ago, but she never arrived. I'm going to Bramingham Place to see if I can find out why."

"I thought you didn't want that Lord St. Clair seein' you," Kim objected. "Ain't—isn't that why you sent me over there yesterday?"

"It is, which is why you're coming with me. Don't argue, Hunch; you've had a long ride and you should rest. Keep the shotgun handy in case that Stower fellow turns up again. I'll set up the warding spells when we get back."

"Now, see 'ere, Master Richard!" Hunch said. "You ain't a-going to take that girl with you, not if I 'ave anything to say about it. Like as not, she's working for that Mr. Laverham."

Kim scowled fiercely at Hunch to hide a sudden, strong inclination to cry. Stower's accusations hadn't gone unnoticed, after all, and she had no way of proving that he was wrong. "I ain't!" she said, but she had little hope of being believed.

"Really, Hunch." Mairelon's tone was mild, but Hunch stiffened and sat back, eyeing his master warily. "You forget," Mairelon went on, "I questioned Kim myself, with the Saltash Bowl to compel her to be truthful. Or do you remember that, and doubt my skill?"

"I'd forgot," Hunch said, plainly chagrined. "But—"

"No," Mairelon said in the same mild tone. "No buts. Spell or no spell, Kim has earned the right to be trusted. You owe her an apology."

"No, he don't," Kim said hastily. Hunch looked at her in surprise, and she hurried on, "I'd forgotten about that spell myself. I thought sure you'd take Stower's gab for truth. I would have. So he don't owe me nothin'."

"Doesn't," Mairelon said.

"What?" Kim said, momentarily at sea.

"Hunch *doesn't* owe you *anything*. We'll leave it at that."

Hunch nodded, still wearing a faint expression of surprise. Mairelon looked at Kim and added in a severe tone, "You have been doing well with your lessons, but you tend to fall back on cant phrases and poor grammar when you get excited about something. Try to be more careful."

Kim fought down a desire to laugh in relief. She felt positively light-headed and didn't trust herself to say anything, so she simply nodded.

"Good. We'll be going, then." Mairelon paused and looked at Hunch, who was chewing on his mustache but wisely refrained from commenting. Mairelon smiled. "I'll send Kim back if I need you for anything, but I doubt that I will. And perhaps you'd better pack while we're gone; we might want to move the wagon in case Stower takes it into his head to come back with a friend or two. Assuming, of course, that he *has* a friend or two. Don't forget the shotgun."

"I won't," said Hunch. "And don't you forget to watch for that there Stower, neither. 'E might follow you instead of coming back 'ere."

Mairelon nodded and beckoned to Kim. With some caution, he opened the wagon door, but there was no sign of Jack Stower. "Come along," Mairelon said to Kim, and started briskly for the road. Kim stared after him for a moment, realizing suddenly that she had let herself in for another two-hour walk out to Bramingham Place and back. Cursing mentally, she ran to catch up.

nineteen

The walk to Bramingham Place was every bit as long as Kim remembered. To make matters worse, Mairelon decided that Kim needed more practice with her speech lessons and drilled her mercilessly as they hiked along. He stopped only when an approaching rider or cart distracted his attention, but as they saw only three during the entire trip this did not give Kim much respite.

At the edge of the manor grounds, Mairelon turned down a narrow side lane along a tall hedge. Kim followed, relieved by the end of the lessons and equally glad that she would not have to face the long trudge up the formal drive. All those rows of trees and carefully positioned shrubs made her uncomfortable.

"There ought to be a gap along here somewhere," Mairelon muttered a few minutes later. "I didn't think it was this far."

"Maybe they've plugged it up since you were here," Kim said.

Mairelon looked at her, then at the hedge. "You know, I think you may be right. Well, we'll just have to push our way through, then."

"Couldn't we go around?" Kim asked without much hope. When Mairelon took a notion, he was stubborn as a hackney coachman wanting full fare in advance. "This ain't—isn't the way we came the other night."

"It isn't dark now, either," Mairelon pointed out. "Unless Bramingham has replanted the entire grounds since I was here last, there's a wood on this side that will screen us from the house. The other way, there's a vista from the South Lawn. We'd be seen at once."

"Right," said Kim gloomily. "What are you plannin' to do when we get up by the house?"

"I'll work that out when we get there," Mairelon said. "I think the bushes are thinner here; follow me, and mind your head." With considerable difficulty and more than a few scratches, they forced their way through the thin spot in the hedge. When they emerged into the little wood on the other side, Mairelon's clothes were covered with leaves and twigs, there were several snags in the previously smooth surface of his coat, and one sleeve sported a long smear of mud that ended in a small tear. Kim had fared little better, but she hadn't been wearing gentry togs.

"Hunch isn't going to be happy when he sees what you've done to them clothes," Kim said.

"Do you think so?" Mairelon said. He brushed the leaves and twigs from his shoulders, ignoring the ones caught in his hair, and studied his mud-flecked sleeve. "It is a little extreme, I suppose. Well, there's no help for it now. I think the house is—"

The echo of a shot from somewhere nearby cut Mairelon off in mid-sentence. His head whipped around and his eyes widened. "That was a pistol," he said, and started running in the direction of the noise.

Kim choked back a shout of dismay and ran after him while her mind listed in a remarkably clear fashion all the reasons why this was intensely foolish. Shots were something you ran *away* from, not toward. Someone else might have heard and roused the house. They would be taken up for poachers. They should sherry off while they had the chance. *She* should sherry off while she had the chance.

The list came to a sudden end as she broke out of the woods into one of the tree-lined alleys she so disliked. Mairelon was several steps ahead of her, slowing to halt beside an anonymous figure in a dark blue coat that lay sprawled on the ground at the edge of the woods. As Kim skidded to a stop next to him, she caught a glimpse of someone running off through the trees. The distance was too great for her to get more than a vague impression of a dark shape, but Kim didn't care. What mattered was that he was going in the right direction: away.

Mairelon went down on one knee and reached under the collar of the blue coat with one hand. "He's dead," he said. He shifted and bent to grip the corpse's shoulders, then gently turned it over.

"Fenton!" said Kim. She felt very odd, looking down at the empty, staring eyes and slack face. She had seen dead men before, and even robbed a few, but a fresh corpse in a shadowy London alley, wreathed in yellow fog, was somehow very different from the same sight in the calm green countryside.

"Get back, Kim," Mairelon said sharply, as though he had just remembered her and was not at all pleased to find her standing next to him.

Nothing loath, Kim backed up a few paces and looked around. A large canvas bag lay on the ground a few feet away. She stared at it with a sinking feeling, then went over and picked it up. It was much heavier than she expected, and she frowned as she tugged at the strings. If it wasn't another platter, what *was* it? She got it open at last, looked inside, and made a strangled noise.

"What's that?" Mairelon asked, looking up. "Another platter?"

"No," Kim said. "It's two of them."

"*Two* of them?" Mairelon stood and came over to her. He took the sack and put his left hand inside for a moment, then shook his head. "And both fakes. Well, at least now we know who was responsible for making them."

"We do?" said Kim.

"Well, nearly. It has to have been either Fenton or the man who shot him," Mairelon said. "One of them brought that bag here, and who would have two false platters except the man who's been making them?"

"You do," Kim pointed out. "Or you did until just now. Now you've got four."

"Yes, well, that's different. We've been collecting them, not making them."

"Why couldn't Fenton do that, too?"

Mairelon sighed. "True. It doesn't seem likely, but it's possible." He stared into the trees for a moment, then shook his head again. "There's no help for it. I shall have to send you back to get Hunch."

"*What?* No! I ain't goin'!" Kim barely stopped herself from shrieking. Leave Mairelon alone for over an hour with a dead body and a killer lurking in the woods, more than likely? Leave without having any idea what Fenton had been doing—or what Mairelon was going to do next? Leave now, and have to pry the story out of Mairelon later?

"I'm afraid you must," Mairelon said. "In case you had forgotten, there is a man around with a pistol. Once he's had time to reload, he'll probably recover his courage, and when he does I would like to have Hunch—and the shotgun—near at hand."

"Then you better go to the wagon yourself," Kim advised. "It ain't goin' to take an hour for the cove to reload, and it'd take that long just for me to walk back."

"True," Mairelon conceded. He frowned down at the bag. "I don't like leaving bodies lying around, but I can't very well march up to the door of Bramingham Place and explain matters, can I?"

Kim stared at him, amazed that he would even consider such a foolish action. "With the Runners after you? Not hardly!"

"Yes, there's that, too," Mairelon said absently. He was still frowning. "Well, let's finish here first, and then decide." He handed the canvas sack back to Kim. "Hold this."

Feeling a bit bewildered, Kim took the sack and watched as Mairelon returned to Fenton's corpse. Her bewilderment deepened when Mairelon began going through Fenton's pockets with the brisk professionalism of a London cutpurse. He ignored Fenton's handkerchief, shook his head over a gold snuffbox and an expensive-looking pair of gloves hidden inside Fenton's waistcoat, and frowned at a note he found in Fenton's jacket. Then, to Kim's complete confusion, he began patting Fenton's sides and pulling at the hems of his clothes.

"What are you doin' that for?" Kim demanded at last.

"I'm checking for—ah!" Mairelon stopped and took a penknife from his pocket. Carefully, he made a slit along the left seam of Fenton's waistcoat; a moment later, he pulled a folded paper from inside the lining.

"Well, well," Mairelon said, shaking the paper open. "What have we here?"

"How should I know?" Kim said. "How did you know to look for it there, anyways?"

"It's a trick the Frenchies used now and then when they had something important to send," Mairelon said. "If it comes to that, it's a trick I've used myself a time or two . . . well, *well.*"

"Well what?" Kim said crossly. "What's it say?"

"Unless someone else finds out about this and gets there before we do, which seems unlikely, I believe we have discovered the location of the Saltash Platter at last," Mairelon said with great satisfaction. He refolded the paper and tucked it into an inner pocket, then rose, dusting his hands.

"You mean he really *was* makin' those fakes?" Kim asked, feeling a little chagrined.

"Probably, but it doesn't matter much any more. The important thing is that Fenton knew where the real platter is, and now we do, too."

"Then we can leave?"

"Not just yet, my dear," said a new voice. "Particularly not if your friend's most recent statement is true. I have a great deal of interest in the Saltash Platter, you see."

Kim whirled and felt the blood drain from her face. "Dan Laverham!" she said.

Dan was standing next to one of the tall, grey-barked trees that lined the avenue. He held a pearl-handled pistol in each hand, and beside him stood Jack Stower, similarly armed. Jack's eyes were fixed warily on Mairelon, and as Laverham stepped into the avenue he said, "Be careful, Mr. Laverham! That there's the frog-maker I told you about."

"Really." Dan smiled. "Richard Merrill, I assume?"

"The same," Mairelon said, inclining his head. "May I inquire how you guessed?"

"Oh, come, now. There aren't many first-class wizards who'd be out chasing after the Saltash Set. You're far too well behaved to be one of the Sons of the whatever, and I am . . . familiar with Lord St. Clair's appearance. Who else could you be?"

"You are uncommonly well informed," Mairelon observed.

"It is necessary, in my business," Dan replied. "Don't try any spells, by the by. After Jack told me his little tale, I prepared a few odds and ends especially to take care of that sort of impromptu effort. You wouldn't have a chance." He gave Mairelon a long, appraising look that made Kim feel cold inside, then said in quite another tone, "Move over by Kim."

Without comment, Mairelon did so. Dan Laverham took two steps forward and glanced down at the body. "James Fenton. Dear me, how dreadful. And just when I thought he was finally going to be of some use to me, after all. Well, it can't be helped. By the way, why did you kill him?"

"I didn't," Mairelon said.

"How interesting," Dan said. "Jack, go get that bag from Kim, there's a good fellow, and see what's in it. Then I think we had all better be going. You can't depend on amateurs to do the sensible thing; whoever shot Fenton might decide to come back and take a shot or two at us, and that would never do. Assuming, of course, that Mr. Merrill is telling us the truth."

Jack stuck one of his pistols into his belt and swaggered over to Kim. Silently she handed him the sack. If she hadn't been so scared, she would have enjoyed the way his expression changed when he opened the bag and saw what was inside.

"It's *two* of them wicher cheats, Mr. Laverham!" Stower said. "That there frog-maker's gone and doubled the thing!"

"Bring it here," Dan commanded.

Stower did so, eyeing Mairelon nervously the whole time, as if he thought the magician might make twins of himself if he were not watched carefully. Dan felt around inside for a moment, just as Mairelon had, then shook his head. "They're forgeries. Fenton was probably hoping to pass one of them off as the real thing. Leave them."

Stower gaped at Dan in disbelief. "*Leave* them? But they're *silver.*"

"I said, leave them," Dan said sharply. "I don't need any more complications. This—" he gave Fenton's body a casual kick, "—is more than enough."

The canvas sack hit the ground with a thud and a clatter. "Very good," said Dan. "Now, drag our late friend back into the woods a little, where he won't be so likely to be noticed. I don't want him found until we're well on our way back to London.

"I see you were acquainted with the late Mr. Fenton," Mairelon said as Jack Stower, glowering, complied with Dan's commands.

"James was one of my least reliable men," Dan said. "I was positively looking forward to disposing of him myself. If I'd realized he was getting ideas above his station, I'd have done so long before this." He gave the canvas sack a disapproving look.

"Then Fenton *was* the one who made all the fakes!" Kim said before she could stop herself.

"All the fakes? You mean there are others besides these?" Dan gave the sack a look that should have made it crumble to dust on the spot. "My, but he was ambitious. Or perhaps greedy is the proper word; under the circumstances, it's difficult to be sure. It was James, all right. His eldest brother is a silversmith."

"The black sheep of 'is family; they're mostly respectable tradesman,'" Mairelon murmured. "I should have asked Hunch for details."

"Speaking of platters, I think it's time you told me where the real one is," Dan said pleasantly. "It's what I came for, after all."

"I'm afraid your Mr. Fenton didn't say," Mairelon said with equal affability.

"I don't care whether he told you where he put it or simply gestured so eloquently that the knowledge sprang into your mind unbidden," Dan said dryly. "I want to know the location of the Saltash Platter. I'm sure you don't need a list of the various painful things I could do to your young companion to make you talk."

"Quite so," Mairelon said in the gentle tone he used only when he was particularly angry. Kim glanced apprehensively at Dan, but he seemed oblivious to Mairelon's reaction, and Kim realized with a sense of shock that Dan did not know Mairelon at all. She was so used to taking for granted that Dan Laverham knew everyone and everything better than she did that she barely heard Mairelon continue, "It's somewhere in the druid lodge. I'm afraid he wasn't any more specific than that, but a little searching should turn it up without too much difficulty. The place isn't that large."

"Very good," said Dan. "Jack! Leave that and come along." He gestured with one of his pistols. "That way, Mr. Merrill, and not too fast. Follow him a little to the side, Kim."

"What d'you want them for?" Jack demanded, emerging from the woods with a sour expression. "Pop them and leave them with the other cove."

"You have no imagination," Dan responded. "Get that sack out of sight and meet us at the carriage. And don't linger; I won't wait for you."

As they started up the avenue in the direction Dan had indicated, Kim glanced back and saw Jack glare after Dan. He bent and grabbed the open end of the sack, and, with a strong heave, sent it flying into the trees before he ran to catch up with Laverham.

twenty

Dan Laverham directed them down the tree-lined avenue and along a bridle path to a wooden gate in the hedge. Kim, remembering how difficult getting through the hedge had been, gave Mairelon a reproachful look as Stower opened the gate and waved them through. Mairelon did not seem to notice; he was studying Stower in a way that made Kim very nervous. After all, Dan was still behind them with a pair of guns.

To Kim's relief, Mairelon did nothing to annoy Dan, and they reached the lane with no more than a few dark looks from Jack Stower. A closed carriage waited near the roadside, the driver's perch occupied by a figure muffled in a shabby, ill-fitting coat that, to Kim's experienced eye, had the indefinable aura of the London back streets. The horses were placidly chewing wisps of grass, and Mairelon gave them the same long, considering look he had just given Jack.

"Ben!" Dan called as he came through the gate. "We have another stop or two to make. Mr. Merrill will give you the direction."

Mairelon glanced back over his shoulder at Dan. Dan smiled very slightly and lifted one of his pistols a fraction of an inch. "And they will be clear and without any deliberately misleading bits. Won't they, Mr. Merrill?"

"Of course." Mairelon inclined his head, then turned and went forward to speak with the coachman. Dan kept his eyes—and his pistol—fixed on them as he waved Jack forward with his other hand.

"I think you had better ride with Ben," Dan told him. "Put the guns under your coat; we don't want to attract attention."

"You ain't riding in there with two of 'em!" Jack protested. "What if they jump you?"

"A point," said Dan, showing no signs of concern. "Have the goodness to hold your gun on Mr. Merrill while I see to it that they won't."

Jack nodded with unnecessary force. He stepped forward and pointed both of his pistols at Mairelon's stomach. Dan looked at him, nodded, and turned to Kim. "I trust you will not attempt to do anything foolish in the next few minutes," he said. "It would have most unpleasant consequences."

Kim didn't trust her voice, so she nodded. Dan smiled coldly and set his right-hand pistol on the step of the carriage. "This will only take a moment," he said, putting his hand in his pocket. He withdrew it almost immediately, and when he uncurled his fingers, Kim saw two balls resting in his palm. One was a silver sphere, covered with tiny vines and fruit, that would have fit comfortably in the circle of Kim's thumb and forefinger. The other was a small, faceted crystal the size of her thumbnail.

Behind her, Kim heard a sharp intake of breath from Mairelon. Dan looked past her and said, "I see you recognize these, Mr. Merrill. I hope that means you will be sensible enough not to interfere. The pieces of the Saltash Set are temperamental to work with when they aren't together."

Without waiting for a response, Dan stretched his hand toward Kim and began murmuring sharp, crystalline words. They hung in the air, twisting over and under and around each other like the streets of London, making an intangible net between Kim and Dan. Kim shuddered and took an involuntary step backward. Dan Laverham raised his left hand and made a complicated gesture, his voice rising as he did so. The invisible web of words swirled and swept forward, settling around Kim. She froze, waiting for it to do whatever it was meant to.

Dan gestured again, commandingly, and shouted a final phrase. The two spheres began to glow with a clear, silver light. Kim felt the razor-edged words close in, but the air between her and the spell was full of a strong, sweet, smoky scent, and the net of magic could not touch her. She swayed, light-headed with relief, and the spell swayed with her, maintaining its fractional distance.

"There," Dan said. He sounded breathless, as if he had been running, but he spoke in a tone of great satisfaction. He returned the two still-glowing balls to his pocket and bent to pick up his pistol.

"An interesting demonstration," Mairelon said in a cool voice from behind Kim's shoulder. "But what is it supposed to accomplish?"

"Dear me, I thought you would be able to puzzle that out for yourself," Dan replied, straightening. "Even under these admittedly adverse conditions."

"You have a high opinion of me," Mairelon answered. "I recognized parts of it, but I've never seen anything quite like the whole. You adapted the Saltash truth spells to do something else, didn't you?"

"Shut your gob," Jack Stower growled, gesturing with his pistols.

"Now, now, don't get carried away, my dear," Dan said to Jack. "After all, he's quite right." Dan turned to Mairelon. "It's a control spell, or rather, a minor reworking of the control portions of the Saltash spells. It therefore has the same limits as its original, an annoyance I hope to correct once I have the whole set to study."

"The same limits as the Saltash spells?" Mairelon looked from Kim to Dan and shook his head. "That can't be very convenient. Only one person at a time, only one use per person, time limit—what is the time limit on your control spell, by the way? I know how long it is for the Saltash spells."

"Two hours," Dan answered. "Long enough for me to retrieve the Saltash Platter and Bowl and be well on my way back to London. Providing, of course, that we don't waste any more time. Into the carriage."

Kim blinked, realizing that this last command was directed at her. She felt no particular compulsion to follow Dan's orders, though she could still sense his spell hovering around her. She stared at Dan for a moment, her mind whirling, and suddenly the pieces came together. Dan had adapted the Saltash spells into a control spell, but his spell still had the same flaws as the Saltash spells. It only worked once on any particular person. And over a week before, on their first night out of London, Mairelon had cast the Saltash truth spell on Kim to find out what her lay was. That was why Dan's control couldn't touch her!

There were, however, two pistols still pointed at Mairelon, and he and Kim were outnumbered three to two, counting the phlegmatic coachman. It would clearly be much better to follow Dan's directions for a while. As long as he thought his spell was working, he wouldn't pay too much attention to Kim, and she might get a chance to pike off and get Hunch. Kim took a deep breath and climbed into the carriage.

"You next, Mr. Merrill," Dan said. "Sit there, next to Kim. Good." Dan climbed in after Mairelon and settled onto the seat opposite him. He pointed his pistols at Mairelon, then called out the window, "Up on the box with Ben, Jack. Keep your pistols handy, but try not to let anyone see them. We don't want to attract attention, remember."

Jack said something Kim could not hear, and Dan frowned. "Nonsense. Don't dally, my dear; I haven't time to waste."

There was a muffled curse, followed by an assortment of thumps as Jack climbed up to sit with the coachman. A moment later, the coach jerked and started off. "Not much of a driver, your man Ben," Mairelon commented. "Did you bring him out of sentiment, or economy?"

"Neither," Dan said with unimpaired good humor. "He has talents other than driving that I thought I might find useful."

There was an undercurrent in Dan's voice that made Kim shiver. She was all too conscious of the various unpleasant ways a man could find to survive in London's rookeries; Jack Stower was the Archbishop of Canterbury compared to some. She knew nothing of the driver, but she knew enough of Dan to be sure that she didn't want to learn. Anyone he spoke of in those tones was sure to be an ugly customer.

Dan either did not see Kim's quiver or attributed it to the motion of the carriage. Mairelon shot her a flickering glance, then returned his attention to Dan as if he had noticed nothing. A moment later, however, the carriage lurched as he was shifting his position, and he fell sideways against Kim's shoulder.

"Don't fret," he breathed into her ear, his lips barely moving "Sorry, Kim," he added in a louder tone as he straightened and resumed his seat.

Kim forgot her worries long enough to glare at him. "Don't fret" was probably his idea of a reassuring message, but he couldn't have picked a more ridiculous thing to say if he'd thought about it since the day they met. Don't fret, with Dan Laverham pointing a pistol at them, Jack Stower on the box with a gun of his own, a dead man in the woods behind them, and not the faintest hope of a way out of the mess that she could see? Don't fret, when Dan was about to get his hands on the blasted platter that all the rogues and half the gentry for miles around were chasing after? Did he take her for a Bedlamite, or hadn't it occurred to him that any reasonable person would fret himself to flinders in a situation like this?

"I think you should stay firmly seated from now on," Dan said to Mairelon. "It would be unfortunate, don't you think, if you were to careen into me that way and my pistol were to go off."

"Unfortunate is certainly one word for it," Mairelon agreed. "You know, as long as we have time for a chat, I was wondering whether you'd tell me a little more about that control spell of yours. It's terribly interesting. Don't you think it's terribly interesting, Kim?"

"A more tactless comment I have seldom heard," Dan said.

"What?" Mairelon blinked, then looked from Dan to Kim for a moment and back to Dan. "Oh, yes, I see what you mean. But even so—"

There was a loud report from outside the window, and the coach jerked to a sudden and unceremonious halt. For a moment, Kim was convinced that Jack Stower had fired at something or someone; then she heard an all-too-familiar voice cry in ringing tones, "Stand and deliver! In the name of the Four Holy Things!"

"Jonathan Aberford," Kim said, feeling stunned. "That bufflehead!"

"Oh, Lord, not again," Mairelon said, rolling his eyes.

Laverham's eyebrows rose. "A holdup, in broad daylight? On a country road going from nowhere to nowhere else? It seems unlikely, on the face of it."

Jack Stower seemed to share Dan's opinion. "You're dicked in the nob," they heard him shout. "Mr. Laverham's in this coach!"

"Stand and deliver!" Jonathan cried again. "Drop your weapons, or I fire!"

"We've stood, we've stood," Jack snarled. "Now what?"

"An excellent question," Mairelon murmured. "I wonder whether he's thought of it?"

"If this is some trick of yours—" Dan raised a pistol.

"It's not a trick," Mairelon said. "It's a druid. In a manner of speaking, that is. He's harmless, I think, unless he happens to have taken the notion that highwaymen always shoot someone just to prove they're serious."

Before Dan could respond, they heard a wordless yell, a horse's shrill, frightened neigh, and the sounds of a scuffle outside. Dan leaned over and glanced out the window. When he returned his gaze to Mairelon, his expression had not changed, but there was an air of satisfaction about him. A moment later, Jack's face appeared at the window. He was breathless, and there was a smear of mud across his left cheek.

"We got the rum padder, Mr. Laverham," Jack panted. "What d'you want us to do with him?"

"Kill him," Laverham said.

"Right." Jack smiled, showing crooked brown teeth. "Now?"

Dan nodded, then, as Jack turned to go, he frowned and said, "No, wait. Are you—" he gestured at Mairelon with his pistol, "—quite sure this person is a druid?"

"Well, you can see that he's not much of a highwayman," Mairelon said in a reasonable tone. "It probably didn't even occur to him to bring a spare pistol."

"It don't matter," Jack objected. "The cull tried to pop the lot of us!"

"With only one pistol?" Dan said. "I think not. In any case, if this inept highwayman is a druid, he'll know where to look for the platter once we get to the lodge. We'll bring him along."

"But, Mr. Laverham—"

"Don't argue, my dear, just do it." Dan studied Mairelon for a moment, then smiled unpleasantly. "You'll have to be tied, of course," he said to the magician. "I'm not fool enough to leave you free with the carriage as crowded as it's going to be. Kim!"

Kim jerked, startled by the unexpected command. "What?"

"There's a bit of rope under the seat." Dan pointed with his left hand. "Get it and tie your companion's hands. And see you do a good job of it. I won't—"

The carriage door swung open, and Jack Stower shoved the unfortunate Jonathan forward, so that he staggered against the step. "Where do you want him, Mr. Laverham?" Jack asked.

"In a moment, Jack," Dan replied. "Tie him, Kim."

Remembering suddenly that she was supposed to be under Dan's spell of control, Kim bent and rummaged under the seat for the rope. She straightened and turned sideways to face Mairelon. "Hold out your hands," she said in a flat voice.

Mairelon did so, his gaze fixed on Kim's face. Kim dropped her eyes, wondering whether Mairelon knew she was faking. Well, he'd figure it in another minute. She looped the rope around his wrists and pulled hard for Dan's benefit, then fed the ends through the complex pattern Mairelon had shown her on their first day out of London.

When she finished, she looked up. Mairelon was still staring fixedly at her face, his expression unreadable. "There," Kim said. "You won't get out of *that* in no hurry."

"No?" Mairelon said. He looked down at last, and went still as he recognized the trick knot. He raised his head to look at Kim again and said very deliberately, "I see."

"Kim learned to tie knots down on the docks," Dan said, misinterpreting Mairelon's reaction. "Now, Jack, let's have the druid highwayman."

Jack shoved Jonathan again, and it was more by luck than planning that this time Jonathan stumbled up the step and into the carriage. He was hatless, one of the capes on his coat was torn, and there was a reddened area on his left cheek that would make a splendid bruise in another day or so. His awkward progress was due to the sock he had used as a mask. At some point during his encounter with Dan's men, the sock had slipped to one side, and the holes Jonathan had cut in it were now centered over his nose and right temple. Kim almost laughed aloud.

"This is entirely unnecessary," Jonathan said in a calm voice, but his hands shook as he raised them to pull the sock off his head. "I'm Jonathan. It was just a bet, and—" He stopped short as the sock came off and he saw the occupants of the coach.

"I see you weren't expecting us," Dan said, pointing his pistols impartially at Jonathan and Mairelon. "Not that it matters. Tie him, too, Kim."

"What?" Jonathan stared as if he couldn't believe what he had just heard. "You don't mean it! Look, my name's Aberford; if you stop at the next house, they'll vouch for me. You don't have to bring a magistrate into it."

"I don't intend to," Dan said. He lifted his pistol again for emphasis and added, "Just hold still while Kim works."

"What's going on here?" Jonathan demanded, finally taking in Mairelon's bound hands and rumpled appearance. "This is an outrage!"

"No more so than a holdup in the middle of the morning," Dan said. "You're hardly in a position to criticize. Jack!"

While Jonathan spluttered and Kim repeated her performance with another piece of rope, Dan held a brief conversation with Jack through the open carriage door. According to Jack, Jonathan had come galloping out of the trees, blazing away with his pistol. The frightened carriage horses had reared, tangling their harness and causing the coach to bounce to a halt. When Jonathan, with typical single-mindedness, had turned his back on the coachmen in his eagerness to open the carriage door, Jack had jumped him.

"Not badly done," Dan said. "However, we've wasted enough time here. Go help Ben with the horses."

"I ain't no horse coddler," Jack grumbled, but did as he was told, and in a few minutes the coach began to move again.

twenty-one

"Now, Mr. Aberford," Dan said, settling back against the rear wall of the coach, "tell me what you thought you were going to accomplish with your little masquerade. And please, don't try to put me off with that tarradiddle about a bet. What were you really after?"

"I had a bet," Jonathan repeated doggedly. "With—with Robert Choiniet. He said I couldn't pull it off without being recognized."

"He was right," Mairelon murmured.

"Quiet," Dan said. "I'm afraid I don't believe you, Mr. Aberford. I think you were after something else. The Saltash Platter, perhaps?"

"The what?" Jonathan's puzzlement was unfeigned. "I've never heard of it."

"You call it the Sacred Dish," Mairelon put in.

Jonathan jerked upright in his seat as if someone had stuck a pin in him, banging his head against the roof of the coach. "What do you know of the Sacred Dish?"

"Not nearly as much as I'd like," Mairelon said. "For instance, how did you and your druids get hold of it? And how does it happen that you don't have the smallest notion what it really is?"

"I told you to be quiet," Dan said.

"When Queen Dick rules," Kim muttered, her annoyance with Mairelon momentarily getting the better of her fear of Dan. She was as curious as Mairelon about the druid's behavior, but she knew enough to keep her mouth shut when someone had a pistol pointed at her.

Dan gave her a piercing look, but just then the coach slowed and lurched through a sharp turn, distracting him. He leaned sideways and peered out the window. "It doesn't matter now. We appear to be arriving."

"Not quite yet, but soon," Mairelon said. "The lodge is around the back side of the hill."

"You aren't—you can't—what are you going to do?" Jonathan said.

"Look for something I . . . mislaid a few years ago," Dan answered. "And you are going to help."

Jonathan's jaw tightened. "No. I won't. I won't let you desecrate our meeting place."

"Let? My dear boy, how do you propose to stop me?" Dan said, shifting his pistol just enough to call attention to its presence.

"Yes, and what do you expect us to do?" Mairelon asked Jonathan in tones of great interest. "Or to put it another way, just what would 'desecrate' a place where you and your friends drink, dice, and wench until almost dawn?"

Jonathan turned a dull red and did not answer. The coach bumped to a stop and Dan reached through the window and unlatched the door. "Out," he said. Mairelon shrugged and climbed out, steadying himself awkwardly with his bound hands. Jonathan sat back, looking stubborn.

Dan sighed. "Don't be foolish, dear boy. If you stay here, you have no hope of keeping me from doing whatever outrageous things you think I am planning. And I assure you that if you decide to be obstinate, I shall make it a point to think of something particularly outrageous."

Jonathan hesitated, then gave in. Wearing a ferocious scowl, he crawled out of the coach. Kim started to follow, but Dan put out an arm and blocked her. "After me," he said. "And from now on, you are to do nothing and say nothing unless I tell you. Do you understand?"

"I understand," Kim said sullenly.

"Good. Now, after me."

When Kim came blinking out into the light, she saw Jack Stower holding his pistol on Jonathan Aberford while Dan kept Mairelon covered. She glanced longingly at the woods, but she did not try to run. There was no cover close by, and Dan wouldn't so much as pause to consider before shooting her. Even the unexpected failure of his control spell wouldn't slow him down. She'd stand a better chance of nicking the Queen's garters at high noon on the steps of Buckingham Palace than she would of getting away now. Reluctantly she joined the others.

"Ben, you wait for us here," Dan commanded. "The rest of you will come inside and help look for the platter. You first, Mr. Merrill."

Mairelon walked over to the door of the lodge. "It's locked."

"It shouldn't be. We never—" Jonathan stopped short and pressed his lips together, as if he were afraid he was giving vital secrets away to an enemy.

"No matter," Dan said. He waved his free hand in a sweeping invitation. "Kim! Open the door."

Even more reluctantly than before, Kim walked forward and pulled her bit of wire out of her pocket. As she knelt in front of the lodge door, Mairelon gave her an encouraging wink. She did not dare respond, for Dan was watching her, but her hands did not shake at all as she inserted the wire in the keyhole and began wiggling it against the tumblers.

The lock was nothing special, but Kim took her time with it. After her experience with Mairelon's magic trunk, she was not inclined to take chances, particularly since this lodge also belonged to a bunch of frog-makers. Then, too, she didn't much want to flaunt her skill in front of Dan. It'd only give him another reason for wanting to get his dabbers on her.

"Losing your touch, dear boy?" Dan said. "I hope not."

The threat below the words was plain. Kim gave her wrist a final turn, wondering as she did whether Dan had forgotten that she was supposed to be acting under his command or whether he just enjoyed threatening people. "It's open," she said, rising.

"Good. Mr. Merrill?" Dan nodded toward the door. Mairelon gave him an ironic bow, shoved the door open, and went in. Jack followed, at Dan's direction, then Jonathan and Kim. Dan himself came last.

The interior of the lodge was dark and smelled of smoke and old wine. "Who's pulled the shutters to?" Jonathan demanded. "Blast it, can't anyone do anything right?"

"I fail to see—" Dan began, when a voice from the far corner of the room interrupted him in mid-sentence.

"Jon? That you? Well, of course it is. Nobody else would be so put about by a little thing like shutters. It's all right, Marianne, it's only Jon."

"Freddy!" said an agonized female voice in a piercing whisper. "Sshhh!"

"But it's only Jon," the first voice said, and a shadowy male figure rose from behind a clump of high-backed wing chairs. He stepped forward, peering through the gloom, then stopped short and said with considerable indignation, "I say, Jon, who are all these people you've brought along? Not the thing, old boy, not at all the thing. This lodge is supposed to be private, y'know."

"Meredith! I might have guessed," Jonathan said in tones of loathing. "What are you doing here?"

"Might ask you the same thing," Freddy pointed out. "*I* ain't the one who came barging through a locked door with a country fair's worth of people."

"That door isn't supposed to be locked! The Sons of the New Dawn should be free to come and go as they please; we agreed on that at the very beginning!"

"This is all very interesting," Dan said in a bored voice, "but I do have a few things to do here, and time presses. If you—and your no doubt charming companion—will just join the others here, Mr. Meredith, we can begin."

"Who's this?" Freddy said without moving. "Some jumped-up Cit? Really, Jon—"

"Freddy!" The female whisper was, if possible, more agonized than before. "Make them go away!"

Freddy turned his head back toward the corner. "I'm trying, Marianne. But it ain't an easy sort of thing. Jon's a stubborn fellow. Maybe he would if you asked him," he added hopefully. "I mean, favor to a lady and all that. Jon's a gentleman, after all."

"But I can't! Oh, I can't!"

"The lady doth protest too much," Mairelon murmured.

"It doesn't matter," Dan Laverham said, ignoring Mairelon. He seemed a little put out by Freddy's determined thick-headedness. "Mr. Aberford isn't the one you have to convince. Do as I tell you."

Freddy looked at Dan with an expression of polite hauteur that changed quickly to incredulity. "Jonathan! That fellow has—" He broke off and glanced back over his shoulder, then lowered his voice and continued, "I think that fellow has a gun."

"He certainly does," Jonathan said, disgusted. "And only a sapskull like you would take ten minutes to notice it."

"Enough of this nonsense," Dan said. "Kim, find something to tie them with, and open the shutters while you're about it. We can't hunt for the platter in this light. Jack, get that blithering fool and his doxy over with the rest of them."

"Right," Jack said with an evil smirk, while Freddy spluttered a half-hearted protest. He sidled between a settee and a low, solid-looking table toward the darkened corner from which Freddy had emerged. Kim threw back the first pair of shutters, letting the dusty grey sunlight light up

another cluster of chairs and a side table stacked with cards and mother-
of-pearl marker chips.

A moment later, there was a quavering feminine shriek from the far
corner. "A pistol! Oh, it isn't loaded, is it?"

"Be a lot of use that way, wouldn't it?" Jack sneered. "Move it."

Kim glanced back as she opened a second set of shutters, and her
eyes widened in surprise. The distraught and somewhat disheveled young
woman whom Jack was pulling, with evident relish, from her hiding place
was the lovely blonde who had been with Lady Granleigh in the carriage
at the inn, that first day in Ranton Hill. Kim cudgeled her brain and
summoned up the girl's name: Marianne Thornley. She blinked as a few
other bits of information came together in her head, and almost smiled.
So this was the heiress Lady Granleigh intended for her scapegrace
brother! From the look of things, Jasper wouldn't have much luck, no
matter how persuasive his sister was. Miss Thornley seemed to have her
own plans.

"My, my," Dan said. "Gently, Jack; it's not a doxy, it's a lady."

"Miss Thornley!" Jonathan gasped. "Freddy, have you run mad?"

"Freddy! Oh, Freddy, do something!" Marianne cried. With a sudden spurt of strength, she jerked her arm from Jack's grasp and ran to
Freddy, where she wrapped her arms around his neck and buried her
head in his shoulder, effectively preventing him from doing anything even
if he had wanted to.

"Now see what you've done," Freddy said reproachfully to Dan. He
patted Marianne's shoulder in awkward and meaningless reassurance.

"Kim, where's that rope?" Dan called.

"There ain't none," Kim said, throwing open a third set of shutters.
Even with three windows uncovered, the room was not well lit, but at
least it was now possible to move around without tripping over a footstool
or a bench. From where she stood, she could even make out the wreaths
carved into the mantel above the big fireplace, if she squinted.

"Well, find something! And hurry it up." Dan's temper was beginning to fray.

"Are you quite sure you want to keep on with this?" Mairelon asked
with an air of polite concern. "You're accumulating rather a lot of wit-
nesses, you know, and these three—" he indicated Jonathan, Freddy, and
the shrinking Marianne with a theatrical wave of his bound hands,
"—will be missed before long."

Marianne looked up, as if she were about to say something, but before
she could speak, the door behind Dan swung open. "Good day," said

Gregory St. Clair. "I hope I'm not interrupting, but I was getting tired of waiting."

In the momentary silence, St. Clair stepped into the lodge and pushed the door closed with his silver-headed walking stick. He was dressed for all the world as if he were paying a morning call at the height of the Season in London: Wellington coat, striped pantaloons, and Hussar buskins. His cravat was a snowy expanse of starched linen, and his gloves were grey kid. Looking at him made Kim's fingers twitch acquisitively.

Both Mairelon and Dan Laverham were staring at St. Clair with unconcealed dislike. Jack didn't seem to know whether to aim his pistol at the new arrival or continue pointing it at Jonathan and Freddy, who wore identical blank expressions. Marianne, on the other hand, clung more closely to her puzzled escort and said in faltering tones, "Oh, Freddy, it's Lord St. Clair!"

"Good," said Freddy, relaxing. "For a minute, I thought it was another Cit."

"St. Clair," Mairelon said in a flat voice. "I should have expected you."

"Gregory has a habit of turning up where he is not wanted," Dan said. He spoke as if responding to Mairelon's comment, but his eyes stayed on Lord St. Clair and his voice was cold.

"You have a great many unappealing habits of your own, Daniel, but I don't regard them." St. Clair's expression made Kim want to crawl behind one of the wing chairs; he looked exactly like Dan in his worst and most unpredictable moods. He glanced around the interior of the lodge, then added, "This time you seem to have outdone yourself, however. I expected Merrill, but who are all these other people?"

"Lord St. Clair!" Marianne shrieked as his gaze reached her. "You must do something, or we shall all be killed!"

"I doubt it," St. Clair replied. "Even Daniel isn't that foolish."

"But he wants to bind us!" Marianne said dramatically.

"Typical." St. Clair looked at Dan. "You should have gagged her. I begin to see why you're still standing here waving a pistol about instead of collecting the Saltash Set."

"The Sacred Dish is not for the likes of you!" Jonathan cried. St. Clair raised his eyebrows in polite incredulity. "That is, if we still had it," Jonathan added in a resentful tone, glaring at Freddy, "which thanks to him, we don't."

"You ain't still harping on that, are you?" Freddy said. "Burn it, Jonathan, I told you what happened!"

"You had no right—" Jonathan began hotly.

"Quiet," Dan commanded without turning. "How did you get past Ben?" he asked St. Clair.

"I employed my talents to good effect," the Baron answered. "Which is to say, I put him to sleep."

"I took precautions against that sort of thing."

"Not very good ones; at least, not by my standards."

Kim could almost hear Dan's teeth grinding. "What do you want?" he demanded.

"The same thing you do, more or less," St. Clair said. "The Saltash Set." He looked around again with an air of languid disappointment, and Kim hoped she was only imagining that his eyes lingered on her. "I had hoped you'd have found the rest of it by this time, but then I hadn't expected you to have so much . . . assistance."

"However reluctant," said Mairelon, who had been observing this exchange with interest. "You have some unusual associates, St. Clair."

"No more unusual than yours," the Baron responded with a significant look at Kim.

"But definitely more long-standing," Mairelon shot back. "Or am I mistaken in thinking you and Mr. Laverham here are well acquainted?"

"This isn't getting us anywhere," Dan put in. "Jack, put them all in the corner and then start looking. Not him," he added as Jack started warily toward Lord St. Clair. "I'll deal with him myself."

"Will you, indeed." St. Clair sounded both bored and skeptical, but Kim thought she heard darker undercurrents in his voice. "Not the way you did before, I hope? You owe me for that, Daniel, and I intend to collect. In full."

"*I* owe *you?*" For an instant, Dan let his rage show; then he had himself under control again. "It doesn't matter. As soon as I have the platter, we'll leave. You won't be able to stop us."

"The platter?" St. Clair said sharply. "Is that all? What about the bowl?"

"I'll have no trouble finding the bowl once the platter is in my hands," Dan said with renewed confidence.

"Finding it? You mean you weren't aware that Merrill has the bowl?" St. Clair shook his head. "And you seemed so well informed."

Laverham frowned. "Is this true?" he demanded of Mairelon.

"Yes," Mairelon said. "Though it's not the sort of thing one carries around in one's pockets, you realize."

"Why didn't you tell me this before?" Laverham said, and his eyes narrowed as he spoke.

Mairelon shrugged. "You didn't ask."

"We'll get it when we're finished here," Laverham said.

"That would be foolish," St. Clair commented.

"Why?"

"Merrill's got a man at his wagon."

"That's the turnip-pated cove I told you about, Mr. Laverham," Jack Stower put in. "He ain't no problem."

"And even if no one was waiting, it is generally considered . . . inadvisable to assault a wizard on his home ground," St. Clair finished.

Jack's enthusiasm waned visibly. Laverham stared at Lord St. Clair, his face expressionless. "What would you suggest?"

"Send the girl with a message," St. Clair replied. "She can tell Merrill's man that Merrill wants the bowl brought here to help locate the platter. He'll believe that."

"Not if she's the one telling him," Dan responded with a contemptuous glance at the quivering Marianne. "Besides, I wouldn't trust her to keep her story straight."

"Not that girl," St. Clair said. "The one you've cast the control spell on." He gestured at Kim.

Kim swallowed hard, half terrified that Dan knew her secret at last and half hoping against hope that he would adopt Lord St. Clair's suggestion. If she could get away and warn Hunch . . .

"Ah," said Dan on a long, slow breath, staring at Kim. "Yes, perhaps that would be a good idea."

"Hunch won't believe Kim," Mairelon said a little too quickly. "He doesn't trust her."

"No?" Dan said. "Kim, tell the truth: could you make Merrill's man believe you?"

"Yes," Kim said, trying to sound sullen and reluctant. "He'll believe me."

"Good." Dan gave her a slow smile that chilled her to the bone. "We'll discuss the other business later. You know what I mean. Meanwhile, we'll wait here while you go—"

"No!" Marianne cried.

Everyone turned to look at her. She cringed back against Freddy and said, "We can't stay any longer; we can't! It's nearly teatime, and Lady Granleigh will look for me and find . . ." She faltered to a stop under the circle of astonished stares and buried her face against Freddy's coat once more, her shoulders shaking with sobs.

"Find what?" St. Clair asked. "Find you gone? Embarrassing and unfortunate, to be sure, but it's too late to do anything about it now."

"Even if we would let you," Dan added.

Marianne turned a damp face to the group once more and said defiantly, "Freddy and I are going to be married!"

"Oh, Lord," said Jonathan. "Freddy, you fool! Your uncle will cut you off with a shilling!"

"It don't matter," Freddy said. "Rather have Marianne than a whole mountain of shillings."

"Congratulations," St. Clair said politely. "I fear you'll have to postpone your arrangements a little, however. We can't just let you go, you know."

"But you must!" Marianne cried. "I—oh, you must! You must!"

"Are you trying to say that you left a note for your guardian?" Mairelon asked.

"Oh!" Marianne turned back to Freddy's comforting shoulder and hid her face against his by now damp and wrinkled coat. Safely hidden from hostile eyes, she nodded. In the silence that followed, the noise of an approaching horse came clearly from the drive outside.

twenty-two

No one spoke as the hoofbeats grew louder and slowed to a walk. "Hi, you there, wake up," someone shouted. "Who's here?"

"Putting Ben to sleep may not have been one of your best ideas," Mairelon said to Lord St. Clair. "Is he the sort that wakes up cross, do you suppose?"

"He won't wake up at all until I let him," St. Clair said. "Be quiet, Merrill."

"You take a deal of liberty with my men," Dan Laverham observed.

"I am only following your example," Lord St. Clair replied sweetly. "Your handling of my former footman, James Fenton, for instance, left much to be—"

"Austen! Edward! George!" the voice outside shouted, coming nearer with every name. "Out and about, you're needed. Jon's gone and been thrown by that fire-breathing nag of his, and—Jonathan!"

The lodge door had been flung open during the latter part of this speech, revealing the speaker as Robert Choiniet. He stopped short when he saw Jonathan, then said in a more moderate tone, "I'm glad to see you weren't hurt, but you might have sent a message home. Your mother was frantic when your horse turned up without you."

"She's always frantic," Jonathan said callously. "She should know better, and so should you. How did she talk you into haring off after me?"

"Well, what was I supposed to do?" Robert asked. "There was the horse, all over lather and frightened out of its wits, with an empty saddle.

The obvious assumption was that you'd been thrown. For all we knew, you were lying under a hedge somewhere with a broken leg."

"You didn't tell me you'd taken a toss, Jon," Freddy put in with interest. "That'll teach you not to call names. I've told you and told you, it's the sort of thing that can happen to anyone."

"I didn't take a toss," Jonathan snarled. "And even if I had, I'd still say you're cow-handed, because you are."

"Don't you say that about Freddy!" Marianne said, raising her head and looking daggers at Jonathan.

"Can't you keep them under control?" Lord St. Clair asked Dan, while Jonathan, Freddy, and Marianne embarked on a noisy quarrel that relieved their feelings even if it accomplished nothing else. "None of us will ever get anything done at this rate."

Dan gave St. Clair a glare that should have melted steel. "If you think you can do better, you're welcomed to try."

"Here, you lot!" Jack shouted, waving his pistol. "Stow your gob and listen to Mr. Laverham!"

This command did not produce the desired result. Instead, Freddy and Jonathan turned on Jack, demanding an apology for the interruption. Dan was obliged to intervene to keep Jack from shooting Freddy out of hand, while Robert did his best to distract the other combatants. Unfortunately, Jack's threats were all too clear to Marianne, who immediately went into strong hysterics.

Lord St. Clair stood calmly watching, as if he were observing a raree show that did not please him above half, though he made a point of keeping an eye on Mairelon as well as the row in the middle of the room. Kim realized suddenly that, for the time being, no one was watching *her*. She slid quietly behind a tall chair and crouched down, eyeing the path to the door. Two more chairs and a card table provided some concealment, but she would have to cross an open stretch of floor to reach the exit itself. Kim shrugged and began moving.

She was not even halfway to her goal when the door swung open yet again. "Villain! Unhand that girl!" cried Jasper Marston as he strode into the room. He stopped short, looking completely nonplussed, as he took in the scene in front of him.

The noise died as the adversaries became aware of their new audience and turned to stare at him. "Ah, Mr. Marston!" Mairelon said cheerfully. "I'm afraid you'll have to be more specific about whom you were addressing. There are several persons present who admirably fit the description 'villain.' Which of them did you have in mind?"

"Really?" Robert Choiniet said. "You mean this isn't all one of Jon's queer starts?"

"My queer starts? What do you mean, my queer starts? Are you saying you think I *arranged* all this?"

"It has all the earmarks. I mean, just look at those two—waving pistols all over the lodge and threatening Freddy, of all people. How do you expect me to take it seriously?"

"You'd better," Dan said. He sounded a little wild, and Kim was glad to be out of sight behind the card table. "Get over in the corner there, all of you, and *be quiet.* You, too, Marston, or whatever your name is."

"Ah, I don't want any trouble," Jasper said, eyeing Dan's pistol with misgiving. "I'll just leave quietly. It's no problem, really."

"Yes, it is," Dan said, recovering himself somewhat. "Into the corner."

" 'Ere, now, what's all this, then?" a deep, slow voice said from the doorway.

"I should think it was perfectly plain, even to someone of your limited understanding, Stuggs," a female voice answered acidly. "My brother has bungled things again."

"Lady Granleigh!" gasped Marianne. She turned as white as St. Clair's cravat and fainted into Freddy's arms. Unfortunately, Freddy was as dumbfounded as she by the new arrivals, and he failed to catch her in time. He overbalanced, and the two of them toppled backward into a chair and crashed to the floor in a shower of splinters.

Mairelon sank onto a nearby footstool, propped his head on his bound hands, and began to laugh. Lady Granleigh gave him a look of displeasure and marched into the room, followed by Stuggs. Her gaze swept imperiously around the assembly, barely checking at the sight of the pistols Dan and Jack still held. She passed over the struggling Freddy and the unconscious Marianne, dismissed Jonathan and Robert as inconsequential, and fixed at last on Lord St. Clair.

"Good day, St. Clair," Lady Granleigh said with a dignity that did not conceal her annoyance.

"Lady Granleigh," Lord St. Clair responded, nodding a cordial greeting.

Below the table, Kim ground her teeth and made a rude gesture with her left hand. Lady Granleigh had left the door wide open, but tempting as the sight was, Kim still could not reach it. Lady Granleigh had stopped too close to the door, and what little space she had left was taken up by the overly large Stuggs.

"I confess I had not expected to find you here, but I thank you for your efforts on behalf of my ward," Lady Granleigh went on, smiling insincerely at Lord St. Clair.

"Efforts!" Freddy said, outraged. He extracted himself from the tangle at last, with some help from Jonathan, and climbed to his feet, staring at St. Clair the whole time. "What efforts? He ain't done anything but stand there and annoy people."

"Your conduct hardly bears examination, Mr. Meredith," Lady Granleigh responded. "I should be careful about casting aspersions, if I were you." She looked pointedly down at Marianne.

Robert, who had knelt beside the unconscious girl and begun chafing her wrists, glanced up and said to no one in particular, "Could one of you get a glass of wine?"

"No, but there's brandy," Jonathan answered. He started toward a small cabinet near the fireplace, but came face-to-face with Jack Stower before he had taken two steps. Jack's pistols and threatening glare were eloquent. Jonathan shrugged and went back to his original position.

"Aspersions! Well, I like that!" Freddy said to Lady Granleigh, undaunted by her arrogance. "*I* didn't barge in through a locked door without so much as a by-your-leave. *I* didn't wave any pistols about or make any threats. *I* didn't frighten any ladies into a fit of the vapors, and *I* didn't scare her straight into a faint!"

"You lured Miss Thornley here," Jasper charged.

Robert looked up, visibly impressed. "Did you really, Freddy? I hadn't thought you had it in you."

"I didn't lure anybody," Freddy protested.

"You made Miss Thornley extravagant promises you had no intention of fulfilling!" Jasper said.

"I dunno," Stuggs put in. " 'E don't look like the type, if you take my meaning."

Jasper gave his henchman a withering look. "Why else did you bring Miss Thornley here, to this lonely place?" he demanded, turning back to Freddy.

"Hardly lonely," Mairelon said in a low but clearly audible tone.

"Had to meet her somewhere," Freddy said reasonably. "It would have looked dashed odd for me to pick the girl up off the side of the road."

"No doubt," Jasper sneered with an ironic glance at Jack Stower's gun. "You and your ruffians would have looked odd anywhere."

Freddy frowned. "Here, now! What are you insinuating?"

"I think it is perfectly plain," Lady Granleigh said. "If Lord St. Clair and his friends had not arrived in time to stop you and your kidnappers, who knows what might have happened?"

"Marianne and I would have gotten married, that's what would have happened!" Freddy retorted, too angry to continue trying to be polite. "What's more, we're going to tie the knot as soon as we get out of here, no matter what you say."

"Freddy, you're crazed!" Jonathan said.

"No, I ain't, and I ain't as foolish as you think, either. Got the special license right here in my pocket."

"What!" Jasper's eyes widened; then he whirled to face his sister. "Now see what you've done, Amelia! If you hadn't set the girl on to this buffoon, we wouldn't be in this pickle!"

"Be quiet, Jasper!" Lady Granleigh commanded. "There is no need for you to worry. Lord St. Clair, be so good as to have your men assist Miss Thornley into our coach. After we have gone, you may deal with these felons as you see fit."

Before St. Clair could reply, there was a loud crash. Everyone jumped and turned. Dan Laverham was standing beside one of the long windows, which he had just broken, his pistols leveled at the assembly.

"I am afraid you have mistaken the situation, Lady Granleigh," he said. He stepped forward, and shards of glass crunched under his feet. His face was a cold, expressionless mask. "I am not in St. Clair's employ, nor have I the slightest interest in you, your ward, or any of your companions. I am here for one thing, and only one thing. Once I've got it, you may sort yourselves out in any manner that suits you. Until then, I have heard too much of your brainless chatter. I shall shoot the next person who speaks out of turn."

St. Clair nodded. "Crude, but generally effective."

"That includes you, St. Clair," Laverham said, glaring.

Lady Granleigh drew in her breath at this breach of manners, which seemed to disturb her more than Dan's pistols. St. Clair smiled, but said nothing.

"Much better," Laverham went on. "Now, you, the highwayman. Is there somewhere in this pile to lock up this lot of lunatics while we search the rest of it?"

"Highwayman?" Freddy said with interest. "I say, Jon, you never told us anything about—" He broke off as one of Dan's pistols swung in his direction.

"There are private rooms upstairs," said Jonathan sullenly. "I think one of them has a lock."

"The one on the end," Freddy put in. "But it's broken. The lock, I mean."

"This is an outrage!" Lady Granleigh said, finding her voice. "Who is this person? Lord St. Clair—"

"I told you to be quiet," Dan said. "Get over there with the others."

"Better do as 'e says, mum," Stuggs warned. " 'E looks the sort as 'ud do you without blinkin'."

Kim held her breath as Lady Granleigh, stiff with disapproval, moved away from the door at last. Now, if they would all stay busy at the other end of the room for a few minutes longer . . .

A shadow fell across the doorsill. Kim frowned and sank back into her uncomfortable half-crouch. Had Lady Granleigh brought a coachman, or had Ben awakened in spite of Lord St. Clair's precautionary spell? Either way, she would be running into trouble. Not that she wasn't in a proper mess already, of course, but Dan's temper looked to be deteriorating rapidly, and she didn't like to think what he might do if she didn't get away on her first try. It would be better to wait for a more certain chance.

The motley company was slowly assembling in the corner, with occasional low-voiced grumbling that Dan pretended not to hear. Robert and Freddy between them supported the slowly recovering Marianne, while Jonathan stalked past and Lady Granleigh glowered impartially at everyone. For a moment or two, it looked as if Dan had gotten things under control at last; then Jasper said in a cross, too-loud voice, "But what is it the fellow *wants*?"

"The Sacred Dish!" Jonathan answered. He gave Dan and Jack a dark look. "But he shall not get it, however he tries."

"The what?" said Jasper.

"The sacred dish," Lady Granleigh said, giving her brother a sidelong glance full of meaning. "The platter that we gave to Mr. de Mare this morning." She nodded in Mairelon's direction.

"What?" several voices said at once. Lord St. Clair examined Mairelon with angry speculation, and both of Dan's pistols swung to point at the magician. Kim cursed mentally and swiveled her head from side to side, trying to watch Dan and the door at the same time.

"I told you not to try any tricks with me, Merrill," Dan said. "Where's the platter? And this time, tell me the truth!"

The shadow on the doorsill shifted and withdrew, but Kim stayed where she was. With Dan so jumpy, she'd be shot before she was out the door if she made a run for it. She edged toward the front of the table with a vague idea of doing something, she wasn't sure what, if Dan looked like shooting Mairelon.

"Merrill?" said William Stuggs, giving Mairelon a swift, sharp look. "Well, well."

"What does that mean, 'well, well'?" Jasper demanded, rounding on his servant.

Stuggs's expression instantly resumed its usual appearance of placid stupidity. "Ain't 'e the cove you was lookin' for in London?"

"Answer me!" Dan said to Mairelon. "Where is the platter?"

"Which one?" Mairelon asked. "The one your man Stower left by my campfire, or the one Lady Granleigh was so anxious to get rid of? Or one of the other fakes Fenton seems to have been peddling?"

"The Saltash Platter, you buffoon!" Laverham shouted.

"Infidel! What have you done with the Sacred Dish?" Jonathan cried at the same moment.

"Fenton?" said Freddy, frowning. "I've got a footman by that name. What's he got to do with Jon's dish?"

Mairelon lifted his bound hands and scratched his ear. "I don't have any better idea where the Saltash Platter is than you do, Laverham."

"Do you expect me to believe that?"

"Why not?" Mairelon shrugged. "It's true."

"I gave you the Saltash Platter this morning," Lady Granleigh insisted in her most superior manner. "How dare you suggest otherwise!"

"Oh, you gave me a platter, all right, but it was a forgery and you knew it," Mairelon said. He gave her a charming smile that expanded to include the entire ring of surprised, confused, and skeptical faces. "By the by, how do *you* happen to know anything about the Saltash Platter, hmmm?"

"Never mind!" Dan said. "I don't care about her, and I don't believe you." He raised his pistol and slowly and deliberately cocked it. "For the last time, *where is the Saltash Platter?*"

"I don't have it," Mairelon said.

"But of a certainty you do not," said a new voice. Dan whirled, and everyone else's head flicked toward the door. Kim bumped her head on a table leg, cursed, and turned to see Renée D'Auber standing in the doorway. Her auburn hair was dressed in ringlets and threaded with a peach-colored ribbon that exactly matched the delicate muslin of her walking dress, and she smiled brightly when she saw the faces turned toward her. "I have it."

"Renée!" Mairelon said. "What are you doing here?" Then his face went blank as a stocky, sandy-haired man stepped into the doorway beside her, and he added in a thunderstruck tone, *"Andrew?"*

twenty-three

"Hello, Richard," said the sandy-haired man. He sounded nervous and uncertain, which Kim thought was understandable under the circumstances, but his attention was fixed on Mairelon rather than on Dan or Jack Stower. "I, um, it's been a while."

"Well, well," said St. Clair. "This is becoming quite the family gathering."

Dan Laverham glared at St. Clair. Mairelon did not move; he seemed as oblivious to the crowd around him as the man he had called Andrew. Kim frowned, puzzled both by St. Clair's comment and the unusual strength of Mairelon's reaction. Then her head jerked and almost hit the underside of the table again as several fragments condensed into the memory of Mairelon's voice saying in a flat tone, "The evidence was overwhelming. Even my brother Andrew believed it."

"What are you doing here?" Mairelon said in the same tight voice Kim remembered.

"Trying to keep your head out of a noose," Andrew replied. Now that Kim had remembered who he must be, she could see how much he resembled Mairelon in his middling height, neat build, and rounded face. Andrew glanced at Renée D'Auber and added, "At least, that was the original idea."

"What do you mean by—"

"Then you *do* have the Saltash Platter?" St. Clair interrupted, looking fixedly at Mademoiselle D'Auber.

"Nonsense," Lady Granleigh said. She made an urgent motion at

her brother, but Jasper, who did not appear to have the slightest idea
what she wanted of him, remained where he was.

"But, yes, I have it," Renée D'Auber told Lord St. Clair. "Though
I do not at all see why it is you who ask, when it is this person with the
pistols who was so very curious before."

"Where is it?" Dan demanded.

"Don't tell him," Freddy advised. "Fellow ain't the thing at all, that's
my opinion."

"For once, I agree with you, Freddy," Robert murmured.

"Freddy!" Marianne had recovered enough to pull away from Robert
and clutch at Freddy's arm in protest. "Oh, be careful! That man might
shoot you!"

"It would be a singular service to humanity if he did," St. Clair said.
"I have seldom met a more tiresome group, or one more foolish. Mademoiselle D'Auber—"

"Quiet!" Dan commanded. "Or I'll shoot *you*, Gregory! I'm tired of
your interference."

"You seemed in need of some assistance," Lord St. Clair said with
unruffled calm. "I was only trying to help."

"I don't want your help, you insufferable—"

"But you know each other!" Renée D'Auber said in tones of pleased
surprise. "It is a thing remarkable, I think."

Mairelon shook himself and tore his eyes away from the man in the
doorway. "Yes, St. Clair, how *do* you come to know Laverham? And how
long have you been, er, acquainted? At least five years, I think?"

"Oh, much longer than that," St. Clair replied. "I expect you would
be vastly interested in the details, but unfortunately I don't intend to give
them to you."

"Perhaps Laverham can be persuaded?" Mairelon said.

"Not by you," Dan snarled. He turned back to Renée. "Give me the
platter."

Behind Renée, Andrew made a gesture of protest, but he had enough
sense not to say anything. Renée D'Auber tilted her head and considered
Dan Laverham with an air that suggested something unsatisfactory about
the object of her scrutiny. "It is not at all possible for me to give you the
platter now," she said at last, as if granting a great concession in answering
at all.

"Renée," Mairelon said warningly.

A muscle in Dan's jaw jumped. "Don't lie to me," he said in a tone that made Kim shrink back from the edge of the table, just in case he turned in her direction.

"I tell the truth," the Frenchwoman said, affronted. "And it is quite true that I cannot give you the platter now. I am not a fool, me, and I do not wish to lose it. So I do not carry it about with me, especially when there are housebreakers and highwaymen and persons with pistols everywhere. If you were not yourself without sense, you would have comprehended that and not bothered me with silly questions."

Mairelon made a muffled, choking noise. Dan lowered his pistols slightly and studied Renée through narrowed eyes.

"She ain't no dull mort," Jack Stower offered. "I bet she done it like she says."

"I have no doubt of it," St. Clair said. "If, that is, she has done anything at all."

"Ain't no knowing," Stuggs said with an air of deep gloom. "She's French."

"It's easy enough to tell whether she's lying," Dan said. He walked over to the card table and set something heavy down just over Kim's head. She flinched and backed away slowly, hoping he would not drop anything. If he bent over, he could hardly miss seeing her. At the rear of the table, she stopped and curled into a lumpy, motionless ball, waiting for Dan to move away again.

"What do you think you're doing, Laverham?" St. Clair said sharply, and Kim had to suppress an urge to peer over the edge of the table to see what he was referring to.

"I'm going to find out which of them is telling the truth," Dan answered. "If it's Merrill, the Saltash Platter is in this building somewhere. That's close enough for me to find, even with only two of the indicator balls to use as a base for the location spell."

"Freddy!" Marianne said in a carrying whisper. "Is he going to cast a *spell*?"

"You know not what you do," Jonathan said in his best master-druid voice. "Beware the consequences of defiling the hall of the Sons of the New Dawn!"

"Quiet," said Dan. "I've had as much of your posturing as I can stomach. Jack, keep an eye on them."

This last instruction seemed unnecessary to Kim, since, from the way his pistols had been waving about, Jack had been trying to watch everyone at once for some time. She could just see him out the side of the table and through the latticed back of a wooden chair, his jaw clenched and his eyes compressed to slits of grim concentration. Stuggs was creeping around the outside of the group toward him, craning his neck to get a look at Dan. Did the great looby think this was some kind of show, or was he fool enough to try a trick on a real magician in the middle of a spell? Then Dan began to speak diamond-sharp words Kim could not understand, and every other thought left her mind instantly.

She knew at once that something was wrong. Always before when she had heard magicians at work, the too-solid words had settled quickly into an orderly arrangement, full of dangerous corners and edges but as firm and stable as the words themselves. Dan's words were floating free, jostling against each other like a market-day crowd, fighting the structure the magician sought to impose on them.

The magicians in the room were also quick to realize that Dan was in trouble. Renée D'Auber stepped backward into Andrew, her eyes widening, and brought up her left hand in a contorted gesture.

"Renée, don't!" Mairelon cried. "You'll only cut what's left of the basic binding!"

"Break off, you fool!" St. Clair said to Dan at the same moment. "You'll have the house down in another minute."

"He can't break off," Jonathan said with bitter satisfaction. "If he does, he'll lose what control he has. He'll lose it soon, in any case. His obstinacy has doomed us all."

Jasper Marston made a gobbling noise and collided with his sister as he tried to leap for the door. Marianne gave a ladylike shriek and fainted again. This time, Freddy caught her without mishap. Dan's voice droned on. Robert stared at Jonathan and demanded, "What do you mean by that, Jon?"

"He has fallen afoul of the protections of the Sons of the New Dawn," Jonathan answered. "I warned him not to meddle!"

"You might have tried warning him you had a protective spell up, you young idiot!" Mairelon said acidly as, with two swift motions, he undid the special knot Kim had used and stripped the binding cords from his wrists. "What did you use? Quick now!"

Jonathan mumbled something, and Kim stopped listening. No matter what he said, no matter what Mairelon thought he could do, there wasn't time. She could hear the note of desperation in Dan's voice; she could feel his words twisting like oiled eels. The very air inside the lodge was beginning to shine with reflections from the invisible, impossible crystal words, and with every syllable Dan spoke, the glow grew stronger. He had to be stopped *now*, before he put so much power into his distorted spell that it really would destroy them all when he finally lost control of it.

Kim took a deep breath, swallowed hard, and stood up with a surge, pushing the heavy wooden card table up and forward with all her strength. Cards and markers slid off and scattered across the floor; the pistol Dan had set on top of them followed with a metallic scraping noise. The table hit Dan hard, knocking him sideways. He staggered briefly, then regained his feet, but his concentration had been shattered and the spell broke free.

There was a brilliant flare of light, and sharp-edged words flew in all directions. Mairelon, Renée D'Auber, and Lord St. Clair flung their arms up in identical gestures of repudiation and simultaneously shouted the same unintelligible phrase. Kim ducked behind the upturned table as the unseen words bounced back toward her. Something hit the floor with a metallic ping, and something else with a clear ringing noise. Dan cried out and fell heavily against the table. Kim heard a peculiar muffled noise that sounded like Jack Stower's voice; then the remnants of the spell swirled and settled around her like dust. They lay in shimmering silver drifts on the wooden floor for a long moment before they melted into nothing.

"Well done," St. Clair's voice said to someone.

"Thank you," Renée D'Auber responded.

"Kim!" Mairelon called. He sounded very close; an instant later, he appeared, bending anxiously over the end of the table. "Kim?"

"I ain't hurt," Kim assured him. "Is that spell done with?"

"For the most part," Mairelon answered.

Judging this to be as near a "yes" as she was likely to get from him, Kim climbed cautiously to her feet and looked around. Freddy, his arms locked around the unconscious Marianne, was trading icy stares with Lady Granleigh and Jasper Marston. Jonathan alternated between baleful muttering and attempts to untie his hands with his teeth. Meanwhile, Jasper's man, Stuggs, had a firm and very professional-looking armlock on Jack Stower. Stower's pistols had vanished, and his clothes were even more rumpled and disreputable than usual. Kim was sorry she had missed seeing their encounter. Robert Choiniet and Mairelon's brother, Andrew, were standing over Dan Laverham, who looked and smelled somewhat singed but seemed otherwise unhurt. Renée D'Auber stood next to the door, her face composed, her eyes bright and alert; on the opposite side of the room, Lord St. Clair watched the others with a cold, speculative expression.

" 'Ere, now," Stuggs said to Jack, who was struggling in vain. "None o' that."

"Get your hands off me!" Dan said to Robert and Andrew. They had considerately helped him to his feet and then neglected to let go of his arms.

"And give you a chance to grab one of those pistols again, or start some more magic?" Robert said. "Not likely."

"Someone should find those guns and get them out of the way," Andrew added.

"Did you say something about brandy a bit ago, Jon?" Freddy asked. "Like to get some for Marianne."

"Get me out of this first," Jonathan said crossly, holding out his hands and the tangle he had made of Kim's knots.

Mairelon was studying Kim with an abstracted air, as if she were wearing her coat inside out and he couldn't puzzle out why she should do such a thing. "Now what?" Kim asked him in a low voice. "We ain't much better off than when we started."

"Aren't," Mairelon said without thinking. He blinked. "Aren't we?"

"Well, Dan don't—doesn't have his guns any more," Kim admitted. "That's something. But we still haven't found that platter. The real one, I mean. And we ain't—aren't going to with this lot of Bedlamites muddling everything up proper."

"Ah, yes; thank you for reminding me," Mairelon said. He glanced around, then took two steps sideways and reached under a chair. He straightened and held up the vine-covered silver sphere that Dan had used to focus the spell he had cast on Kim. "You don't happen to see the other one, do you?"

"It's next to Mr. Aberford's foot," St. Clair said. Mairelon gave him a sharp, suspicious look, then retrieved the second sphere without comment. "I do hope you aren't planning to repeat Daniel's lunacy, Merrill," Lord St. Clair went on. "Not only was it an uncomfortable and dangerous bit of sorcery, it was pointless as well. I doubt that you could do any better."

Mairelon raised an eyebrow and smiled slightly. "You think not?"

"Richard, don't be a fool!" Andrew said.

"It matters not at all," Renée announced. "For that annoying person with the pistols was not so altogether unsuccessful as you think. Look!" She pointed toward the fireplace.

Kim blinked, not understanding; then she saw the silver shimmer on the hearthstone. Mairelon immediately lost all interest in St. Clair. "Well,

well! Andrew—no, you'd better keep hold of Laverham. Aberford and Marston, then; come and lend a hand."

It was not quite as easy as that; Jonathan had first to be extracted from the rest of the cords on his wrists, and Jasper only stood and glowered until Lady Granleigh poked him and pointed eloquently. It took the three of them longer than Kim expected to find the notches in the edge of the stone and pry it out.

Mairelon reached down into the gaping hole and lifted out a familiar-shaped bundle. Kim held her breath as he pulled the canvas wrapping away and took hold of the silver handles.

"The Sacred Dish!" Jonathan breathed.

"Is it another fake?" Kim demanded, unable to bear the suspense.

"No," Mairelon said. He looked up with a broad smile. "This is the real Saltash Platter."

twenty-four

There was a long silence while everyone stared at the heavy silver tray. Then Lady Granleigh swept forward.

"I believe that belongs to my dear friend, Mr. Charles Bramingham," she said. "It should be returned to him at once."

"By you?" Mairelon's tone was polite; too polite.

Lady Granleigh lifted her chin. "Certainly," she replied without blushing.

"No!" Jonathan Aberford leaped to his feet and planted himself between Mairelon and Lady Granleigh. "The Sacred Dish belongs to the Sons of the New Dawn! It will not leave this house!"

"No, no, really, Jon," Freddy protested. "I lost it to Henry at play; told you that ages ago. So it doesn't belong to the Sons. Doesn't belong to this Charles person, either, if it comes to that. It's Henry's."

" 'Ere," said Stuggs, "somebody give me a 'and with this cove afore 'e breaks 'is arm accidental-like."

Kim grinned malevolently at Jack and crossed the room to retrieve the cord that had been used to tie Mairelon and Jonathan. She tossed it to Stuggs, who snatched it out of the air and had his grip back on Jack's arms before Jack realized he had missed a chance to get free. Kim grinned again to hide her unease and kicked a broken chair rung out of her way. Between the chair Freddy had smashed, the window Dan had broken, and the table Kim herself had overturned, walking across the room was becoming decidedly hazardous. Kim retreated to the back wall, where she could see everyone without getting in the way.

Lord St. Clair looked up from the platter at last and turned a cool, thoughtful gaze on Renée d'Auber. "So you were lying," he said.

"But of course," the Frenchwoman replied with a Gallic shrug. "I did not at all like that person with the pistols; whom I hope Monsieur Andrew is holding very hard. Why should I not lie to him?"

Dan lunged, almost breaking free of Andrew's hold. *"Salaude!"*

"What?" said Freddy. Lady Granleigh stiffened in outrage, from which Kim deduced that whatever Dan had said was disrespectful, if not actually shocking. Stuggs and Jack Stower wore identical expressions of bafflement, while Robert glanced warily at Renée. Andrew was plainly appalled, but Mairelon seemed to be holding back a smile. St. Clair was watching everyone with an expectant air, like a cat waiting for the right moment to pounce.

Renée D'Auber raised an eyebrow, looking faintly puzzled. "Pardon? Your accent is not at all good, monsieur. If you wish for me to understand, you should speak the English."

"I think not," said St. Clair. "It might distress the ladies."

"You!" Dan transferred his glare from Renée to the Baron. "You won't get away with this!"

"With what?" Lord St. Clair asked in a reasonable tone.

"You're not getting that platter! You've had everything else—the money, the title, everything—just because *you* were born on the right side of the blanket, but you're not getting this."

"That remains to be seen," St. Clair said calmly.

"Does it?" Mairelon said. "By whom?"

"The Sacred Dish is the property of the Sons of the New Dawn," Jonathan repeated stubbornly. No one paid him any more attention this time than they had the last.

"Richard," Andrew put in uneasily, "you're not going to keep that thing, are you? If you're found with it—"

"—there are at least thirteen people here who can say that I didn't have the smallest idea where it was until Laverham there did his locating spell," Mairelon interrupted. "I'm sure that at least one or two of them would be willing to say as much in court. Don't be a fool, Andrew."

"Ah, but you might have been acting," Lord St. Clair said with a cold smile. "I think Mr. Merrill's point is well taken."

"You would," Mairelon said.

"They don't like each other much, do they?" Freddy commented sagely to Robert.

"Freddy?" Marianne Thornley was coming around again, and the sound of her beloved's voice had caught her attention. "Oh, Freddy, what has happened?"

"You have behaved very badly," Lady Granleigh answered in a severe tone. "We shall, however, discuss it later, in private. Jasper! We have wasted enough time. Bring the platter out to the carriage at once. Come, Marianne."

"You aren't taking Marianne anywhere," Freddy said, stepping in front of the shrinking Marianne.

"Nor you the Saltash Platter," Mairelon said to Jasper.

"Amelia . . ." Jasper said, waffling visibly.

"Really, Jasper! You're larger than he is," said Lady Granleigh over her shoulder. "Just take it."

"Allow me to get out of the way first," said Lord St. Clair.

Kim frowned as St. Clair moved farther away from the hearth where Mairelon, Jonathan, and Jasper stood. She could understand a gentry cove not wanting to get involved in a turn-up, but St. Clair hadn't been close enough to be inconvenienced by a fight. She watched as he crossed the room to join Lady Granleigh, and saw him stumble as he passed a footstool. Her frown deepened. Had he scooped something from the floor? She couldn't be sure; he had turned away from her as he straightened.

The sound of a scuffle distracted her. She turned in time to see Mairelon shove the handle end of the Saltash Platter into Jasper Marston's stomach. Kim winced in sympathy as Jasper doubled over with a huff of exhaled breath. Mairelon yanked the platter back, grabbed the free handle, and brought it down on the back of Jasper's head. There was a satisfying clang, and Jasper collapsed without another sound.

"Very impressive," St. Clair said without enthusiasm. Kim looked quickly back at him, but his hands were empty; if he had picked anything up, he had hidden it under his coat.

Mairelon turned and flourished the platter in an elegant stage bow. "Would you care to be the next to try to take it?"

"Richard!" Andrew said, sounding horrified. "You can't go around assaulting peers of the realm!"

"Oh, really, Andrew, he's only a Baron," Mairelon said irritably.

Renée D'Auber rolled her eyes. "It is not how it must be done," she declared.

"And giving St. Clair the Saltash Platter is?" Mairelon asked, his jaw tightening.

"I did not say such a thing at all," Renée said with dignity.

Lady Granleigh turned, her attention momentarily diverted from
Freddy and Marianne. She raked Mairelon with a haughty look that had
no apparent effect whatever, and sniffed loudly. "Lord St. Clair seems an
infinitely more proper person to have charge of that object than you, Mr.
de Mare, or whatever your name is."

"Just so," said St. Clair. "And after all, Mr. Merrill is a wanted man.
I wonder what the Bow Street Runners would make of this little scene?"

Mairelon's lips thinned. Jack Stower lurched sideways, whimpering,
in spite of William Stuggs's grip on his arms and the cord Stuggs had
knotted around his wrists, dragging the two of them several feet nearer
the door. Jonathan Aberford shifted uncomfortably and ran a hand
through his hair as if in search of the stocking mask that had been taken
from him in the carriage. Lady Granleigh turned a shade paler and raised
her chin imperiously.

"Oh, no," Dan Laverham said softly. He was staring at Lord St.
Clair with single-minded intensity, and Kim had never heard so much
hatred in anyone's voice before. "Not this time, Gregory. This time, if I
lose, you lose, too."

"You had better think what you are saying," St. Clair replied, frowning. "In any case, this is not a suitable place for that discussion."

"I have thought," Dan said. "You lied to me before and tried to use
me; I won't make the same mistake again. You call the Runners in,
Gregory, and I'll tell them whose idea it was to nick that bloody platter,
yes, and exactly how it was arranged, too. Shall I tell this lot right now?"

"Please do," Mairelon said.

"Don't be absurd, Daniel," Lord St. Clair put in quickly. "No one
will take your word for anything."

"St. Clair?" Andrew said. "You mean *St. Clair* stole the Saltash Set?
I don't believe it."

"There, you see?" said the Baron.

"Not so fast," Mairelon said. "I want to hear him out."

Robert nodded. "Let him have his say."

"He's a gutter-bred criminal!" St. Clair snapped. "I give you my word
as a peer of the realm—"

Dan's high, half-hysterical laughter cut off whatever Lord St. Clair
had planned to say. "Peer of the realm! The only reason you're the peer
and I'm the gutter brat is that our blue-blooded father was too high in
the instep to marry a kitchen maid, though he wasn't above giving her a
tumble."

"Good Lord," breathed Mairelon, looking from Dan to St. Clair. "So that's it."

"This discussion is highly improper," Lady Granleigh announced. "Marianne, cover your ears. I recommend that you do the same, Miss D'Auber, though I am well aware that French persons do not have any real delicacy of mind."

Everyone, including Marianne, was too busy studying the two men to pay any attention to Lady Granleigh. The resemblance between them was marked. Kim remembered how shaken she had been by her first glimpse of Lord St. Clair, when she had thought for a moment that he *was* Dan Laverham, and cursed herself mentally for not guessing the truth before. But who would have pegged Dan for gentry blood, even on the wrong side of the blanket?

St. Clair looked a trifle pale, but seemed otherwise unmoved by the intense scrutiny. "This does not change matters at all," he said. "Your wild accusations are clearly the delusions of a mind deranged by jealousy. I am very sorry you have been subjected to this, Lady Granleigh, but I venture to hope that you will not hold my father's indiscretion against me."

Dan laughed again, bitterly. "Still wanting to have your cake and eat it, too, Gregory? You were pleased enough with me as long as you could make use of my services. You shouldn't have lied to me about the Saltash Set, though. If I'd known it was magical, I'd never have split it up to sell."

"You 'ad this 'ere dish as all the fuss is over?" William Stuggs put in unexpectedly. " 'Ow did that 'appen?"

"Fenton was my man," Dan said, speaking directly to St. Clair. "He wouldn't have dreamed of cracking a crib without cutting me in. You didn't know that when you told him to keep mum about it, did you?"

"Be quiet, Daniel," Lord St. Clair said.

"Why? I told you, this time you're going to lose, one way or another."

"No." St. Clair sounded regretful, almost sad. "You may make my life a little difficult for a time, but even if everyone here believes you, it won't make any real difference. Bow Street won't take the word of a criminal against that of a Baron, and without Fenton you have no proof of anything you say. There will be rumors, of course, and one or two houses may shut their doors to me for a time, but nothing more serious than that. It's one of the advantages of my position, you see."

Dan Laverham growled and lunged again. St. Clair stood quietly, smiling slightly as Andrew and Robert fought Dan back under control.

"There, you," Robert panted. "Now, before you continue, would one of you mind explaining why that—" he waved a free hand at the Saltash Platter, then had to grab Dan's arm again, "—is so all-fired important? I'm getting tired of not knowing what, exactly, is going on."

"It's perfectly plain," Jonathan said. "The Sacred Dish—"

"Oh, stop nattering about the Sacred Dish," Robert begged. "This is serious, Jon."

"Quite serious," Mairelon said over Jonathan's spluttered protests. "This is—"

"—the Saltash Platter, part o' a set as was stolen from the Royal College of Wizards upwards o' five years ago, by a person or persons unknown," said William Stuggs. He smiled seraphically over Jack Stower's shoulder at the circle of surprised faces, and before the surprise could turn to speculation he added, "I 'ate to disconvenience the Quality-like, but I 'ave to inform you that you, Lord Gregory St. Clair, and you, Mr. Daniel Laverham, and this cove 'ere, 'oose name I ain't 'ad the dubious pleasure of bein' told, are all under arrest in the name o' the Law, for the theft o' the Saltash Set, breakin' an' enterin', 'olding a lot o' respectable folk at gunpoint, an' one or two other things as are against the Law o' the Realm."

"He's a Runner!" Kim burst out before she thought.

"Jasper, you fool!" said Lady Granleigh, too angry to remember that her brother was still comatose on the hearthstone.

"Good Lord!" said Andrew. "Miss D'Auber, did you know?"

"It is to me a great surprise also," Renée D'Auber assured him. "It is entirely a good thing after all, however, since Monsieur St. Clair and that person with the pistols are arrested, so I shall not repine in the least."

"Well, well," Mairelon said. He stepped forward, holding out the Saltash Platter to Stuggs. "I expect you'll want this as evidence?"

"I fear not," St. Clair put in. Kim looked back at him and froze. He was holding one of Dan's pistols trained on Stuggs, who stood between him and the door, and his expression was grim. "Or rather, you may want it, but you won't have it."

"Don't shoot!" Jack Stower pleaded, twisting in Stuggs's grip in a vain effort to get out of Lord St. Clair's line of fire. "I ain't no nabbing cull! Don't shoot me!"

"You can't shoot all of us with only one pistol," Mairelon said gently to St. Clair, ignoring Jack's frantic cries.

"Quite true," Lord St. Clair agreed. His left arm shot out and grabbed Marianne, who shrieked loudly as he pulled her close and pointed the pistol at her head. "But I doubt that any of you will let the young lady be hurt just to keep me here. I shall let her go in Dover, when I board the packet for France—provided, of course, that no one does anything foolish."

"Here, now!" Freddy expostulated. "What d'you think you're doing?"

"Lord St. Clair!" Lady Granleigh exclaimed in tones of shock.

"You wouldn't dare," Andrew said to St. Clair.

"He certainly would," Mairelon said to Andrew. "I think you had better move away from the door, Stuggs. Your superiors will have to be content with half a haul this time."

St. Clair smiled and started forward, dragging Marianne along with him, as Stuggs reluctantly moved aside. "Don't forget the platter, Merrill," St. Clair said, turning his head slightly.

At that precise moment, Freddy Meredith stepped in front of Gregory St. Clair and astonished the entire company by knocking him down. His success was due only partially to his catching St. Clair completely off guard; Kim had to admit that the blow had been a regular wisty castor. Lord St. Clair fell backward, discharging his pistol into the ceiling above the hearth. A shower of plaster descended on Jonathan and the unfortunate Jasper, who coughed, choked, and sat up at last, holding his head and moaning.

"Well struck!" Robert said after a stunned moment.

"Dash it all, Freddy, that was a stupid trick to pull!" Jonathan complained, brushing at the plaster dust that covered his shoulders. "I might have been shot!"

"Oh, *Freddy!*" said Marianne, throwing her arms around him in ecstasy. "How *brave!*"

"Get up, you villain, and I'll do it again," Freddy said. "Dashed lot of nerve you've got, bullying ladies and frightening Marianne."

St. Clair did not reply. He lay sprawled on the floor, his top hat gone and his hair disarranged, staring at Freddy as if he could not believe what had happened.

"I knew he was a regular Captain Sharp," Kim said with considerable satisfaction to no one in particular.

To her surprise, Mairelon answered her. "Yes, you did, and very right you were, too. Just hand that other bit of cord to Andrew, will you, Kim? Then look around for something to tie St. Clair. I'll feel considerably happier when all three of them are, er, secure."

"That's good sense, gov'ner," Stuggs said approvingly. "An' pick up them other pops while you're at it. They 'adn't ought to be lyin' about for the likes o' 'im to get 'is 'ands on."

"There ain't no rope or string or anything," Kim said, picking up the second piece of cord and Dan's other pistol. "I already looked."

"Amelia?" Jasper's voice rose querulously from the hearth. "What's happening? Have you got the platter?"

"You imbecile!" Lady Granleigh stalked to her brother's side, the better to berate him. "Fool! That man of yours is a Bow Street Runner!"

"Stuggs? Don't be silly, Amelia. Monkton recommended him; he'd hardly send me a Runner, now, would he?"

Mairelon glanced at the two of them, then took the cord and pistol from Kim and walked over to Laverham, Robert, and Andrew. He handed the cord to his brother and said, "Tie him up."

"Of course," Andrew answered. "Richard—"

"In a minute, Andrew. Mr., er, Stuggs, I believe you'll find this useful, at least until we've gotten things sorted out." Mairelon handed Stuggs the pistol, then tapped Freddy, who was still glaring pugnaciously at Lord St. Clair, on the shoulder.

"I think this would be a good moment for a discreet departure," he said when Freddy turned. He nodded his head in the direction of Lady Granleigh and her brother, quarreling in front of the fireplace.

"What?" said Freddy. "Oh, I see. Good of you to mention it. Come on, Marianne." He abandoned St. Clair to Stuggs and the pistol, and he and Marianne slipped out the open door.

"That was very kind," Renée D'Auber said to Mairelon. "But have you not perhaps made for yourself more trouble?"

"I'm sure of it," Mairelon said cheerfully. "But I believe I owe Lady Granleigh one, for setting her unspeakable brother on me, and I can't think of a better way of evening the score."

"It seems singularly appropriate," Robert said, stepping forward. "But I would like to point out that I still haven't had my explanation. Not in any way that is remotely satisfactory, that is. I don't suppose you'd care to try again?"

"Good luck," Kim said under her breath. She gave the rest of the dropped pistols to Mairelon, then sat on a nearby footstool to watch. Andrew and Renée were both looking expectantly at Mairelon, Jonathan was scowling at him, and any minute now Lady Granleigh would realize that her wealthy ward had managed to escape again. It ought to be better than a Drury Lane comedy.

twenty-five

Mairelon set the Saltash Platter on the seat of a high-backed chair and put the pistols Kim had given him on top of it. When he turned back to the group, he was no longer smiling. "Yes, there do seem to be a number of loose ends," he said. "For instance, what are you doing here, Renée?"

"It is as your brother has said," Mademoiselle D'Auber replied. She thought for a moment, then added scrupulously, "For the most part."

"We came because Miss D'Auber had heard there was a Runner on your trail," Andrew put in.

"And you wished to assist him?" Mairelon said politely.

"No!" Andrew looked hurt. "I—we came to warn you. And to help you, if we could, though I suppose you've no reason to believe that."

"Why didn't you just tell Kim the Bow Street Runners were about?" Mairelon asked Renée. "Why the meeting? And why weren't you there?"

"Meeting?" Andrew stared at Renée D'Auber in surprised speculation. "You didn't tell me anything about a meeting."

"But of course not," Renée said. She gave the brothers a brilliant smile. "You have both got the heads of pigs, and if I had told you—" she nodded at Mairelon, "—that Monsieur Merrill the elder was here, you would have said a great many things of no politeness and gone away without seeing him, because you thought he did not believe you. And if I had told you—" she glared at Andrew, "—that we were to meet with your brother, you would have made a great many excuses of no merit and not have come, because you did not want to face him and admit you made the mistake five years ago. That is why I was late," she added, turning to Mairelon. "He was being difficult."

"Difficult? *I* was being difficult?" Andrew was almost beyond speech.

"Do you mean to say that you dragged Andrew down here to force the two of us to make up with each other?" Mairelon demanded with equal incredulity.

Renée opened her eyes very wide. "But of course. This feud was all very well when you were in France and he was here, but it would be altogether tiresome if you were both in England, and me, I do not like the things tiresome. So I thought I would arrange it."

The brothers exchanged a look of complete accord, and Kim suppressed a grin. That served Mairelon a bit of his own sauce! Stuggs shook his head sadly. "French," he explained to the room at large.

"And you weren't looking for the Saltash Platter?" Mairelon asked Renée, though Kim could tell from his tone that he did not really have doubts any longer.

"It would have been a very good thing, I think, if I could have gotten it," Renée answered, unperturbed. "For then we should not have had all this confusion which you have still not explained in the least."

"But for yourself?"

"For me?" Renée looked at Mairelon with convincing horror. "But no! Only consider! The Saltash Platter makes persons speak the truth, and that would have been of all things the most inconvenient."

Kim laughed. Mairelon looked at her with an affronted expression, which only made her laugh harder. Slowly Mairelon began to smile. "Yes, under the circumstances, I can see where it would have been, er, inconvenient."

Lady Granleigh chose this moment to stop abusing her brother and turn back to the rest of the room. "Marianne, it is high time—where is Marianne?"

"Gone," Mairelon answered helpfully.

Jonathan snickered, and Lady Granleigh rounded on him. "It is not humorous, young man! Stand aside," she commanded Stuggs. "I must leave at once, to prevent my ward from throwing herself away on that lamentably foolish young man."

"I 'ave my duty," Stuggs said, not moving. "And I 'ave one or two questions as you ought to answer, beggin' your pardon for the inconvenience."

"Of course, you could always pay a call in Bow Street later," Mairelon put in as Lady Granleigh stared, unable to believe that Stuggs had not immediately followed her orders. "It would cause quite a sensation among the *ton*, you might even set a new fashion."

"Amelia!" Jasper had gone pale. "We can't! The duns would be after me the minute they got wind of it."

"What is it you wish to know?" Lady Granleigh said stiffly.

" 'Ow did you come to 'ave an interest in that there platter? An' what sort o' interest did you 'ave?"

"I am very much afraid that I can answer that," a new voice said from behind Stuggs.

Stuggs jumped back and whirled, so that he could cover both the doorway and the corner where Laverham, Stower, and St. Clair stood. Then he smiled and relaxed. "Sir!" he said, and stepped aside.

Four men entered behind him. Hunch was the only one Kim recognized; the other three were gentry toffs, middle-aged and dressed for riding, but she didn't recall seeing any of them before. She glanced around the room, sizing up the reactions of the rest of the group. Lady Granleigh was staring at the man who had spoken, and she had gone rather pale. Jonathan Aberford turned red when he saw the second toff, but Robert smiled in relief at the same man. Laverham and Stower wore blank expressions; St. Clair's eyes narrowed and his lips thinned as he stared at the newcomers, and Kim got the impression that he was not at all pleased. Stuggs was watching the third man with a respectful expression. Andrew, Renée, and Mairelon all looked startled to various degrees.

"What 'ave you been a-doing now, Master Richard?" Hunch demanded, ignoring the rest of the company entirely.

"An excellent question," Robert murmured. "Perhaps you'll do better at getting an answer than we have."

"Well, well," Mairelon said. He blinked, smiled, and swept a bow. "Your servant, Granleigh, Bramingham. I'm afraid you've missed most of the excitement, Edward."

"I am desolated," the third man replied. With a start, Kim recognized his voice: he was the Earl of Shoreham, who had sent Mairelon off to Ranton Hill in search of the Saltash Platter. "Richard, I hate to be overly particular, but I seem to recall telling you not to attract atten—*Andrew*? What the devil are you doing here?"

"No, no, we've already had that bit," Mairelon said. "I want to know what Granleigh here meant when he said he could account for Lady Granleigh's, er, actions. And how you all happen to be here," he added as an afterthought.

"I received some information last night, after Hunch left," the Earl replied. He glanced toward Laverham and St. Clair. "I thought it sufficiently urgent to post down, but it seems to have been an unnecessary effort."

"If you're talking about the irregular relationship between Mr. Laverham and St. Clair, yes, that's come out," Mairelon said. "But where did you pick up these others?"

"Hunch told me you'd gone to Bramingham Place," Shoreham said. "Naturally we went looking for you there. Mrs. Bramingham had just discovered that most of her houseguests had vanished, and Bramingham and Granleigh elected to come with me in hopes of hunting them up."

"And in hopes of getting away from the excellent Mrs. Bramingham's frenzy," Mairelon murmured. "Quite understandable. Now, what was that you were saying about Lady Granleigh?" he asked, turning to the tall, distinguished man who had been first through the door.

The first man sighed and glanced toward the Earl of Shoreham. "My wife has a tendency to meddle," he explained. Lady Granleigh stiffened and recovered her usual color, but her husband gave her a look that caused her to subside without saying anything. Kim was impressed; there must be more to this stuffy-looking cull than at first appeared.

"A tendency to meddle," Lord Granleigh repeated. "And considerably more ambition than I had realized. I believe she was trying to arrange for me to be the next Minister of Wizardry." He gave the Earl of Shoreham another sidelong look as he spoke, as though checking his reaction.

"Nonsense, Stephen," Lady Granleigh said unconvincingly. "You are perfectly capable of managing such matters yourself."

"True," Lord Granleigh replied. "A fact which you would be well advised to remember in the future, Amelia. Your interference this time could very easily have had unpleasant consequences."

"I don't know what you are talking about," Lady Granleigh said even more unconvincingly than before. "I am only here to keep Marianne from ruining herself with Freddy Meredith."

"I don't believe it," the last of the three toffs put in. "Freddy's a good lad. He wouldn't do anything, er, dishonorable."

"Freddy said something about a special license before he left, Mr. Bramingham," Robert said, ignoring Lady Granleigh's glare.

"Yes, I believe he has one with him," Mairelon said. "Amazingly sensible of him, too. Any number of things might have gone wrong between here and Gretna Green, if he'd chosen that route."

"Sensible?" Jonathan goggled at Mairelon. *"Freddy?"*

"There, you see?" Mr. Bramingham said to the room at large. His eye fell on St. Clair, and he frowned. "Shoreham, what's Baron St. Clair doing in the corner with this fellow pointing a pistol at him?"

"'Es under arrest, in the name o' the Law," Stuggs informed him. "Along with these other two. I 'aven't got straight yet which o' 'em did what, but they 'as all done somethin', and I 'ave my duty."

"You ought to be arresting *that* man as well," Jonathan Aberford grumbled, pointing at Mairelon. "Whoever he is. Didn't someone say he was wanted?"

Andrew's face set in grim lines. Mairelon only smiled and looked at the Earl of Shoreham. Shoreham returned the smile, then said to Jonathan, "He is certainly wanted by the French, but though our relations with them have improved a good deal, I don't think our cooperation would stretch so far as to turn one of our people over to them. Particularly a man with such a distinguished record."

"You're too kind," Mairelon said.

"Probably," Shoreham agreed blandly.

Andrew's mouth had dropped open, as had Lady Granleigh's. St. Claire had gone white; Renée D'Auber and Hunch looked smug. "What are you talking about?" Jonathan demanded.

The Earl of Shoreham sighed. "For the past five years, Richard Merrill has been one of the best agents the War Office has had the good fortune to employ. Is that clear enough for you?"

"But—but I thought he stole the Saltash Set," Jonathan said, frowning.

"Merrill?" the Earl of Shoreham said. "It's your turn to explain."

"In a minute. I don't think we were quite through with Lord Granleigh yet," Mairelon answered. "I still don't understand what Lady Granleigh's ambitions for her husband have to do with the Saltash Set, or how she found out about it in the first place."

"She listened at doors, that's how," Jasper Marston said waspishly, lifting his head for the first time since the Earl and his companions had arrived.

Lady Granleigh gasped. "Jasper, how dare you—"

"Oh, stop it, Amelia," Jasper said. "There's no use pretending to injured innocence. They already know most of it. They know *you*," he added spitefully.

"You are not thinking about what you are saying," Lady Granleigh said in a tone that could have frozen the Thames at mid-summer.

"I know exactly what I'm saying! This whole mess is your fault, Amelia, and I'm not going to take the blame for it."

"My fault? You are the one who brought along that Bow Street Runner! I suppose you are going to claim you knew nothing about it."

"As it 'appens, 'e didn't," Stuggs put in. "I know my business, and it ain't lettin' no buffle'eaded toff in on the nick, beggin' your pardon, sir."

"It was your idea to get hold of that blasted platter!" Jasper said, ignoring Stuggs. "The whole thing was your idea, start to finish!"

Mairelon cleared his throat, which recalled the presence of an audience to the combatants. Lady Granleigh closed her mouth on whatever she had planned to say, and Jasper subsided on the hearth once more, holding his head. Mairelon smiled blandly. "And how would Lady Granleigh's, er, acquiring the Saltash Platter advance you with the Ministry, Lord Granleigh?"

Lord Granleigh looked at Mairelon in surprise. "Good Lord, man, recovering the Saltash Set and catching the thief would give anyone a boost! One of those chaps down at the Royal College came up with a gadget that said so, and the whole Ministry has been buzzing ever since."

"A gadget?" Mairelon frowned, distracted. "Not one of Fotherington's crystals? He's been trying to get them to make accurate predictions forever; do you mean to say he's finally succeeded?"

"As it happens, yes," the Earl of Shoreham said. "You can discuss it with him later."

"How did he get it to—"

"*Later*, Richard. Right now, we want your story, and you must admit we've been very patient."

"Too patient," Hunch said darkly.

"Oh, very well. I think I have enough of the pieces to put together a fairly good picture. It's a long tale, though; you'd best make yourselves comfortable."

The Earl suppressed another sigh and leaned against the door. Mr. Bramingham, looking mildly puzzled, held a chair for Renée D'Auber, while the rest of the company (with the exception of Stuggs and his prisoners) settled themselves around the room. Watching Lady Granleigh and Jonathan Aberford vie for a chair, Kim was glad she'd bagged the footstool before it had occurred to anyone else to sit down.

"The story begins about five years ago," Mairelon said, and Kim smiled, recognizing the familiar lecturing tone. "The Saltash Set, of which this is part, was being displayed in the antechamber of the Royal College of Wizards, to which I had recently been elected.

"Lord St. Clair—" Mairelon gave him an ironic half-bow, "—had for some time been attempting to obtain the Saltash Set from the College, but for one reason or another, the College refused to sell. So he decided to steal it. Having no experience with the finer points of theft, he approached his illegitimate half brother, Daniel Laverham, for assistance.

"Laverham sent St. Clair a young man named James Fenton, who I must suppose was both an accomplished housebreaker and extremely loyal to Laverham. Laverham, you see, disliked and distrusted St. Clair—"

"With reason!" Dan Laverham interrupted, glaring at Lord St. Clair.

"Quiet, you," Stuggs said. "You'll 'ave your chance to talk later."

"St. Clair arranged for Fenton to steal the Saltash Set," Mairelon continued. "St. Clair must have taken care of the Royal College's magical precautions against theft, and Fenton did the rest, including dropping one or two items he'd stolen from me in the antechamber to make it look as if I were the thief. He had even timed things so that I'd be on my way home alone from my club when the theft occurred, so he had no reason to worry about laying information at Bow Street against me.

"Unfortunately for St. Clair, things began going wrong at that point. I ran into Shoreham here outside the club, and we got to arguing about the use of invocations in wards and protective spells. We ended up at Renée's, experimenting with catnip and powdered pearls until the watchmen made their morning rounds."

"Then why didn't you say so?" Andrew burst out. "Why did you let everyone believe—"

"At first, because I didn't see the need," Mairelon said. "I didn't think anyone would take the accusation seriously. And there was Renée's reputation to consider."

"Which was a great foolishness," Renée D'Auber said emphatically. "I am the eccentric, me, and no one pays the least attention when I do odd things."

"Not *now*," Mairelon agreed. "But five years ago you were barely eighteen, and it would not have done."

"Bah!" said Renée, dismissing these imaginary terrors with a wave. "You are altogether English, and very silly besides. Papa and I would have contrived something."

"But once you knew the Runners intended to arrest you—" Andrew said and stopped, looking from Mairelon to Renée uncertainly.

"By then I had asked them not to say anything," the Earl of Shoreham said. "It was the perfect excuse for Richard to fly the country and take up residence on the Continent, and we needed someone like him to do just that. Someone who could deal with any level of society, someone who wouldn't look too suspicious, and above all, someone who knew magic. Richard was perfect."

"So Hunch and I fled to France," Mairelon resumed. "Meanwhile, Fenton took the Saltash Set to Laverham instead of St. Clair. Since Laverham didn't know the set had magical properties, he broke it up and sold it to spite his brother. By the time Fenton learned that the set was more useful together than apart, it was too late. The pieces were scattered, and practically impossible to trace."

Laverham and St. Clair were looking at Mairelon as if he had suddenly acquired two heads; the rest of the company was listening with rapt attention. Kim shook her head in admiration. Mairelon had put it together so neatly that he might have been eavesdropping on Laverham and St. Clair the whole time.

"One of the pieces of the set, the bowl, was purchased by a German Baron," Mairelon said. "I got wind of it, and after the war I stayed on the Continent to track it down. It took me nearly a year. Meanwhile, Laverham had recovered two of the four spheres, and the platter had fallen into the innocent hands of Mr. Aberford's little group."

Jonathan Aberford scowled, and Kim wondered whether he was more annoyed by Mairelon's reference to the druids as a "little group" or by his characterizing them as innocent.

"That was the situation some four weeks ago when I returned to England," Mairelon said, giving Jonathan a charming smile. "And things began to get complicated. Naturally I couldn't return as myself; the Runners were still after me, and I have a great deal of respect for their abilities." He and Stuggs exchanged nods. "So I chose the role of a market performer. No one expects a real magician to work for pennies and the occasional shilling in a market, so I didn't expect anyone to look for me there. But I did send word to Shoreham, and I presume he told you, Lord Granleigh."

Mairelon paused and looked at Lord Granleigh expectantly. Lord Granleigh nodded. "He did. We discussed the implications at some length." He glanced at his wife and added, "In my study."

"That will be how Lady Granleigh heard about it," Mairelon said with supreme lack of tact. "She, ah, persuaded her brother to help her find me, intending, I suppose, to collect me and as much of the Saltash Set as possible and present the lot to the Royal College on behalf of her husband."

"And a proper mull 'e made of it," Stuggs put in, looking scornfully at Jasper Marston "Went around askin' this one an' that one, with no more sense nor a baby. Word was all over St. Giles before the day was out."

"How was I to know?" Jasper complained. " 'Find this Merrill person,' she said; well, how do you find one man in the whole of London without asking?"

"Which explains how Bow Street heard of my return," Mairelon said, "and undoubtedly how Mr. Laverham heard of it, as well." He glanced at Dan, who glared and said nothing. "Bow Street arranged for Mr. Stuggs here to keep an eye on Mr. Marston. At least, I presume it was Bow Street." He threw a sidelong look at the Earl of Shoreham.

The Earl laughed. "Right again, Richard. Stuggs has done a job or two for me before, though this wasn't one of them. How did you guess?"

"He recognized you when you arrived just now," Mairelon answered. "And only one of your people would call you 'sir' and not 'my lord.' "

Lady Granleigh sniffed, but a look from her husband kept her from saying anything.

"Once he found Mairelon the Magician, Mr. Marston hired Kim here to look through my wagon for the Saltash Bowl. I, er, found her in process and persuaded her to come with me after she completed her commission from Mr. Marston."

"Cloth-head," Kim muttered, not entirely sure whether she meant Marston or Mairelon.

"I suspect it was Laverham's men we gave the slip to on our way out of London," Mairelon went on blandly. "It doesn't matter, though. Shoreham told us where the platter was, and we came here to recover it. I'm not sure how Renée found out where we were headed—"

"Lord Shoreham told me," Renée said. "And since Monsieur Andrew Merrill was of an unhappiness, and had besides heard some of the rumors, and since I also heard that the Bow Street Runners were of an interest, I thought, me, that it would be best to come here and arrange matters myself."

"Renée!" Shoreham looked horrified.

"Oh, I was very discreet," Renée assured him. "No one knew I was not in London, except of course Madame Bramingham and her guests, and Monsieur Andrew stayed at the inn in that town with the dreadful name I cannot remember."

"Swafflton?" Mairelon murmured.

"Yes, that is it," Renée said. "And it has all turned out well, so there is no reason for you to pull your mouth down, so, and make faces as if you have the stomachache."

"You should have left matters to me," Shoreham said, shaking his head.

Renée opened her eyes very wide. "Truly? But it does not seem to me that you have done very much."

"It wasn't necessary," Mairelon said. "Any more than it was necessary for you to come."

"Well, but it might have been," Renée replied, unperturbed. "And it is better to be too ready, is it not? Also, I do not see that you would explain anything at all to me if I had stayed in London, and I do not wish to perish of the curiosity. So I am glad I came, and I do not care if you look very sour about it."

Mairelon rolled his eyes, and Kim laughed. She was beginning to like Renée in spite of herself.

"I don't know whether Lady Granleigh knew that the Saltash Platter was in Ranton Hill when she came down to Mrs. Bramingham's house party," Mairelon went on after a moment, "but I rather think not. It didn't take her long to discover it and send for her brother, though, and the roads and weather being as they've been, both of them were settled in before we arrived.

"Laverham must have known the platter's whereabouts for several months, at least, but he was being very cautious. He arranged for James Fenton to take a job as footman to Freddy Meredith, intending to have Fenton steal the platter for him later. Fenton had other ideas."

Dan Laverham muttered something under his breath and glared at Mairelon. Mairelon smiled, and Kim shook her head. He was enjoying this altogether too much, she thought.

"Fenton's family was respectable, and his brother was a silversmith. Fenton persuaded him to copy the Saltash Platter exactly. Perhaps the original idea was to cover up the theft of the platter for as long as possible, but he must have realized fairly soon that he could make a tidy sum selling copies of the platter to each of the, er, interested parties. Since he wasn't a magician himself, he didn't know that the forgeries would be childishly easy to spot.

"When the copies were finished, Fenton replaced the real platter with a copy and hid it in the druid's lodge." Mairelon waved at the gaping hole in the floor in front of the hearth. "But he was stretching his luck; making the copies had taken a long time, and Laverham was beginning to worry, particularly since by then he'd heard that I was back. So Laverham sent Jack Stower there down to Ranton Hill to check on Fenton."

"Then he didn't follow me at all!" Kim exclaimed, remembering how frightened she had been by Jack's unexpected appearance at the inn in Ranton Hill.

"No, but it was as well that you kept out of sight," Mairelon said. "Think of the trouble we'd have had if Laverham had arrived a few days earlier than he did."

Kim shuddered.

"Richard," the Earl of Shoreham said. His tone was mild, but Mairelon sighed and returned to his story.

"Just to thoroughly confuse matters, at about this time Freddy Meredith lost the false platter to Henry Bramingham in a game of cards. Henry knew that his uncle," Mairelon nodded at Gregory St. Clair, "collected oddities of that sort and proposed to give it to him. That brought St. Clair down to Ranton Hill posthaste and set off an interesting round of burglaries at Bramingham Place. Kim and I were privileged to observe most of the parade."

"What, what?" said Mr. Bramingham.

"We hid in your priest's hole," Mairelon explained.

"Priest's hole!" Kim said, disappointed. "Is that what it was? I thought it was a spell."

"Bramingham showed it to me last time I visited," Mairelon said. "Next time your household is roused in the middle of the night, Bramingham, you should remember to check inside it."

"Yes, but what's this about burglaries?" Bramingham said. "Somebody broke into the library a couple of nights ago, but—"

"Several somebodies," Mairelon interrupted. "Actually, I believe Renée was the first, but she recognized the platter for a fake and left it where it was. She was long gone when Kim and I got there."

"I knew I 'adn't ought to 'ave gone to London and left you 'ere with 'er," Hunch said.

"It wasn't my idea!" Kim protested.

"I didn't figure as it was," Hunch said dryly, and Kim blinked in surprise. Then she grinned at him.

"We were interrupted by Mr. Stower's arrival," Mairelon said with a quelling look at Hunch. "Stower was interrupted in turn by Marston and Stuggs, who were interrupted by Jonathan Aberford."

"Jonathan?" Robert Choiniet said, startled. "Are you sure?"

"He has a turn of phrase that is unmistakable," Mairelon answered.

"Have you got maggots in your head?" Robert demanded, glaring at Jonathan. "Or have you suddenly gotten as bacon-brained as Freddy Meredith? Why in heaven's name would you try to burgle Bramingham Place?"

"I thought it would work," Jonathan said sullenly.

"He hadn't counted on the, er, competition," Mairelon said. "In the end, Lady Granleigh managed to obtain the platter by as neat a trick as I've seen. You might consider taking her on, Shoreham; she's got the nerves for it."

Lady Granleigh looked as if she did not know whether to be pleased or insulted by this remark, and Kim hid a smile.

"Lady Granleigh quickly discovered that her platter was a forgery, which left her in something of a dilemma. She couldn't return it to the Braminghams without awkward explanations, but she didn't want to keep it, either. And Jonathan Aberford was hanging about Bramingham Place and making a nuisance of himself; if Lady Granleigh and her brother made any attempts to locate the real platter, Jonathan was sure to notice. So she decided to give the forgery back to the druids and solve two problems at once.

"Miss D'Auber and I had agreed to meet this morning near here to compare what we had each learned. She was delayed—" Mairelon gave Andrew a quick look, and Andrew smiled wryly, "—so I was here alone when Lady Granleigh and her party arrived. I, ah, accepted the platter on Mr. Aberford's behalf."

"By what right?" Jonathan demanded.

Mairelon looked at him without answering. Stuggs made a peculiar noise that Kim realized, after a moment, was a smothered chuckle. Jonathan turned very red and subsided, muttering, and Mairelon turned back to the Earl of Shoreham and continued his tale.

"Meanwhile, Fenton was proceeding with his own plans. He gave or sold the second of his fakes to Jack Stower and presumably made arrangements to meet with a couple of other prospective customers." Mairelon glanced toward St. Clair, who did not react. Jonathan Aberford, however, scowled and shifted uneasily. Mairelon smiled. "Yes, I thought so."

"Get on with it, Richard," the Earl said. He sounded amused but determined.

"You have no sense of the dramatic, Shoreham," Mairelon complained.

"I have as much as I need," the Earl replied in a dry voice. "Though

I will readily admit that I have not spent the last few years on a stage. No doubt it's a grave failing in my education."

"No doubt," Mairelon said, looking somewhat disgruntled. "Well, Stower was on the point of returning to London with his platter when he spotted Hunch in Ranton Hill. He followed Hunch to our camp and attempted to take the false platter we had collected; instead, he lost his own and prompted me to head by Bramingham Place to find out what was going on.

"I found more than I expected." Mairelon paused, staring at the far wall, and something in his stance kept the others from commenting. Then he shook himself and looked at Mr. Bramingham. "When you get back, you'd best send someone down to the wood by the Long Avenue. There's a body and two more copies of the Saltash Platter hidden there."

"Richard!" said the Earl, his voice carrying clearly over the confused babble that broke out among the rest of the listeners. "Who? What happened?"

"The body was the unfortunate and ambitious James Fenton," Mairelon answered. "As to what happened, I can only speculate; Kim and I heard the shot, but we didn't get a look at the man who fired it."

"Speculate, then!"

"I think Fenton had arranged to meet someone in the Long Avenue. Two someones, actually; he couldn't very well have sold both fakes to the same person. I think he miscalculated badly—remember, he didn't know that a magician could easily tell the difference between his forgeries and the real platter. So when he tried to pass off one of the fakes, St. Clair shot him."

"Unlikely," Lord St. Clair said into the horrified silence that followed.

"Not at all," Mairelon said with exaggerated politeness. "You, Laverham, and Aberford there are the most logical people for Fenton to pick as possible customers for his remaining forgeries. Laverham, or rather, Laverham's man Stower, already had a platter. Aberford would clearly do a lot to get his hands on his, er, Sacred Dish, but I doubt he'd commit murder. Besides, if he'd killed Fenton, he wouldn't have held up Laverham's coach half an hour later, looking for the platter."

Jonathan jerked. "How did you know—"

"It's the only reason you've done anything for the past week," Mairelon said. "You were supposed to meet Fenton, too, weren't you? How did you find out that he was hoping to sell the platter to someone else?"

"I heard him bragging about it at the inn," Jonathan said sullenly. "I didn't kill anyone!"

"Yes, I know," Mairelon said. "You thought you'd save yourself some time and trouble, not to mention money, and hold up the coach instead of paying Fenton."

"This is all speculation," St. Clair said. He acted as if he were calm enough, but there were small lines of tension at the corners of his eyes, and a muscle in his jaw twitched now and again when he was not speaking.

"Not entirely," Mairelon told him. "A moment ago, you told Laverham and Stuggs that they couldn't prove anything against you without Fenton, but no one has mentioned Mr. Fenton's unfortunate demise until now. If you didn't kill him, how did you know?"

"I was not referring to this Fenton's death," Lord St. Clair said coldly. "I merely meant that no one knew where he was."

"Convince the Runners of that." Mairelon nodded at Stuggs.

"You were the man he was to meet!" Jonathan said suddenly, staring intently at St. Clair. "You were the one to whom he would have sold the Sacred Dish!"

Robert Choiniet rolled his eyes. Lady Granleigh looked shocked. The Earl of Shoreham frowned. "How do you know?" he demanded.

"He was at the inn; I saw him hanging about while I was . . . following Fenton."

"Hardly convincing," St. Clair said.

"I doubt that the Runners will have any trouble finding proof, one way or another," Mairelon said.

"Now that they're looking at the right man," Andrew muttered.

"In any case: St. Clair shot Fenton, but Kim and I interrupted him. Laverham and Stower interrupted us and brought us here. I presume St. Clair followed us. Fenton had hidden the platter under the hearth; we found it and had a small disagreement over its ownership. I expect Stuggs can tell you the rest; he was here for most of it. And that's all."

twenty-six

It wasn't all by a long shot. Everyone wanted a chance to object, explain, or ask questions, and it took all the Earl's considerable force of character to keep them more or less under control. Mairelon was no help whatever; he took immediate advantage of the commotion to dodge past Hunch and corner Lord Granleigh, whom he began cross-questioning about recent magical developments at the Royal College of Wizards.

After a few minutes of chaos, Stuggs brought the confusion to a halt by pointing out that he ought to take his prisoners into town and make arrangements for them to be transported to London.

"There's another one asleep on the box of the coach outside," Mairelon said, turning his head. "I don't know what he's done, but I'm quite sure it's something nasty."

Stuggs frowned. " 'E ain't a wizard, too, is 'e?"

"What, driving a coach?" Jonathan said scornfully.

"No, he's just another of Laverham's crew," Mairelon said. "Unpleasant enough, but quite ordinary so far as his skills are concerned."

"Still, that makes four of them," Shoreham said. "Which is a bit much to expect one man, however competent, to handle alone."

"Well, I could go along as far as the town," Mr. Bramingham offered. "It's not much out of my way, you know. I can't stop there, though; my wife will be waiting to hear what's happened."

"And to spread it over as much of the county as she can reach," Mairelon murmured. "I'm afraid St. Clair is going to be a social outcast no matter how the trial turns out."

"I should think so," Lady Granleigh sniffed. "His behavior to me, and to poor Marianne, has been simply unpardonable. If it hadn't been for him, Marianne would not have run off as she did."

Everyone looked at Lady Granleigh in patent disbelief, including Jasper. Lady Granleigh stared haughtily down her nose at the lot of them. "Pointing that pistol at poor Marianne clearly disordered her intellect. I am quite confident that, had you behaved as a gentleman ought, wiser counsels would have prevailed, and she would not have dashed off to be married in such a hole-in-the-corner fashion."

"I congratulate you, Lady Granleigh," Lord St. Clair said after a moment. "I have never before met anyone with so great a talent for seeing the world as she wishes it to be."

Lady Granleigh stared through the space occupied by Lord St. Clair as if he were not there, then turned to her brother. "Come, Jasper, it is time we were going."

"Time and past," Kim muttered. Mairelon glanced sharply in her direction, but no one else seemed to hear.

"I'll accompany you, my dear," Lord Granleigh said in a tone that brooked no argument. "Bramingham's right; we should be getting back."

Lady Granleigh did not look at all pleased by this development (nor did Jasper), but they had no choice but to go along. Kim wondered whether Lord Granleigh would give them both a dressing-down in the carriage. She hoped so; the bracket-faced mort deserved a tongue-lashing and then some for the way she'd been mucking about in everyone else's affairs, and Jasper was no better.

"Now, then, Stuggs," Lord Shoreham said when the Granleighs were safely out the door. "You'll want someone besides Bramingham to help with the prisoners, I think. No sense in taking chances."

"We'd be happy to help, sir," Robert Choiniet volunteered. "That is, if you think we'd be useful." He nudged Jonathan with his elbow.

"Happy?" Jonathan said bitterly. "Oh, yes, of course, certainly. The Sacred Dish is gone for good, the lodge is in ruins, and the Sons of the New Dawn will be a laughingstock. Naturally we're happy."

Mairelon looked at him. "I hardly think one broken window, a displaced hearthstone, and a couple of overturned chairs constitute being in ruins."

"Yes, we've done more damage ourselves on a good night," Robert agreed. "Do stop playacting, Jon."

"Playacting? *Play*acting? You don't seem to realize how serious this is! We *need* to consecrate the Sacred Dish before we can make any more progress in the Mysteries."

Robert rolled his eyes and Mairelon hid a smile. Kim felt sorry for Jonathan. She knew what it was like to lose something she'd depended on having, even if she didn't know anything about druids or magic. And after all, it wasn't *his* fault he'd gotten hold of the Saltash Platter instead of some ordinary silver tray that no one else would have cared about. A thought occurred to her, and she said suddenly, "Why'd you pick the Saltash Platter for your Sacred Dish? I mean, would any old wicher cheat do, or does it have to be this particular one?"

"It was perfect," Jonathan said sullenly. "It's exactly the right dimensions, and the pattern has the proper balance of natural form and abstract design. It took me two years of hunting to find it, and it had to be stolen!"

"Well, if all you need is something that size and shape, can't you use one of the fake platters? There's enough of 'em around."

Everyone looked at Kim, and she flushed. "It was just an idea."

"And a very good one," Mairelon said. "One of the false platters should suit you admirably, Aberford. Better than the real thing, in fact; you won't have to worry about your spells getting tangled up with the ones that are already in the Saltash Platter and exploding, or doing something equally unexpected."

Jonathan, who had opened his mouth, closed it again, looking suddenly very thoughtful. The Earl of Shoreham's lips twitched, and Renée D'Auber put up a hand to hide a smile. Andrew only looked bewildered, and St. Clair and the other prisoners studiously ignored the exchange.

"I doubt that there will be any fuss over ownership of one of the duplicates, either," Mairelon added.

"I think I can guarantee that no official questions will be asked," Shoreham put in. "Provided there is no fuss made at this end, of course. I should warn you, though, that I can't do a thing about gossip." He glanced in the direction of the door, where Lady Granleigh and her party had long since vanished.

"Gossip won't do anything but increase our membership," Robert commented. "We might even get a couple of fellows who'll pay their subscription fees. That would please Austen no end."

"Yes, wouldn't it?" Jonathan said, failing to sound anything like as offhanded as he plainly wanted to. "Very well, we'll do it."

"Good. I have two at my wagon; you can come by this evening and pick one up," Mairelon said. "It's just down the road, on the left-hand side as you head toward the village."

"This evening? But I thought—"

"I have a few things still to do here," Mairelon interrupted, "and it won't be convenient for you to wait. Trust me."

"Yes, and your mother was in an awful taking when I left, Jon," Robert put in. "God knows what she's like by now. She'll have half the county out hunting for you if you don't get home soon, depend on it."

"Oh, very well," Jonathan said ungraciously. He swirled his cloak unnecessarily and stalked to the door of the lodge. "I shall wait upon you this evening," he told Mairelon in portentous tones, and left.

"Silly young chub," Mairelon said, but not loudly enough to be heard outside.

Andrew frowned. "Wait a minute. Didn't somebody say his horse ran off? How is he planning to get home, wherever home is?"

"Oh, Jon never plans anything," Robert said in a resigned tone. "Except ceremonies. He'll probably take my horse. I think I had better come along with you and Bramingham, after all, Mr. Stuggs. I can stop in the village for as long as you need help with that lot, and then borrow a horse to get home on."

Stuggs nodded and handed him a pistol. "Right, then. Move along, now, you lot."

"I think I'd best go with them, at least as far as the coach," the Earl of Shoreham said to Mairelon as St. Clair, Jack Stower, and Dan Laverham started toward the door, flanked by Robert and Mr. Bramingham. "Two of them are wizards, after all, and it wouldn't do for them to take advantage, so to speak."

"You always were a cautious one," Mairelon told him. "Shall I come and help?"

"No, no, you've done enough already," Shoreham replied quickly. "And it'll only take a moment. You stay here." He followed Bramingham, who was bringing up the end of Stuggs's little procession, out the door.

Mairelon gazed after him with an abstracted air. "Now, do you suppose he was being subtle, tactful, or merely cowardly?" he asked the window Laverham had broken.

"'E's a-doing of 'is job," Hunch said. "Which you ought to 'ave been, too, instead of breaking into 'ouses and things while I was gone."

"That *was* my job," Mairelon pointed out. "Or part of doing it, anyway, which comes to the same thing."

"You might 'ave got shot," Hunch said doggedly.

"Yes, well, I didn't, so there's no need to go on about it, especially since the main reason you're so nattered about it is that you missed out on the fun."

"Nattered about it?" said Andrew in a puzzled tone.

"It's one of Kim's expressions," Mairelon said. "Very descriptive."
He paused, looking at Andrew, and Hunch closed his mouth on whatever
further comment he had been about to make. "It's good to see you again,
Andrew," Mairelon said after what seemed a very long time.

"It's good to see you, too, Richard," Andrew answered in a low voice.
"For a while I . . . wasn't sure I was going to."

"What? You haven't been listening to Hunch, have you? That business on the Peninsula wasn't anything like as serious as he claims."

"I can see that Hunch and I are going to have to have a long talk,"
Andrew said with a crooked smile. "But that wasn't what I meant."

"Yes, well, actually I know that, but it doesn't matter," Mairelon
said quickly.

"It matters to me," Andrew persisted. He took a deep breath and
went on, "I misjudged you very badly five years ago, and I want to tell
you that I know it now, and I'm sorry."

Renée D'Auber gave a small nod of satisfaction, and a slow grin began
to spread across Hunch's face. Kim felt like cheering, but she didn't dare.
She was almost afraid to breathe, for fear someone would notice, and
remember she was there, and make her leave.

"All right," Mairelon said gently, his eyes on Andrew's face. "You've
told me. Apology accepted. Can we leave it at that?"

"You mean I—you'll—that's all?"

"Really, Andrew, were you expecting me to demand satisfaction?"
Mairelon said in the mildly exasperated tone he used with Hunch and
Kim. "A pretty thing that would be; you are my brother, after all, not to
mention that dueling's illegal. Or did you think I'd throw a fit of temper?
I could turn you into a frog for a few minutes, if it would make you feel
better, but I'd really rather not. It's the devil of a nuisance to measure
out all the ingredients for the powder, and I can never remember the
proper endings for the verbs."

Andrew laughed. "I—well, thank you, Richard. Will you be coming
home now?"

The words were a question, but his tone made it clear that he expected Mairelon to answer yes. Kim's heart lurched as she realized just
how inevitable that yes was, and how much it would mean. The Mairelon
she knew was an act, a trick to fool the Runners, and the trick was no
longer necessary. He would become Richard Merrill again, and go back
to a gentry life she could hardly imagine. She tried to be glad, but all she
could think was that there would be no place in that life for her. She

wrapped her arms around herself and hugged hard. At least she had the five pounds Jasper Marston had paid her, and the clothes Mairelon had bought. Maybe Mairelon or Shoreham would give her a few guineas more for her help with Laverham. It was as much as she had wanted when she got into this; she couldn't help it if her wants had changed somehow since then.

"Home," Mairelon said, rolling the word as if he were checking its taste. "Not just yet, I think. Until the word gets out, I prefer to lie low. We'll stay here for a few days, then start back to London. Is the old stable still there?"

"In London?" Andrew asked, bewildered.

"No, in Kent. The one we used to climb on the roof of, when we were boys."

"Oh. Yes, it's there. Why?"

"It would be a good place to leave my wagon. I'll send Hunch down with it once I'm settled in London."

"And not before," Hunch put in darkly. "You ain't fobbing me off with no tale this time, Master Richard."

"You're going to stay in London for the Season, then?" Andrew said with an uncertain look in Hunch's direction.

"It is an excellent plan," Renée D'Auber said. "You will be the nine days' wonder, and it will be entirely plain to everyone that you had nothing to do with the robbery."

"I expect I'll have more to do than attend social events," Mairelon said with a hint of sarcasm. "Shoreham is bound to want me for all sorts of things. Which reminds me, there was one other thing I wanted to attend to. Kim!"

Kim jumped and nearly fell off her footstool. "What?" Her throat felt scratchy, and she experienced a sudden desire to run. She knew what he was going to say, and she didn't want to hear it.

"Why did you tip that table over on Laverham when he was in the middle of that spell a few minutes ago?" Mairelon asked.

"The *table?*" Kim said blankly. The question was so completely different from what she had expected that she couldn't quite grasp it.

"Yes, the table." Mairelon looked at her sternly. "I've told you more than once that interrupting a wizard is dangerous, and if you claim you forgot, I won't believe you. So why did you interrupt Laverham?"

"Because his spell was queer as Dick's hatband anyway," Kim said. "You know that."

"Yes, *I* knew it," Mairelon said. "But how did *you* know?"

"It was the words," Kim said. She frowned, trying to think how best to describe what she had sensed when Laverham's spell began to go wrong.

"You speak the Latin, then?" Renée D'Auber said, raising her eyebrows in polite incredulity. "Or the Greek, perhaps?"

"I ain't got no need to speak it," Kim snapped, wondering why they were staring at her like that. "Laverham's words weren't . . . They weren't lined up neat and proper like they should of been."

"Should *have*," Mairelon murmured. "And I did warn you, Kim, about reverting under stress."

"Do not be hard with her," Renée reproved him. "It is not at all wonderful that she should have the difficulties after all that has happened."

"No, the wonderful part was the bit about the words," Mairelon said. "Kim, do you mean that you can feel when someone is casting a spell?"

"I don't know about that, but I can tell when somebody says some of them—of *those* shiny, sharp words you use for spells," Kim replied carefully.

"You mean like *apbeteon*? Or perhaps—" Mairelon rattled off a long, humpy sentence and raised his eyebrows at Kim.

"No," Kim said, happy to be sure of something. "Those sound right, but they don't have no edges. They're just nonsense."

"And these?" He said a short phrase that crackled and glittered.

Kim flinched and nodded. Mairelon stared at her. "My Lord," he said in a low voice. "No wonder you weren't hurt when the spell shattered."

"There ain't nothin' wonderful about *that*," Kim said, staring in turn. "I ducked, that's all."

Renée and Mairelon exchanged glances. "Nothing wonderful about it at all," Mairelon agreed. "For a wizard."

"What?" Hunch gasped. "That Kim, a wizard? She ain't no such thing!"

"Not yet," Mairelon said, smiling. "But with proper training she will be."

"Me?" Kim said, stunned. "Me, a wizard? Me?"

"Ah, bah!" said Renée to Mairelon. "You do not explain at all well, I find, and so you are frightening her." She stepped forward and put a comforting arm around Kim's shoulders. "It is because you can feel the magic, which is a thing very difficult for most people to learn and for some quite impossible. So you have the talent for magic, and now, if you wish, you will come to London and get the training."

"Of course she wishes," Mairelon broke in. "Kim likes London. We'll start the lessons as soon as we've found a house to hire for a few months, and—"

"Richard!" Andrew sounded horrified. "Are you mad? You can't live with this . . . girl in the middle of London!"

"Really, Andrew, you're as bad as Hunch," Mairelon said. He gave Kim an uncertain, sidelong look that Kim, in her confusion, found impossible to interpret. "I'll make Kim my ward; that will satisfy the proprieties."

"But, yes!" Renée said before Andrew could object again. "That will do entirely well. And you and Mademoiselle Kim will stay with me to begin, and there will be no foolish gossip such as Monsieur Andrew Merrill fears, because I will be there and everything will be proper." She tilted her head to study Kim, ignoring the brothers Merrill.

"It is a great pity we cannot take you to France," Renée went on. "But there is a dressmaker I know who will do well enough, although she is entirely English. You will be quite charming in a gown, I think." Her eyes flickered from Kim to Mairelon and back, and she smiled to herself, as if contemplating a private joke.

"Hold on a minute, Renée," Mairelon interrupted. "I'm not spending hours at some dressmaker's. I refuse. Positively."

"But of course you will not," Renée said gently. "You will be spending hours with Milord Shoreham. He will want the details of all your work, and he is very persistent."

Mairelon looked at her with a blank expression that changed slowly to chagrin. "Oh, Lord, you're right again. It'll take hours. Days."

"Naturally," Renée said. "And while you and Milord Shoreham talk, Mademoiselle Kim and I shall shop for the kind of clothes that will be proper for your ward to wear in London." She turned back to Kim and leaned forward conspiratorially. "But we will save the boy's clothing for other times, because, all the same, Monsieur Richard Merrill is not at all proper and of a certainty you will need them."

"It ain't fitting, Master Richard," Hunch grumbled, but he was not chewing on his mustache at all, and Kim decided he was only complaining for the form of the thing.

"Well, Kim?" Mairelon said. "You do want to come, don't you?"

"Come?" Kim shook herself, thinking *Me, a wizard!*, and gave

Mairelon a look full of scorn. "Do I look like a looby? Of course I want to come!"

"Good," Mairelon said, relieved. "That's one thing settled. Now, Hunch, about the wagon—"

He half turned, to include his henchman and his brother in his conversation, and Kim stopped listening. She was going back to London. She'd never have to sleep on the streets again as long as she lived, or bear the cold and the nagging hunger. She had escaped Dan Laverham and the looming shadow of the stews for good. She was going to learn real magic, and not just tricks, but proper wizard's training. She was going to stay with the notorious Mademoiselle Renée D'Auber, who might be willing to teach her a thing or two of a different kind. And she was going to be Mairelon's ward. She wasn't quite sure what that would mean, but it was certain to be interesting. She looked at Mairelon, who was arguing with Hunch and Andrew about the passability of some obscure road in Kent, and shook her head. Interesting wouldn't be the half of it. Slowly she began to smile. After this, anything might happen.

Anything at all.

MAGICIAN'S
WARD

For Lois Bujold,
without whom this would still be stuck in Chapter 7.
Twice.

Acknowledgments

This book would not have been possible, let alone finished, without the aid and comfort of the following people:

Pamela Dean Dyer-Bennet, Beth Friedman, Raphael Carter, Sarah Withee, and Elise Matthesen, who helped with sundry accents and foreign languages, and James Bryant, who provided the answer to a tricky research question. Any errors are, of course, my own.

My critique group, The Usual Suspects past and present, who were amazingly good about sitting through the same scenes over and over until I got them right, and who performed prodigious feats during the final days of production: Lois McMaster Bujold, Peg Kerr Ihinger, Elise Matthesen, Bruce Bethke, and Joel Rosenberg.

My editors, Delia Sherman and Patrick Nielsen Hayden, who were supernaturally patient when patience was most required, and who somehow knew exactly when it was necessary to crank up the heat.

Caroline Stevermer, Rosemary Ighel, Lois Bujold, and Pamela Dyer-Bennet, who provided much appreciated moral support, encouragement, lunches, and a careful eye to period detail.

My family, who were exceedingly understanding as regards late Christmas presents and last-minute cancellations.

one

Cold rain drizzled on the dark London streets—at least, it *looked* cold. Kim peered out her bedroom window at the deserted square two stories below and pulled her shawl closer around her shoulders, though the fire in the grate was almost too warm for comfort. She hadn't had to shelter, shivering, in a doorway for nearly a year, but the memories lingered.

Still no sign of Mairelon. Is he going to stay out all night? Kim thought resentfully. *He gets to jaw with Lord Shoreham and eat at the Royal College of Wizards, and I'm stuck here with a great thick square book and that poker-backed aunt of his.* She shook her head. It was not what she had expected, a year ago when she had agreed to become Mairelon's ward and learn reading and magic. Then, she had thought it would be a great adventure.

" 'Anything might happen,' I thought," Kim said aloud to her reflection in the rain-dark window. " 'Anything at all.' I must have been touched in the head." She crossed her eyes and stuck out her tongue at her mirror image.

"Dicked in the nob, that's what I was," she muttered.

The bedroom door opened. "What did you say, Kim?" Mrs. Lowe asked in a mildly disapproving tone.

With a faint sigh, Kim slid off the window seat and turned. The relentless respectability of Mairelon's paternal aunt was very wearing. It seemed much longer than a week since they'd found her ensconced in the townhouse on their arrival in London. And since they were all technically guests of Mairelon's brother Andrew, who as elder son had inherited the townhouse, there was nothing to be done about Mrs. Lowe except spend time elsewhere. Which Mairelon had been doing rather a lot. Kim wished she had that option. "I didn't say anything," she told Mrs. Lowe in as mild a tone as she could manage.

"I was sure I heard your voice." Mrs. Lowe hesitated. "It wasn't any of that . . . that thieves' cant, was it?"

"Flash lingo," Kim said helpfully.

Mrs. Lowe frowned. "After all my nephew has done for you, the least you could do is to be more careful of your language."

"Mairelon doesn't mind the way I talk."

"My nephew is not always as conscious of the social niceties as he should be," Mrs. Lowe said. "Nonetheless, they must be observed. And you really should refer to him as 'Mr. Merrill.' He is your guardian, and it would show a proper respect."

"Did you want me for something?" Kim asked, hoping to dodge the discussion. "I have studying to do." She waved at the fat, leatherbound book on the nightstand beside the bed, and suppressed a grimace. Three more volumes were waiting for her in the library below. *Why he keeps shoving them at me when he knows I'm no great hand at reading. . . .*

"More magic, I suppose." Mrs. Lowe shook her head. "I'll speak to Richard about that in the morning."

"Speak to him?" Kim said, beginning to be alarmed. For the past week, Mrs. Lowe had made Kim's life a respectable misery. She had insisted that Kim accompany her to pay interminable morning calls on dull but acceptable acquaintances, forbidden all walks alone, and made it quite clear that, in the unlikely event of Kim's encountering any of her former friends, Kim was to cut them dead. Thus far, however, she had not attempted to interfere with Kim's magic lessons.

"I am sure you will have plenty of opportunity to study when you are back in Kent," Mrs. Lowe said. "Magic is all very well, but it is hardly a necessary branch of knowledge for a young woman in your situation. While you are in London, we must make the most of your chances. I cannot say I have any great hope of success, given your . . . circumstances, but there are one or two possibilities—That is why I wished to talk to you tonight."

"I don't understand," Kim said warily.

"Mrs. Hardcastle knows a gentleman who sounds as if he will do very nicely. Well, perhaps not a *gentleman*, but respectable enough. She has arranged for us to meet him tomorrow afternoon, and I wished to warn you to be on your best behavior."

"Best behavior—You can't be thinking of getting me leg-shackled to some gentry cull!"

"If what you just said was some sort of reference to arranging a suitable marriage for you, yes, that is precisely what I was referring to," Mrs. Lowe replied stiffly.

Kim didn't know whether to be amused or appalled. Her, married to a toff? In her wildest notions, she had never thought of such a thing. She looked at Mrs. Lowe, and her amusement died. The woman was serious. "It'd never work."

"It certainly won't if you burst out with a remark like that over Mrs. Hardcastle's tea table. Consider carefully what I have said, and be prepared tomorrow, if you please. I am afraid that your . . . interesting background means that you are unlikely to have many opportunities of this nature; you would be ill advised to waste this one. Good night."

Kim stared at the closing door, then flung herself back into the window seat. *Marriage!* She's *the one who's dicked in the nob. There isn't a toff in London who would marry a penniless, nameless sharper, even if I have gone all respectable.* She shifted restlessly in the window seat. Respectability did not sit comfortably with her, but what other choices did she have?

She couldn't go back to the streets, even if she were mad enough to want to. What with all the regular eating, she'd filled out more than she'd have thought possible; posing as a boy now would be out of the question. She hadn't the training to be a housemaid or take up a trade, even if she could find someone to hire her. Mrs. Lowe's "respectable gentleman" wasn't a serious possibility, but sooner or later Kim would have to think of something. She couldn't stay Mairelon's ward forever.

Though that doesn't seem to have occurred to him.

But Richard Merrill—whom she still could not think of as anything but Mairelon the Magician—didn't look at things the way other people did. *Well, if he did, he'd never have got himself made my guardian.* For all the awareness he showed, you'd think he was perfectly willing to go on feeding, clothing, and housing Kim until they both died of old age.

Maybe she should ask him about it. Maybe she would, if she could figure out what "it" was, exactly—or at least well enough to explain. "I'm bored" would only get her a larger stack of books to study; "I'm not happy" sounded ungrateful; and "Your aunt is a Friday-faced noodle" was insulting. But there had to be some way to put it.

Meanwhile, she had three more pages of Shepherd's *Elementary In-*

vocations to decipher before morning. She didn't want Mairelon to think that she wasn't working at her lessons, not if that Mrs. Lowe was going to ask him to stop them. Sighing, Kim climbed out of the window seat.

The text on magic occupied Kim for several hours, but when she finally laid it aside and went to bed, she found it impossible to sleep. She lay in darkness, staring up at the plaster ceiling and listening for the clatter of Mairelon's carriage on the cobblestones outside. Around her, the household quieted as the housemaids and sculleys finished their days' work and climbed the narrow servants' stair to their beds under the eaves. The watchman's cry, muffled and perfunctory, came faintly through the window. *Poor old cull,* Kim thought as a gust of wind sent raindrops rattling like gunfire across the panes. *I'm glad I'm not out in this.*

Suddenly she sat bolt upright in the bed. *That sounded like . . .* The noise came again, soft but clear. *Someone's downstairs. Someone who's got no business being there.*

Kim slid out of bed. Her eyes slid past the bellpull without pausing. If she summoned a maid, she'd only have to send the girl for a footman, and by the time all the running around was done, the cull downstairs would have gotten away. And if she was wrong, if there wasn't anyone, she'd have to endure endless lectures from Mrs. Lowe. She could call someone when she was sure.

She started for the door, then stopped. Her white nightdress stood out in the darkness; she didn't want the cracksman to spot her and pike off before she got a footman or two to help catch him. Her dressing gown was a dark, rich blue that would blend with the shadows; she picked it up and struggled into it. Then she eased the door open and slipped into the darkened hallway.

Moving lightly, she made for the stairs. Another soft, scuffing sound came from below, followed by a distinct creak; hadn't *anyone* else noticed? *Probably a novice, on his first crack lay. Somebody should have told him to stick by the walls. Mother Tibb wouldn't have sent anybody out that didn't know at least that much.*

Suiting her own actions to her thoughts, Kim plastered herself against one wall and started down the stairs, setting her bare feet as near the wall as she could. No creaks betrayed her. Halfway down, she caught the flash of a dark lantern and froze. The light flickered past. A moment later, a figure skulked down the hallway, opening doors and peering through them. The strong smell of a cheap lard candle and the scent of wet wool preceded him; he must have been standing in the rain for some time to be so drenched. Finally, with a grunt of satisfaction, the man let the last door swing fully open and disappeared into the library.

The *library?* What could a thief want from the library? The silver was downstairs, on the ground floor, and Mairelon's brother didn't keep valuables on display in his townhouse. The whole thing had more of a rum look by the minute. Kim frowned, considering; then a hastily stifled expletive decided her. There was no knowing what this cove was up to. She'd just make sure he couldn't pike off, and then she'd call the footmen.

Silently, she crept down the remaining steps. A cautious look showed the cracksman bent over the end table, peering at the shelves behind it by the light of the dark lantern. Kim smiled grimly and, holding the handle to prevent the betraying click of the latch snapping into place, carefully closed the library door. Now, if she could just lock it in place somehow . . . But the door had no lock, and there was nothing nearby she could use to jam it. Magic, perhaps? She ran over in her mind the short list of spells she could cast with some reliability. There was one that might do the trick, if she could get it right.

She took a deep breath, then focused her eyes on the handle. In her mind she pictured it as it was, staying as it was, motionless, frozen, immovable, and in a voice barely above a whisper began the spell that would make the image real.

An outraged bellow and a loud crash from inside the library rattled her concentration. "—*sta, atque*—" she continued, and then the door burst open, knocking her sprawling. An instant later, the escaping housebreaker stumbled over her and went down. Kim shouted and grabbed at him. Her hands slid against silk, then tightened around thick, damp wool. The burglar twisted and something tore; the man scrambled away from her, leaving her holding a scrap of cloth.

Kim tried to roll to her feet and ended up tangled in her dressing gown. The man regained his feet and pelted down the hall, just as a sleepy-eyed footman appeared on the far stairs. The burglar shoved the hapless footman against the wall and dashed down the stairs and out of sight. Crashing noises and yells marked his continued progress. The footman recovered himself and plunged after his assailant. More shouts drifted upward.

As Kim, muttering curses, struggled to a standing position at last, she heard footsteps on the stairs behind her. She turned and found Mrs. Lowe, lamp in hand, staring at her with shock and disapproval.

"Kim! Whatever have you been doing? And in such a state!"

Kim glanced down. Her dressing gown had come undone, and she showed distinct traces, even in the lamplight, of having rolled about on the floor. A torn and ragged bit of lace trailed off the hem of her nightdress, and her hair was probably every-which-way, too. Mrs. Lowe, of course, was turned out in more proper style—not a wisp of gray hair escaped from under her dainty lace cap, and her dressing gown was crisper and neater than Kim's had been even before her encounter with the burglar. Kim pulled her dressing gown closed and discovered that several of the buttons were missing.

"I heard someone in the library," Kim said as she scanned the floor for the buttons. One of them lay next to the baseboard, beside a piece of wood with a splintered end. Kim bent toward it.

"Nonsense. You were dreaming, I'm sure."

"I wasn't asleep." Kim reached for the button, and her fingers brushed the splintered wood. A light tingling ran up her arm, and she jerked her hand back in surprise. *Magic?* She touched it again. *Not a strong spell, but recent. Mairelon'll want a look at this.* Frowning, she picked up wood and button together and shoved them in the pocket of her dressing gown.

"If you *did* hear something, it was probably one of the maids. They keep different hours in town, and I expect you are not yet accustomed—"

Kim tucked another button in the pocket of her dressing gown and looked back at Mrs. Lowe. "It wasn't one of the maids. They wouldn't be carrying on like that if it had been," she added, waving at the stairs. The shouts and crashing noises had ceased, but it was nonetheless obvious that there was far more activity on the ground floor than was normal at this time of night.

"At least you had the good sense to put on your dressing gown before you came down," Mrs. Lowe said, tacitly conceding the point. "Still, wandering about the house en *déshabillé* at this hour is most irregular, no matter what your reasons."

"I bet Mairelon won't think so." The injudicious words slipped out before Kim thought.

Mrs. Lowe's thin lips pressed together in a hard line. Then, in deceptively soft tones, she said, "Mr. Merrill, Kim, not Mairelon. Showing proper respect is—Where do you think you are going?"

"To find out whether they've caught the flash cull that was turning out the library."

"Indeed you shall not," Mrs. Lowe said. "You will return to your room at once, and we will discuss matters further in the morning."

"What matters?" said a new voice from the lower stairs.

"Mairelon!" Kim said, turning toward the voice with a sigh of relief.

two

Richard Merrill climbed the last few steps and stood eyeing Kim and Mrs. Lowe with a quizzical expression on his round, cheerful face. His dark hair looked damp and a little disheveled, but his coat and pantaloons were immaculate. Kim wondered what he had done with his cloak. *Probably left it in a heap in the front hall because the footmen were too busy chasing burglars to take it.*

"What matters?" he asked again. "And why wait to discuss them? From the look of things, no one's going to get any sleep for hours. Kim, Harry says he rescued you from someone, or possibly several someones, who from his description were apparently seven feet tall and more indestructible than the strong man down at Astley's Amphitheatre. Ought I to congratulate him, or should he merely be sent to the kitchen to sleep it off?"

Before Kim could answer, Mrs. Lowe frowned and said in tones that promised dire retribution for someone, "Who is Harry?"

"One of the footmen. He's on his way to the pantry to receive a hero's due, on the strength of a bruised shin and a knock on the head. The question is, does he deserve it?"

"He got banged up against the wall when that cracksman piked off, that's all," Kim said. "Unless they had a run-in later."

"No, the fellow got clean away. Still, I think we'll leave Harry to his laurels, well-earned or not. What I want now is the rest of the story." He looked at Kim expectantly.

"I was upstairs when I heard—"

"Not tonight, Kim," Mrs. Lowe broke in. "You have had quite

enough excitement for one evening, and tomorrow is going to be a busy day. I'm sure that if Richard thinks about it, he'll agree that you ought to be in bed. You'll have plenty of time to talk in the morning. Come along."

Mairelon put out a restraining hand. "I appreciate your concern, Aunt, but I wish to speak to Kim now, if she's agreeable. It won't take long."

"Of course I'm agreeable," Kim said.

"That's settled, then." Turning his head, he called down the stairs, "Hunch! Bring a lamp when you come up."

Mrs. Lowe looked startled. "Kim is not the best judge of what is most appropriate, Richard. If you will stop for a moment and think, you will see that."

"What? No, no, Kim is quite good at this sort of thing. Go on, Kim—you were upstairs, and you heard something."

"She will catch a chill, running about half dressed at this hour," Mrs. Lowe said firmly. "She belongs upstairs in her bed."

"Half dressed?" Mairelon said with mild interest. He looked at Kim and shook his head. "Nonsense. She's wearing a dressing gown. Now, I'll grant you, it wouldn't be quite the thing if she were going to go walking in Grosvenor Square in the rain, but I promise you I won't let her. We'll stay right here in the library."

"Kim needs her rest, Richard."

"She's more likely to get it if she has a chance to talk first," Mairelon said, frowning slightly.

"I'm not sleepy," Kim put in.

Mrs. Lowe sighed. "If you insist, Richard. I shall join you as chaperone, of course."

"I think not." Mairelon's attention was firmly fixed on his aunt at last, and his expression had gone bland and unfathomable, the way it did when he was about to be particularly stubborn about something. Mrs. Lowe did not seem to realize it.

"Richard, Kim's reputation—"

"—is quite safe. I'm her guardian, remember." His tone was polite and gentle, but brooked no contradiction.

Mrs. Lowe hesitated, then acquiesced. "Very well, Richard. No doubt you have your reasons. I must tell you, however, that it is most irregular, and the possible consequences—"

"In the morning, Aunt," Mairelon said. He glanced at Kim and gave a tiny nod in the direction of the library. Turning back to Mrs. Lowe, he went on in a soothing tone, "As you said, it is late, and I'm sure this has been a strain on your nerves. Things will look different when you've had a good night's sleep."

Kim slipped quietly around behind him and into the darkened library. The murmur of voices in the hall continued; then she heard heavy footsteps on the stairs, and Mairelon's voice: "The library, Hunch." She stepped back as Mairelon's manservant came through the door, carrying a candle. He was tall and thin, and everything about him drooped: his shoulders, his mustache, the baggy trousers he insisted on wearing.

" 'Ere now, Kim, where—oh, there you are. Stay still; I'll 'ave these 'ere lamps lit in no time."

Light flared, then steadied as Hunch adjusted the lampwick. "There. Now—'Struth! That 'Arry wasn't 'alf right, by the look of it. What 'appened?"

The burglar's dark lantern lay on its side next to an overturned end table; it was a good thing the candle had gone out. A dozen books were scattered across the floor, some looking as if they had fallen when the table went over, others as if they had been dropped or thrown.

"An excellent question, Hunch." Mairelon entered, closing the door firmly behind him. "We've heard Harry's tale; I trust yours will be somewhat . . . less imaginative, Kim."

"I thought I heard something, so I came down to have a look," Kim said. "A man with a dark lantern was in the hall, looking in all the rooms. He went into the library. I was going to lock him in and call a footman, except he must of heard me working the spell or something, because he came charging out while I was still in the middle of it. He tripped over me, and I yelled, and he got away from me. The footman—Harry?— was coming up to see what the noise was, and the rum cove ran slap into him before he piked off down the stairs. That's all."

"Brief and to the point," Mairelon said. "Though not, perhaps, up to Aunt Agatha's standards of elocution. What a good thing we sent her off to bed."

"I found this in the hallway after the turn-up," Kim said, pulling the scrap of wood from her pocket and laying it on top of the books. "I don't know what it is, but it's been magicked."

Mairelon picked up the scrap and turned it over in his hands. It looked like a piece of a wooden rod, about four inches long and as big around as Kim's little finger. "Technically, the term is 'infused,' not 'magicked,' but in a general sort of way you're quite right."

"What's the difference?"

"Something that's been enchanted, or 'magicked,' as you put it, has had a spell cast *on* it. Something that's been infused has had a spell stored *in* it." Mairelon frowned at the piece of rod.

"What kind of spell?" Kim asked.

Mairelon blinked, then smiled. "That *is* the next question. One of them, anyway. Normally, once the spell has been invoked, it's used up— there's no way to tell what it was."

"That's normally," Kim said, recognizing the tone. "What's weird about this?"

Mairelon's smile broadened. "Whoever made it was exceedingly clumsy; it's as if he put the spell together from bits and pieces. And not all the bits and pieces went off when the wizard invoked it."

" 'E's a beginner, then?" Hunch said.

"Mmm. Possibly. But Kim's a beginner, and she could do a better job than this."

"Well, are there enough bits left that you can tell what it was supposed to do?" Kim said, trying to decide whether she should be pleased or insulted by the comparison.

"Let's find out, shall we?" Mairelon pointed the piece of rod at the nearest bookcase and muttered something under his breath.

Nothing happened. Mairelon frowned and said something longer that sounded like Latin to Kim. As he spoke, he waved the rod in a slow circle.

Several of the books began to glow with a soft, golden light. Mairelon gave an exclamation of satisfaction, then began muttering rapidly, moving the rod in a rapid, complex pattern. The glow dimmed, then steadied. After a moment, Mairelon relaxed and set the rod on the table.

Kim looked down. The books that lay scattered about the floor were all glowing as well. "This is crazy! He couldn't of sherried off with all those."

"If it were that simple, we wouldn't have books all over the library floor," Mairelon said. "I'll wager he was looking for one or two particular volumes. The question is, which ones?"

"If you was to clean up a bit o' this 'ere mess, you might 'ave an easier time figuring it out," Hunch said.

"An excellent notion." Mairelon stepped forward and lifted the little table back onto its crocodile paws. "Put the books here, and we'll have a look."

Hunch picked up the scattered volumes, while Kim rather gingerly helped Mairelon pull glowing books from the shelves When they were all piled on the end table, they made an impressive heap.

"Now, what have we here?" Mairelon murmured. "*The Mountains of Doubt, Collegium Sorceria, Discoverer, Après Cinq Cents Ans, Fire Keepers Vol. VI*—I wonder why he didn't want the first five?—*A Pottery Pigeon, Reflecting Quadrille, Maturing Without Heaviness* . . . Our housebreaker appears to have excellent taste."

"Well, 'e can just taste things somewheres else next time," Hunch muttered.

"I am inclined to agree with your recommendation, Hunch," Mairelon said. "I don't suppose you got a look at his face during all the excitement, Kim?"

"No," Kim said with regret. "I got a piece of his coat, though. He's a toff, or someone as wants to be."

"Really?" Mairelon looked at Kim with interest. "How did you deduce that?"

"He was wearing a silk waistcoat. I felt it. And this isn't homespun." Kim pulled the torn piece of wool from her pocket. Two buttons came with it, and bounced off under the settee.

"Ripped his coat, did he?" Mairelon said. "How lucky for us."

"Lucky?" Kim said, mystified.

"Yes, of course." He crossed to the heavy table in the middle of the library and studied it a moment, frowning. "Help me move this closer to the center of the room. Hunch, get me the blue chalk and a pot of ink. Oh, and an unused candle for Kim."

"You ain't doing nothin' dreadful now, Master Richard," Hunch said in a stern tone. "Not in Master Andrew's 'ouse."

"Hmm? Oh, not at all, Hunch," Mairelon said as he and Kim shifted the table. "It's only a spell Shoreham's been working on for a while—an adaptation of the standard scrying spell. He showed it to me the day before yesterday; it's quite clever. You'll see."

"All right, then," Hunch said, though he continued to frown. "Lord Shore'am is a proper gentleman."

Mairelon shot his servant an amused glance and pulled a handkerchief from his pocket. Carefully, he spread it over the tabletop, smoothing the creases with his fingertip. The corners of the handkerchief hung over the center of the table's sides, so that a triangle of bare wood was left in each corner.

"Yes, but what is this spell supposed to *do?*" Kim said.

"Help us catch our burglar, with luck," Mairelon replied. "Hunch, where's that ink? Thank you. Give Kim the chalk." He set a small ink bottle on one of the bare corners of the tabletop.

"*Mairelon—*"

"You'll see in a minute. Now, what can I use—ah, yes, this will do nicely." He plucked a small silver salver from a shelf beside the door and positioned it carefully in the exact center of the handkerchief. "There. Hand me that scrap of cloth you found."

"Mairelon, I'm never going to learn any magic if you don't give me any explanations," Kim said in exasperation as she gave him the piece of wool.

"And you'll never be a great magician if you can't make half an understanding do for a start," Mairelon said, dropping the scrap into the salver. "A competent one, perhaps, but not a great one. The chalk, if you please."

Sighing, Kim handed him the chalk. He sketched three careful crosses in the remaining corners of the table, then drew an unsteady circle around the salver on the handkerchief. Absently, he stuck the chalk in his coat pocket as he surveyed the setup. Then he looked up at Kim. "Now you may demonstrate the results of your studies for me. I want you to set the ward."

"Me?" Kim stared at the candle in her hand, suddenly appalled. The warding spell was nearly always set when a complex or dangerous enchantment was being attempted; in theory, it protected the mage from outside interference, and any bystanders from the consequences of a spell gone wrong. In practice, the degree of protection such a spell afforded was directly related to the skill of the spellcaster. An apprentice's ward was unlikely to stand up to more than an apprentice-level mistake. And Mairelon wanted Kim to set a ward while he worked a new spell.

"Don't worry," Mairelon said. "This is a relatively simple enchantment. Normally, I wouldn't bother with a ward at all, even though this is the first time I've ever cast it. But you can use the practice, and it will keep our work from disturbing anyone. Or from attracting attention outside the house," he added as an afterthought.

Only partially reassured, Kim nodded. She thought for a moment, to make sure she had the steps of the warding spell clear in her mind. Then she took a deep breath. "*Fiat lux,*" she said, concentrating on the candle.

The candlewick burst into flame. Kim held it still for a moment, until the smell of melted beeswax reached her and the tingly pressure of a spell in progress ran up and down her arms. Then, keeping her eyes

fixed on the candle, Kim turned and walked in a slow, clockwise circle
around Mairelon and the table. As she walked, she recited the words of
the warding spell four times, once for each side of the table. She had
more difficulty than she had expected in judging her speed correctly so
that the words came out even, but she managed it. When she reached
the spot where she had begun, she turned to face Mairelon and said the
final "*fiat*." With considerable relief, she felt the ward rise around them
like an invisible curtain.

"Very good," Mairelon said softly. "I couldn't have done better myself. Now, watch carefully, and try to split your concentration so that you
can still hold the ward while you watch. You may not always have someone handy to cast a ward for you when it's needed, so you'll need to learn
to hold it without even thinking about it."

"Sort of like picking a lock and listening for the nabbing culls at the
same time," Kim said, nodding carefully. She felt the ward shift as she
spoke, and hastily returned her attention to it. When it was steady again,
she whispered, "Only trickier."

Mairelon laughed. "Yes, I imagine it would be. Very well; it's my
turn."

He picked up the scrap of cloth and concentrated for a moment,
then crumpled it and dropped it into the salver. The springy wool flattened out immediately, but the scrap was too small to cover much of the
salver. Uncorking the bottle of ink, Mairelon poured it slowly over the
cloth. The ink soaked quickly into the wool, then rose around it in a flat
black pool. Mairelon studied it a moment, then picked up the salver and
tilted it this way and that until the ink coated the bottom with shiny
blackness.

When he was satisfied at last, he set the salver on the handkerchief
once more. Holding his left hand over it, he began speaking, too rapidly
for Kim to follow. The tingling sensation of a spell in process struck her
with renewed force, and she had to concentrate to keep control of the
ward. Mindful of his instructions, she tried to pay attention to Mairelon's
spellcasting, but her Latin and Greek were still rudimentary. She recognized perhaps one word in twenty, but even the unintelligible phrases
had the hard-edged feel that only came with magic. They hung in the air
around Mairelon's hand, building the invisible, dangerous structure of
the spell.

Kim suppressed a shiver. She did not want to distract Mairelon; even
a small mistake would send razor-edged words flying like shards of shattered glass. She wondered whether she would ever be sure enough of her

control to risk building a spell around her own hand. It seemed unlikely, but a year ago the thought of learning magic at all had seemed not merely unlikely, but impossible.

Mairelon finished speaking and, without moving his arm, folded his outstretched fingers in toward his palm. The hovering spell slid past his hand onto the ink-covered salver. "Now, we look," he said.

Puzzled, Kim stared at him; then she realized that he meant for her to look at the salver. She lowered her gaze, and saw that a picture had formed on the surface of the ink, like a reflection in a mirror or a puddle of water.

A man muffled in a scarf, top hat, and long cloak hurried along a narrow street. The shop windows behind him were dark and shuttered, and the wind whipped his cloak out behind him. "Well, well," Mairelon murmured. "It looks as if you were right, Kim. Our housebreaker is a gentleman. Let's see. . . ."

The picture in the ink wobbled, then shifted so that the man was hurrying directly toward them. His head was down, and one hand gripped the brim of his hat; between that and the scarf, little of his face was visible. Gold gleamed on his middle finger, and Kim leaned forward to look more closely.

"Blast!" said Mairelon. "I wanted a look at his face. Perhaps if we try another angle—"

The image wobbled and distorted, like a reflection in water when a pebble drops into it. Kim got a brief impression of blue eyes and a damp wisp of hair plastered wetly to a high forehead, and then the picture was gone. The shiny surface of the ink reflected only a glimmer of light from Kim's candle.

Mairelon scowled at the salver, then reached for the ink-soaked wool. As he lifted the cloth, the ink slid off like hot oil running out of a pan, leaving the threads clean. "You can drop the ward now, Kim," he said as he pocketed the scrap.

Obediently, Kim recited the closing phrase and blew out the candle. Hunch collected it and the empty ink bottle and carried them off. Mairelon continued to frown at the salver. "That was not nearly as useful as I'd hoped," he said. "Perhaps I should have waited; we might have gotten a glimpse of his rooms. But I was hoping to see his face, and I didn't want him to have a chance to change his coat."

"Well, if you'd waited much longer, he wouldn't of had the coat at all, I'll bet," Kim said.

"Why do you say that?"

"Why else would a toff be on Petticoat Lane at this time of night, unless he had something for the togs-men?"

Mairelon blinked. "Petticoat Lane? You're sure?"

Kim snorted. "I spent enough time there. He was just down from Flash Annie's, by where Willie Bast used to lay up. It's a good job for him that it's a mucky night out, or he'd be rid of more than his coat."

Hunch returned and picked up the salver with a disapproving look. "Are you done with this, Master Richard?"

"What? Yes, of course. Did you notice anything else, Kim?"

"He has blue eyes," Kim offered. "And he wears a gold ring with a flower on it and a ruby in the center."

"And he has his boots from Hoby," Mairelon said. "It's not much to go on, but it's a help. Now, let's make a list of these books and see what we can tell from it."

The pile of books on the table had stopped glowing sometime during Mairelon's scrying spell. Mairelon sat down and began sorting through them, while Hunch brought him a pen, paper, and a fresh bottle of ink. As Mairelon wrote titles, Kim shifted books so he could see the ones he hadn't written down yet, and in ten minutes the list was complete.

"There," Mairelon said, and glanced around the library. "I believe that's all we can do tonight." He picked up his list and, in the absence of a blotter, blew gently on the ink to hasten its drying.

"What about tomorrow?" Kim said.

"Tomorrow, I'll take this over to the Royal College and see whether Kerring has any thoughts on it."

"Who's Kerring?"

"Lord Kerring is head archivist at the Royal College of Wizards," Mairelon replied. "If there's a connection among all these titles, he'll spot it. He might even have some idea which wizards would be likely to know a bit about burglary."

"That cove didn't know the first thing about the crack lay," Kim said. "I wouldn't of heard him at all, if he had."

Mairelon looked thoughtful. "Possibly he's more of a magician than I'd been thinking. If he was depending on magic to pull off his theft—"

"He was still a clunker," Kim said firmly. "And I didn't notice any spellcasting."

"He invoked the spell he had stored in this," Mairelon said, holding up the broken rod.

"Then why didn't I notice it?"

"Because it was *invoked*, not *cast*," Mairelon replied. "The spellcasting took place when the spell was originally stored in the rod, which could have been hours ago, or even days. When the spell is invoked, you wouldn't notice anything unless you were touching either the storage container or the object the spell was intended to affect."

"I think I see," Kim said.

"If our burglar had another trick or two like this, he could have used them without alerting you," Mairelon went on, fingering the rod. "Rather a good precaution to take if you're going to burgle a wizard's house, now that I think of it. I believe we should set a few wards around the house tomorrow, just in case he comes back."

"What if that there burglar comes back *tonight?*" Hunch said.

"Then the library will no doubt be a wreck when we come down in the morning, Harry will probably collect another lump on his head, Aunt Agatha will be prostrate with the vapours, and I shall have to apologize to everyone for my carelessness." Mairelon smiled sweetly at Hunch. "Unless, of course, you spend the night here, on watch."

"I might 'ave known you'd think of that," Hunch muttered. "Well, as long as you don't go 'aring off after 'im while I'm busy elsewhere."

"Hunch! Would I do such a thing?"

"You 'ave before."

"I'm a reformed character."

Kim choked back a snort of laughter. Mairelon turned and looked at her with mock disapproval.

"I seem to recall telling Aunt Agatha that I'd send you up before you took a chill. As we appear to be finished here, for the time being—"

"As long as you don't go haring off after that burglar without me," Kim echoed.

"You're getting to be as bad as Hunch," Mairelon said, and Kim laughed and left him.

three

When Kim came down to breakfast the following morning, Mairelon was there before her. Mrs. Lowe was fortunately not in evidence, and Kim bolted her meal in hopes of getting away before she turned up. After five minutes, Mairelon looked up and said mildly, "What's the rush?"

"Mrs. Lowe," Kim replied, then flushed as she realized how it must sound. Well, she'd wanted to talk to Mairelon about his aunt, hadn't she? She just hadn't planned on blurting it out over breakfast. She must be more tired than she'd thought.

"Ah." Mairelon looked suddenly thoughtful. "Has Aunt Agatha been so much of a problem?"

"Nothing I can't manage," Kim said. Then honesty forced her to add, "Yet."

Mairelon glanced at Kim's almost empty plate. "I see."

Gathering her courage, Kim said, "Yesterday, she said something about—"

The far door opened, and Mrs. Lowe entered. "Good morning, Richard. You're up early. Good morning, Kim."

"I've a busy day ahead of me," Mairelon said, rising politely to greet her.

Mrs. Lowe helped herself to eggs and herring from the platters on the sideboard, then joined them at the table. Much to Kim's relief, she took the chair beside Mairelon. "I hope all this running about will not go on indefinitely," she said, picking up her fork.

"Some things are difficult to be definite about," Mairelon said.

"Your levity is unbecoming, Richard, and not at all to the point," Mrs. Lowe said, giving him a stern look. "In another week, the Season will be upon us, and as you have chosen to come to Town for once, I shall expect you to find a little more time for your social and family obligations."

"Oh, you may expect whatever you like, Aunt." Mairelon's tone was careless, but there was a set to his shoulders that told Kim he was not pleased.

"People are already arriving, and I fear there are still quite a few who are . . . confused about your proper standing."

"I can't imagine why. I'm the least confusing person I know."

Kim choked on her toast. Mrs. Lowe frowned, but it was impossible to tell whether it was at Kim or at Mairelon.

"I think you are being deliberately dense, Richard," Mrs. Lowe said after a moment. "I am of course referring to your role in the theft of the Saltash Set from the Royal College of Wizards seven years ago."

"I had no role whatever in the *theft* of the Saltash Set," Mairelon said, frowning. "I had a role in its *recovery*. Rather a large one."

"Yes, of course, Richard, but still . . . Your innocence may have been established in a legal sense—"

"Not 'may have been,' " Mairelon put in, his frown deepening. "Has been."

"—but there are those in Society who still have doubts. Your . . . eccentricities since your return have done nothing to reassure the *ton*."

"Eccentricities?" Mairelon raised his eyebrows.

"As you chose not to appear socially during last year's Season, you perhaps do not realize just how much talk there has been." The muscles in Mrs. Lowe's neck tightened, and Kim realized that she was carefully not looking in Kim's direction.

Kim tensed angrily, then forced herself to relax. It wasn't exactly a surprise that Mrs. Lowe disapproved of her, and it might be true that the existence of Mairelon's unusual ward had somehow tarnished his reputation. Toffs were odd that way; even after a year of life among the gentry, Kim knew she didn't understand them.

"Gossip drives the Season," Mairelon said, and there was a faint edge beneath the outward blandness of his tone. "I'm glad to have been of service."

"It is no service to yourself or your family," Mrs. Lowe said severely. "If you do not exert yourself a little this year, I shall have to wash my hands of you."

Kim looked up hopefully, but managed to bite her tongue before anything untoward slipped out. Mairelon, however, caught her expression and laughed. His reaction drew his aunt's attention to Kim, and, after giving them both a quelling look, Mrs. Lowe said, "There is another thing I have been meaning to speak to you about, Richard."

"And what is that?"

"Your ward's education," Mrs. Lowe replied, and Kim's stomach clenched.

"Kim has been doing very well," Mairelon said. "She's learned to read, and her magic skills are coming along nicely. It will be a while before she has the necessary Latin and Greek, of course, but she has a remarkable memory for chants and invocations, and an eye for detail that will be very useful when she gets to more advanced work."

Pleased and a little surprised by the unexpected compliment, Kim looked down at her plate.

Mrs. Lowe coughed. "I was referring to her *social* education, Richard. It has been sadly neglected. No doubt you had your reasons, and it could not matter much while she was safely in Kent, but now that you have brought her to London it is imperative that she learn how to go on."

"Why?" Kim demanded, looking up. "It's not as if I'm going to balls or anything."

"So long as you are my nephew's ward, you will undoubtedly meet persons of consequence from time to time," Mrs. Lowe said. "Your behavior toward them will reflect on your guardian, and on the rest of his family. And while the Merrill family is undeniably well-connected and well-off—"

Forty thousand pounds in the Funds is only "well-off"? Kim barely managed to stop herself from shaking her head in disbelief.

"—connections are no protection from scandal." She turned to Mairelon. "So long as her time is so completely occupied by her magic studies, Kim is unlikely to learn what she needs to know in order to cope with Society."

"But does Society know how to cope with Kim?" Mairelon murmured. "Still, perhaps you're right." He looked at Kim. "How would you like to come along to the Royal College of Wizards with me this morning? It's time you had a look at it, and I'm sure you'll like Kerring."

Kim, caught with her mouth full, could only nod emphatically. Mrs. Lowe frowned. "Richard! That is not at all what I meant."

"No? Well, I'm sure it will work out."

"Furthermore, Kim and I have an important engagement this afternoon for tea," Mrs. Lowe said. "She can't possibly spend the day at the Royal College."

"Oh, it won't take all day," Mairelon assured her. "Kim, if you're finished lingering over your breakfast, we should be going."

Kim dropped her cutlery at once and stood up. Mrs. Lowe frowned. "Richard, you can't take that girl out in—I mean, her conduct is not always to be depended upon."

Mairelon smiled seraphically. "According to you, neither is mine. We'll make a splendid pair. But don't worry; Hunch will keep us on the near side of acceptable behavior. Kim?"

Choking back laughter, Kim followed him to the door, while Mairelon's aunt sputtered in annoyance behind them.

The Royal College of Wizards occupied a long, rectangular building on the Thames, across from Westminster Abbey. The central section dated back almost to the Conquest; the rest was the work of latter-day heads of the college who had maintained their privileged position against subsequent kings and bishops alike. Westminster Hall, where Parliament met, had had to expand into a palace upriver, instead of onto the desirable land already occupied by the wizards.

Kim did not have much chance to study the outside of the building. As soon as their coach pulled up at the entrance, Mairelon jumped down before the footman could reach the carriage door. He headed briskly for the weathered oak doors of the college, leaving Kim no choice but to hurry after. Inside, they whisked past the main hall, allowing Kim only a glimpse of threadbare banners and stone pillars, and a brief whiff of musty air. They climbed a narrow flight of stone stairs, whose centers had been worn down a good two inches by centuries of magicians hurrying up and down. At last, they emerged in a small, bare entrance room with two other doors. Without hesitation, Mairelon crossed to the far door and tugged sharply on the faded bellpull beside it.

"Now, if Marchmain hasn't got all the apprentices busy hunting out historical documents for some project or other—Ah, here we are."

The right-hand door opened, and a slender, brown-haired young man entered and peered at them nearsightedly. "May I be of assistance?"

"I'm Richard Merrill, and this is my apprentice, Kim. We need to see Lord Kerring, if he's here. Is he?"

"I believe so," said the young man, "but he's busy."

"Kerring's always busy. We'll see him anyway. Come along, Kim."

"I don't think that's a good—" The young man broke off. Mairelon had already brushed past him and disappeared through the doorway.

"Don't worry," Kim told him as she followed Mairelon. "If this Lord Kerring cove knows Mairelon—I mean, Mr. Merrill—then he'll know who to blame for interrupting him. And it won't be you."

With the apprentice trailing after, they made their way through a maze of narrow corridors. Finally, Mairelon stopped before a door that, to Kim, looked exactly like all the others they had just passed. He waited just long enough for Kim and the apprentice to catch up, then opened the door and went in.

The room on the other side was much larger than Kim had expected, but there was very little space to walk in. Bookcases not only lined the walls but poked out at right angles to them, leaving only narrow aisles which were further choked by occasional precarious stacks of books on the floor. A narrow table beside the door was piled shoulder-high with books, and there were more books under it. The room smelled of musty paper, old leather, and dust. Kim sneezed.

From one of the alcoves, a deep voice boomed, "What's that? Who's there? Never mind, just go away. I'm working."

"You're always working, Kerring," Mairelon said. "We'll leave as soon as we've gotten a couple of answers."

A very hairy head poked around the side of one of the bookcases. "You're not going to get them that—Richard Merrill! Why didn't you say it was you? What have you gotten into this time?"

As he spoke, Lord Kerring emerged from behind the bookcase, and Kim could not help staring. At first, she thought he was short, but as he came toward them she realized that he was actually of average height; he only looked short because he was so round. He was of middle age, and his clothes looked like something out of one of the ragbags on Threadneedle Street—they had clearly been of excellent quality when they were new, but now they were so rumpled and dusty that they would not have looked out of place on a costermonger in the Hungerford Market. A tuft of cat hair clung to the back of one sleeve. He had dark, curly hair and a bushy beard, both much in need of trimming.

Kim stared. *He's a* lord? *And a wizard to boot?*

"Come in, sit down," Lord Kerring said, waving the relieved apprentice out the door. "Is this that young wizard you found last year? Introduce me."

"I'll be happy to, when you give me a moment's breathing room,"

Mairelon said. "Kerring, my ward and apprentice, Kim. Kim, this is Lord Kerring, one of the senior wizards of the college."

"Enchanted," Kerring said, and bowed with unexpected grace. His eyes twinkled as he added, "Though not in the literal sense. Why haven't you brought her before? Will you be coming out this year, Miss Merrill?"

"Just Kim. I don't think so." *Or rather, when hell freezes over.* She had a momentary, dazzling vision of herself whirling across the dance floor at an elaborate ball, then shook her head. *Even if I got an invitation, I'd end up sitting out. The Society toffs agree with Mrs. Lowe.* "Mr. Merrill has been very kind, but I don't really belong in Society."

Kerring gave her a sharp look, as if he knew exactly what she had been thinking. "Nonsense, my dear. A wizard is the social equal of anyone."

The beginnings of a frown vanished from Mairelon's face. "You're quite right, Kerring, and it's a solution I hadn't thought of. Thank you."

"You're welcome. I think." Kerring looked at Mairelon blankly; when this was not enough to produce an explanation, he opened his mouth to continue. Mairelon forestalled him.

"Now, if you'll just give me a hand with this other matter, we'll leave you to your books." Mairelon drew a piece of paper from his pocket and handed it to Kerring. "Can you tell us anything about these books? What they might have in common, or why anyone might want them?"

Kerring studied the list, frowning. "It's an odd assortment. What is it, someone's collection that you're thinking of buying?"

"Part of my brother's library, actually," Mairelon said.

"They don't seem much like his kind of thing," Kerring said. "I wonder . . . Wait here for a minute." He disappeared behind one of the bookshelves, and Kim heard the sounds of drawers opening and closing, and paper rustling. Finally Kerring reappeared, carrying Mairelon's list and a little sheaf of documents.

"Found it!" he said triumphantly. "I thought these were familiar. They're part of a collection your father had me assess about, oh, fifteen years ago."

"Only part?" Mairelon said.

"The part I recommended he buy." Kerring waved the sheaf of documents. "The whole collection was much more extensive. It belonged to a Frenchman, an *émigré* who ended up in debtor's prison. De Cambriol, that was his name. His wife was a French wizard, one of the group they called *Les Griffonais;* she was just beginning to make a name for herself when she died. That's why your father was interested in her books."

"Her books?" Kim said. "I thought you said they belonged to her husband."

"He inherited them," Kerring said. "It was quite a nice little collection, actually, but he wasn't a wizard himself and had no interest in magic, so when he fell on hard times, he sold them off. Didn't do him much good, I'm afraid. Too many gambling debts; the proceeds from the sale didn't even begin to buy him out."

"And my father bought them," Mairelon said in a thoughtful tone.

"Some of them," Kerring corrected him. "Madame de Cambriol's magic collection, to be precise, plus one or two others he thought looked interesting. I thought he'd bought her *livre de mémoire*, too, but I don't see it on your list. Pity; there's a deal of interest in the *Griffonais* these days. Your brother could have gotten a nice price for it."

"What's a . . . a *livre de* thingumy?" Kim asked, at the same moment that Mairelon said, "Interest?"

Kerring's beard split in a grin. "One at a time. A *livre de mémoire* is a sort of book of notes that a lot of French wizards keep. A memory book, we'd call it."

"Just who is interested in *Les Griffonais*?" Mairelon said. "And why?"

"Everybody," Kerring replied, gesturing expansively. "Because of the restoration of the French monarchy, you see. Now that they've finally gotten rid of that pushy little Corsican they let take over the country, there's a lot of curiosity about things under the old regime."

"I believe there was rather more to Napoleon than that," Mairelon murmured. "Thank you very much for the information, and if you hear of anyone asking specifically about *Les Griffonais* or Madame de Cambriol, do let me know. Andrew might be interested in selling off some of the books."

Lord Kerring gave Mairelon a sharp look. "You're up to something, Merrill, and don't think I don't know it. I expect a full account for the archives once it's over, whatever it is."

"If you insist," Mairelon said. "I believe we have what we came for. Good day; perhaps I'll see you at the club next week."

"No doubt. Good day, Miss Merrill. I expect I'll see more of you when you start your journeyman's work. And I assure you that it will be a pleasure," Kerring bowed.

"Thank you, my lord," Kim stammered, and managed to curtsey without losing her balance. Kerring gave her an avuncular smile, and a moment later she and Mairelon were outside the library once more.

Mairelon was frowning slightly as they started down the hall. *Think-*

ing again, Kim told herself. *Well, he can just think out loud where I can hear it.* "Now what?" she asked him.

"Mmm? Kerring is an old reprobate at times, but he's a sound man and there's no denying he knows his work."

"Fine for him," Kim said. "But what do *we* do now?"

"We go back to the house and see whether we can turn up Madame de Cambriol's memory book. If it's not there, we'll know our burglar got what he was after."

"But you don't even know whether it was in the library to begin with," Kim said.

"If Kerring thinks my father bought it, I'm willing to wager he did," Mairelon said. "There might even be an inventory around somewhere. We'll have to check. Come along; we haven't time to waste."

four

Mairelon was extremely cheerful all the way home, but he refused to tell her anything more and she could not think of a way of questioning him that was likely to get a useful response. Not when he was in such a fey mood, anyway. When they reached Grosvenor Square, the opportunity was lost; Mrs. Lowe was hovering by the door, and took Kim in hand at once.

"You'll have to hurry, or we'll be late," she said as she bustled Kim up the stairs. "I've sent for Sally to do what she can with your hair. It ought to have been in papers all morning, but that can't be helped now."

"It wouldn't have helped then," Kim muttered.

"What did you say?"

"Nothing."

"I hope you don't intend to be difficult about this," Mrs. Lowe said. "Mrs. Hardcastle has gone to a good deal of trouble to arrange this meeting, and it is probably the best opportunity you will have to settle yourself comfortably."

As if that's the reason I came back to London, Kim thought, frowning. Fortunately, Mrs. Lowe had stepped forward to open the bedroom door, and did not see Kim's expression. Mrs. Lowe's maid, Sally, bobbed a curtsey as they entered. A pair of curling tongs lay heating in the fire, and a pale yellow walking dress waited on the bed. Kim rolled her eyes. "You mean I have to change clothes, too, as well as having my hair fussed with? What's wrong with what I have on?"

"Mrs. Hardcastle informs me that Mr. Fulton is partial to yellow,"

Mrs. Lowe said coldly. "Now, sit down and let Sally fix your hair. We have barely half an hour before we must leave."

Kim considered briefly, then sat. She could, she supposed, delay their departure if she worked at it, but delaying or avoiding this call would only make Mrs. Lowe more determined to arrange another. She had to think of a way to put an end to the matter once and for all, or she'd fall in the soup sooner or later.

"You have lovely hair, Miss, though it's a bit short," Sally ventured as she wound the first strand around a curl-paper. "I dare say it'll look that nice when it's all done up proper."

"That will do, Sally." Mrs. Lowe studied Kim for a moment, and then she and Sally went to work. With considerable effort and ingenuity, they produced a passable arrangement of curls from Kim's dark, unruly hair. At least, Mrs. Lowe said it was passable, but even to Kim's unpracticed eye the coiffure bore no resemblance to the elegant styles worn by real ladies. *I look like a fishmonger's daughter trying to ape Quality,* she thought gloomily. *I bet it'll be all straggly before we've gone three blocks. If it stays up that long.* She shook her head experimentally, and Mrs. Lowe clucked at her.

Getting into the gown without disarranging her hair was an effort, and Kim was glad that Sally was there to do most of the work. When Mrs. Lowe was satisfied with Kim's appearance at last, they descended the stairs once more.

Mairelon was waiting in the hall. "There you are at last! I thought you were in a hurry. I've had the coach waiting for half an hour." He picked up his gloves. "Shall we go?"

Mrs. Lowe stared at him, for once bereft of speech.

"You're coming, too?" Kim said with relief.

"Oh, yes." Mairelon smiled seraphically at his dumbfounded aunt. "After all, Aunt Agatha said only this morning that she expects me to pay more attention to my social duties. I thought I had best begin at once, before I forgot." He signaled the footman, who opened the door wide, and offered his arm to his aunt. By the time Mrs. Lowe recovered from her shock, they were in the carriage and on their way. Mrs. Lowe could hardly rip up at Mairelon as long as Kim was present, so the journey was accomplished in silence.

They emerged from the carriage in front of a sturdy brick townhouse of modest proportions. Two of the lower windows had been bricked over. An iron railing enclosed a yard or so of space in front of the house, where an extremely ugly pottery urn stood empty. Three slate steps, freshly scrubbed, led up to the wooden door. An impeccably correct butler opened the door and led them up the staircase inside. Kim, noting the empty candle sconces on the wall and the half-hidden darns in the linen drape covering a table in the upstairs hall, was not impressed. *Mrs. Hardcastle may be bosom-bows with Mrs. Lowe, but she's not as full of juice. This place wouldn't be worth the time—let alone the risk—to a decent cracksman.*

They found Mrs. Hardcastle in the saloon, a dark and austerely furnished room whose narrow windows did little to lighten the atmosphere. Mrs. Lowe checked briefly in the doorway, and when Kim entered close on her heels, she saw why.

Mrs. Hardcastle had more guests than they had expected. Not only that, the young woman shaking her golden-guinea curls at the offer of a slice of cake was a diamond of the first water. From the top of her high-crowned hat to her heart-shaped face and perfect complexion, to her slender figure, to the elegantly turned ankles and dainty feet set off by neat kid boots, she was everything that current fashion demanded of a Beauty. *No wonder old poker-back's nose is out of joint,* Kim thought with satisfaction. *She didn't bargain for any competition, let alone a regular out-and-outer.*

Beside the Beauty sat an undistinguished girl, also turned out in expensive (though in her case, unbecoming) fashion. A sober-looking gentleman and their middle-aged hostess completed the company.

Though Mrs. Lowe must have been annoyed, she gave no sign of it beyond that initial hesitation. She greeted Mrs. Hardcastle with the warmth due an old friend, and acknowledged the necessary introductions with perfect aplomb. The Beauty was a Miss Letitia Tarnower; her companion, Miss Annabel Matthews. The sober gentleman was, of course, Mr. Henry Fulton.

As the newcomers seated themselves, Kim studied Mr. Fulton. He looked to be in his mid-thirties, which was considerably younger than she had expected. His morning-dress was neat and correct, but lacked a certain elegance. *He's a Cit, and well enough off for Mrs. Lowe to think he's "reasonably respectable," but he doesn't follow Society fashion. Well, most Cits don't.* She wondered whether he had been informed of the purpose of their meeting.

Then Mr. Fulton caught her eye, reddened slightly, and looked away. *He knows.* And if he had come intending to inspect a potential bride, then she could no longer simply dismiss Mrs. Lowe's maunderings about marriage and her opportunities in London.

She glanced at Mr. Fulton again. His face was pleasant enough. *I ought to jump at him. There can't be very many well-to-do Cits willing to take up with a girl off the streets, even if I am the ward of a gentleman now. So why is the idea so . . . repellent?*

"Tea, Miss Merrill?" Mrs. Hardcastle said.

"Yes, thank you."

Mrs. Hardcastle beamed as if Kim had said something clever. Kim blinked, then accepted the teacup with a noncommittal murmur. This earned her an encouraging nod and a not-too-subtle significant look in Mr. Fulton's direction.

Kim chose to ignore the hint. She sat sipping at her tea, in the faint hope that a polite lack of interest would discourage any more attempts to draw her into conversation with Mr. Fulton. There was also a slim chance that sitting quietly might keep her from committing any of the social solecisms that would earn her a trimming from Mrs. Lowe once they returned home.

"I am pleased to find you here, Mr. Fulton," Mrs. Lowe said. "My nephew's ward was particularly eager to make your acquaintance."

"Yes, it is so nice to meet new people," Miss Tarnower said with a dazzling smile before Mr. Fulton could respond. "Mrs. Hardcastle's acquaintance is so very *varied* that one never knows who will turn up. I would not be astonished to find the Prince of Wales himself at one of her saloons."

Mrs. Hardcastle looked quite struck for a moment, then shook her head. "It is kind of you to say so, but I fear that His Highness is considerably above my touch."

"Oh, pooh! You are too modest. Everyone knows you, and you know everyone. I'll wager that if I gave you a name, you could tell us all about that person, no matter who it is! There now, you cannot say it is untrue."

"Ah, but it would be inhospitable of her to correct a guest," Mairelon said.

"That was not what I meant at all," Miss Tarnower said with a puzzled frown. "Oh! I see. You are bamming me."

"Letitia!" Miss Matthews said in an urgent undertone that carried rather better than she intended it to.

Miss Tarnower glanced at her companion, then turned back to Mairelon. "Is your acquaintance as wide as Mrs. Hardcastle's, sir?" she asked with another dazzling smile.

"Oh, at least," Mairelon murmured.

"Richard," Mrs. Lowe said softly, in the same warning tone that Miss Matthews had used. Being more experienced, her pitch was better-chosen; if Kim had not been sitting next to her, she would not have heard a thing.

"Mr. Merrill is well known in France, I believe," Mrs. Hardcastle told Miss Tarnower.

"Too well known," Mairelon said. "Even under the new king."

"But I am not interested in the king of France." Miss Tarnower frowned, as if suddenly struck by a thought. "Unless he is to be in London this Season?"

"I believe that to be unlikely," Mrs. Hardcastle said.

Mr. Fulton leaned forward. "I take it you were in France during the war, then, Mr. Merrill?"

"Some of the time," Mairelon acknowledged with a faint smile.

"I thought your name was familiar," Mr. Fulton said with some satisfaction.

"It is of no consequence," Mrs. Lowe said hastily. "It was a . . . personal matter."

"What, still?" Mr. Fulton looked from Mrs. Lowe to Mairelon and said apologetically, "I am very sorry if I have been indiscreet, but since my brother saw no harm in relating the story to me, I thought—"

"Tommy Fulton!" Mairelon said, snapping his fingers. "Last time I saw him was in that little French town where Old Hooky set up his, er, coin exchange. St. Jean de Luz, that was it. Good heavens, are you his brother? How is he?"

"He was badly wounded at Waterloo, and I fear his health has not been the same since," Mr. Fulton replied. "Still, he does tolerably well."

"I'm glad he made it through." Mairelon's face clouded. "Too many didn't."

Mrs. Lowe was frowning in a mixture of relief and mystification that Kim found puzzling. Didn't she know or care what Mairelon had really been doing during those years when London Society thought he had run off with the Saltash Set?

"Tom speaks very highly of your . . . work," Mr. Fulton said to Mairelon.

"No need to mince words," Mairelon said. "Not now, anyway." He smiled at the puzzled expressions of the two young ladies opposite him. "I met Tommy Fulton while I was on the Peninsula, spying on the French. He was one of the pickets who made it possible for me to cross back and forth across the lines when I needed to. Very solid."

Mr. Fulton inclined his head. "He will be pleased to know you remember him so kindly."

"Remember him? I could hardly forget him. Did he tell you about the incident with the chickens?"

Seeing that the conversation was about to degenerate into military reminiscence, Mrs. Lowe and Mrs. Hardcastle both hurried into speech.

"I am sure you have many fascinating tales, but—"

"Perhaps Richard can visit your brother some other—"

The two ladies both stopped short and waited politely for each other to continue. Since Mr. Fulton was also waiting for one of them to finish her speech, this gave Letitia Tarnower the opportunity to reenter the conversation.

"I dislike chickens," she announced. "They are stupid birds, and they have nothing whatever to do with who one knows, which is what we were discussing."

"Yes, and I quite agree that it is pleasant to meet new people," Mrs. Lowe said, though her tone was at odds with her words. She managed a stiff smile at Miss Tarnower, then turned to Mr. Fulton with a warmer expression. "It is, for instance, very pleasant to make your acquaintance at last, Mr. Fulton. We have heard so much about you."

"I, too, have heard much about you, Miss Merrill," Mr. Fulton said, and smiled. "I must say, it did not do you justice."

Beside Mrs. Hardcastle, Mairelon frowned suddenly. Mrs. Lowe nudged Kim and gave her a pointed look. Annoyed, Kim raised her teacup and sipped again. *Old fusspot. It would serve her right if I did disgrace her in public.* Then she blinked and began to grin. *And I bet it'll send Fulton to the rightabout in a hurry, too.*

Mairelon was watching her, and his frown deepened. Before he could queer her pitch, she looked at Mr. Fulton and said very deliberately, "Don't go pitching me no gammon. You ain't heard near enough, acos I'll lay you a monkey the gentry-mort ain't told you I was on the sharping lay afore Mairelon took a fancy to adopt me."

Mrs. Lowe's breath hissed faintly between her teeth in anger; Mrs. Hardcastle looked shocked, and the two younger ladies, merely puzzled. Mr. Fulton seemed taken aback, but he rallied enough to say, "No, I don't believe she did."

"Well, I ain't no mace cove, and I don't hold with bubbling a flash cull, not when it comes to getting priest-linked, anyways."

"Kim!" Mrs. Lowe had recovered from her surprise-induced paralysis; it was a tribute to her good breeding that she kept her voice low despite her anger and chagrin. "Hold your tongue, at once."

Kim set her teacup on the table. Looking up, she met Mr. Fulton's eyes. "And I'll tell you straight, this ain't been my lay, right from the beginning," she continued, as if Mrs. Lowe had never interrupted. "I ain't never been no Madam Ran. So I ain't going to get in a pucker if you was to shab off."

"I . . . see," Mr. Fulton said in a dazed voice.

"Well, I do not," Letitia Tarnower said crossly.

"I should hope not!" Mrs. Hardcastle groped in her reticule and produced a bottle of smelling salts, which she at once made use of. "I have never heard anything so vulgar in my life! Not that I understood the half of it myself."

"Really?" Miss Matthews's wide eyes were fixed on Kim. "Was it so very bad?"

"It was certainly intended to be," Mairelon said. His eyes, full of amusement, met Kim's, and she felt light-headed with relief. As long as he hadn't taken her antics in bad part, she didn't give a farthing for Mrs. Lowe.

Unexpectedly, Henry Fulton laughed. "Miss Merrill, I think we are both correct. I had not heard nearly enough about you, and what I did hear *certainly* did not do you justice."

Kim blinked and said cautiously, "Well, that ain't my lookout."

"Kim!" Mrs. Lowe said. "Be *still!*"

"It is much too late for that," Mrs. Hardcastle said acidly. "Really, Agatha, you might have told me."

"Told you what?" Mairelon said. "That my ward was once a street thief? I didn't think it was a secret."

"A street thief?" Letitia wrinkled her nose and looked at Kim with disfavor. "How horrid."

"I think it is the most romantic story I have ever heard," Miss Matthews said with conviction.

Mr. Fulton gave her an approving look, which caused Miss Matthews to blush in confusion.

Kim shook her head. Abandoning cant language, she said soberly, "It may sound romantic, but living on the street isn't very pleasant. Horrid describes it much better."

"I do not believe that was what Miss Tarnower was referring to," Mrs. Hardcastle said. She seemed even more upset by Kim's reversion to standard English than she had been by the string of thieves' cant.

Mrs. Lowe rose to her feet. "We must be going," she said stiffly. "At once."

"But you have only just arrived," Letitia objected. "And I *particularly* wished to ask Mr. Merrill something, because he has been on the continent."

Kim had not thought it possible for Mrs. Lowe to get any stiffer, but she did. "Another time, perhaps."

"Nonsense, Aunt," Mairelon said, leaning back in his chair. "We can spare another few minutes to gratify the young lady's curiosity."

"Richard . . ."

"What was it you wanted to ask, Miss Tarnower?" Mairelon asked.

"Why, only if you had ever heard of a Prince Alexei Nicholaiovitch Durmontov," Letitia said.

"Durmontov?" Mairelon said in a thoughtful tone. "No, I can't say that I met anyone of that name while I was in France, though there were a number of respectable Russians there from time to time. Of course, most of the people I dealt with there were not respectable at all."

"That appears to continue true." Mrs. Hardcastle sniffed and looked pointedly in Kim's direction.

"Well, it's only to be expected," Mairelon said consolingly. "London Society isn't what it once was."

Both Mr. Fulton and Miss Matthews experienced sudden fits of coughing. Kim found herself entirely in sympathy with them; she was having trouble choking back her own laughter at Mairelon's deliberate outrageousness.

Mrs. Hardcastle, however, was neither amused nor misled. "I was speaking, sir, of your so-called ward."

Mrs. Lowe bristled and began to say something, but Mairelon held up a restraining hand. "Were you, indeed?" he said in a deceptively gentle tone to Mrs. Hardcastle. "Then you will certainly not wish to attend her come-out ball. I must remember not to send you a card."

Kim's stomach did a sudden flip-flop. *Come-out ball? He's got windmills in his head. Doesn't he?*

"Richard!" Mrs. Lowe gasped.

"Ah, yes, you wanted to be going," Mairelon said, ignoring the reddening Mrs. Hardcastle. "I find that for once I am in agreement with you, Aunt." He rose and nodded to Mr. Fulton. "Give my regards to your brother. If you'll send me his direction, I shall stop in to see him. Your servant, ladies." He made an elegant bow that managed to include Miss Matthews and Miss Tarnower while excluding Mrs. Hardcastle, and ushered Kim and his thunderstruck aunt from the room.

five

They were hardly out of Mrs. Hardcastle's house before Mrs. Lowe turned to Mairelon. "Richard, I fear that your unfortunate impulses have landed you in difficulties once again."

Mairelon raised an eyebrow. "I do hope that you are not referring to my ward. I thought I was finished with that subject for today."

"Not at all," Mrs. Lowe said with a look at Kim that spoke volumes, none of them pleasant. "But *that* I intend to discuss with you privately, at a later time." She climbed into the carriage and waited for Kim and Mairelon to find their own seats. Then, as the carriage began to move, she said, "No, I was referring to your invention of a come-out ball for Kim. While I fully understand your desire to give Mrs. Hardcastle a set-down, I must tell you that it will certainly have precisely the opposite effect, once she realizes that no such party is being planned."

"I'm sure she feels just as you do," Mairelon murmured. "But think of her chagrin when she discovers that it will, in fact, be held."

"Richard, your flights of fancy take you too far," Mrs. Lowe said severely. "You can't possibly introduce a girl of dubious antecedents into Polite Society." She gave Kim another look. "Particularly a girl whose behavior cannot be depended upon."

"That's three," Mairelon said with apparent interest.

"Three what?" Mrs. Lowe asked, clearly at a loss.

"Three mistakes in one speech. First, Kim's, er, antecedents aren't dubious, they're completely unknown. That is, if you're referring to her parents. Second, her behavior is entirely dependable and shows a great deal of good sense."

"If you call using vulgar cant phrases in Mrs. Hardcastle's drawing room *showing good sense*—"

"And third," Mairelon went on implacably, "I am quite capable of introducing my ward to Polite Society—though judging by this afternoon, I'd say the adjective is extremely ill-chosen."

Kim found her voice at last. "Mairelon—"

"Kim, I have told you a dozen times: Refer to your guardian as Mr. Merrill, if you please," Mrs. Lowe snapped.

"I don't please," Kim said. "And I'm no good at wrapping it up in clean linen, so there's no use my trying. Mairelon—"

"You are being deliberately impudent and unmannerly," Mrs. Lowe said crossly. "I don't know which of you is worse."

"Yes, it's why Kim and I deal so well together," Mairelon said.

Before Mrs. Lowe could respond to this provoking remark, the carriage came to a halt and the footman sprang to open the door, putting a stop to further conversation. As they descended, a ragged boy of nine or ten materialized next to the front stoop, and stood staring up at Mairelon. Automatically, Kim moved her reticule to her far hand and backed off a step.

The boy ignored her. "You that Merrill cove?" he demanded of Mairelon. "The frogmaker?"

"I'm a magician, and my name is Merrill."

"Got something for you to give to a chap named Kim," the boy said. "A bob cull up by Threadneedle told me you'd give me a bender for delivering it."

Mairelon studied the boy for a moment, then reached into his pocket and pulled out a coin. "There's your sixpence. What have you got?"

"Here you go, governor." The boy dropped something into Mairelon's outstretched palm, snatched the sixpence from his other hand, and ran off down the street.

"Fascinating," Mairelon murmured, looking after him. "Now, who do we know who would use such an . . . unusual method of communication? And what does it mean?"

Kim leaned over to see what Mairelon was holding. It was a cheap wooden button, scratched deeply from one side to the other. "It's from Tom Correy," she said. "He's got a secondhand shop on Petticoat Lane, off Threadneedle. This is how he always used to let me know he wanted to see me. How did he know to send it to you? I never told anyone where I was going."

"I did," Mairelon said, handing her the button. "In a general sort of way. I wonder what he wants? Somehow, I doubt that the timing is coincidental."

"Tom didn't have nothing to do with that filching cove last night!"

"Kim!" Mrs. Lowe said. "Mind your language."

" '*Anything* to do with,' " Mairelon said calmly. "And I didn't claim he had. If he's heard something about the business, though, that might account for his summons." He frowned suddenly. "Or our mysterious burglar may be hoping to hire you to complete his work."

"As if I would!"

"Yes, well, he doesn't know that, does he?"

"*Need* we discuss this in the street?" Mrs. Lowe said with a significant look in the direction of the interested footmen.

"A reasonable enough point," Mairelon said, and they proceeded into the house.

Inside, Mrs. Lowe looked at Mairelon and said, "I wish to speak further with you about all this, Richard. I will expect you in the drawing room. Immediately." Without waiting for an answer, she swept up the stairs, leaving Mairelon and Kim standing just inside the door.

"I have a few questions, too," Kim said.

"Aunt Agatha got in before you, I'm afraid," Mairelon said. "You'll have to wait. Unless you want to join us?"

"No," Kim said hastily. "I'll talk to you after."

"In the library. You can study your orisons and invocations while you wait," Mairelon said, and disappeared down the back hall before Kim could say anything more.

Fuming, Kim went up to the library and flopped into a chair. *Introduce me to Polite Society! He's dicked in the nob. And anyway, the last thing I want is to spend more time having tea with widgeons like that Tarnower gentry-mort.* She glared at the book of invocations, but didn't bother picking it up. Even if she could calm down enough to puzzle out the letters, nothing she read while she was in this state would stick. *And what in thunder does Tom Correy want? He can't have a job for me; if he knows about Mairelon, he knows I don't need to go on the sharping lay any more. And how am I going to sneak down to Petticoat Lane in skirts?*

Tom wouldn't have sent for her if it wasn't urgent, but he didn't know that Kim was a girl. She'd dressed and acted as a boy for all her years on the London streets, and only Mother Tibb had known the truth. The back alleys of London were dangerous places at the best of times, and doubly dangerous for girls. Petticoat Lane wasn't quite as bad as the rookeries of St. Giles, or the stews around Vauxhall and Covent Gardens, but it was still far from safe.

If I go well after dark, in boy's clothes, I might still be able to pass. But she had no idea what had become of her old garments, and even if she had, they wouldn't fit her now. Mrs. Lowe would never countenance a shopping expedition for an appropriate jacket and breeches, let alone Kim's actually wearing them anywhere. Mairelon . . . Mairelon wouldn't mind the boy's clothes, but Kim felt oddly reluctant to ask him for help in this. She owed Tom a lot, from the bad times before she'd met Mairelon, and the debt was one she had to pay herself.

When Mairelon arrived fifteen minutes later, Kim was no nearer a solution to her problem. She looked up as he came in, and with a particularly cheerful grin he said, "Well, that's settled, more or less. Now, what was it you wanted to ask?"

All thoughts of Tom Correy fled from Kim's mind at once. "Settled?" she croaked. "What's settled?"

"The business of presenting you to Society," Mairelon said. "Aunt Agatha doesn't like it, of course, but it's clear enough that she'll agree to sponsor you eventually."

"Eventually?" Kim grasped at the slim hope.

Mairelon's grin widened even more. "Right now, she's too furious with me to agree to anything, but she'll come around as soon as I propose letting Renée D'Auber sponsor you instead. She's far too conventional to let my ward be presented by someone who's not a member of the family."

"You *enjoy* annoying her," Kim said in surprise.

"Nonsense. It's much too easy—everything annoys Aunt Agatha. Now, you had some questions, I think?"

"Not exactly. It's just that you forgot to ask me."

Mairelon blinked, then looked a little sheepish. "I'm sorry about springing it on you, but I wanted it to be clear to Aunt Agatha that you hadn't been scheming for a come-out all along. It worked, too."

"That's not what I meant," Kim said. "That just explains why you didn't *tell* me what you were planning. I'm talking about *asking* me whether I wanted to be launched into Society."

"I didn't think I had to," Mairelon said. "It's obvious that you haven't been happy since we got back to London. I thought you wanted a change."

So he did *notice*, Kim thought, but the knowledge only added to her growing annoyance with him. "Well, I haven't been, and I did want a change, but that's not the point. A year ago, I wanted to get off the streets, but I didn't want it badly enough to go to the stews."

"I should hope not," Mairelon said, and for an instant he sounded exactly like his aunt. Then he gave her a worried look, and the resemblance vanished. "It's not just a matter of presenting you, you know. I'm hoping that if we circulate a bit during the Season, we'll run across our mysterious toff burglar."

"That's *not the point*," Kim repeated. "A year ago, you *asked* me if I wanted to be your ward, when it was a lot plainer that I'd jump at the chance. But you didn't ask me about coming out in Society, and you didn't ask me about 'circulating during the Season.' You're as bad as Mrs. Lowe."

"What?" Mairelon looked startled, and for the first time, Kim felt as if she might have gotten through to him.

"Mrs. Lowe didn't ask me whether I came to London to catch a husband, she just decided that's what I wanted. Or that it would be best for me. And you didn't ask about this. You both act like I'm some fog-headed mort who ain't got sense enough to make up her own mind about anything."

"I'm sorry."

"*I'm sorry* don't fix it."

"What would? Do you want me to tell Aunt Agatha you refuse to be presented?"

"Yes," Kim said. "That's exactly what I want."

Mairelon looked startled. "Why? It's not because of that Hardcastle woman's remarks this afternoon, or the Tarnower girl's attitude, is it? Their opinions really don't matter in the slightest."

"Not to you. But I ain't been out with your poker-backed aunt every day for a week without noticing that the opinions of bubble-brains like those two matter a lot to some people. Your aunt, for one."

Mairelon frowned. "And do they matter to you? Is that why you're so . . . overset?"

"*No*." Kim flung her hands up in exasperation. "Not the way you mean, not now. But if I was to get launched into Society, their opinions would *have* to matter, wouldn't they? Because that's what Society is, mostly."

"What an unfortunately truthful observation," Mairelon said. "I take your point. I shouldn't have sprung this on you in front of them."

"You shouldn't of sprung it on me at all! You ought to of asked me about it first, and not just because you thought I'd give you a trimming

if you didn't." Kim stopped and took a deep breath. Then she said quietly, "It's *my* life. And I ain't—I'm not a noodle."

"No one said you were."

"You act like it." She shook her head. "Maybe it's just how you toffs
are, deciding what other people should do. But I wasn't born and bred
to it. I don't like it. And I ain't never going to get used to it."

There was a brief silence. Then Mairelon shook his head. "Very well,
if you really don't wish to have a come-out, I'll talk to Aunt Agatha again.
Tomorrow, I think; that will give her time to calm down, and I can
probably convince her that her excellent arguments persuaded us to reconsider, which might even put her in charity with both of us."

"Good," Kim said, trying to convince herself that she meant it. After
all she'd never have thought of it herself, the fairy-tale images of being
presented at a real Society ball were hard to dismiss now that they'd been
offered to her. *Just like the ash-girl in the stories Red Sal used to tell. But it
ain't a story. Cut line,* she told herself severely.

The library door opened, and Hunch came in. " 'Ere's that list of
books you wanted."

"The inventory? Excellent." Mairelon took the papers that Hunch
held out to him and scanned the first page. After a moment, he shuffled
it to the bottom of the stack and began on the next. Kim watched, feeling
an odd mixture of relief, curiosity, and regret. Halfway down the fourth
page, Mairelon paused. His frown deepened momentarily; then he smiled.
"Found it at last!"

"Found what?" Kim said. "That liver book Lord Kerring was talking
about?"

"*Livre de mémoire,*" Mairelon corrected, "and yes, I have. *Le Livre
de Sept Sorciers: un livre de mémoire* by Madame Marie de Cambriol. It
was in this library, all right; now let's find out whether it still is. According
to this, it should be a smallish volume with a blue leather binding."

Kim took a quick look at the page in Mairelon's hand, to make sure
she would recognize the title when she saw it, then started going through
the shelves on one side of the room. Mairelon took the other side, and
Hunch, muttering under his breath and chewing on his mustache, began
on the cabinets under the windows.

Three-quarters of the way down the second set of shelves, Kim found
it—a short, slim volume sandwiched between two much larger ones. "Is
this it?" she called, holding it up.

Mairelon joined her. "It certainly is," he said, scowling at it.

"What's the matter?" Kim said. "I thought you'd be pleased that it hasn't gone missing."

"Oh, I am, I am," Mairelon said. "But you must admit, this confuses things considerably."

Hunch look up. " 'Ow's that, Master Richard?"

"Well, if it had been missing, we'd have had a good idea that this was what our burglar was after," Mairelon replied. "Now, we can't be sure, especially since that spell we used last night didn't make it glow like the other books he'd pulled off the shelves."

"It was in between two big books," Kim said. "They might have hidden it enough that the glow didn't show."

"Or Madame de Cambriol might have done something rather special to safeguard her notes," Mairelon said in a thoughtful tone.

"Or that there cracksman might 'ave piked off with something else," Hunch put in. " 'Ow would you know if 'e 'ad?"

"You're starting to pick up thieves' cant from Kim," Mairelon observed. "I'll have a look at this tomorrow; perhaps it will give me some ideas. Oh, and that reminds me—Kim, what do you intend to do about that button?"

"Button?" Kim stared, wondering why Mairelon would care about the buttons she'd ripped from her dressing gown during her row with the burglar; then her mind made another connection, and she said, "You mean, the one Tom Correy sent?"

"Yes, of course. You said it was a sort of summons. Do you want to go?"

Kim looked at him in mild surprise. "Tom wouldn't ask me to come if it wasn't important. Of course I'm going, if I can figure out how."

"We'll take the coach. Aunt Agatha won't need it; when I left, she was talking about having a spasm, and that generally occupies her for at least a day. Up High Holborn to Threadneedle, isn't it?"

"That's not what I meant," Kim said, but she couldn't help smiling. *All that fretting about whether to ask him, and he just barges into the middle of things without a second thought.* "I meant . . ." She gestured, taking in her yellow walking dress, kid boots, and painstakingly curled hair.

Mairelon's eyes focused on her. A startled expression crossed his face; then he nodded. "Yes, I see. You can't very well go wandering about the London back streets dressed like that, no matter what time of day it is. Particularly if Correy still thinks you're a boy."

"That's it," Kim said, relieved that he had understood without more explicit explanation.

"Hunch," Mairelon went on, "do you think you can find a suitable set of boy's clothes? Something a bit better than what she had when we met, but not fine enough to attract attention."

"And loose," Kim put in, then sighed. "I hope it works. I wouldn't fool a blind man in broad daylight, but I might still be able to pass for a boy at night."

"Nonsense. You won't have any trouble at all," Mairelon said.

Kim stared at him. It was so like Mairelon to have overlooked the inconvenient physical changes in his ward that she could not help being amused, but she was a little hurt as well. Hadn't he looked at her even *once* in the past six months?

"She's right, Master Richard," Hunch said unexpectedly. "Look at 'er. She ain't skinny enough no more."

Mairelon gave Hunch a startled glance, then looked at Kim for a long, considering moment. Slowly, he nodded. "I . . . see. I apologize, Kim." Kim felt herself beginning to flush; fortunately, Mairelon turned toward Hunch and did not see. "Do as well as you can, Hunch."

"Cook might 'ave somethin' from the last errand boy," Hunch said. "I'll check."

"Don't forget something suitably disreputable for me," Mairelon called after him as he left the library.

Kim looked at Mairelon. "You expect to come with me?"

"I *am* your guardian," Mairelon said.

All Kim's annoyance with his high-handed ways boiled over once again. "If that means that I get no say in anything I do, I'd rather go back to the streets."

There was a brief, stunned silence. Then Mairelon said, "You don't mean that."

"Not yet," Kim admitted. "But even Mother Tibb *asked* what we thought of a job before she sent us out."

The silence stretched again. Finally, Mairelon said, "You said you wanted to go."

"I do." Kim took a deep breath. "But I don't think you should come with me."

Mairelon tensed. "Why not?"

"I'll have a harder time with Tom if you do. He won't be expecting no toffs, just me. If you show up, even dressed like a dustman, he'll muffle his clapper and I won't find out a thing."

"You can't go to that end of town alone."

"Why not? I *lived* there alone, for five years after Mother Tibb swung."

"But you haven't been on the streets for a year," Mairelon came back swiftly. "You're out of practice."

"You're more out of practice than I am," Kim retorted. "Especially seeing as you weren't ever *in* practice. I've got a better chance of not getting noticed if I go alone."

The library door swung open, and Hunch entered, carrying a large bundle. Mairelon waved him toward the table and raised his eyebrows at Kim. "Not in practice? While you were living on the back streets, I was nosing about in France, if you recall."

"Huh." Kim sniffed. "France ain't London."

Hunch choked. Kim eyed him with disfavor. "Well, it ain't," she said.

"*Isn't*, Kim," Mairelon said.

"Ain't," Kim said firmly. "I got to talk to Tom tonight; if I sound too flash, he ain't going to be comfortable."

"Very well. Just don't slip in front of Aunt Agatha, for I won't be responsible for the consequences."

Kim nodded. "I won't. But you still ain't coming with me."

Hunch frowned and began nibbling on the left end of his mustache. Mairelon sighed. "Kim—"

"If you try, I won't go. And Tom won't talk to you alone, whatever he's got to say. If he'd meant for you to come, he'd have let us know somehow."

Mairelon studied her for a moment, frowning slightly. Finally, reluctantly, he nodded. "If you're determined. But I still don't like the idea of you crossing half of London on your own at that hour. Hunch and I will take you up High Holborn in the carriage."

"That's going to be inconspicuous for sure," Kim said scornfully, "Me, pulling up at Tom's door in a coach at midnight."

"Much as I'd like to do just that, I hadn't planned on it. I *have* done this sort of thing before, you know. We'll wait at the bottom of Threadneedle Street, or somewhere else nearby if you can think of a better place."

It was Kim's turn to nod reluctantly. She had, for a few wild minutes, hoped for a night run through the back streets of London, an opportunity to visit some of her old haunts besides Tom Correy's place. But Mairelon's points were well-taken. The London rookeries were a dangerous place even for the experienced, and her experiences were a year out of date. The less time she spent on the streets, the better her chance of avoiding robbery or murder. Memories were no good to the dead.

"That's settled, then," Mairelon said briskly, and handed Kim a stack of wrinkled clothing. "Now, do go and try these on while there's still time for Hunch to find more if they don't fit. And for heaven's sake, don't let Aunt Agatha see you, or we'll both be in the suds."

six

A heavy London fog had settled over the dark streets by the time Kim approached Tom Correy's shop in Petticoat Lane. Here there were no streetlamps to mark the road with flickering yellow light, and Kim was grateful. In the dark and the fog, she was only a shadow moving among shadows. This close to the St. Giles rookery, anyone who was noticing enough to spot her would likely be knowing enough to pretend he hadn't.

Even so, the thought of Mairelon and Hunch, waiting in the carriage a few streets away, was more comforting than she had expected. The smells of coal smoke and uncollected horse dung, the sounds of drunken revelry from the public house on the corner, and most of all the penetrating chill of the fog brought back the constant undercurrent of fear that she had lived with for so long. She had almost forgotten the fear, in her year of safety and security with Mairelon.

A church clock chimed the quarter hour. Kim jumped, then shook herself. *Past midnight already. I'll be home as late as a fashionable lady coming back from a ball.* She frowned at the thought, then dismissed it. Pulling her jacket firmly into place, she knocked at Tom's door.

An unfamiliar dark-haired youth opened it and looked at her suspiciously. "Who are you and what d'you want?"

"I come to see Tom Correy," Kim said.

"And I'm a valet to His Majesty," the youth sneered. "You're lookin' to unload something you pinched from your betters."

"What if I am?" Kim said. "You ain't one of 'em, so it ain't no lookout of yours."

"Ho!" The doorkeeper made an awful grimace and raised his fists. "See if I ain't!"

"I can see it just by looking at you," Kim said. He was sturdy enough, but his movements were too slow; even out of practice, she had little to fear from a scrap with him, unless he landed a lucky punch. She shook her head. *I'm not here to pick fights.* "You're wasting time. Tom's expecting me."

"No, he ain't," the youth retorted. "He ain't expecting nobody what would come sneaking around the back. He—"

"Here, Matt, what's the racket?" Tom's voice drifted out of one of the inner rooms, followed by Tom himself. His face split in a broad grin when he saw Kim. "Kim, lad! You got my message, then. Come in, come in, and tell me how you're keeping."

"Hellfire!" said the doorkeeper in obvious chagrin. "You told me you was expecting some flash frogmaker!"

"Well, so I am," Kim said in her best Grosvenor Square tones. If Tom had already said that much, there was no point in pretending. "But I didn't want to be noticed, and walking the alleys in pantaloons and a silk cravat would have gotten me noticed for sure."

"Garn!" said Matt, obviously impressed in spite of himself. "You ain't no frogmaker."

"Oh, ain't I?" Kim glanced quickly around. The door was closed, and the windows shuttered; no one but Tom and Matt was likely to see. Raising her right hand, palm upward, she focused all her attention on it and said, *"Fiat lux!"*

The tingling sensation of magic at work swept across her hand and arm. An instant later, a ball of light flared into being in the air above her palm. It was brighter than she'd intended; either she really was getting better at spellcasting, or annoyance had given her spell a boost. She rather suspected it was the annoyance. However it had happened, the effect was impressive. She heard Tom's breath hiss against his teeth in surprise, and Matt's startled exclamation, but she was concentrating too hard to respond.

Kim let the light float above her hand for several seconds. Then, one by one, she folded her fingers inward. The light dimmed, and as the last finger touched her palm, it vanished. The tingling sensation vanished as well, leaving her hand feeling unusually sensitive. She let it fall to her side, resisting the temptation to flex her fingers; it would spoil the effect.

"Coo," said Matt, his eyes bulging. "Ain't that a sight! What else can you do?"

"Get along with you," Tom said, cuffing Matt's shoulder. "Do you think a real magician has nothing better to do than show off tricks like a Captain Podd with his puppets? Kim's got things to do, and so have you."

With a resigned nod, Matt started for the inner door. Tom stood aside to let him pass, then called after him, "And if you say one word about this to anyone, I'll have Kim's master turn you into a frog!"

Kim couldn't make out the words of the muffled response, but it was apparently an affirmative, for Tom nodded in satisfaction and pulled the door to. Looking gravely at Kim, he said, "You hadn't ought to have done that."

"It was just light," Kim said uncomfortably.

"That's not the point, but it's too late to mend matters now." Tom sighed. "I just hope Matt has the sense to keep his jaw shut. If his uncle hears about this, we're grassed."

"What are you talking about?"

"I forget, you don't know what's been going on." Tom studied Kim for a moment, and forced a smile. "You're looking well. I guess that Mairelon cove wasn't gammoning me about feeding you up and teaching you magic and all."

"No, he's done all that, right enough." Kim said

Tom gave her a sharp look. "So? And what hasn't he done?"

"Nothing. It's just . . . different. Toffs take a bit of getting used to, that's all. I'm fine."

"You're a sight better off than you'd have been if you'd stayed here, and don't you forget it," Tom said emphatically.

"I ain't likely to, what with regular meals and all," Kim said. "Why did you want to see me? And what was that about Matt's uncle? Who is he, anyway? You never used to have anybody to help out."

"Matt is one of my Jenny's nephews," Tom said, and Kim grinned at the possessive fondness in his tone when he spoke of his wife, even in passing. Some things hadn't changed. Oblivious, Tom continued, "Her sister's eldest boy, come to London to learn a trade."

"So? Ain't he working out?"

"He was working out fine, until somebody talked Jack Stower off the transports. That's why I wanted to talk to you."

"Stower's loose? When did that happen?" Kim was surprised, but not unduly alarmed. Jack Stower was Tom's brother-at-law, and a bad lot if there ever was one. Kim had never had much use for him, but she'd never feared him as she had his boss, Dan Laverham. And both Jack and

Dan had been arrested a year ago, when she'd first hooked up with Mairelon. A twinge of uneasiness shook her. "Laverham ain't loose as well, is he?"

"No, he danced on air last November. It's just Jack."

Kim blew out a long, noisy breath. "Then I don't see what you're nattered about. Jack will have it in for me, but I can handle Jack now."

"I thought that's what you'd say," Tom said gloomily. "And if it was just Jack Stower, I wouldn't have sent for you to come here. But he's hooked up with Mannering, and if that don't worry you, it ought to."

"Why? Jack may think he can borrow enough to turn himself into a toff, but it ain't going to happen. And if he's in over his head with Mannering and the other cent-per-cents, he'll have more to worry about than me."

Tom stared at her for a moment, then shook his head. "I forget how much has changed since you've been gone. Mannering ain't just a moneylender, these days. He's got ambitions."

"Like what?"

"Like rounding up anyone with a hint of magic to 'em, and persuading them to work for him."

Kim snorted. "Laverham tried that once, and Ma Yanger gave him a week's rash, and Sam Nicks pitched him out a window, and George and Jemmy and Wags gave him an earful in the middle of Hungerford Market. You're telling me a creaky old moneylender's had better luck?"

"A lot better luck, one way and another, and nobody knows why. George and Jemmy and Wags turned him down when he first tried, right enough, but two weeks later they were working for him. Sam was stubborner, and he woke up one morning in an alley with his throat slit. Ma Yanger ain't working for Mannering, but she ain't working for nobody else, neither."

"Ma Yanger's given up witching people?" Kim said incredulously.

Tom nodded. "She's holed up in her rooms, and she won't see nobody. Been that way for two months now. And that's how it is with everyone else—they're working for Mannering, or they ain't working at all. And since Stower came back, Mannering's lads have been asking about you."

"Me?"

"Stower told him you can do magic, *and* that you were getting training from some fancy toff wizard. I think Mannering would like to get his hands on both of you. I figured the toff could look out for himself, but I thought somebody ought to tell you what was up afore you found out the hard way."

"Thanks, Tom." With a shiver, Kim remembered that Jack was one of the few people from her old life who knew of her masquerade. *It doesn't matter any more if people know I'm a girl,* she told herself, but the old habits and fears kept her tongue locked.

"So you see why you hadn't ought to have been showing off in front of Matt," Tom went on. "Jack Stower is his uncle, and they've been thick as treacle since Jack turned up again. Jenny's after me to keep Matt away from him, but how she expects me to do that I don't know," he added gloomily. "It ain't like I can put leg-irons on the boy."

"I wish I could help," Kim said, but Tom shook his head.

"That ain't why I asked you to come. Matt's my business, and I'll deal with him. But I don't know that I can keep him from talking to Jack about this, and if he does, Mannering will be after you like a shot."

"Maybe he already has been," Kim said thoughtfully. "You wouldn't know something about a green cracksman who bungled a job in Grosvenor Square last night?"

Tom considered for a moment. "No, but I can ask around if you like."

"Let it go," Kim said, shaking her head. "If Mannering's got you that flattered, you hadn't ought to get any more mixed up in this than you are already. I'll find out about it some other way."

"Kim, if Mannering has already made a try for you—"

"It wasn't anything like that," Kim said hastily. "Somebody tried to nobble a book from Mairelon's library, near as we can tell, and botched the job. It probably didn't have anything to do with Mannering. He's a deep old file; he wouldn't send an amateur on a crack lay like that."

"You're sure it wasn't bungled apurpose?"

Kim snorted. "The cull didn't know the first thing about housebreaking. Mairelon thinks he was depending on a spell to keep from getting nabbed, and even that didn't work."

"I still don't like it," Tom said. "He's a sneaking one, Mannering is."

"All the more reason he'd know better than to send a green 'un to mill a ken in Grosvenor Square. It's pure luck the cull wasn't laid by the heels right then." Seeing that Tom still looked unconvinced, Kim shook her head. "I'm sorry I mentioned it. And I really am glad of your warning."

"I don't know what good it'll do you," Tom said in a gloomy tone.

"Jemmy and Sam and the others knew what was up, and knowing didn't help them none."

"Jemmy and Sam ain't proper wizards from the Royal College," Kim said. "I ain't, neither, but Mairelon is. And Mairelon won't take kindly to nobody messing with his ward. If Mannering knows anything about toffs, he'll twig to that as soon as he finds out where I am. If he finds out at all."

"Maybe you're right," Tom said thoughtfully. "Mannering deals with toffs all the time, what with his business and all. He ain't like Laverham, passing off sham gentility."

"It wasn't no sham with Laverham," Kim said. "He was born on the wrong side of the blanket, but he was a toff, sure enough."

"No! Laverham? You're bamming me."

Thankful to have found a neutral topic to take Tom's mind off fretting, Kim allowed herself to be drawn into gossip about old acquaintances. Tom reciprocated as well as he was able. Many of her former fellows were in Newgate Prison, "polishing the King's iron with their eyebrows" as they looked out through the barred windows. Some had been transported; a few, like Laverham, had been hung. On the whole, it was a depressing catalog, and Kim was almost glad when time came to give Tom a final "Thank you" and slip away at last.

The shadows on the streets and alleys seemed darker and more threatening as she made her way down Threadneedle toward the Thames. Even at this hour, the street was not quite deserted, and she kept a wary eye on the bingo boy staggering from one public house to the next and the tired costermonger pushing his barrow home from Covent Garden.

Mairelon's carriage waited at the end of the street, just where she had left it. Hunch sat in the coachman's seat, chewing on the ends of his mustache. When he saw Kim, his gloomy expression lightened in relief, and he thumped on the carriage roof. "She's 'ere, Master Richard."

There was a muffled noise from inside, then Mairelon's head poked out of the carriage window. "There you are, Kim! I was just about to come and fetch you."

"It hasn't been that long," Kim said. "Tom and I had things to talk about."

"You can tell me about it on the way home," Mairelon said. He sounded somewhat disgruntled, and when Kim climbed into the carriage, she saw that he had changed into a workingman's wrinkled shirt, vest, and breeches.

He's disappointed because he couldn't go larking about the alleys, Kim thought, and shook her head. He ought to have better sense. She smiled suddenly, remembering her own eager response to the thought of a night out. *Seems like neither of us is strong on good sense.*

"Well, what happened?" Mairelon said as the coach began to roll. "Did Correy just want to talk over old times?"

"Not exactly," Kim said. "Jack Stower's loose, and Tom thinks he's trying to make trouble." She repeated what Tom had said about Mannering, his ambitions, and his apparent interest in Mairelon and Kim.

When she finished, Mairelon rubbed his chin, frowning. "What else do you know about this Mannering fellow?"

Kim shrugged. "He's a moneylender. He never had much to do with the canting crew, that I heard, but he wasn't above laying out a bit of the ready to folks like Laverham, that had some security to offer. It don't—doesn't—make sense that he'd want to take Laverham's place. He's more of a gent already than Laverham ever was."

"Perhaps he's not interested in climbing the social ladder. Or perhaps he has . . . unusual methods in mind." Mairelon smiled suddenly. "Perhaps I should drop in at his office one day soon."

"There ain't no call for that," Kim said, alarmed. "We got enough on our plates already, what with that cove poking around after that book and all. There's no reason to go *looking for trouble.*"

"Of course not," Mairelon said, but the impish smile still hovered around the corners of his mouth. Kim resolved to have a talk with Hunch. Maybe the manservant could get some sense into Mairelon's head, or at least keep him from going off half-cocked and stirring up a pot of problems. Maybe. Not that anyone seemed to be able to check Mairelon's queer starts when he got the bit between his teeth.

"I wish I hadn't said anything about it at all," Kim muttered as the coach drew up behind the townhouse.

"What?" Mairelon said.

"I said I wish I hadn't told you about Mannering," Kim repeated.

"Why?" Mairelon studied her face for a moment. "You're really worried about this, aren't you?"

"Tom doesn't get all nattered over nothing. And he's nattered about Mannering and Stower, right enough."

"I see." Mairelon hesitated, then nodded slowly. "Very well. I won't pursue the matter until we've dealt with our literary housebreaker, unless we get some further indication that pursuing it would be advisable. And I'll speak to you beforehand."

"Fair enough," Kim said, slightly dazed. *He wouldn't say it if he didn't mean it. Don't that beat everything?*

"Then if that's settled, I suggest you turn your attention to sneaking inside without waking Aunt Agatha. I see no reason to precipitate another scene if we can avoid it."

"Right," said Kim, and slid out of the carriage.

seven

Kim woke late the following morning, to sunlight and the clatter of carriage wheels on the cobbles below her window. As she dressed, she considered what to do with the little heap of boy's clothes in the corner of the wardrobe. If a housemaid found them, she'd report to Mrs. Lowe and there was sure to be a row. Finally, Kim stuffed them in a hatbox, tucking them around the hat as best she could, and shoved the box back onto the top shelf of her wardrobe. With luck, she could think of some excuse to give the box to Hunch later in the day, and he could dispose of the clothes without causing comment.

Feeling unreasonably cheerful, Kim left her bedroom and started downstairs. Halfway down the first flight of stairs, she heard muffled thumps and shouts drifting up from the lower floors. She quickened her pace, wondering what was going on now. It couldn't be the cracksman again, not in broad daylight.

As she turned onto the last landing, she heard an unfamiliar feminine voice below shriek, "Darby! Close that door at once!"

"He's headed for the stairs!" a second voice cried. "Catch him!"

An instant later, a small, yellow-brown monkey leaped onto the banister railing just in front of Kim and directed a high-pitched shriek of defiance at his pursuers. Kim, momentarily unnoticed, reached out and collected him in a firm hold. The monkey shrieked again, this time in surprise. Then, wrapping his long tail firmly around Kim's wrist, he relieved himself on her skirt.

"Don't think you're getting out of it that easily," Kim told him. Maintaining her hold with some care, so as to be sure that she would neither hurt the monkey nor be bitten herself, she rounded the corner and looked down.

The entry hall was full of people, boxes, and trunks. At the bottom of one of the piles of luggage, a large wicker cage lay on its side, its door open wide. Several disheveled footmen and an elderly, bright-eyed man in a coachman's many-caped cloak were scrambling over boxes and trunks toward the stairs; in the far corner, one of the housemaids was having hysterics. In the center of the commotion stood a tiny doll of a woman, looking upward with anxious hazel eyes. Her brown hair, where it curled out from under an exceedingly elegant wide-brimmed hat, was liberally streaked with gray. When she saw the monkey in Kim's arms, her worried expression broke into a cheerful smile that was the mirror of Mairelon's.

"Ah, you have captured Maximillian! Thank you very much. Would you be so kind as to bring him here and restore him to his cage? It is by far the simplest thing, when he is so nervous and upset. I am afraid he dislikes traveling."

Willingly, Kim made her way to the foot of the stairs and deposited the monkey in the wicker cage, which one of the footmen had hastily righted. The woman secured the latch with a small padlock and said to the footman, "Now, take him up to the library, and be sure to put the cage in a corner where it will not be overturned again. I will bring him water and a bit of fruit presently, when he is more settled." She turned to Kim. "You must be my son's ward, Kim. I am so pleased to meet you at last. I am Lady Wendall."

Kim stared, her brain scrambling in several directions at once. *Lady? Her son's ward? This is Mairelon's mother, and she's a Lady Wendall?* Feeling a strong sense of ill-usage, she belatedly bobbed a curtsey. *Somebody ought to have warned me!*

As she straightened, she found herself being critically examined by the diminutive new arrival. "I thought so," Lady Wendall said cryptically after a moment. "My dear, who has—"

A door down the hall opened. "Whatever is going on?" Mrs. Lowe said as she came out into the hall, and then, in thunderstruck tones, "*Elizabeth?*"

"Good morning, Agatha," Lady Wendall said. "I should think that what is going on is obvious; the footmen are moving my trunks in."

"What . . . how . . . why wasn't I informed?"

"I told them not to disturb your breakfast." Lady Wendall nodded at the footmen, then favored Mrs. Lowe with a charming smile. "Speaking

of breakfast, I am positively famished; these early hours are not what I
am accustomed to. Do join me, and we shall talk while we eat."

With that, Lady Wendall swept past Mrs. Lowe into the dining room.
Mrs. Lowe pursed her lips as if she had bitten into a bad orange, glared
at the footmen, and went after Lady Wendall. Kim hesitated; they might
not want her to join them. But neither of them had said anything, and
the temptation was irresistible. She followed them in.

Lady Wendall had gone straight to the sideboard and was shaking
her head over the dishes as she lifted the covers. Mrs. Lowe watched for
a moment, her face a politely frozen mask, then took her seat. As she
picked up her fork, she saw Kim in the doorway, and her eyebrows
twitched together. "Whatever have you done to your dress, Kim?"

"It was the monkey," Kim said.

"Monkey?" Mrs. Lowe blinked, for once at a complete loss.

"Yes, and quite unpleasant for you, I'm sure," Lady Wendall said,
turning toward the table with her hands full of loaded dishes. "Use one
of the napkins to clean it off for the time being."

"She can't sit down to breakfast like that!" Mrs. Lowe protested as
Kim set to work with the cloth. "She must go and change at once."

"I'm sure Kim is just as hungry as I am," Lady Wendall said with a
smile. "It wouldn't be kind to make her wait. Unless you'd rather change
first, Kim? We can all wait for you, if you'd prefer."

Kim shrugged. "It's no matter to me." Having food at all had always
been far more important to her than the condition of the clothes she
wore to eat it. She set the napkin on a side chair and began filling her
plate.

"The stain will set and ruin the dress," Mrs. Lowe said.

"So much the better," Lady Wendall responded with unimpaired
calm. "It's not a good color for her at all, and I intend to have it disposed
of as soon as possible."

Mrs. Lowe stared, and her chin lifted. "Disposed of?" she said in
ominous tones.

Lady Wendall nodded. "Unless you're particularly fond of it, Kim.
It's well enough to wear about the house in Kent, but not for your first
Season in London."

"It is entirely appropriate for a girl in her situation," Mrs. Lowe said
firmly.

"I didn't say it was inappropriate," Lady Wendall said gently. "I said
it was unbecoming. And Kim will want to look her best during her come-
out."

"Elizabeth, I do hope you are not going to encourage Richard in this notion he has taken of having the girl presented."

Kim's half-formed protest stuck in her throat. She wasn't going to have a come-out, she'd settled that with Mairelon, but she couldn't quite say so if it meant agreeing with Mrs. Lowe in public. She coughed, trying to clear away the obstruction, but before she could find a good way to phrase her comment, the door opened and Mairelon entered.

"Good morning, Mother," he said. "I thought it must be you when I heard the commotion in the hall, and I was sure of it when I found a monkey in the library. Why a monkey, of all things?"

"Yes, isn't he charming?" Lady Wendall said. "Pahari Singh sent him to me. Actually, he sent three of them, but I'm afraid the other two didn't survive the voyage from India."

"*Three* monkeys?" Mrs. Lowe said.

"Who is Pahari Singh, and why on earth would he send you one monkey, let alone three?" Mairelon demanded.

"He was a good friend of your father's, from his days in India, though that, of course, was before you and Andrew were born. He was in London a few years ago on business, and he made a point of renewing the acquaintance."

"That explains who he is," Mairelon said, "but not why he should choose to send you a batch of monkeys."

"I believe he wanted to make sure I would have more than one serving," Lady Wendall replied. "Though his note was not exactly specific on the subject."

"Serving?" Mrs. Lowe said faintly. She set her fork carefully beside her unfinished breakfast. "Elizabeth . . ."

Mairelon looked at Lady Wendall with considerable misgiving. "Mother, are you saying that Mr. Singh sent you this creature as a . . . an addition to your dinner menu?"

"In a way. Monkey brains are considered a delicacy in India, and—"

"You're going to eat a *monkey brain?*" Kim broke in, thoroughly taken aback.

Lady Wendall gave a regretful sigh. "Not any time soon, I am afraid. I simply couldn't bear to have Maximillian slaughtered. It will just have to wait until the next time I visit India."

"Thank goodness for that," Mairelon said. "You know, monkeys are filthy creatures. You're lucky he doesn't have lice. Or fleas."

"Oh, he had both, when he arrived," Lady Wendall said imperturbably. "I had him bathed, naturally."

"I should hope so," Mrs. Lowe put in. She appeared to have recovered her equanimity, though she had not yet returned to her breakfast. "That does not explain, however, why you have chosen to introduce him into this household."

"Well, Lord Wendall couldn't very well take Maximillian to Suffolk with him, and I couldn't very well leave him in Russell Square with the renovations going on. So of course I brought him with me."

"Renovations?" Mairelon frowned. "Mother . . ."

"Renovations?" Mrs. Lowe stared. "Elizabeth, do you mean to say that you intend to stay *here* for the entire Season?"

"Yes, of course," Lady Wendall said. "Lord Wendall and Andrew are going to be in Suffolk discussing canals for the greater part of it, so Andrew offered to let me use the townhouse. He did warn me that Richard and Kim—and you, of course, Agatha—would be here, and I was of two minds about it until I heard that Richard was planning to give Kim a formal come-out."

"And when did you hear that?" Mrs. Lowe said, with a look at Mairelon that would have set fire to a heap of coal.

"Yesterday, at Lady Weydon's saloon," Lady Wendall replied. "Sally Jersey told me; she had it from someone who had been having tea with Richard. And I can already see that I was quite right to come." She turned to Mairelon. "Really, Richard, I thought you'd have had better sense. You've got her rigged out like a greengrocer's daughter."

"Kim's clothes are entirely suitable for her situation," Mrs. Lowe said, bristling.

Kim shifted uncomfortably. "It's not slap up to the nines, but neither am I."

"Nonsense," Mairelon said. "You look perfectly all right to me."

"That is precisely the problem," Lady Wendall told him. "Why on earth didn't you ask your friend Mademoiselle D'Auber to help you? If there's one thing the French know how to do, it's dress."

"She offered," Mairelon admitted, looking a little guilty, "but we didn't have time before Kim and I went down to Kent, and since we've been back, there have been other things. . . ."

"Well, you had better send her a note today," Lady Wendall said. "I shall be occupied in going through Kim's clothes, to see which of them are suitable, and in engaging an abigail for her."

Mrs. Lowe frowned. "Surely one of the housemaids will do well enough."

"I don't want an abigail," Kim said. "And—"

"I don't blame you in the least," Lady Wendall told her, "but an abigail you must have if we are to launch you into Society." She studied Kim for a moment, her expression disconcertingly like Mairelon's when he was concentrating all his attention on something. "Someone young and flexible, I think, who will know when to make allowances for the eccentricities of wizards."

"Kim is hardly eccentric, Mother," Mairelon said.

"Nor is she the only wizard in this household," Lady Wendall replied. "Though if you can think of a more socially acceptable description of her background than 'eccentric,' I will be delighted."

"I am relieved to see that you are aware of the problem," Mrs. Lowe said stiffly.

"Perhaps Renée can recommend a suitable abigail," Lady Wendall went on. "You must remember to ask her when you speak to her about Kim's clothes."

"Mairelon—" Kim said, feeling desperate. The whole conversation was getting out of hand. If one of them didn't say something soon, she was going to find herself presented whether she wanted to be or not. And Mairelon had promised to speak with Mrs. Lowe about it. . . .

But Mairelon's face had the peculiar expression he wore when he had just had an idea, and he was oblivious to anything else. "Renée. Of course; I should have thought of that myself. You haven't anything planned this morning, have you, Kim? Good; finish your breakfast, and we'll go see Renée."

"I'm finished," Kim said. "But—"

"Change your clothes first," Mrs. Lowe said. "You positively cannot be seen on the street like that."

Lady Wendall nodded. "*Just* what I have been saying. I'll send a note to Madame Chandelaine this afternoon; there's no better dressmaker in London."

There was no use talking to any of them now. Maybe Renée D'Auber would have some advice; she was a lot more sensible than most toffs. Kim rolled her eyes and left.

When Kim and Mairelon arrived at Renée D'Auber's townhouse, a formidably correct butler showed them up to the drawing room at once. There they found Mademoiselle D'Auber busy at a small writing table. Her auburn hair was braided close to her head, and there was a smudge of dust or ink on the point of her chin; she resembled neither an elegant lady of fashion nor a wizard of power and skill, though she was both. A stack of books stood on a side table next to her. A faint scent of incense lingered in the air; Mademoiselle D'Auber must have been spellcasting recently. As the butler announced them, she looked up and smiled.

"Monsieur Merrill! And Mademoiselle Kim. It is of all things good to see you."

"And it is always good to see you, Renée," Mairelon said with a warm smile.

"You are kind, but it is not often that you come so early," Renée said, returning Mairelon's smile. "Sit down, and tell me what it is that brings you."

As she took a chair covered in wine-red silk, Kim watched her two companions with curiosity bordering on bafflement. Though she had known both Mairelon and Renée D'Auber for a year now, she could not begin to pretend that she understood their relationship. There seemed to be no element of romance between them, and she had observed them closely enough to stake her position as Mairelon's ward that there was no physical intimacy, either. Yet there was an undeniable warmth and familiarity in their conversation that, if Mrs. Lowe were to be believed, was not fitting between an unattached man and a respectable young woman of quality. Maybe it was because they were both wizards, or perhaps it had something to do with the years Mairelon had spent gathering intelligence in France.

"Two things," Mairelon said. "First, can you tell me anything about a group of French wizards called *Les Griffonais*? They apparently had something of a name in France before the Terror."

Renée looked at him with considerable amusement. "And you expect that I will know something of them? The Terror was nearly thirty years ago, and me, I was not yet born." She held up a hand to forestall Mairelon's next comment and continued, "I do not say I have not heard of them, but I wish to know why you have this interest before I say any more. Otherwise you will not tell me anything, and I shall perish of the curiosity."

"My father bought part of a library collection that once belonged to a Madame Marie de Cambriol. Lord Kerring down at the Royal College says she was one of the group."

"And?"

Mairelon sighed. "And somebody seems a little too interested in Madame's collection for my peace of mind."

Mlle. D'Auber looked at him with disfavor. "You, my friend, are entirely English, which is a thing impossible to understand. And you are even more impossible to get answers from than other English persons. Kim! What is it that he means by this 'too interested for his peace of mind'?"

"Some toff wizard broke into the house night before last," Kim said. "He was looking for something in the library, and he had a spell with him that lit up all the books from the Cambriol mort's collection."

"We think he only wanted one of the books," Mairelon said, "but Kim ran him off before he could take it."

"You are sure?"

Mairelon shrugged. "Andrew had an inventory done when my father died; everything on the list is still there."

Renée nodded. "Very good. Now I will tell you what I know, which is not much. I never met this Marie de Cambriol, but the Sieur Jacques de Cambriol was a friend of my father's. His wife died very suddenly, a year or two after they emigrated, and when I was very little he used to come to dinner with my parents."

"Was the Sieur de Cambriol a wizard?"

"No. I do not know what he was in France, before the Terror, but afterward he was a gambler. Papa spoke of him often, and tried to help when he could. He died nearly ten years ago, I think, in the debtors' prison."

"So they escaped the Terror and came to England—"

"No," Renée corrected. "They left France before the Terror began, the Sieur Jacques and his wife and their friends." She frowned. "The Sieur used to tell me the story, with much waving of hands. I am afraid I do not recollect the details at all clearly—it was not a daring escape, you see, but simply prudent. And the prudence, it did not at all interest me when I was a child."

Mairelon straightened. "The de Cambriols *and their friends* left France before the terror? That wouldn't by any chance be the rest of the group of wizards?"

"I think it was," Renée said after some thought. "But I am not positive, you understand."

"Do you know who the others were?" Kim asked.

"*Les Griffonais?* Let me think. Madame de Cambriol, of course, and the Comte du Franchard and his wife, the Comtesse de Beauvoix. The duchesse Delagardie. The Hungarian, M. László Karolyi. M. Henri d'Armand. And Mademoiselle Jeannette Lepain, who as a child I thought was of all things most romantic because she married a Russian prince."

"Do you know whether any of them are in England now?" Mairelon said.

"No, I do not know," Renée said. "They were not, you understand, friends of mine; I do not think even Papa knew any of them except Sieur de Cambriol."

"Well, at least now I have some names," Mairelon said. "Thank you, Renée. I wonder whether Shoreham is still keeping track of the *émigrés*; I believe I'll stop in and ask him tomorrow."

"And your other reason for coming to visit me?" Mlle. D'Auber said. "You said there were two."

"What? Oh, yes, well, that's Kim's, actually. Mother arrived this morning and says she's not dressed properly; she thought you might be interested in helping out."

"*Mairelon*," Kim said, thoroughly exasperated.

"Yes, he is of all persons the most excessively trying," Renée said, nodding. "Now you will tell me what it is he is trying to say."

"He said, it, but—Lady Wendall only wants me to dress better because she thinks Mairelon's going to present me to Society. And he isn't."

Renée's eyebrows rose expressively. "Not?"

"Kim doesn't wish it," Mairelon said shortly.

The eyebrows twitched, then rose even higher. "Indeed. Then how is it your so-estimable mother is of the idea that you will do so?"

"Gossip," Mairelon said.

"It ain't just gossip!" Kim said. "It's what you said at that tea. Your mother believes it, and the way she's going on, I'm like to be presented tomorrow whether I want it or not."

"I'll explain to Mother as soon as we get back," Mairelon said. "She'll understand. Though she would certainly enjoy managing it."

"One moment," Renée said, looking from one to the other. "I wish first to know why it is that Mademoiselle Kim does not wish to be presented."

"I—" Kim swallowed hard. "Look, this ain't—isn't going to sound right, but I just don't like it. Making up to a bunch of old cats just because they say who gets invited to a lot of boring teas and balls . . . Doing the wizard stuff is hard enough. And I'm not good at watching what I say." She gestured helplessly. "It just wouldn't work."

"But of course it would work!" Renée shook her head reprovingly. "You are a wizard. It is expected that you will be entirely original. And there are many advantages, you know."

"Like what?" Kim said, half wanting to be convinced but not really believing it was possible.

"M. Merrill's Mama is exceedingly well known; if it is she who introduces you to Society, you will be accepted by everyone. And it is often useful for a wizard to know a great many persons. Also, if you are not presented, there will always be persons who wonder why. Some will think that you cannot truly be a wizard."

"I hadn't thought of that," Mairelon said slowly, "but you're right. They would."

"Why?" Kim said. "That doesn't make sense!"

Renée shrugged. "To them, it does. They cannot conceive that anyone would not wish to be presented. If you are not, they will say it is because you *cannot* be, and since a wizard can always be presented, you must not be one. It is very foolish."

"Well . . ."

"There is also M. Merrill to consider," Renée went on. "A great many people thought he had stolen the Saltash Set, and now they do not think he is enough respectable even though the set is returned and milord Shoreham has arrested the real thieves."

"That is ridiculous!" Mairelon said.

Renée waved his objection aside. "I say only what people think. And since you do not often go to balls or parties, a great many persons of no intellect whatever think that it is because you are not invited and not because, like Mademoiselle Kim, you do not find it interesting. It would have been altogether better if you had spent the Season in London last year, as we talked of then."

"I did," Mairelon objected.

"You spent it with milord Shoreham, and not at the balls and parties," Renée said. "It is not at all the same. But if Mademoiselle Kim is presented, you will *have* to go to balls, and people will see that you are quite enough respectable after all. Or at least, that you are not so unrespectable as they had thought."

Kim stared at Mlle. D'Auber, speechless. This was an aspect of the matter that she had never considered. From the look on his face, neither had Mairelon, though she couldn't tell whether his look of chagrin came from the realization that some of Society thought he was not "enough respectable," or from the realization that if his ward were to come out properly, he, too, would be required to attend balls and parties. Knowing Mairelon, she suspected the latter.

"I do not think it will be nearly so boring as you fear," Renée said

to Kim, smiling. "Not with M. Merrill's Mama in charge. And once you
have been presented, it is done, and you may attend the balls or not, as
it pleases you."

"And if you do it, Aunt Agatha will turn positively purple," Mairelon
murmured, recovering quickly.

The silence that followed stretched on for what seemed forever. Finally, Kim sighed. "All right, then. I'll try it. But I still think you all have
windmills in your heads."

"Of a certainty," Mlle. D'Auber said. "How else is one to deal with
M. Merrill?"

eight

After leaving Mlle. D'Auber's, Mairelon ordered the coach to stop at the Horse Guards, where Lord Shoreham had his office. Unfortunately, Lord Shoreham was unable to give him any more information regarding the French wizards, though he promised to have his records checked for anything that Mairelon might find useful. They arrived home early in the afternoon, and Kim was immediately swept up by Lady Wendall.

"Is there anything in your wardrobe of which you are particularly fond?" she demanded of Kim almost as soon as Kim entered the house.

"I don't think so," Kim said, considerably startled.

"Good. Then I will have one of the footmen take all of it to the used clothing shops tomorrow," Lady Wendall said. "Except of course for the outfit you have stored in the hatbox; that clearly has uses other than fashion to recommend it. Did you speak to Mlle. D'Auber about shopping tomorrow?"

"I forgot," Kim said. "Mairelon had other things he wanted to talk about."

"Richard always does. Well, I'll send a note around this afternoon. I suggest you spend the time on your magical studies; tomorrow, you will be quite thoroughly occupied."

Nothing loath, Kim escaped to the library, where she alternated between watching the monkey's antics in its wicker cage and trying to puzzle out a few more of Mairelon's assigned texts. Since all of them included occasional examples in foreign languages that were quite beyond Kim's comprehension, she had a long list of questions ready for Mairelon by the time he came to check on her progress. Mairelon readily agreed to translate and explain the questionable bits, but his answers only frustrated Kim more.

"Don't these coves know how to say anything straight out in English?" Kim demanded after Mairelon had finished explaining a particularly convoluted paragraph written in Greek, which boiled down to *Don't try this; it doesn't work.*

Mairelon laughed. "It wouldn't sound nearly as impressive in plain English."

"I thought the point was to tell wizards how to do magic," Kim said crossly. "Not to sound impressive."

"Wizards are at least as vain as anyone else," Mairelon said. "Possibly more so."

"Well, I don't see why I have to learn all this foreign talk just so some cull who's been dead since before I was born can sound flash when he says, 'Wiggle all the fingers on your right hand.'"

"You'll just have to trust me when I tell you it's worth the effort," Mairelon told her. "You could probably learn quite a few of the simple spells by rote, but it would be very difficult for you to get much beyond that."

"Why? I have a good memory."

"Yes, but magic isn't just a matter of memory. It takes understanding, too. Here, I'll show you." Mairelon set the book aside and went over to his mother's desk. After a moment of rummaging and a few more of scribbling, he returned with a sheet of paper bearing a peculiar diagram and four words.

"This is a spell," he said, thrusting the paper into her hand. "You ought to be able to handle it at your level. You cast it by drawing this diagram, starting with this—" he pointed "—and ending with these. As you draw each of these points, you say one of these words, in order."

"How do I say them?" Kim said, staring at the unfamiliar jumble of consonants and vowels.

Mairelon obligingly pronounced each word in turn. "Now cast it."

Kim gave him a startled look, then lowered her eyes to study the paper. The drawing was of a circle quartered by two double-headed arrows, the heads of which protruded on all four sides. *Draw the circle first, then the cross, and then the arrowheads, and say one word at each arrowhead. Fine.* She took the pen and ink Mairelon handed her, and bent to her task.

As she spoke the first word, she felt a faint tingling. It strengthened a trifle with each additional command, and when she looked up, she thought she saw a faint greenish haze around several of the bookcases, and a brief shower of green sparkles near Mairelon's coat. The effect faded almost at once. Mairelon nodded in approval.

"Not bad. But look here. The circle represents magic; the four arrows are four directions. *Epistamai* is Greek for 'to know,' *videre* is Latin for 'to see,' *l'herah* is Hebrew for 'to show,' and *revelare* is Latin again, meaning 'to reveal.' Put it all together, and you have a spell that lets a magician find out what things around him have been enchanted."

"You can tell that most of the time just by touching them," Kim objected.

"You can't go around touching everything you suspect of being magical," Mairelon said. "Quite apart from the attention you'd attract, it's not always wise."

"Trap spells, you mean."

"Among other things. Now, cast it again."

Frowning slightly, Kim did so. This time, two of the bookcases glowed a steady green, the third button on Mairelon's coat was a shower of green sparks, and one of the candlesticks was briefly surrounded by a faint green mist.

The effect took longer to fade, too. A greenish haze still remained around his button when he finally said, "It was clearer that time, wasn't it?"

Kim gave him a startled look. "Couldn't you tell?"

"It's not a general spell to show *everyone* what's enchanted. It's only supposed to show *you*."

"Oh. Yes, everything was brighter."

"That's the difference between knowing a spell by rote and actually understanding what you are saying."

"But—" Kim paused, frowning. Then she dipped the pen once more and began to draw the figure. "To know," she said as she completed the first arrow. "To see. To show. To reveal . . . Ow!" An instant too late, she flung a hand over her eyes to shut out the blinding light that flared from the bookcases and the searing flashes from Mairelon's button.

"And *that* is why you can't just learn spells in English in the first place," Mairelon said in a tone of smug satisfaction.

"You might of warned me!" Kim said, keeping her eyes closed.

"Some things take better if you aren't told about them first," Mairelon said. "Besides, I wanted to see whether you'd think of it on your own."

"You still could of warned me." Cautiously, Kim opened her eyes.

Green spots still danced in front of them, but the light had weakened to a bearable level.

"If it's any comfort, you're doing rather well. I didn't think of trying a spell in English until my third year of formal study, and I was fool enough to pick a translation spell to try it on. For the next week, everything I said or wrote came out in a garble of French, Spanish, Italian, Russian, and some outlandish tongue I didn't even recognize. I couldn't explain to anyone what had happened, and with everything I said coming out in a muddle, I couldn't use magic to correct matters."

"What did you do?"

Mairelon grimaced. "There wasn't much of anything I *could* do. Fortunately, Mother knows a bit of the Art herself, and when I came in sounding like all the workmen at the Tower of Babel rolled into one, she could tell there was magic involved. She sent for my tutor, and of course once he did the spell properly, he understood me. He told the family, which settled things down considerably. There was nothing to be done about me, though, except wait for the enchantment to wear off. I had to make do with sign language for a week."

"Are you trying to say that if I'd waited until next year to try that, it would have been even worse than it was?" Kim demanded.

"Much worse," Mairelon said cheerfully. "The further you get in your study of magic, the more power you use without thinking about it. Using a foreign tongue keeps it all from spewing into a spell uncontrollably. And the reason most spells are in ancient Greek and Latin is that nobody grows up speaking those languages any more, so every wizard can use spells written in them without having to translate them first."

"So if I was to say this spell in French, it would work just as well as it does in Latin?" Kim asked.

"Yes, exactly. Of course, the more complex the spell, the more important the precise shades of meaning become. When we get to advanced work, you'll find that some spells have completely different effects, depending on whether you say them in Latin or Greek or Hebrew."

"And Mlle. D'Auber could do spells in English if she wanted, but I can't."

Mairelon beamed. "Yes. As far as the Royal College can determine, mere fluency in a foreign language does not cause the same problems as growing up speaking it. English is a foreign language to Renée, so she could certainly cast spells in it." He paused, then added absently, "I sometimes wonder how the Jewish wizards manage. Hebrew is used in quite a lot of spells, and one would think— But then, if they *have* found a way around the language problem, one can't blame them for keeping it secret. Not after the way they've been treated over the centuries."

Ignoring this novel viewpoint, Kim frowned. "All right, but why do I have to learn *three kinds* of foreign talk? Isn't one enough?"

"It is an unfortunate side effect of history," Mairelon said. "The ancient Romans couldn't cast their spells in Latin, so they used Greek. The Greeks couldn't cast spells in Greek, so they used Latin. And mixing in a little Hebrew kept spells from being quite so easy to steal, because the spellcaster had to know at least two languages."

"I still say it's too tangled," Kim grumbled. "And what do all those spells *do*, anyway? The ones I saw—on the bookcases and your waistcoat button and the candlestick."

"Finding that out is a different spell," Mairelon said. "And we're not through with the theory of this one, yet. Now, if you alter the order, like this, nothing happens, but if you change the arrowheads to triangles . . ."

An hour and a half later, Kim's head was buzzing. She was amazed by the number of changes that could be wrung out of the simple spell merely by changing the order of the words or the way in which the diagram was drawn, and she had a new respect for the reasons behind Mairelon's emphasis on accuracy in spellcasting.

The following morning, Lady Wendall appeared at Kim's room, accompanied by a plump, middle-aged woman whose sharp eyes belied her outward appearance of placid respectability.

"Wilson will be your abigail," Lady Wendall informed Kim. "If you must go out without Richard or myself, take her with you."

"Even to St. Giles?" Kim said, nettled.

"Not at all, miss," the plump woman responded. "St. Giles ain't no place for a respectable woman, let alone a young lady of Quality. So if you go there, it'll be for wizardly doings, and you won't be needing me. My lady meant more usual places. Shopping and such."

Kim made a face, and Lady Wendall laughed. "Wilson is quite right. Wizards do not require an abigail when they are on magical business, though of course it is wise to bring one with you even for most of that. You will become accustomed in time, I am sure."

"That doesn't make any sense," Kim objected. She didn't feel up to explaining that it was the thought of shopping, and not of being shadowed by a respectable abigail, that had made her grimace.

"Of course it doesn't make sense," Lady Wendall said. "The rules of

Society seldom do. One must simply learn them, no matter how little sense they make."

"Oh. It's exactly the opposite of magic, then."

Lady Wendall laughed. "Yes, I am afraid so. But if you transgress the rules of Society, you may well find yourself an outcast. Wizardry cannot protect one from everything." She paused. "I do hope you will try not to err, my dear. You may not find social ostracism much of a threat, but it would be so uncomfortable for Richard."

Kim frowned. "You mean that Mrs. Lowe was right?"

"I doubt it," Lady Wendall murmured. "Right about what?"

"About how me being his ward makes him look bad to the nobs."

"Not at all. It is a minor eccentricity on his part, but wizards are allowed considerably more freedom in some regards than most people. Were you to create a great scandal—if you eloped to Gretna Green or attempted to turn His Highness into a toad—that would certainly reflect on Richard, the same as if his brother or I were to do such a thing. I don't think you need to worry too much, however. A little common sense is really all that is needed."

Maybe that's all it takes for you, Kim thought, but she held her peace. Lady Wendall was trying to be reassuring, but Kim could not help feeling that she would be facing less obvious pitfalls than a runaway marriage or a misdirected spell.

Lady Wendall smiled. "Now, if you will put on your green walking dress, we will proceed to Madame Chandelaine's to procure you a proper wardrobe."

With a sigh, Kim nodded. She let Wilson dress her and arrange her hair, then joined Lady Wendall. She was still considering Lady Wendall's comments, and wondering whether the whole come-out business wasn't really a mistake after all, and so they had almost reached Madame Chandelaine's before she thought to ask whether Renée would be accompanying them.

"Mlle. D'Auber is to meet us at Madame's," Lady Wendall told Kim. "We will have a certain amount of time to talk while you are being fitted, but I warn you that Madame is an inveterate gossip. If you do not wish to find the whole of London discussing your affairs, you will have to watch what you say."

When they arrived, they were ushered immediately into a private room at the back of the establishment. Renée was already there, engaged in a spirited conversation with a black-haired woman of formidable proportions. Unfortunately, the conversation was in French, so Kim did not understand a word. Lady Wendall greeted the two in the same language, and for a moment Kim was afraid that all three of them would speak French for the entire afternoon. After her greeting, however, Lady Wendall returned to English and said, "Has Mlle. D'Auber explained our requirements, Madame?"

"A wardrobe for the young lady, I believe?" The formidable Frenchwoman studied Kim with a critical eye.

Lady Wendall nodded. "Garments suitable for my son's ward, whom I shall be presenting this Season. And also suitable for an apprentice wizard, recognized by the Royal College, who is having her first Season."

"A wizard in her first Season?" Madame's gaze sharpened with curiosity and interest.

"It is not at all uncommon for wizards to enjoy the Season," Mlle. D'Auber pointed out gently.

"It is, however, uncommon for the young ladies to admit that they are wizards—especially in their first Season," Madame said. "It is not a thing the Mamas believe is of help in catching a husband. Last Season, I had the dressing of only two such; this Season, none at all."

"My son's ward is uncommon," Lady Wendall said. "In fact, her antecedents are somewhat . . . unusual."

"Wizards are always unusual." Madame waved dismissively. "But of a certainty, they do not always admit it. I will find it a pleasure to have the dressing of one who does. Turn around, Mademoiselle, if you please."

Kim complied.

"Charming," Madame said. "Entirely charming. It will be well, I think. Elspeth! The green-figured muslin, and the yellow silk. And the China blue crêpe."

"Not yellow," Renée put in firmly. "For Kim, it is a color entirely unbecoming."

"So?" Madame studied Kim a moment, frowning. "Yes, yes, I see. The white sarcenet, then, and the lilac. What will she be doing for her display? Roses?"

"We have not yet decided," Lady Wendall said. "I can assure you, however, it will not be anything so usual."

"Display?" Kim said, her head already spinning from the talk of so many colors and fabrics. "What display?"

"If you wish me to design a dress for her presentation ball, I must know what illusion she is to perform," Madame said. "Something in peach would be well with Mademoiselle's coloring, but not if she is to perform red roses or a fire."

"Perform?" Kim said, now thoroughly alarmed. "What do you mean, perform?"

"We will leave the dress for her ball until later," Lady Wendall informed Madame. "There are still three weeks before it will be needed." She turned to Kim. "It is customary, on those occasions when a wizard is being presented, for her to perform some magical illusion with her magic tutor before she opens the dancing. Climbing roses have been very popular in the last few years, though in the Season following Waterloo a Miss Taldworth attempted an image of Napoleon surrendering his sword. She did a very bad job of it, quite apart from the fundamental inaccuracy of the image, and it was an *on dit* for weeks. Since then everyone has kept to things that are simpler."

"Or they avoid it entirely," Renée said. "The Mamas, they presented last year more than two young ladies who were wizards, I think."

"You mean I'm going to have to do a spell in front of a bunch of *toffs*?" Kim said, outraged that no one had mentioned this before she had agreed to this come-out.

"Yes, exactly," Lady Wendall said serenely. "You and Richard have plenty of time to design something that will reflect your unique background, as well as demonstrating your abilities as a wizard. I am looking forward to seeing what you decide upon."

"I could pick everyone's pockets at once with magic," Kim said, still disgruntled. "That'd 'reflect my unique background,' all right."

Lady Wendall considered. "I don't think so. Unless Richard has been pushing you far harder than he ought, spells of that magnitude and scope are still beyond your abilities. An illusion along those lines, however, would be just the thing. You must discuss it with him when we get home."

A teetering pile of fabric bolts, supported by Madame's young assistant, staggered into the room. "Ah, Elspeth!" Madame said. "On the table, if you please. Now, Mademoiselle. . . ."

Kim spent the next several hours being measured, draped, fitted, and paraded before the critical eyes of Lady Wendall, Renée D'Auber, and Madame Chandelaine in a variety of dresses. Lady Wendall began by ordering a cream walking dress that needed only to be shortened and a morning dress in the green-figured muslin, both to be delivered on the morrow. After that, she became more particular, choosing a sleeve from this dress and a flounce from that one, to be combined with a different bodice and a fuller skirt. Renée added advice and suggestions of her own, and Madame also put in a word from time to time. No one asked for Kim's opinion.

The number and cost of the dresses appalled Kim. Lady Wendall's idea of an acceptable wardrobe was considerably more lavish than Mairelon's or Mrs. Lowe's; in her days on the street, Kim could have lived comfortably for two years on the price of a single walking dress. The ball gowns were naturally much worse, and there were far more of them than Kim could imagine ever needing. But both Lady Wendall and Renée D'Auber looked at her in complete incomprehension when she tried to explain her objections, so eventually she gave up and let them do as they wished.

When they had finished negotiating with Madame, there were more things to be purchased elsewhere: gloves, bonnets, stockings, slippers, and all manner of other small items. By the time they returned to Grosvenor Square at last, they were laden with packages and Kim was exhausted. Even Mrs. Lowe's disapproving comments over dinner failed to penetrate her fatigue. She fell into bed that night, thankful that at least the shopping part was done with.

nine

Kim discovered her mistake over the course of the next week. Not only was the shopping not done with, there were an enormous number of preparations necessary for the ball Lady Wendall proposed to hold. Everything, it seemed, had to be done immediately, beginning with writing out and sending invitations to some four hundred persons of Lady Wendall's acquaintance. Kim's poor handwriting kept her from helping with that chore, but plenty of other things needed to be done.

Her magic lessons were a welcome break from the sudden plunge into social arrangements. Mairelon had begun focusing more on specific spells, which Kim found far more interesting than the dry tomes full of jaw-breaking foreign languages that she had been studying earlier. When she thought about it, she realized that she was learning a great deal of magical theory along with the practical specifics of the spells they reviewed together, but working with Mairelon made theory intriguing instead of dull.

In the evenings, Mairelon gave her dancing lessons, while Lady Wendall played the pianoforte. Kim picked up the patterns of the country dances very quickly, but waltzing made her nervous. For too many years, she had carefully avoided getting near people, for fear they would discover that she was not the boy she had pretended to be. Allowing anyone, even Mairelon, not only to come close, but to circle her waist with his arm brought back old fears, though she had to admit that the sensation was pleasurable on those rare occasions when she could relax enough to enjoy it.

The mysterious burglar did not reappear, for which Kim could only be thankful. Between shopping, preparations for the ball, and lessons in magic, dancing, and etiquette, her days were too full to admit any additional activities. It was almost a relief when Lady Wendall announced over dinner that they would be spending the following evening at the opera.

"Most of your gowns have arrived, so you will be sure of making a good appearance," Lady Wendall said.

Mrs. Lowe looked up. "You will understand, I am sure, if I do not choose to join you."

"Of course," Lady Wendall said. "Though I think you refine too much on Kim's misadventure at Mrs. Hardcastle's."

"Nonetheless, I prefer a peaceful evening at home to the . . . uncertainties of a public appearance at this time."

"Nonsense, Aunt!" Mairelon said. "What can happen at the opera? You go, you sit in a box and listen to a lot of caterwauling, you wave at other people during the interval, and you come home."

"I sincerely hope that your evening will be as unexceptionable as you say," Mrs. Lowe said. "But I remain at home."

"In that case, I shall invite Renée D'Auber to accompany us," Lady Wendall said.

The whole thing sounded less than appealing to Kim, but she had agreed to this come-out business, and she would see it through. Her misgivings increased when Wilson, the abigail, helped her get ready. Apart from fittings, it was the first time Kim had worn formal evening dress. The apricot crêpe hung smoothly over the matching satin slip, but she was not at all sure she could walk without stepping on the deep flounce of blond lace that trimmed the hem. The bodice was fashionably tight and low cut—too low cut, Kim thought. Her shoulders and breasts felt decidedly exposed. It hadn't seemed nearly as skimpy during the fittings. A thin scarf woven with gold threads did little to mend matters. Feeling nervous, Kim went down to join the others.

"Excellent," Lady Wendall said as Kim came down the stairs. "That color is perfect."

"I'm sorry I kept you waiting," Kim said. Lady Wendall's dress was at least as low cut as hers, and the drape of lace trim that fell over the dark green silk of the bodice made it look even more precarious.

"It's only to be expected," Mairelon said. "It always takes longer to put on a costume the first time."

"Richard!" said his mother. "You are talking as if we were going to a masquerade instead of the opera."

"Am I?" Mairelon said vaguely. "Ah, well. Hadn't we better be going?"

Lady Wendall rolled her eyes and took Mairelon's arm. *But Mairelon is right*, thought Kim as she followed them out to the carriage. *It is a costume, and I am only playing a part, the same way I played the part of a boy for so long.* The thought was depressing; it made her wonder whether she would have to play at being something other than what she was for all her life. *But what am I, if I stop playing parts?* She shivered and thrust the thought away. *This* part was what mattered tonight, dispiriting as it might be. And on top of everything, Mairelon hadn't even said that she looked nice.

Her depression lifted when they entered the opera house. The ornate foyer was crowded with toffs. Most of the men wore dark coats and pantaloons; the younger women wore muslin gowns in soft colors; and the older ones wore silks, velvets, and a profusion of jewels that almost made Kim regret having given up thieving. Lady Wendall, Renée, and Mairelon seemed in no hurry to reach their box. They moved slowly through the crowd, greeting acquaintances, chatting with friends, and introducing Kim to more people than she could possibly remember.

Eventually, they reached the box, but this only set off another round of socializing as people in other boxes saw them and left their places to come and visit. Kim was not at all sure how they decided who stayed in a box and who came to visit, but there had to be some sort of system, or too many people would pass each other in the hall.

After what seemed hours, the traffic lessened and a few people began to take their seats in preparation for the overture. Many, however, continued talking and visiting despite the music. As the curtain rose, Kim noticed a slender young man watching them from the opposite box. She leaned over to mention this to Lady Wendall, but was frowned into silence. The show began.

On the whole, Kim decided, opera compared favorably with the puppet shows, hurdy-gurdy men, and balladeers of the marketplaces. The actors had better costumes, and everybody sang on key, and every so often a thoroughly implausible fight would erupt, with lots of leaping about and everyone still singing at the top of their lungs. On the other hand, she couldn't understand a word of it, and without the words, the actions didn't make much sense. She wasn't entirely convinced they were supposed to. It didn't seem to matter to anyone else; most of the audience was more interested in talking to each other or observing the toffs in the boxes than in the events on stage.

Halfway through the first act, Kim felt the unmistakable tingling sensation that heralded a spell in process. She stiffened, and looked around for the wizard, noting absently that Mairelon, Lady Wendall, and Renée D'Auber were doing the same. No one else seemed to notice; on stage, the opera continued forward without pause, and the audience was as rapt as they had ever been, which was not much. Mairelon spoke two rapid sentences in a low voice, and the tingling intensified. Then, abruptly, the feeling vanished.

Kim wanted desperately to question Mairelon, but again Lady Wendall gestured to forbid speech. Renée, Mairelon, and Lady Wendall continued watching the performance with outward calm, while Kim shifted restlessly in her seat for the rest of the act. As the curtain closed and the stage crew rushed to replace the candles in the giant candelabra that provided light to the stage, she turned to Mairelon and demanded, "What was that?"

"A scrying spell, I think," Mairelon said. "Someone wanted to know where we were."

"You *think?*" Renée said, lifting her eyebrows.

"The spell had an unusual construction. It was similar to the basic look-and-see spell everyone learns as an apprentice, but it wasn't identical by any means." He smiled. "It will be interesting to see who turns up during the interval."

An expression of mild relief crossed Lady Wendall's face. "You think that's all—oh, good evening, Lady Lidestone. Allow me to present my son's apprentice and ward, Miss Kim Merrill."

Kim rose and bobbed a curtsey as an elderly woman in a purple turban entered the box. "I am pleased to make your acquaintance, Lady Lidestone," she murmured.

Lady Lidestone raised a gold lorgnette and studied Kim. "Better than I had been led to believe," she pronounced after a moment. "So you really do intend to introduce her to Society, Elizabeth?"

"Of course," Lady Wendall said. "It will add a bit of spice to this year's Season."

Lady Lidestone gave a crack of laughter. "You always have been one for spice. I'll look forward to more entertainment than I've had in a long while." She gave a nod of approval that included Kim, and moved on.

She was replaced almost at once by a tongue-tied young woman and her Mama, who had ostensibly come to give their regards to Lady Wendall, but who seemed far more interested in being presented to Mairelon.

They were followed by several amiable young men who wished to pay their respects to Renée, and the box began to seem more than a little full. Kim frowned, feeling hot and a little dizzy but not knowing quite what to do about it.

"You're looking a bit overheated," Mairelon's voice said in her ear. "I believe we should take a turn in the corridor."

Kim jumped, then nodded gratefully. With a few words, Mairelon extricated them from the polite conversation, and a moment later they were in the relative cool and quiet of the corridor.

"That's a relief," Kim said with a sigh as they walked toward the foyer.

Mairelon raised an eyebrow in inquiry.

"This is all . . . it's just . . . it's so *much*," she said.

"A bit overwhelming?" Mairelon nodded. "You'll become accustomed."

"Maybe," Kim said dubiously.

They walked in companionable silence to the foyer, nodding in passing to several people on their way to visit boxes. The foyer was, once again, full of toffs and the scent of candle smoke. They stood in the doorway for a moment, watching as people surged and shifted, then moved sideways to stand against the wall and out of the traffic.

A few enterprising vendors had slipped into the opera house with baskets of fruit or comfits to sell to the toffs; one had even managed a tray of steaming drinks. Kim watched in professional admiration as he maneuvered through the crowd without spilling a drop. His customers were not always so fortunate; even as she watched, someone jostled a tall gentleman holding one of the drinks. The liquid sloshed over the rim of the mug and over his hands and sleeves. Cursing, the man set the mug on the vendor's tray and stripped off his gloves. As he scrubbed uselessly at his sleeve, light gleamed on a gold ring carved in the shape of a flower with a red stone in the center.

Kim clutched at Mairelon's arm. "Mairelon! That toff burglar's here. Or somebody with a ring like his, anyways. Over there!"

Without hesitation, Mairelon shook off her hand and plunged into the crowd. Kim tried to keep the burglar in sight, but the constant motion of the crowd made it impossible. *If I'd known it was him sooner, I could have gotten a look at his face. Oh, well, maybe Mairelon will catch him.* But she knew that under these conditions, it would be the sheerest luck if he did. *At least now I know he's got light hair. I wish I could have seen his face, though.* She backed up to avoid being stepped on by a portly gentleman in a very great hurry, and bumped into someone standing behind her.

"Excuse me," she began, turning, and stopped short. Looking down at her was an impressively handsome man with sandy-brown hair and warm brown eyes. He appeared to be in his early thirties, and his clothes proclaimed him very well-inlaid. Without thinking, Kim glanced down at his hands, and was unreasonably relieved to see that he was not wearing a ring. *He can't be the cove Mairelon's chasing, anyway—he couldn't have gotten here from over there, not this fast.*

"It was my fault entirely, Mademoiselle, and I beg your pardon," the man said, bowing. His voice was deep and faintly accented, but all Kim was certain of was that he was not French. He straightened and smiled. "We appear to have no one to make proper introductions. Permit me to be incorrect. I am Alexei Nicholaiovitch Durmontov."

"I'm Kim."

"I am most pleased." Durmontov bowed again. "You are alone; may I return you to your party, to amend my clumsiness?"

Kim glanced over her shoulder, but there was no sign of Mairelon. *Well, Lady Wendall and Renée D'Auber keep saying that wizards can do what they like. So I will.* "Yes," she said, then added belatedly, "Thank you."

Durmontov offered her his arm, and she directed him down the hall to the box. Lady Wendall looked mildly startled when they entered, and gave Kim a pointed look of inquiry.

"Mairelon saw somebody he wanted to talk to," Kim said. "Mr. Durmontov offered to bring me back."

"Ah." Lady Wendall's expression cleared. "Thank you, Mr. Durmontov. I'm sure my son also appreciates your kindness to his ward. I am Lady Wendall."

"It is more correctly Prince Durmontov," Durmontov said almost apologetically. "Prince is not the most correct term, but it comes as close as your English can."

A prince? Kim suppressed the urge to shake her head in wonder as Lady Wendall went through the rest of the introductions, extracting the prince's full name in the process. *A prince, bowing to me. Tom Correy would never believe it.*

"You are, then, Russian?" Renée said with considerable interest once the courtesies had been attended to.

"Since my birth, Mademoiselle," Durmontov replied. "I currently stay with Countess Lieven, though next week I remove to the George."

"I will look forward to seeing you at the countess's when I call upon her Friday," Renée said.

"And what brings you to England, Prince Durmontov?" Lady Wendall asked.

The prince's smile vanished. "Family business," he said shortly.

"Forgive me if the question was indiscreet," Lady Wendall said, unperturbed. "I find your country fascinating, but I fear I am not well acquainted with your customs."

"In your country, it is I who must comply with English customs," Durmontov replied.

"Ah, Kim, you made it back," Mairelon said from the entrance to the box. "I had no luck, I'm afraid; he got away in the crowd. Did you get a good look at his face?"

"No," Kim answered.

"Richard." Lady Wendall's voice held just the faintest note of reproach. "Allow me to present Prince Alexei Durmontov. Prince, my son, Richard Merrill."

"It is a pleasure," the prince said, but his eyes were skeptical and faintly wary.

Mairelon did not appear to notice. "Durmontov, Durmontov. Now where have I . . . ? Oh, yes. You don't happen to know a Miss Letitia Tarnower, do you?"

"I do not believe so," he replied, looking startled. "Why is it that you ask?"

"I expect you'll meet her fairly soon, then," Mairelon said. "That would explain it nicely."

"Explain what?" Lady Wendall said.

"Monsieur Merrill is very often most provoking, particularly when it is a matter of information," Renée informed the puzzled Russian prince. "Do not mind him in the least."

"I shall do my best to take your advice, Mademoiselle," Durmontov said. "It would be less difficult, however, if I had some small idea to what he refers."

"We met Miss Tarnower at that tea party last week," Kim said to Lady Wendall, feeling some explanation was called for. "She asked about Prince Durmontov."

"Yes, she put on a splendid show of hen-wittedness," Mairelon said. "Nobody is that silly by accident. I wonder what, exactly, she has in mind?"

"It is entirely unimportant," Renée said with somewhat more emphasis than was strictly necessary. "And I very much regret it, but it is nearly time for the second curtain."

"I regret it also, Mademoiselle, and I look forward to our future meeting," Durmontov said, and took his leave.

There was no time for more; the curtain rose almost as the prince left the box. It was not until they were in the carriage on the way home that the conversation resumed.

"*Did* anyone else interesting turn up in the interval?" Mairelon asked as they rattled over the cobblestones toward Renée's townhouse.

"A Russian prince is quite enough, I think," Renée said.

"But was he the one who cast the scrying spell?"

"How is it that I would know that?" Renée demanded. "It is not a thing one can tell by looking."

"The Marquis of Harsfeld, Lord Franton, arrived after you left," Lady Wendall said with some satisfaction. "He wished to be presented to Kim, and was quite disappointed to find that she was not there."

"Harsfeld? He must be nearly eighty," Mairelon said, frowning. "What does he want with Kim?"

"No, no, Richard, you're thinking of the fourth Marquis of Harsfeld," Lady Wendall said. "He died last year; it is the fifth marquis who was asking after Kim. He is quite a young gentleman—not much above twenty, I think. He was the grandson of the previous marquis."

"Oh. I expect that's all right, then," Mairelon said, but he continued to frown.

Lady Wendall looked at him, and turned the topic to the evening's performance. As this involved much comparison with previous performances, and speculation as to what certain different singers might have done in some of the roles, the discussion lasted until they reached the house in Grosvenor Square. Lady Wendall and Mairelon were arguing amicably as they entered, only to be interrupted by a loud thump from upstairs.

"What was that?" Mairelon said.

The unmistakable sound of china shattering, followed by an inarticulate shout, was the only reply.

"Maximillian!" Lady Wendall cried, and flew up the stairs.

ten

Mairelon and Kim exchanged glances and followed Lady Wendall, though somewhat less rapidly. Halfway up the stairs, Kim unexpectedly felt the tingling pressure of magic. Her eyes widened; whatever was going on up there, it wasn't just the monkey. Mairelon must have felt it, too, for he started taking the stairs two at a time and elbowed his way rapidly through the little crowd of servants that had gathered in the upstairs hall, following his mother. He paused only once, to speak briefly to Hunch. Kim, hampered by her skirts, followed as fast as she could manage, only to bump into Mairelon from the rear when he stopped dead in the library doorway. The magical pressure was stronger here, and for a moment Kim thought that was what had brought Mairelon to a halt. Then he moved aside, and she got a clear view of the library.

Shards of white pottery littered the hearth, and one of the unlit candlesticks from the mantel had fallen among them. The heat from the fire was in the process of melting the candlewax, gluing everything firmly to the hearth rug. The table in the center of the library had tipped over, strewing books and papers across the floor. Harry, the footman, hovered uncertainly by the monkey cage. Inside the cage, Maximillian swung from bar to bar in high agitation, chattering loud reproaches. Kim's first thought was that their burglar had returned; then she saw Mrs. Lowe.

She stood in the far corner, her back to the bookshelves. Her expression was grimly determined, and her hands were wrapped around the fireplace poker, brandishing it as if it were a club. Behind her, one of the housemaids cowered in terror. In front of them, at about chest height, hovered a small book with a blue leather binding—Marie de Cambriol's *livre de mémoire.*

Lady Wendall had stopped two paces inside the library. "What on earth—"

The monkey shrieked loudly, and the blue book hurled itself forward. Mrs. Lowe whacked the book with her poker, and it dipped and retreated. An instant later, it streaked toward the bookcase beside her. It hit with considerable force, knocking several volumes to the floor. Apparently, this was not the first time the book had performed this maneuver; two of the shelves were already empty, and a third held only one book lying flat. The monkey shrieked again as the book backed up and made a dive at Mrs. Lowe. She hit it with the poker once more, square on.

"A nice flush hit!" Mairelon said. "Have you ever thought of playing cricket, Aunt?" Though his words were careless, Kim noticed that his hands were already moving in the gestures of a spell.

"Richard, your levity is singularly ill-timed," Mrs. Lowe said, keeping a wary eye on the floating book. "You are supposed to be a magician; do something about this ghost, if you please."

The housemaid wailed. The book wobbled, then angled upward and flung itself at the bookcases again. It hit the top shelf, which was still filled, and all of the books jumped. Fortunately, this time none of them fell.

"It isn't a ghost," Lady Wendall said calmly. "It's a spell." She picked a candle from the candlebox on the side table next to the door. "*Fiat lux,*" she said, and the candle burst into flame. Kim blinked; she hadn't realized that Mairelon's mother was a wizard. Lady Wendall held the candle out to Mairelon. "If you'll assist with the warding spell, dear. . . ."

"Not just yet, Mother," Mairelon replied. "I'd like to analyze this first."

"Stop it and *then* analyze it!" Mrs. Lowe gave Mairelon a withering look, then hastily returned her attention to the flying book. It was now making short runs against the bookcase, and its edges looked rather battered.

"But it's much simpler to analyze a spell in process," Mairelon said. "*O xenoi, tines este, pothen pleith' hugra keleutha.*"

The book paused in midflight, hovered for a moment, and then fell to the floor with a thud. The suffocating sense of magic eased. Mairelon looked startled, then began muttering rapidly under his breath. Lady Wendall, imperturbable once again, began pacing slowly around the room with the lighted candle, reciting the familiar warding spell as she went.

Mrs. Lowe hesitated, then lowered the poker and pulled the whimpering housemaid out of Lady Wendall's way. Kim waited a moment longer, to be certain that she would not accidentally disrupt the spells Mairelon and Lady Wendall were working, and then began picking up the books and papers littering the floor. She kept away from the blue volume that had apparently caused all the trouble. After a moment, the footman joined her.

"There," Lady Wendall said, placing the lighted candle in a holder next to the candlebox. "That should hold things for a little, I think."

"For a little?" Mrs. Lowe's voice wavered, then steadied into indignation. "Do you mean that we may expect a recurrence of this . . . this *event?*"

The housemaid apparently did not find Lady Wendall's comment very reassuring either; she shook off her paralysis at last and began having strong hysterics instead. Kim rolled her eyes, set down the books she was carrying, and looked around for a water jug or a vase of flowers. If the library had ever had any such things, they had not survived the activities of the flying book.

Lady Wendall moved swiftly to the housemaid's side and gave her a resounding slap. The maid gasped and coughed, then began sniveling quietly. When she was sure the girl was not going to begin screeching again, Lady Wendall turned to the footman and said, "Thank you for looking after Maximillian, Harry. Why don't you take Tess down to the kitchen and give her something to settle her nerves? And yourself as well, of course. You've both had a very trying evening, I'm sure."

"Thank you, Mum," the footman mumbled, and ushered the housemaid out.

"He'll be into the brandy for certain," Mrs. Lowe said sourly when the door had closed behind them.

"That is precisely what I intend," Lady Wendall said. "I think they deserve it, and if it makes the rest of the servants wonder whether this is all the result of some odd drunken revel, they will be less likely to give notice due to fear of ghosts."

"Ghosts? Not at all," Mairelon said, looking up from his observation of the now-quiescent book. "Good heavens, this house has had magicians and wizards in it for donkey's years. No ghost would dare come near it."

"Well, perhaps it would be a good idea if you explained that in the servants' hall tomorrow morning, Richard," Lady Wendall said. "Otherwise we may end up doing the cooking and floor-waxing for Kim's ball ourselves."

"Hmm? No, I'll get Hunch to do that. He'll be much more convincing.

"So long as it *is* convincing, dearest," Lady Wendall said. "Are you quite finished? Because if you are, we had better set up a ward around the house."

"I thought you were going to do that after the cracksman piked off," Kim said to Mairelon.

"Yes, well, it slipped my mind," Mairelon said. "It wouldn't have helped with this, anyway, not with as much power behind it as it had."

"You will not forget this time," Lady Wendall said firmly. "Only think of the difficulties another such disturbance would create! We are going to cast a full ward; we shall do so as soon as possible; and we shall maintain it at least until Kim's ball."

"A full ward?" Mrs. Lowe looked inquiringly at Lady Wendall.

"To keep this from happening again." Lady Wendall's wave encompassed the entire library. "All this excitement is very bad for Maximillian."

"I should think that that monkey would be the least of your worries!" Mrs. Lowe said. "If that was some sort of spell, I want to know who was responsible." She looked suspiciously from Mairelon to Lady Wendall to Kim.

"I'd like to know that myself," Mairelon said. Bending, he picked up the blue book that had caused all the commotion. Mrs. Lowe flinched. Apparently oblivious, Mairelon went on, "It was another puzzle-spell, stuck together out of pieces that didn't quite fit. A bit of summoning here, a bit of levitation there, a few other odds and ends, and a really awkward binding holding it together like a piece of string. It couldn't have lasted much longer, even if we hadn't arrived when we did."

"That book didn't look to me as if it were getting tired," Mrs. Lowe said. "And it had been bashing itself against the wall for a good half hour."

"Half an hour?" Mairelon blinked at his aunt. "Oh, come, you can't have been holding it off with the poker that long."

"I didn't say I had," Mrs. Lowe replied dryly. "It's only been about five minutes since that extremely foolish girl panicked and ended up in the corner. Your precious heroic footman was no use whatever, and something had to be done. I trust it will not be necessary again."

Lady Wendall tilted her head to one side and looked at Mrs. Lowe. "If you were not belaboring it with the poker for half an hour, what *were* you doing, Agatha?"

"Writing a letter to Lady Percy in my room," Mrs. Lowe replied.

"The noise in the library disturbed me, so I rang for a footman—who took an amazingly long time to arrive—and sent him to put a stop to it. He proved unable to do so, but did not think to report back to me when he discovered the cause of the disturbance. When the noise did not subside after ten minutes, I came down to see for myself what was going on. By then, half the household had gathered, and while I was considering what was best to be done, the book made a more than usually erratic swoop and that silly girl panicked. I make it approximately half an hour from the time I first noticed the noise to your arrival."

Mairelon looked down at the book in his hand with a thoughtful expression. "This gets more interesting all the time."

"Why's that?" Kim demanded. She could see that neither Lady Wendall nor Mrs. Lowe was going to ask, and she knew that if no one asked, Mairelon wouldn't think to explain.

"For one thing, it means I was mistaken about the scrying spell at the opera," Mairelon said. "The caster wasn't looking to see whether we were there; he was looking to make sure we *weren't* here."

"Very clever of him," Lady Wendall murmured encouragingly.

"Furthermore, the spell on that book was an incredible mishmash. Holding it together for even a few minutes would take a lot of power," Mairelon went on. "To hold it together for half an hour—well, there are only two or three wizards in England who could manage it. That I know of."

"Then one may presume this wizard is no one you know of," Lady Wendall said.

"More than that," Mairelon said. "I think he's someone I *couldn't* know of. I think he's either largely self-taught, or foreign. *Very* foreign."

Kim thought instantly of the handsome Russian prince at the opera, and she could see the same thing occur to Lady Wendall. "Why?" she said again.

"Because I've found very little trace of any traditional spell structures in any of the spells he's cast so far," Mairelon said, waving the blue book for emphasis. "That scrying spell this evening, for instance—no one who's had a proper magical education would bother reinventing something like that, not when every apprentice learns the standard scrying spell by the end of the second year. So our mystery wizard hasn't had the kind of magical education magicians get in England, which means he's either self-taught or foreign."

"If it's a he," Kim said. Something was niggling at the back of her brain, something important that she couldn't quite get hold of.

"That fellow who tried to burgle the library last week was a man," Mairelon pointed out.

"He was a toff," Kim objected. "You said this wizard had to be self-taught; toffs get training. At least, more training than this." She looked around at the library.

"An excellent point," Lady Wendall said. "Though very few gentlemen practice, any more than they read Catullus in the original once they have left school."

"They read Catullus if they read anything," Mairelon said. "He's too salacious to be so easily forgotten."

"Virgil, then," Lady Wendall said impatiently. "The point is that anyone who attended Oxford or Cambridge has learned at least a little magic."

"I should rather say they have been exposed to a little magic," Mrs. Lowe said austerely. "Whether they have learned any of it is another matter."

"Ladies are not so universally educated in magic as gentlemen are," Lady Wendall went on. "And such a display of vindictiveness as this—"

"What display of vindictiveness?" Mairelon said with a puzzled frown.

Lady Wendall gestured eloquently. Mairelon looked around as if seeing the chaos for the first time, and his puzzled expression vanished. "Oh, the mess. That's all just a side effect, really."

"A side effect?" Mrs. Lowe said indignantly. "Next I suppose you'll tell me that this object wasn't attacking me!"

"It wasn't," Mairelon said. "It was simply trying to get somewhere in as straight a line as possible. If this house were on the east side of the square instead of the west, the book would have smashed through a window in one or two tries and been gone."

"East?" Lady Wendall looked at the wall of bookcases. "Yes, I see. What a pity; practically all of London is east of us. If it had been heading south or north, we could have eliminated a great many more possibilities."

"If that book was just trying to get somewhere, why *didn't* it just smash a window and go?" Kim asked.

"That's one of the things that makes me think we're dealing with a self-taught wizard," Mairelon said. "The way that spell was cobbled together was so thoroughly inefficient that he didn't have room for an additional element, and so unstable that my analytical spell unbalanced it completely. What he left out were the comprehensive directional controls and the visual component. He could make a bit of change up and down and side to side, but he couldn't adjust the primary axis of movement at all, and he had no way of knowing which way he ought to send it. He's either very stupid, very careless, very ignorant, or very close; even if he'd gotten the book out of the house, it couldn't have gone far without running into something else."

"Do you mean to say the person responsible for this outrage may be standing in the street outside at this very moment?" Mrs. Lowe demanded.

"Possibly," Mairelon said. "I thought he might be, even before I came into the library, because of the power level. So I sent Hunch to look. He should be—"

Someone knocked at the library door. "That will be him now," Mairelon said. "Come in, Hunch."

The door opened and Mairelon's manservant entered, wearing an expression even more dour than usual. He nodded respectfully at Lady Wendall and said to Mairelon, "There weren't nobody around but a couple of toughs in back. They ran off when they saw me."

"Possibly a coincidence," Mairelon said. "Or possibly they were hired to catch Mme. de Cambriol's book when it flew out a window, and then bring it to our mysterious spellcaster. That would have gotten around the problem of flying the thing through the London streets."

"I ought to 'ave stopped them," Hunch said, chagrined.

"I told you to look for a spellcaster," Mairelon said. "I didn't realize, at the time, that there might be other possibilities."

"I still ought to 'ave stopped them," Hunch said stubbornly.

The thing that had been niggling at the back of Kim's brain suddenly came clear. "Ma Yanger!" she said before she thought to stop herself.

Everyone looked at her. "She's a witcher that lives up on Ratchiffe Row by the Charterhouse."

Mairelon's eyebrows rose. "And you think she's involved in this?"

"I might have guessed it would be something like that," Mrs. Lowe said, giving Kim a dark look.

Kim shook her head. "Not exactly. She used to do spells for people, though, and I think she put them together out of bits and pieces, like you said this one was. Tom Correy told me she's given up witching people, but she's got to do *something* to eat. Maybe she sold the idea to somebody, or sold them part of the spell they used."

"An interesting idea," Mairelon said. "We'll pursue it tomorrow. In the meantime, Mother, you and I should get to work on that warding spell. Kim, you'll watch; you're not quite ready for a long-term spellworking yet, but watching one will give you some idea what's ahead of you."

"I'll leave you, then," Mrs. Lowe said. "Kindly let me know when it will be convenient to have the servants come and clean up."

"I will see to that," Lady Wendall said. Mrs. Lowe nodded and left. As the door closed behind her, Mairelon let out a long breath. "Good. Now, Kim, I take it you wish to visit this witch friend of yours tomorrow?"

"It's a place to start," Kim replied with a wary look at Lady Wendall.

"When, exactly, were you thinking of going?" Lady Wendall asked. "There's a new bonnetmaker I wished to investigate, and we are engaged for dinner with the Blackburns."

"It'll have to be after dark," Kim said, resigning herself to the bonnetmaker. "I won't pass for a boy in daylight."

"I'll make your excuses to Lady Blackburn, then," Lady Wendall said.

"Mine as well, Mother," Mairelon said, and looked at Kim. "The same procedure as last time, I think? Hunch and I waiting in the carriage."

Kim was too surprised by the ease with which everything had been arranged to do more than nod.

Lady Wendall looked thoughtful, then smiled. "I shall tell Lady Blackburn that you have both been called away on some magical project. It will raise your stock with her considerably; she's terribly intrigued by wizards, though she's not in the least magically inclined herself. And it has the additional merit of being entirely true."

"That's settled then." Mairelon tucked the battered little book absently into his jacket pocket. "Now for the general warding spell. We'll need four candles, Kim, as closely matched in size and shape as you can manage. Hunch, will you fetch the largest lump of coal you can find from the kitchen? Mother, would you like to be the Respondent or shall I?"

Hunch nodded and left, Kim began hunting through the candlebox, and Lady Wendall moved to Mairelon's side to discuss their respective parts in the upcoming spell.

eleven

For the second time in less than a fortnight, Kim slipped through the dark London streets in her boys' clothes. She was considerably more nervous, though she did not have as far to go—Ma Yanger's rooms were only a block and a half down Ratchiffe Row from Bath Street, where Mairelon and Hunch waited with the carriage. Because she was not answering a summons from Tom this time, it was earlier in the evening, and there were more people about. Several bricklayers clustered around an iron brazier on the corner, warming their fingers, while on the opposite side of the street a toothless old woman offered a cup of soup to anyone with a ha'penny to pay for it. A collier strode toward the bricklayers, possibly hoping to sell them another lump or two of coal before they packed themselves up. Huddled in a doorway, a young girl with haunted eyes took a swig of bottle courage from a flask. As Kim passed, the girl pulled the neck of her dress lower and started toward the bricklayers in a cloud of gin fumes, her hips swaying suggestively.

It was with a degree of relief that Kim arrived at the tenement at last. Like most such buildings, it was a rickety wooden structure—Ratchiffe Row was an alley well away from the center of London, and no one enforced the laws that, since the Great Fire, had required bricks to be the principal building material. The rates, however, were collected regularly, and as a result most of the windows had been blocked up to avoid the window tax, giving the exterior a hodgepodge look and making the interior gloomy and airless.

Kim climbed the dark stairs with care; it was early to find squatters sleeping on the steps and landings, but some liked to stake out a space before the competition got too intense. She stepped over one man who was already snoring loudly, but from the smell of him, it was liquor and not opportunity that had put him to sleep.

Ma Yanger had two rooms on the third floor, a palatial home by the standards of the place. No one had ever dared to complain that she was taking more than she should—not when the occupant of the rooms was commonly known to be a witch. So long as the landlord received his rent on time, the rooms were hers . . . and possibly longer. It was widely speculated that the only reason this building hadn't collapsed like so many others was because of Ma Yanger's spellworking.

Once, Kim had believed those speculations like everyone else. Now, with her magical training and her sensitivity to spells, she was fairly certain that the only thing holding the building up was good fortune. Even right outside Ma Yanger's door, there were no traces of magic.

Frowning, Kim rapped at the door. There was no answer; well, Tom Correy had said that Ma had holed up in her rooms and wasn't seeing any customers. But unless she'd cut off her friends as well, she'd have to answer the door to find out which it was. Kim's frown deepened, and she rapped again.

There was still no response. Kim glanced quickly up and down the hall to make certain that no one was in sight or earshot, then pulled a bit of wire from her pocket. She was out of practice, but the locks in a place like this wouldn't be much. She bent toward the lock, then hesitated. The locks wouldn't be much, but Ma Yanger was a magician of sorts, and she'd know that as well as everyone else. And Ma was too canny to rely on her reputation to keep the cracksmen away. If she'd witched the lock . . .

Kim straightened and returned the wire to her pocket. That spell Mairelon had taught her last week would tell her whether the lock was enchanted, but she hadn't thought to bring paper or ink with her. Well, Mairelon was always working spells without actually drawing the diagrams; maybe she could, too.

Slowly and carefully, she traced the diagram in the air, visualizing it as her hands moved. "*Epistamai, videre, l'herah, revelare,*" she said, and with the final word she felt the spell take hold.

The lock did not glow even faintly green. Puzzled but relieved, Kim retrieved her wire and bent to her work. Two minutes later, the lock clicked open, and she slipped inside.

Ma Yanger's front room was one of those that had had its window blocked up to save taxes; it was nearly pitch black and smelled suffocat-

ingly of herbs. Nothing in it glowed green, either, though Kim could feel
that the spell she had cast was still active. *How come a witch doesn't have
anything magic in her rooms?* But Tom Correy had said that Ma hadn't
done any witching for two months; maybe she had let her personal spells
lapse, too, if she'd had any.

"Ma?" Kim called into the darkness. "Ma Yanger? It's Kim, from
the Hungerford Market. I got to ask you something."

There was a shuffling noise in the next room, which subsided almost
immediately. "Ma?" Kim called again.

No one answered. Kim thought about working the light spell she
had shown Tom Correy, but Mairelon was always warning her about
overextending herself, and she had a great deal of respect for his advice
in matters magical. Her eyes were adjusting to the gloom, and there was
no great hurry. She waited a moment longer, then began picking her way
toward the far door, past a table strewn with anonymous packets and a
set of shelves laden with jars. At the far door, she hesitated again. "Ma?
Ma Yanger?"

On the other side of the door, something grunted. Kim's throat
clogged, and she almost turned and ran. *It's just one of Ma Yanger's tricks
to discourage visitors,* she told herself firmly. *And anyway I probably know
more magic than she does, now.* Whether it was the sort of magic that
would do her any good in a confrontation with Ma was something about
which Kim refused to think. Taking a deep breath, she opened the door.

Ma Yanger was clearly visible in the faint green-glowing haze that
surrounded her. She sat on the edge of a low, lumpy bed, one corner of
which was propped up by an orange crate because the leg was broken.
Gray hair hung in rat-tails around her face. Her eyes were empty and her
mouth hung slack; a thin trickle of drool trailed from one corner.

"Ma?" Kim whispered.

"Uuunh," said the woman on the bed. The noise was clearly only a
reflex; no trace of sanity or intelligence showed, even for a moment, on
her face.

Kim started forward, then paused. Mairelon hadn't glowed green
when she cast the magic-detecting spell before; only the button on his
jacket that he'd enchanted to foil pickpockets had responded. Ma Yanger
wasn't glowing green because she was a witch. She was glowing because
someone had cast a spell on her. And there was no knowing what the
effect would be if Kim touched her while the spell was active; the contact
might cure her, or it might kill her, or it might afflict Kim with the same
bizarre malady.

This is too much for me. I'm getting Mairelon. Kim backed out of the bedroom and hurried across the front room. By the time she reached the stairs, she was running. She vaulted the drunk and pelted up the street at top speed, ignoring the attention she attracted.

By the time she reached them, Mairelon and Hunch were out of the carriage and scanning the street behind her for pursuers. "Easy, Kim," Mairelon said as she leaned against the coach, panting. "No one's after you."

"I know," Kim said, forcing the words out between gasping breaths. "That . . . ain't it."

"What is it, then?"

Still panting, Kim told them. Mairelon's face grew grim as she described what she had found. "No wonder you were shaken," he said when she finished. "Do you want to stay here with Hunch while I go back?"

"No!" Kim and Hunch said together. They exchanged glances of perfect understanding, and then Kim went on, "You'll need someone to cast a ward, if you're going to do anything about that there spell on Ma."

Mairelon studied them for a moment. "Very well, then. The sooner, the better, I think. Though I'm afraid you will have to stay with the horses, Hunch."

"O' course I 'as to," Hunch said sourly. "And I'll 'ave them ready to move the minute you come running back."

"Very good," Mairelon said, oblivious to his servant's tone. "Let's go, Kim."

They started up the street in silence. Half a block later, Mairelon said in a musing tone, "You know, you were very fortunate with that spell of yours. There are a number of unpleasant things can happen to a wizard who dispenses with written diagrams too soon."

"Like what happened when I tried it in English?"

"Worse. If you get the diagram wrong—if the lines don't quite connect in the right places, or they overlap somewhere because you can't actually see what you are doing—then the energy of the spell will not be correctly shaped. At best, the wizard can be drained of all magical ability for weeks or months. At worst, one can end up in a condition similar to your friend Ma Yanger."

"But not dead?"

"I said *at worst*," Mairelon pointed out.

Kim digested this while they continued. "You haven't told me not to do it."

"I don't intend to tell you that," Mairelon said as they entered the tenement. "You've done it once; you obviously have the capacity to visualize a diagram clearly without having an actual, physical drawing. Just make certain that you always know the diagram well enough. Simple ones are easiest; the more advanced spells require too much precision, even for the very few wizards with absolutely perfect recall."

They reached the top of the stairs and turned down the hall. "Did you leave the door open?" Mairelon said, nodding at a wide-open entrance just ahead.

"That's Ma Yanger's place, but I don't think I left it open," Kim said. "I'm . . . not positive, though. I was kind of in a hurry."

Mairelon nodded. "We'll go carefully, then. *Fiat lux.*"

A ball of light appeared on Mairelon's palm. Resisting the impulse to point out that a light spell was not consistent with her ideas of "going carefully," Kim followed him into Ma's rooms. Mairelon took only a cursory look at the front room. "Workshop and business parlor both, hmm?" he said, and headed for the far door.

Ma Yanger was gone. Nothing else had changed; the lumpy bed still bore the dent where she had been sitting during Kim's first visit.

"She *was* here," Kim said.

"Yes, well, given your description of her condition, she can't have gone far if she's just wandered off."

"*If she's just wandered off!*"

"Someone may have come and fetched her," Mairelon said. "Let's have a look around, shall we?"

They did not find Ma Yanger, and no one they spoke to would admit to having seen her in weeks, with or without companions. A small boy on the lower floor admitted to leaving food at her door every day for several months, but said he never saw her. He would give a special knock, a shilling would slide out under the door, and he would depart, leaving the package of food behind. No one else had had even that much contact with her. After half an hour of fruitless searching, they returned to her rooms, where Mairelon made a quick but thorough investigation that made Kim blink in respect.

"You would of made a top-drawer cracksman, the way you sort through things," she said with considerable admiration.

"I got plenty of practice when I was in France," Mairelon replied absently. "And it's easy to be fast when there's nothing of interest to find." He frowned, then glanced toward the bedroom. "Wait here a minute."

"What are you planning?" Kim demanded.

"Something I should have done at once," Mairelon said. "Check for residuals." He made three sweeping gestures and spoke a long, involved sentence. Kim felt the spell, but nothing seemed to happen. She looked at Mairelon. He was turning slowly, studying everything in the room with narrowed eyes.

It must be something like that magic-detecting spell, that only shows things to the wizard who casts it, Kim thought.

Mairelon crossed to the bedroom and stood in the doorway, looking at it for a moment. "That's odd."

"What's odd? What did that spell do?"

"I told you, it's a check for residuals. Spells leave traces, and these rooms are full of them—but every last one of them is over two months old. No one has done any magic here in all that time."

"Tom said Ma Yanger had given up witching people," Kim said, uncertain of what point Mairelon was trying to make.

"Yes, but she can't have been incapacitated until very recently," Mairelon pointed out. "From your description, she doesn't sound as if she can clean or cook any longer; she'd have starved to death if she'd been like that for two months."

Kim thought of the empty eyes and the expression void of intelligence, and shuddered. "You're right about that. Maybe someone has been taking care of her."

"Possibly," Mairelon said. "But would whoever-it-is also take care of her herbs and spellworkings? There's no dust on these shelves; they've certainly been cleaned in the past day or so. And look at the table."

Kim looked. A candle stub sat in a puddle of melted wax; next to it, a wilted violet lay on top of a heap of crushed herbs. "It looks like the makings of a spell," she said cautiously.

"It is," Mairelon said. "It's a traditional spell for averting harm or bad luck. It's very old and not terribly reliable, which is why I haven't bothered to teach it to you—there are much better spells available nowadays."

Kim looked at the table again. "That flower isn't much wilted. Somebody set this up yesterday, or maybe the day before."

"Exactly. I'll wager that the somebody was your Ma Yanger. Somehow, she knew that something was going to happen to her, and she tried to avoid it."

"But you said nobody's done magic here in two months!"

"They haven't," Mairelon said, and his tone was grim. "She set this up, but she either didn't have time to use it, or couldn't for some other reason."

"Maybe that spell hit her and . . . and made her like that before she could cast this," Kim said.

"Possibly. But if it was a spell that incapacitated her, it can't have happened here, because there's no trace of it. And as far as we know, she hadn't left these rooms in two months."

Kim stared at Mairelon. "Then what happened?"

Mairelon looked at her. "That *is* the question, isn't it?"

twelve

Mairelon and Kim stayed a few minutes longer, turning out Ma Yanger's bed and checking the iron kettle they found underneath it, but they came no nearer to answering Kim's question. When they returned to the coach at last, Hunch was wearing his most sour expression, from which Kim concluded that he had been worried. He refused to drive anywhere, or to allow Mairelon to do so, until Mairelon set up a protective spell around the coach. Mairelon eventually did so. Once they arrived home, he informed Hunch with insufferable smugness that the spell had not even been tested during the drive.

It was something of a shock to return to the trivialities of a social schedule the following morning. The London Season was under way at last, and invitations were pouring in. To Kim's surprise, many of them included her.

"At present, people are merely curious," Lady Wendall said. "That will change when they meet you, and I am quite certain that between us we can see to it that the change is a positive one. To that end, I should like you to accompany me on a few morning calls."

Kim sighed. "Morning calls are boring."

"That depends largely on just whom one is calling upon," Lady Wendall replied gently. "Wear your jaconet morning dress with the pink ribbons, I think."

Kim rolled her eyes, but nodded. She let Wilson dress her and arrange her hair, then joined Lady Wendall in the salon. Shortly thereafter, they were on their way. The first two stops were houses Kim had visited during the horrible week with Mrs. Lowe, but to Kim's astonishment, Lady

Wendall did no more than send in her card. As they pulled away from the second house, Kim ventured to ask why.

"One cannot cut someone dead simply because they are dull, but one need not endure their conversation in order to maintain the social niceties," Lady Wendall replied.

Their next stop was quite close, and this time Lady Wendall climbed down from the coach to rap on the door. A moment later, they were ushered up to the drawing room, where they found their hostess, Lady Clement, already engaged with several earlier visitors. Kim was dismayed to see that one of them was Miss Annabel Matthews, who had been at Mrs. Hardcastle's disastrous tea.

Lady Wendall presented Kim, and Lady Clement introduced her guests. Miss Matthews was accompanied by her mother; the tall, brown-haired girl beside her was Miss Marianne Farrell. Miss Farrell's aunt completed the company of ladies. Across from them was a handsome, blond man in his mid-twenties, who was introduced as Lord Gideon Starnes. As he rose and bowed, Kim's eyes flashed automatically to his hands. They were ringless.

A little uncertainly, Kim made her curtsey. To her relief, Miss Matthews welcomed her warmly, though her mother frowned disapprovingly. Lord Starnes, Kim noticed, did not seem pleased either; his eyebrows rose slightly and his lips curved in an ironic smile as she took her seat.

"I am so glad to see you again," Miss Matthews said in a low tone. "And if you would be so good as to pretend to be absorbed in conversation with me for a few moments, I would be deeply grateful."

"Why?" Kim asked.

"I do not wish to speak with Lord Starnes," Miss Matthews said. "And he *will* not take a hint."

"Is he—" Kim could not think of a polite way to finish her question.

"There! He has struck up a conversation with Mrs. Farrell, and we are safe."

"Why don't you like him?" Kim asked.

"It is not that I don't like him, exactly," Miss Matthews responded. "But it is very wearing to be solicited constantly as a go-between, particularly when it would be decidedly improper of me to agree."

Kim blinked in surprise. In her experience, the need for a third party to carry messages or arrange other things occurred only when something illegal was involved. But Miss Matthews was an unlikely choice as either a fence or a bawd. "Who does he want you to—to go between?" she asked cautiously.

Before Miss Matthews could answer, her mother looked over and said, "Annabel, dear, come and tell Lady Clement about that Brussels lace we found at the market last Thursday. You are much better at describing such things than I am."

Miss Matthews looked a little surprised by this request, but all she said was, "Of course, Mother," and the two changed places.

"And then I wish to hear all about this ghost of yours," Lady Clement said to Lady Wendall. "I understand it smashed an entire set of Crown Derby china and sent three of the housemaids completely out of their minds?"

Startled and a little worried, Kim looked at Lady Wendall, but Lady Wendall only smiled. "Nothing so dramatic as that. An extremely ugly Sèvres vase was broken, and one of the housemaids had hysterics."

"But the ghost?" Miss Farrell said breathlessly.

"A magical experiment that got out of hand," Lady Wendall said.

"I suspected as much," Lady Clement said with satisfaction. Miss Farrell appeared to have suffered a severe disappointment.

"It was really very careless of Richard," Lady Wendall went on, "and I have informed him that in the future he is to use the laboratories at the Royal College."

"An excellent idea," Lady Clement said. "You really cannot have anything like that happening during your ball. It has been an age since your last party, and I am quite looking forward to this one. Though I trust you do not plan to serve frogs' legs this time. Unusual refreshments are all very well, but there *are* limits."

"My son has already made the same request," Lady Wendall replied. "And since it is to be his ward's come-out, I felt it only proper to accede to his wishes."

"So there *is* going to be a ball!" Miss Farrell said. "I thought it must be true when you came in with—That is, how splendid!"

Mrs. Matthews looked slightly startled. "You are indeed presenting your son's . . . ward, Lady Wendall? I had heard some talk of a ball, but I made sure it was idle speculation, circumstances being what they are."

Lady Wendall's smile had very little warmth in it. "Circumstances? I have not the slightest notion what you mean."

"Well . . . that is . . . I was no doubt misinformed."

"Miss Tarnower was probably just mistaken," Miss Farrell said soothingly.

Lord Starnes stiffened, and his expression turned dark as thunderclouds. "I hope you are not criticizing Miss Tarnower," he said.

"Anyone can make a mistake," Miss Farrell said hastily.

"Perhaps she was confused because my sister-at-law, Mrs. Lowe, acted as Kim's chaperone for a few days until I arrived in London," Lady Wendall said. "But it would be quite improper for anyone other than myself to present my son's apprentice and ward to Society."

"Apprentice?" Miss Matthews said, with a puzzled glance at Kim. "Kim is to be a wizard."

"Oh, I *see*." Mrs. Matthews looked relieved. "That explains everything."

"I thought it might," Lady Wendall murmured sweetly.

"Yes, yes, but now you must tell us about this ball," Lady Clement said, and the talk turned to the festivities. Kim found it very dull. So, apparently, did Lord Starnes, for after a very few minutes he rose to take his leave. He bowed punctiliously to each of the ladies, but when he came to Miss Matthews, he gave her a look that, even to Kim's inexperienced eye, was fraught with significance. Miss Matthews reddened and shook her head slightly. Lord Starnes's face darkened once again; with a curt nod to Kim, he left.

"Such a handsome young man," Lady Clement said as the door closed behind him. "What a pity he had not a feather to fly with."

"If someone truly cared for him, his lack of fortune would not weigh with her," Miss Farrell proclaimed, tossing her head.

"Yes, between the title and that face of his, he may do very well in spite of his financial situation," Mrs. Matthews said. "Though I understand he has a penchant for gaming which may add to his difficulties." She looked at her daughter and added pointedly, "It is unlikely, however, that he would express serious interest in any young woman whose means are but modest. He cannot afford it."

"Oh, Mrs. Matthews, you cannot mean that the way it sounds," Miss Farrell said earnestly. "Why, you make Lord Starnes out to be the veriest fortune hunter!"

Although Kim was quite sure that this was exactly what Mrs. Matthews had intended, the woman disclaimed any such intention, and the talk turned to various social events once more. Lady Greythorne's upcoming musicale was the focus of much interest; rumor had it that over a hundred and fifty cards of invitation had been sent out, and that nearly everyone had accepted.

Several well-known singers had been asked to perform, in addition to an Austrian harpsichordist, and there were to be refreshments afterward, and a card room for those who were not musically inclined.

Kim found the conversation alarming. The invitation to Lady Greythorne's musicale had been delivered two days before, and Lady Wendall
had accepted it that morning. Kim was rather vague as to what a musicale
was, and had been picturing something rather like the opera. From the
ladies' discussion, it was clear that there would be considerably more
activity than that. It was also clear from Miss Farrell's remarks that rumors
about Kim and her exact status were already circulating. The thought of
facing over a hundred members of the *ton* was intimidating enough for
a former street thief without adding worries about what they might have
heard.

Kim voiced her concerns to Lady Wendall as soon as they were alone
in the carriage again after leaving Lady Clement's.

"All the more reason for us to make a push to establish you properly,"
Lady Wendall said. "In fact, that is one of the reasons I particularly wished
you to join me today. You may be sure that after this morning Lady
Clement will inform all her acquaintance that you are a very prettily
behaved young woman, and her word carries considerable weight. If we
can stop in to see Lady Harris, and perhaps Lady Jersey as well, we will
have done a good day's work. I do hope Sally Jersey is at home. She is
the dearest creature, and the greatest gossip in London."

Kim prepared herself for another boring morning, but the rest of it
went much better than its beginning. Lady Harris was a lively woman
with a wide range of interests; she had clearly heard of Kim's background
and equally clearly found it fascinating. Lady Jersey was even livelier; she
talked nearly nonstop for the entire visit and at the end of it pronounced
Kim's conversation to be thoroughly unexceptionable.

They arrived home to find Mairelon scowling over Marie de Cambriol's battered book. "Mother, do these ingredients sound familiar to
you? 'A quart of red wine, three handfuls roses, and the pills out of two
pomegranates.' The pomegranates are heavily underlined; they must be
important, though I can't see why. I thought at first it might be a variation
on the de Quincy fire spell, but I can't see why anyone would need that
much wine for it."

"It's a receipt for a cough remedy, dear," Lady Wendall said. "It was
quite popular when I was young, on both sides of the Channel."

"Cough remedies." Mairelon closed the book with a snap.

"You mean it's just a book of recipes?" Kim said.

"Not *just* recipes. There are portions of spells, incantations, at least
two shopping lists, and several lists of directions which are utterly useless
because they don't mention where one is supposed to begin." Mairelon

shook his head. "I cannot think why anyone would go to such lengths to get hold of this book. I've been through it twice, and everything in it is either commonplace or incomprehensible or both."

"A *livre de mémoire* isn't supposed to make sense to anyone except the owner," Lady Wendall said. "She only copied into it the bits of things she couldn't remember. That's probably why the pomegranates are underlined."

"Maybe whoever-it-is doesn't know that there's nothing useful in it," Kim said.

"Yes, but that's no help at all," Mairelon said crossly.

Lady Wendall laughed. "I doubt that our wizard is trying to be helpful. Kim is probably right, and you will only strain your eyes staring at that book. Come and have tea."

Mairelon came, but he was not so easily discouraged. For the next several days, while Kim and Lady Wendall paid social calls and attended teas, he painstakingly catalogued the contents of the book, identifying as many spell-bits as he could. Kim's magic lessons suffered somewhat from this obsession. She missed them sorely, and not only because she was back to studying dry and difficult books instead of discussing theory with Mairelon. She missed the daily quiet hour in the library with him, away from the toffs who crowded the saloons and parlors of upper-crust London.

For despite Lady Wendall's best efforts, and all her assurances that things would improve, Kim was not really enjoying the preliminaries of a London social Season. She would have much preferred tackling burglars in the hallway or chasing down mysterious wizards, but there were no more attempts made to steal the odd little book and no spells tested the strength of the protective ward that Mairelon and Lady Wendall had put in place around the house. Kim was left with shopping, morning calls, and the other activities that occupied ladies of Quality. Lady Wendall's acquaintances were much more interesting than Mrs. Lowe's, but Kim was simply not comfortable among them. Consequently, Kim was not much pleased when Lady Wendall announced that the two of them were going for a drive in the park.

"It will do you good to get a little air, and I can begin to introduce you to the *ton*," Lady Wendall said. "In the future, you may ride, if you wish—that is, *do* you ride?"

"No," Kim said with somewhat more force than she intended.

"Then you won't need a riding habit," Lady Wendall said with unimpaired calm. "What a good thing I hadn't ordered you one yet. Now, go and put on your cream muslin, and we will go to the park. And take care not to disarrange your hair!"

Kim did as she was bidden. It was amazing, she reflected as she donned the walking dress, how much less annoying Lady Wendall's acerbic comments and peremptory commands were than Mrs. Lowe's had been. But then, Lady Wendall at least *listened* to Kim's objections, and if she overruled her, she usually gave a reason. And Lady Wendall didn't seem at all inclined to make bloodless propriety the center of her life; quite the contrary. She knew exactly how near the line of acceptable behavior to tread, and how far over it she went in privacy was an entirely different matter. *But she's a toff born, and I'm not.* Frowning, Kim shoved the thought away, picked up her reticule, and left the room.

Hyde Park was not as crowded as it would be in another week or two, but it was certainly busy. Traffic crawled along as carriages paused to let their passengers converse with ladies and gentlemen on horseback or with the occupants of other carriages. No one seemed to mind; the object of coming to the park, after all, was to see and be seen.

Lady Wendall's landau was one of those most responsible for holding up traffic. She seemed, Kim thought, to be on speaking terms with every one of the gentlefolk in the park, from Lady Jersey on down. After being presented to upwards of a dozen persons in fifteen minutes, Kim stopped trying to remember the names and simply smiled and nodded in acknowledgment of each new introduction.

The brief conversations that followed the introductions all consisted of talk of people Kim did not know and places she had not been. Lady Wendall seemed to be enjoying herself enormously, but Kim was beginning to wonder how much longer the ordeal would last when she saw Renée D'Auber in a carriage ahead of them.

"There's Mlle. D'Auber," she said as Lady Wendall finished her conversation with the latest set of acquaintances and leaned forward to instruct the coachman.

"Where?" Lady Wendall asked. "I don't see her."

Kim pointed.

"Ah yes; how interesting. She's with the Countess Lieven. In the future, do not point in public. Or at least, try not to do it often. Jackson! Pull around by the Countess Lieven's carriage. I wish to speak to her before we return home."

"Is the Countess Lieven a fr—a magician?" Kim asked as the coachman maneuvered the landau through the snarl of traffic.

"Not at all; I never met anyone with less of a sense for magic," Lady Wendall replied. "But she is one of the Patronesses of Almack's, which makes her a power in Society. Now, what was that you almost called her? Fr—something," she added helpfully when Kim gave her a puzzled look.

Kim's face grew hot. "Frogmaker. It's cant."

"I rather thought it might be," Lady Wendall said, nodding. "You must tell me more some evening when we are at home and private."

Kim had no idea how to respond to such a request, but fortunately, she did not have to. The landau drew up beside Countess Lieven's barouche, and yet another round of introductions began. Kim suffered an interesting mixture of feelings when she discovered that the third person in the barouche, who had not been visible when she spotted Renée, was Prince Alexei Durmontov.

"I am enchanted to greet you again, Miss Merrill," he said.

"Thank you," Kim replied, considerably taken aback.

"I see you are determined to make your ball the highlight of the Season," the Countess Lieven said to Lady Wendall. "Five hundred cards sent out, from what I hear."

Lady Wendall smiled. "It is the first party I have given in a considerable time, and since it is in honor of my son's ward, I wish it to be especially memorable."

"It is of all things the most likely," Renée D'Auber said.

"No doubt," the countess said dryly. "Lady Wendall has always had a reputation for . . . originality, even before the curried snails in aspic. I trust such inventive dishes will not be prominent at *this* party?"

"I try not to repeat myself," Lady Wendall said with a charming smile. "May we hope to see you and your guest?"

"I believe you may count upon Lord Lieven and myself," the countess said. "Prince Durmontov will do as he sees fit, though I believe he would enjoy it. Magicians always seem to enjoy talking to one another."

"Ah! You are a magician, Lady Wendall?" said the prince.

"A mere dabbler," Lady Wendall answered. "My son is the true practitioner in the family, though I understand that Kim is coming along nicely."

"Then I look forward to speaking with him of your English enchantments," the prince said. "I, too . . . what did you say? 'Dabble.' I dabble in magic."

"But you are too modest," Renée said. "Have you not just told me that your family is of the finest wizards in Russia?"

"Some of my family are, indeed," Durmontov replied. "But I am not yet among them. One reason I journey here is to enlarge my skills." Kim's stomach clenched. *He can't be the burglar,* she told herself. *He doesn't wear a ring, and he was behind me at the opera when Mairelon went after that other cove.* But the wizard and the burglar weren't necessarily the same person, and if the wizard had to be either self-trained or foreign . . .

"Then you must come to Kim's ball," Lady Wendall said without hesitation. "Some of the greatest wizards from the Royal College of Magic will be there, and I shall be sure to ask my son to introduce you."

"I am in your debt, Madame," the prince replied.

After exchanging a few more pleasantries, Lady Wendall extracted herself and Kim with effortless politeness and gave the coachman orders to return to Grosvenor Square. She was silent and thoughtful through much of the drive home, putting Kim forcibly in mind of Mairelon in one of his brown studies. Had it been Mairelon sitting beside her, she might have attempted a comment or two, in hopes of finding out what he was thinking, but she did not know Lady Wendall well enough to risk interrupting her thoughts, and so she, too, was silent.

thirteen

The rest of the week went by without incident. No spells tested the house-ward that Mairelon and Lady Wendall had set up, nor were there more burglars. Shoreham sent no news regarding the French wizards, and none of Mairelon's spells elicited any trace of Ma Yanger. Hunch made several forays into the lower-class portions of London, but the only information he could obtain was that Ma Yanger was missing. The general presumption was that she had left for parts unknown.

Kim dutifully accompanied Lady Wendall on rounds of calls and attended several small dinner parties, about which she had very mixed feelings. Lady Wendall's friends had, thus far, been very kind, but Kim could not help feeling rather like the central attraction in a bear-garden. She could only be thankful that Lady Wendall had decreed a quiet schedule until after the come-out ball, which she was already looking forward to with considerable apprehension, and she was a bit dismayed that Lady Greythorne's musicale was considered quiet enough to meet Lady Wendall's exacting standards. Her attempts to explain her real worries fell on deaf ears, so she fell back on something the toffs in the household would understand.

"What if that wizard tries something while we're gone?" she asked at dinner the day before the event.

Mrs. Lowe looked alarmed, but Lady Wendall only smiled. "The warding spell can handle anything he is likely to cast, and a great deal that he isn't," she told Kim. "Richard and I renewed it just this morning."

"I meant like that scrying spell at the opera," Kim said. "Not something here."

"I thought of that," Mairelon said with a touch of smugness. "I hope he does; I've been working on something that will give him a surprise. And with any luck, it will let us know the identity of our mystery wizard."

"I would prefer to receive assurances that there will be no disturbance at all," Mrs. Lowe said. "Here *or* there."

"What, exactly, are you planning, Richard?" Lady Wendall said. "Lady Greythorne is an understanding hostess, but for a wizard to cast spells in the home of a nonwizard without being requested . . . well, no matter what the provocation, it is not *done*."

"I won't be casting anything," Mairelon assured her. "I'm using the same technique as our burglar—infusing an object with a spell to be invoked later. The only one who will notice will be the other spellcaster."

"I sincerely hope you are right," his mother said. "Your reputation cannot stand another scandal. And don't tell me that your name has been cleared. Another muddle, and no one will believe it." She paused, considering. "Unless, of course, it's a more *usual* sort of scandal. I would rather you didn't lose your fortune at cards, but if you could contrive to fall in love with someone's wife, that might answer."

"Really, Elizabeth!" Mrs. Lowe said in scandalized tones. "It would be much more to the point to advise him to behave with propriety."

"There is no point to giving him that sort of advice," Lady Wendall said. "Richard would never follow it. But an *affaire* is another matter, and might answer very well to reestablish him in Society, as long as he doesn't take things too far."

"I assume you would consider dueling over the hypothetical lady to be 'too far,' " Mairelon said, amused.

"Much too far," Lady Wendall replied seriously. "That is precisely the sort of extreme you need to avoid."

"I think I can promise you that."

"It is not a joking matter, Richard! You could find yourself a social outcast permanently, not to mention ruining Kim's prospects and damaging the rest of the family." Lady Wendall paused, then laid a hand on Mairelon's arm. "I am only asking you to take care, my dear. You can't deny that sometimes you forget to do so, especially when you are absorbed in one of your projects."

"I most certainly can deny it," Mairelon said. "Of course, if I did, I'd be lying. Very well, Mother, I'll keep your recommendations in mind."

But Kim noticed that Mairelon had not agreed to actually abide by any of them. She was almost relieved. The thought of Mairelon setting

up a flirtation was . . . awkward. Uncomfortable. Unpleasant. She picked
up her fork, and applied herself to food that had gone suddenly tasteless.

Lady Greythorne's townhouse was a palatial residence filled with footmen, silver, marble tables, and delicate, uncomfortable chairs. A cracksman could have made his fortune in ten minutes in the Green Saloon—
except that, Kim judged, this was one of those houses where the guests
did not depart until three or four in the morning, at which point the
kitchen staff and housemaids would already be stirring in preparation for
the following day. The rooms were even more crowded than Kim had
anticipated, and much to her dismay, Letitia Tarnower was the first person to greet them as they entered the drawing room after paying their
respects to their hostess.

"Mr. Merrill!" the Beauty said to Mairelon. "I am so very pleased to
see you again. And you also, Mrs. Lowe."

Mrs. Lowe nodded stiffly, then immediately excused herself to go
and speak with someone who had just entered on the far side of the room.
Miss Tarnower looked up at Mairelon expectantly.

"Miss Tarnower," Mairelon said gravely, and then, with an exquisite
correctness that made Kim instantly suspicious of his motives, presented
her to his mother.

"I am so very pleased to meet you, Lady Wendall," Miss Tarnower
said, curtseying. She gave Kim a small nod; evidently she was not going
to ignore Kim completely until she was sure of her status.

Lady Wendall murmured something politely noncommittal.

"I am so happy to be here tonight," Miss Tarnower went on in a
confidential tone. "I was quite honored to receive a card, for you know
that Lady Greythorne is so very *choosy* in her guests."

"I was certainly used to think so," Lady Wendall said blandly.

Annoyance flashed in Miss Tarnower's eyes; she gave Mairelon the
briefest of calculating glances and then said sweetly, "Oh, but everyone
knows that Lady Greythorne's parties are very nearly as exclusive as Almack's! Surely you are funning me!"

"Not exactly," Mairelon said. "It will do for an interpretation, however."

Miss Tarnower smiled and widened her eyes at him. "I am excessively
bad at interpretations," she said. "Particularly of music, though I do love
it so. And I particularly wish to understand the pieces tonight. Perhaps
you would be good enough to explain them to me, Mr. Merrill?"

"Do forgive us, Miss Tarnower," Lady Wendall broke in firmly, "but we really must pay our respects to Lady Castlereagh. It won't do, you know, to interrupt her once the music has begun."

"Then I hope I will have a chance to talk with you later, Mr. Merrill," Miss Tarnower said, yielding gracefully. As she moved off, several young men closed in around her. Prominent among them was Lord Gideon Starnes, and Kim wondered briefly whether he had ever persuaded anyone to carry his message to Letitia for him.

"That was rather unnecessary, Mother," Mairelon said as they made their way through the crowd toward Lady Castlereagh. "Now it will take twice as long to find out what it was she really wanted."

Lady Wendall gave him a pitying look. "What she wants is obvious, dear."

"Mmm? Possibly, but nobody is that obvious by accident. Or that hen-witted."

"I didn't say it was accidental." Lady Wendall pursed her lips. "I think it is a good thing that Andrew is in Suffolk this Season. I must write and tell Lord Wendall to be sure and keep him there on some pretext, should they finish their business with the canals a bit early."

Kim felt suddenly queasy. Despite Mrs. Lowe's preoccupation with matchmaking, it hadn't occurred to her that Mairelon was an extremely eligible bachelor. *He's a wizard, he's well-born, he's got forty thousand in the Funds, and he's under thirty.* She stole a glance at him. *And he's not bad-looking, either.* That wouldn't weigh with the Mamas of the innocent hopefuls who flocked to London during the Season in hopes of catching a husband, but it would certainly weigh with the hopefuls themselves. *He's a younger son, and he hasn't got a title,* she reassured herself, but that wasn't much help. Forty thousand pounds was more than enough to offset such trifling disadvantages.

At least he wasn't taken in by that Tarnower chit. Somehow, the thought was not entirely reassuring.

They paid their respects to Lady Castlereagh and wandered through the rooms, conversing with the other guests and admiring the furnishings and the figures painted on the pediments above the doors. Several rooms were designed with recessed alcoves in the corners, most of which were lined with narrow tables on which the hostess had chosen to display a variety of enormous, ornate silver urns, marble statuettes, and other valuable items. Kim was particularly taken with a pair of candlesticks that looked to be solid gold—they were small enough to be easily portable, and they'd fetch at least fifty pounds apiece at Gentleman's Jerry's.

As they proceeded, Kim made a point of observing the gentlemen's hands. Though she saw a great many rings of varying value, none was the ruby-centered flower she was looking for. Twice, she saw Renée D'Auber passing into another room. Prince Durmontov was also present; when Kim spotted him, he was listening with apparent attention to Letitia Tarnower while Lord Starnes stood by in barely concealed irritation. Kim found herself hoping that the Beauty was hanging out for a title after all.

"Kim," Lady Wendall said, calling her back from her reverie. "Allow me to present Lord Franton, Marquis of Harsfeld, who particularly desires to meet you."

Kim turned. A slim young man with dark hair bowed immediately; as he straightened, she recognized him as the gentleman she had seen observing her at the opera, before the scrying spell and Prince Durmontov's appearance had driven everything else from her mind. "I am pleased to meet you, Lord Franton," she said.

Lord Franton smiled. He had a very nice smile, and his expression was openly admiring. He looked to be no more than twenty-two or twenty-three, but he had an air of self-confidence that made him seem older. "Not nearly so pleased as I am to meet you at last, Miss Merrill," he said to Kim. "I have been trying to arrange an introduction for a week, but you have been remarkably elusive."

"I have?"

"So it seems to me. Now that I have managed it at last, will you allow me to procure you a seat for the music? I believe they are about to begin."

Feeling a little dazed, Kim looked at Lady Wendall, who nodded encouragingly. Like a puppet, Kim's head bobbed as well, and a moment later she found herself being escorted to the music room by the marquis. His arm was firm under her gloved hand. Her breath had gone odd, and she was abruptly conscious of the depth of her gown's neckline. *Nobody ever really looked at me like I was a girl before*, she thought suddenly. *No man, anyway.* She stole a glance upward and encountered another warm smile that almost made her stumble. She felt tingly all over, rather as if someone were doing magic nearby, only different. *I could get to like this.*

"I hear that you are studying wizardry, Miss Merrill," Lord Franton said. "I have very little skill myself, but I admire those who do. How did you come to it?"

"Mairelon—that is, my guardian decided to teach me," Kim said. "It's a long story."

"I would be happy to call on you next week to hear it at more leisure," Lord Franton said.

"Sure," Kim replied. "I mean, that will be fine, Lord Franton."

They found seats in the fourth row of hard, straight-backed chairs and sat down to wait for the harpsichordist to begin playing. "Are you enjoying your first Season, Miss Merrill?" Lord Franton asked.

"I'm still getting accustomed to it," Kim answered cautiously. She risked another glance upward, and found him watching her face with a keen admiration that renewed her tingling. Hastily, she averted her eyes.

"You find it still so new, even after a year? I understood that you have been Merrill's ward at least that long."

"Yes, but we were in Kent for most of it, and Mairelon—I mean, my guardian isn't much for house parties."

"Why do you call him Mairelon?"

"It's the name he was using when we met." She hesitated, but the circumstances were no secret, and neither Mrs. Lowe nor Lady Wendall had forbidden her to discuss them. "He was working Hungerford Market as a stage magician, and I broke into his wagon. And got caught." She grimaced in remembered disgust. "The toff who hired me forgot to mention that Mairelon was a real frogmaker, and not just a puff-guts making sparkles for the culls."

Lord Franton looked at her, plainly intrigued. "And that was when he made you his ward?"

"No, that came later. I told you, it's a long story."

"I am even more eager to hear it than I was before," Lord Franton said. "And I must remember to compliment Mr. Merrill on his perception. You clearly were meant to grace the drawing rooms and country houses of the *ton*."

No, I wasn't, Kim thought as the first harpsichordist appeared at last and the conversation ceased in a round of polite applause. Though the marquis plainly meant what he said, and though she could not help being flattered by it, she could not pretend, even to herself, that she felt truly comfortable among so many toffs.

Lord Franton, however, was a different matter. *Comfortable* was not, perhaps, quite the right word for the way he made her feel; nonetheless, she found that by the first break she had promised to go driving in the park with him later the following week, and to grant him two dances at her come-out ball. She was profoundly relieved when he offered to bring her some punch and took himself off for a few moments. Finding a quiet spot beside a large marble bust, she waited, scanning the milling toffs for familiar faces.

A corpulent gentleman entered the room, saying something about

the music to a tall woman in a feathered turban. As he went by, waving
his arms with considerable animation, Kim stiffened. *He's wearing that
burglar's ring! But he* can't *have been the cove in the library; I'd have noticed
for sure if he'd been that fat.*

"Your punch, Miss Merrill," Lord Franton said.

Kim turned. "Find Mairelon right away," she said. "Mr. Merrill,
that is. Tell him to come here; it's important."

"I beg your pardon?" Lord Franton said, blinking.

"Never mind," Kim said. "There he is. Excuse me, I got to talk with
him right away."

Abandoning the puzzled marquis and his cup of punch, she threaded
her way through the crowd to Mairelon's side. "Mairelon, the cove with
the ring is here," she said. "Only it's not the right cove."

Mairelon turned, frowning slightly. He blinked at Kim, and then his
expression cleared. "Who is it, then?"

"The jack weight talking to the mort with the green feathers in her
hat," Kim said. "I'll go bail he wasn't the cracksman, but he's got the
ring. Or one near enough like it to be its twin."

"Ah, Lord Moule. Let's find out how he came by it, shall we?"

Mairelon offered her his arm, and they crossed the room together.
Though Mairelon nodded to several of the people they passed, he did
not pause to converse, and Kim could tell that his attention was focused
sharply on the fat man with the ring. Despite her own curiosity, Kim
could not help comparing Mairelon's attitude to Lord Franton's, and she
found herself wishing that Mairelon were not *quite* so single-minded.

They reached the discussion which, judging from the degree of Lord
Moule's animation, was reaching its climax. As Lord Moule paused to
draw breath, Mairelon said, "Excellent point, Moule. I was just saying
something similar to my ward, wasn't I, Kim? Do allow me to present
you."

The ensuing round of introductions completely derailed the conversation and allowed the lady in the green feathered turban to escape. As
soon as she had, Mairelon said, "Interesting ring you're wearing, Moule."

"This?" Lord Moule studied the gold ring that was squashed onto
his littlest finger. "Yes, I thought so. Won it at play last week."

"Naturally," Mairelon said. "From whom?"

"Some young chub or other," Lord Moule replied. "You know how
it is—White's, three in the morning, claret been flowing for hours, things
get a little fuzzy. But it's a nice piece, and I'm glad to have it."

"I should think so. It's not everyone who's that lucky at play. Though I understand there's rather a good game going in the card room."

"Is there?" Lord Moule brightened. "Excuse me, Merrill. Your servant, Miss Merrill." And he departed in a hurry that was barely seemly.

"And that disposes of the one fact we thought we had," Mairelon said, looking after him. "I wonder whether it was cleverness or mere bad luck that led our burglar to stake it?"

"Don't they keep records or something at those clubs?" Kim said.

"The betting-books? Those are for long-term wagers, not for what's won or lost at table of an evening." Mairelon sighed. "It's a pity. Ah, there's Renée and that Russian in the back corner. Let's see what they're up to."

They made their way around the room to the alcove where the other two stood. Prince Durmontov did not look best pleased to have Mairelon and Kim join his nearly private conversation with Mlle. D'Auber, but he greeted them politely nonetheless. Renée gave Mairelon an amused look and said to Kim, "How is it that you are enjoying yourself?"

"It's a little confusing," Kim said.

"It will become less so," Renée told her.

"My mother tells me you're a wizard, Prince," Mairelon said to Durmontov.

"Of no great measure, I fear," Durmontov said. "I hope while I am here to study your English methods."

"You seem more intrigued by French ones," Mairelon murmured in a provocatively innocent tone.

"I have some familiarity with French magic already," replied Durmontov. "One of my aunts—"

A prickle of magic ran across Kim's skin, and she stiffened. So did the other three wizards. Mairelon's eyes lit. "Now, then!" he said, and reached into his pocket. Kim heard a sharp crack, like a twig breaking. An instant later, power ripped across her in a sudden wave.

I thought he said you couldn't tell when someone invoked a spell instead of casting it, she thought fuzzily, clutching at Mairelon's arm, and then the sensation was gone completely.

"M. Merrill!" Renée said, her voice full of concern.

Kim looked up. Mairelon's eyes had gone blank, and his face was gray-white. He swayed on his feet, and she clutched at his arm again, this time to support him. "Mairelon!" she said, her voice wobbling in sudden terror. "Mairelon?"

fourteen

Mairelon blinked and a little color returned to his face. "That was . . . unexpected," he said in a shaken voice.

A little reassured, Kim shook the arm she held. "What happened?"

"I, too, am full of the curiosity," Renée said. "And so will be a great many other persons, and very soon, I think."

"It appears not," Prince Durmontov said. "Your English seem entirely uninterested."

Kim glanced over her shoulder. Lord Starnes stood against the far wall, arms crossed, glowering at the ring of gentlemen hovering around Letitia Tarnower; Lord Franton was deep in conversation with an elderly gentleman; knots of ladies talked placidly with each other or with gentlemen, or moved with studied grace from one room to another. No one gave any indication of knowing that something out of the ordinary had occurred.

"Good," Mairelon said. "Though that, at least, isn't a surprise."

"No?" Renée studied Mairelon for a moment. Her concerned expression lessened, to be replaced by one of annoyance. "My friend, if you are not at once more clear, I shall become what it is that Mademoiselle Kim says wizards are, and turn you into a frog. Why is it not surprising that no one has noticed this spell?"

"No one noticed the spell at the opera, either," Mairelon said. "This was the same thing, I think. I got that much before he . . . broke off."

Renée nodded. "That is a good beginning. Continue, if you please."

Prince Durmontov frowned. "Spell at the opera? To what do you refer?"

"There, you see?" Mairelon said to Renée. "No one but us noticed it. I was rather hoping that wizard would try again, whoever he is; I had an analyze-and-trace spell all ready for him." He shook his head. "I didn't expect him to chop everything off in the middle the minute the trace got to him, and I caught a bit of back blow, I'm afraid. Now, if you'll excuse us, Kim and I have to be getting home immediately."

"What?" Renée said, alarmed once more. "Why?"

"Because the last time whoever-he-is tried this, he attempted to run off with something from my brother's library." Mairelon's cheerful tone sounded forced to Kim, but neither Renée nor the prince seemed to notice. "I didn't catch him here; maybe I can catch him there. Come along, Kim."

"What about Lady Wendall and Mrs. Lowe?" Kim said as they started toward the door, leaving Renée to attempt to explain Mairelon's cryptic utterances to the prince as best she could.

"I'll send the coach back for them as soon as we get home," Mairelon said. There was an undercurrent to his voice that made Kim want to break into a run. *Whatever happened back there, he hasn't told it all yet. And it isn't good.*

In the coach, Mairelon gave the orders to the coachman and then leaned back against the squabs and closed his eyes. Even in the dark interior, Kim could see his face settle into lines of unnatural exhaustion. She waited, not daring to think for fear of what thinking might lead to, watching the rise and fall of Mairelon's chest as if he were a child on a sickbed.

The carriage lurched into motion. After a few minutes, Mairelon spoke, without opening his eyes and in a voice so low that Kim had to lean forward to hear it over the sound of the carriage wheels. "You'll have to check the house-ward as soon as we get home. You shouldn't have a problem; you've watched Mother and me do it enough times, and I'll be there to talk you through it."

"What?" Surprise and shock made her tone sharper than she intended. "Why? If you're there—"

Mairelon's eyes opened, and the bleak despair in them cut Kim off in midsentence. But his voice was steady as he answered, "I won't be doing it because I can't." He hesitated, then shook his head as if to clear it and took a deep breath. "At the moment, I haven't got enough magic to light a candle."

"*What?*"

"Whatever my tracing spell hit, it didn't get cut off and blown up back at me." Mairelon closed his eyes again. "It got sucked into something, and everything else . . . went with it. So you'll have to check the house-ward."

"Oh." Kim wanted to say more, but Mairelon's pose forbade the sympathy and comfort she didn't know how to express anyway. It hurt to look at him, but she couldn't stop. "How long do you think it will last?" she asked carefully after a moment.

There was another long pause. "I don't know," Mairelon said finally. "If I'm very lucky, I'll be back to normal in the morning. If not, perhaps a week or so. Perhaps longer."

Perhaps never hung unspoken in the air between them, and supper congealed in Kim's stomach like three-day-old porridge. *What will he do, if he can't work magic anymore, ever?* she thought, and then, *And what happens to me?* She frowned suddenly, wondering what she had meant by that. It wasn't as if Mairelon were dead, and even then Lady Wendall wouldn't throw Kim back out on the streets. To do her justice, neither would Mrs. Lowe. *What am I worried about?*

Abruptly, she realized the answer, and her eyes widened in shock. *All the wizards in St. Giles—Tom said they were working for Mannering, or they weren't working. Ma Yanger hadn't done any spells for two months, and then she . . . she . . .* The memory of Ma Yanger's vacant expression and the grunting sound that had been all the speech she could manage made bile rise in Kim's throat. *Not Mairelon!*

She looked across at him, suddenly frantic with worry. His eyes were still closed; he hadn't noticed her reaction. She hesitated, but only briefly—they must be nearly to Grosvenor Square, and she didn't have much time left. "*Epistamai, videre, l'herah, revelare,*" she said, too softly for him to hear over the sound of the coach wheels, and sketched the pattern in the air.

A softly glowing green haze sprang up around Mairelon, twin to the one she had seen surrounding Ma Yanger in the tenement the week before. Despite herself, Kim gasped. Mairelon's eyes opened. "What is it?" he said.

Kim swallowed. If she needed further proof, she had it now; he hadn't felt the spellcasting. "I just did that spell you taught me, the one that shows what things are enchanted. And you're glowing green."

Mairelon's eyes narrowed, and his face lost some of its hopeless look in sudden interest. "Brightly? Evenly?"

"Not very bright, just sort of a mist. It's about three inches deep all

over, near as I can tell." She leaned forward to measure more nearly, and
Mairelon jerked away.

"No!" he said, and then, more gently, "Until we have a better idea
just what happened and how, you'd better not try anything like that again.
You don't want it to happen to you."

Kim sat back. The advice was good, but . . . "If you won't let nobody
throw the wind at you, how are we going to figure out what sneaking
bully fitch done this, let alone set it to rights?"

Mairelon frowned, looking yet more like himself. "I hadn't really
thought it out. Shoreham may have run into something like this before,
or one of his men may have. I'll see him in the morning. And Kerring—if
it's a known spell, it'll be in the Royal College's library somewhere, and
if it's there, he'll find it."

And if it's an unknown spell? But she couldn't bring herself to say it,
not when the thought of being able to do something about the spell had
banished the haunted look from Mairelon's face.

The carriage pulled up, and for once Mairelon waited for the footman
to open the door. The house was quiet as they entered. Mairelon nodded
toward the darkened dining room and said, "We'd best check the ward
before we do anything else. The check is a small variation of the warding
spell you already know, like this. . . ."

Kim followed his directions, but found nothing; the warding spell
remained untouched. When she reported this to Mairelon, he frowned.
"Either we've arrived in good time for whatever he's planning, or he isn't
planning to do it here," he muttered.

"Or he's done it already," Kim said.

"Eh?" Mairelon looked up, startled.

"It was a trap," she said patiently. Mairelon's face set, and she went
on quickly, "Maybe that's all he meant to do."

"Ah. If he thinks that I'm the only full-fledged wizard in the household, he'll expect the ward to dissipate in a day or two, because ward
spells require maintenance and I . . . can't do that any longer. All he
would have to do is be patient, and he'd have a free hand." Mairelon
dropped into a chair and began drumming his fingers on the dining-
room table. "But as soon as he realizes that the ward isn't weakening,
he'll know that someone else is maintaining it. Then he'll come after you
and Mother."

"And maybe we can trap him."

Mairelon's expression went bleak. "That's what I thought I was going
to do, and look what happened. No, that's not a good idea at all, un-

less . . ." He paused, and a hint of the familiar gleam appeared in his eyes.
". . . unless we convince him that his first trap didn't work at all."

Kim blinked, then caught on. "You mean, make him think you still
have all your magic?"

"Exactly." Mairelon rose to pace up and down alongside the table.
"When the ward doesn't collapse, he'll wonder; all we'll need is a public
demonstration to convince him. And we have the perfect opportunity in
a week's time."

"What's that?"

"Your come-out ball," Mairelon said with a shadow of his old grin.
"You and I will do the illusion display, just as we've planned. Only you'll
do a bit more of it, and Mother will handle the rest. If we arrange it
correctly, no one will realize that it's not me actually working the spell."

And it would be arranged correctly, Kim was sure. If there was one
thing Mairelon understood, it was showmanship. When she had first met
him, he had been performing stage magic—sleight-of-hand illusions, coin
tricks, and other such things—in the Hungerford Market, and turning
more than a few shillings at it without employing any real magic at all.
But . . . "If this frogmaker thinks you still got your magic, won't he come
after you again?"

"Thinks I still *have* my magic," Mairelon said. "Yes, that's the whole
idea. He can't do anything more to me, after all."

Kim thought of Ma Yanger, and shivered. But Mairelon would think
of that himself, soon enough, and if he didn't she could point it out later.
And as long as he was busy with Shoreham and Kerring and figuring out
how to pretend he still had his magic, he wouldn't go haring off on some
long chance that only a bubble-brained, pigheaded flat would even think
of.

Carriage wheels sounded outside, and a moment later Lady Wendall
burst into the room, followed more sedately by Mrs. Lowe. "Richard!"
said Lady Wendall. "What happened? Why did you and Kim leave so
early?"

"Our mysterious wizard had another try, and Kim and I thought we
should come home and check the ward," Mairelon said. "But it's held
up fine."

Lady Wendall gave Mairelon a sharp look, but held her peace.

"I trust that next time you will bring your mother, instead of dragging Kim away from a promising situation," Mrs. Lowe said. "She will
be fortunate indeed if the Marquis of Harsfeld does not take exception
to the manner in which he was deserted this evening."

"Bosh, Agatha!" Lady Wendall said. "If Kim had gone to the musicale as one of Lord Franton's party, he might justly have been offended, but she came with us. And it will be just as well if he is not too particular in his attentions. It is much too early in the Season for Kim to allow her name to be linked with that of any one gentleman."

"I should think so!" said Mairelon, sounding rather startled.

"If the pair of you intend to encourage Kim to pass up a brilliant match, simply because it does not suit your sense of timing, then I shall say nothing more," Mrs. Lowe announced.

"Really, Aunt Agatha, that's coming on a bit too strong," Mairelon said. "Kim only met Lord Franton this evening."

"The marquis was clearly very taken with her," Mrs. Lowe countered. "I can only hope that Kim will have sense enough to pursue the matter before he comes to his senses."

Everyone looked at Kim; remembering Lord Franton's polite-but-very-interested attention, Kim flushed. Mairelon frowned. Lady Wendall cocked an eyebrow and said, "Well, my dear?"

"He asked for two dances at our ball next week," Kim admitted. "And he said he'd come to call, and asked me to drive in the park."

"There, you see?" Mrs. Lowe said triumphantly to no one in particular.

Lady Wendall smiled. "It is an excellent thing, to be sure. However, Kim still has the remainder of the Season ahead of her. And may I remind you, Agatha, that the purpose of this come-out is to see Kim launched and well-established in Society, not necessarily to find her a husband."

"She could not possibly be more well-established than she would be if she were to marry a marquis," Mrs. Lowe countered.

"She might marry a duke, as Elizabeth Gunning did," Lady Wendall murmured provocatively.

"That was over sixty years ago." Mrs. Lowe pointed out.

Lady Wendall considered. "Only the first time. Her second marriage, which you will recall was likewise to a duke, was not quite sixty years ago."

"If you intend to make a joke of this, Elizabeth, I shall leave you," Mrs. Lowe said. "I hope you will think about what I have said." With massive dignity, she swept out of the room.

"There!" Lady Wendall said. "I began to think she would never leave. Now, Richard, tell me—what scrape have you fallen into this time? I made sure it was something when Renée told me you had run off, and when I saw your face, I was certain of it."

"It's a good deal worse than a scrape, Mother," Mairelon said. "You had better sit down."

Kim glanced at his face, and then away. It had been hard enough for him to admit to her what had happened, even in the darkness of the closed carriage. She didn't think he would want her to watch him tell the story over again to his mother. Silently, she slipped out of the room.

The hall was empty, and Kim hesitated. She wanted to talk to Hunch, but the thought of being the one to break the news of Mairelon's incapacity to him was more than she could face on top of the rest of the evening. Tomorrow—tomorrow she would talk to Hunch, and then go see Mannering. If he was behind what had happened to Mairelon . . . She climbed the stairs to her bedroom, and found Wilson waiting patiently to assist her in undressing.

Kim allowed the abigail to work in silence for a few minutes, her own thoughts and emotions still churning. Finally she said, "Wake me early tomorrow. I got some errands to do before people start calling."

"Very good, miss," the abigail said. "Will you be wanting me to come with you?"

Kim considered a moment, then shrugged. "I don't know yet. It's part wizard things and part . . . personal. What do you think?"

"I'll be ready, then," Wilson said. "I can sit in the coach for the wizardly bits. Turn around, miss, if you please, so's I can undo the back."

The abigail finished her work and left. Kim climbed into bed and blew out the candle, then lay staring into the dark for a long, long time.

fifteen

Kim slept very badly, and she was wide awake and had already made a trip to the library downstairs when Wilson returned the following morning. Wilson made no comment, but went about her work with quiet efficiency. "What will you wear today, miss?" she asked at last.

"I don't know," Kim said. "What have I got that'll impress somebody?" Some of her plans had firmed during the long dark hours before dawn, but clothes were not among them. All she knew was that there was no point in wearing her boy's disguise today. Jack Stower worked for Mannering now; Jack knew she was a girl, so Mannering must, and she couldn't pass for a boy by daylight anyway. What she *would* wear was not something she had considered.

"I suggest the slate-colored walking dress with the Spanish puffs, miss," the abigail said.

Kim nodded and let the abigail help her into it without paying much attention. When she finished dressing, she put the bit of wire she used for lockpicking in the matching reticule and slid her carefully chosen book into her pocket. Then she said, "Now I got to talk to Hunch. Do you know where he is?"

"Below stairs," Wilson replied. "And in a right temper this morning. I'll fetch him at once, miss."

"No, that'll take too long. Just come down with me," Kim said.

"Very good, miss."

They found Hunch out in back of the kitchen, cleaning carriage tack and chewing on his mustache. As soon as she saw his face, Kim knew that Mairelon had told him what had happened. He glowered at her, but Kim ignored it.

"Hunch, I need to get down to the City," she said without preamble.

"What for?" Hunch demanded suspiciously.

"To see a sharper that might have something to do with what happened last night," Kim said.

"You'll want a 'ackney, then," Hunch said, rising. "Master Richard won't 'ave no trouble figuring out that you've gone and done something if you take the carriage." His eyes met hers in perfect understanding.

"I want a pistol, too, if you have one," Kim said.

Hunch stopped. "I better come with you, then."

"No. Mairelon'll want you when he goes to see Lord Shoreham. And I don't know if we'll be back by then."

" 'E'd want me to come with you. And 'e'll raise merry 'ell when 'e finds out, if I 'aven't. I'm coming, or else you ain't going."

None of Kim's arguments moved Hunch in the slightest. Finally, she gave in, feeling secretly relieved. Visiting a cent-per-cent wasn't quite so bad as wandering some of her former haunts in girl's clothes would have been, but it was enough to make her nervous nonetheless.

Hunch procured a hackney coach, and Kim gave the driver the direction. No one spoke for some time as the coach rattled over the cobbles. Then Hunch looked at Kim and said, "You think this'll 'elp?"

"I don't know," Kim said. "Maybe. I got to try, anyway."

Hunch nodded and relapsed into silence. The coach pulled up in front of a row of small, slightly shabby buildings. Kim climbed out carefully and told the driver to wait, then marched toward the near door without waiting to see whether Hunch or Wilson followed. She had to ring the bell vigorously two or three times before there was any response, but finally a watery-eyed clerk opened the door a crack and said, "We're closed."

Kim shoved her foot into the opening before the clerk could shut the door. "Not to me, you ain't."

The clerk's eyes widened as he took in Kim's fashionable and expensive dress, and he gobbled incoherently for a moment. Kim took advantage of his surprise to push the door out of his lax hands and walk through it into the dim, dusty hallway beyond. "Where's Mannering?" she demanded.

"He ain't here," the clerk said. "I told you, we're closed."

"I didn't ask if you were closed," Kim said. "I asked where Mannering is."

"Mr. Mannering ain't here," the clerk repeated sullenly.

Kim looked at his face and decided he was telling the truth. *Now what?* She frowned at the clerk and said irritably, "You told me that before, cully, and I heard you then. Where's his office?"

"It don't matter; there's no use you waiting. He ain't here, and he ain't coming back today."

Forgetting her girl's clothes, Kim reached up and grabbed hold of the clerk's muffler. One good yank pulled his astonished face down level with hers, and she snarled into it, "Listen, you mutton-headed nodcock. For the last time, where's Mannering's office? Or I'll tie your tongue in a bow-knot behind your ears and find the place for myself."

"Th-that one," the clerk said, pointing. "But you can't go in there, it's locked and I ain't got the key, and Mr. Mannering—"

"Ain't here, you said that, too," Kim said, releasing him. She dusted her gloves and stepped back, to find Hunch and Wilson standing in the doorway. "See this cove don't shab off just yet, will you, Hunch?" she said. "I might want to talk to him again after I've had a look at Mannering's office."

Hunch nodded. Kim walked down to the doorway the clerk had pointed out and studied the lock. It was new and shiny against the aged wood of the door; pretty much what you'd expect to find at a moneylender's place of business. But this moneylender had been collecting wizards. Frowning, Kim cast the spell that allowed her to see enchantments. To her relief, the lock did not glow. She fished her lockpicking wire from the bottom of her reticule and set to work.

Opening the lock took some time; Mannering had paid for the best, and gotten it. Kim felt considerable pride when it clicked open at last. The feeling turned to strong dismay when the door opened and she got a look at the room beyond.

Everything indicated that someone had been here before her: the heavy lockbox lying open and empty on the desktop, the dustless squares here and there on the shelves where objects had lain, the half-open drawers, the wrinkled cravat lying forgotten underneath the chair. Kim bit back a curse and started forward. Maybe the other cracksman had left something she'd find useful.

As she sifted through what was left in Mannering's office, she quickly became convinced that this was no robbery. No thief would have bothered to take pages from the ledgers, or missed the pound note stuck under the lockbox. Mannering had taken the things he considered important and piked off, and he'd done it in a tearing hurry, too. Kim frowned.

This didn't make sense . . . unless he thought that Mairelon's tracing spell had worked, and had expected to find the Runners on his doorstep this morning instead of Kim.

Methodically, Kim began pulling out the desk drawers and examining their contents. Most contained paper or old ledgers. The center drawer had a small lock, which had been thrown—but in his hurry, Mannering had not shut the drawer completely, and the lock had not engaged. Pleased to be spared the work of picking it, Kim opened the drawer.

The drawer was half full of notes and partially completed spell diagrams. Kim looked at one or two of them and frowned. They all looked the same, or rather, nearly the same—on this page, the top line twisted up; on the next, it twisted down; on the one after that, it was straight as an old Roman road. *Variations on a spell design*, Kim thought. *But Mannering wasn't ever a frogmaker, and George and Jemmy and Wags don't know this kind of magic. Who's he got helping him?* Some of the notes bore a line or two of almost illegible writing, with frequent crossings-out and insertions. Kim puzzled at one of the inscriptions for a while, then shook her head. Reading was hard enough when she could tell what the letters were supposed to be; Mannering's scrawl was hopeless. Maybe it was instructions for the spell. She gathered up the papers and stuffed them in her reticule. Mairelon or Lord Kerring or Lord Shoreham might be able to make something more of them.

When she finished, she rejoined Hunch, Wilson, and the clerk, who was by turns sullen and terrified. "I'm done, Hunch," she said. "We'd better go."

"You—I—What am I going to tell Mr. Mannering?" the clerk babbled. "You can't do this!"

"Tell him I heard he wanted to see me," Kim said. "Tell him I got something he wants." She pulled a small blue book from her pocket, just far enough for the clerk to get a look, and then shoved it back out of sight. It had taken her half an hour to find one that was a reasonable match for Marie de Cambriol's *livre de mémoire*, and she wasn't going to give anyone a close enough look to see that it wasn't the real thing. "Tell him that if he pulls any more tricks like last night, he won't see this, or me, or anything else he wants. I ain't got much patience with jingle brains or shag-bags."

The clerk nodded dumbly. They left him staring goggle-eyed after them, and returned to the hackney. "Where to now, miss?" the jarvey said.

Kim hesitated, then shook her head. "Back to Grosvenor Square," she said.

"Find anything?" Hunch said as the coach started off.

"Not what I thought," Kim said. "The cull has piked off, right enough. I think he was scared of something."

"Good."

Kim glanced at him, startled by the savagery in his tone. She wasn't really surprised, though; it was the way she felt whenever she thought about what had been done to Mairelon. "He left some notes. Maybe they'll help."

Hunch nodded and lapsed back into his usual silence. Kim stared glumly out the carriage window, watching the tradesmen on the street without really seeing them. Mairelon was not going to be pleased to find out what she had done, but she'd have to tell him; *she* certainly wasn't going to be able to make sense of all those bits and pieces and scrawls.

The other members of the household were at breakfast when Kim and Wilson slipped through the back door. Kim sent Wilson off with her bonnet and pelisse, while she went up to join the family. When she entered the room, she could tell from everyone's faces that this modest attempt at concealment had been pointless; they were already aware that she had left the house, and Mairelon and Lady Wendall, at least, had been worried.

"Kim!" Mrs. Lowe said. "Where *have* you been at such an hour?"

"I had an errand to run," Kim said, heading for the sideboard. "Don't jaw me down now; I ain't had breakfast yet."

"Mind your language!"

"Sorry," Kim said absently as she filled her plate. "I . . . haven't . . . adjusted back yet."

"Adjusted back?" Lady Wendall raised her eyebrows.

"Don't tell me that after all my warnings, you went to see some of those low friends of yours!" Mrs. Lowe said.

"No." Kim took a seat and began tucking in to the sausage. "Not a friend."

Mairelon's eyes narrowed. Oblivious, Mrs. Lowe shook her head at Kim. "Where *did* you go, then? After all the worry you've caused—"

"I'm sorry you were worried," Kim said, glancing at Lady Wendall apologetically. She couldn't quite bring herself to look at Mairelon yet. "I thought I'd be back before anybody noticed I was gone."

"That is no excuse," Mrs. Lowe said. "It is highly improper for a young lady to wander about London unescorted."

"I took my abigail," Kim said. She sneaked a glance at Mairelon. "And Hunch."

"Did you?" Mairelon's expression was closed; she hadn't ever seen him quite like this before. Not knowing how to respond, Kim said nothing.

"Very sensible of you," Lady Wendall put in approvingly.

"I must entirely disagree," Mrs. Lowe said. "Running 'errands' at this hour of the morning is plainly an excuse. I insist that Kim explain—"

"Aunt." Mairelon's voice was quite level and not very loud, but Mrs. Lowe broke off in midsentence and looked at him. In the same level tone, he continued, "My apprentice and ward will explain *to me* immediately after breakfast. I trust that is clear?"

"As you wish," Mrs. Lowe replied stiffly.

Kim finished her meal quickly in the uncomfortable silence that followed. "I'm done," she said.

Mairelon rose. "Then you can explain yourself to me in the library." He waited only long enough to see Kim nod before he left the room.

She caught up with him on the stairs and followed him into the library. As soon as the door closed behind them, he said, "Well?"

"I went to Mannering's office."

"*What?* Are you mad? Didn't you think at all? If Mannering is behind this—"

"I thought for most of the night," Kim said, and looked at Mairelon apologetically. "I saw right off that Mannering was in this somewhere, but I didn't think you had yet."

"Then why didn't you mention it?"

Kim hesitated. "Because I was worried you'd go off and do something goose-witted," she owned at last. "You've done it before."

Mairelon stared at her in silence for a moment. "Not after I said I wouldn't," he said at last.

"When—" Kim stopped. He'd promised her, when she'd come back from seeing Tom Correy two weeks before, that he wouldn't go investigating Mannering without talking to her first. She hadn't remembered . . . but she hadn't remembered because, she realized, she hadn't really believed that he would hold to his promise now that the situation had changed so radically. "I forgot," she said lamely, and then, looking down at her hands, she added, "Nobody ever—I never knew anybody before that . . . that would do that. Not with something this big, not when it was only somethin' they said to me."

"I see." Mairelon's voice had lost its coldness; he sounded torn between amusement and some other emotion she couldn't identify. After a moment, he went on lightly, "So to keep me from doing something goose-witted, you did it yourself. Why? And why in heaven's name didn't you at least tell me what you were planning?"

The bantering tone didn't fool Kim; she could hear the hurt underneath the lightness. She turned away and said to the monkey cage, "I had to do *something*. You looked . . . you were . . . I just had to do something, that's all. And I didn't say because I was afraid you'd stop me. I can see now I should of trusted you, but— Well, I never had nobody I *could* trust like that before. I'm not used to it."

There was a long silence. Kim wiped at her eyes with the backs of her hands. After a long time, Mairelon said, "Anybody you could trust. Not 'nobody.' " His voice sounded hoarse.

"Anybody," Kim repeated. "Anyway, I'm sorry."

"I'm afraid I have to apologize as well," Mairelon said. She turned to find him looking at her with an expression she could not interpret. "I didn't mention Mannering for the same reason you didn't—because I didn't want you haring off after him. I forgot that *you* hadn't promised anyone not to."

"Well, I won't do it again," Kim said.

"Good." Mairelon hesitated. "I suppose you've thought of the possible connection to your friend Ma Yanger, as well?"

Kim licked her lips. "First thing last night, practically."

"Well." Mairelon looked down, and for a brief moment his expression was grim. Then he shook his head and said, "Well, then, how *was* your little visit with Mannering?"

"He wasn't there," Kim said. "Looks like he took all his valuables and piked off in the middle of the night."

Mairelon stared at her, then sat down very slowly in one of the reading chairs. "Gone, is he? Now that *is* interesting. I wonder why?"

"I been—I *have* been thinking about that," Kim said. "What if he doesn't know that *you're* the one he caught in that spell? If he thinks it was me—"

"—then he'd have expected a very angry wizard in his office bright and early in the morning, and he didn't think he could handle it," Mairelon said. He gave Kim a rueful grin. "He appears to have been quite right, too, though perhaps not in exactly the way he'd been thinking."

"He left some notes in his desk," Kim said, and began pulling them out of her reticule. "They look like bits of spell diagrams and such, but I can't read half of them."

"You're right," Mairelon said, glancing at the drawings. "Someone was experimenting." He squinted at one of the scribbled notes and frowned. "This looks as if it could be part of a spell chant, but—"

"But?"

"It's in English."

Kim stared at him. "But if the spell is in English, it won't work right for an English wizard," she said at last.

"Exactly." Mairelon tapped the note. "Now, if you don't mind, tell me just what happened during your visit to Mannering's offices this morning, and then we'll go through these a little more carefully."

sixteen

It took Kim some time to give Mairelon the precise account he wanted. He did not interrupt, but listened with a bemused expression, sorting Mannering's notes into two neat piles as Kim talked. When she finished, he shook his head.

"None of this adds up properly," he said. "You say Mannering isn't a wizard, and is certainly English, but he has a drawer full of magical diagrams and spell bits that no English wizard could use. We have a Russian wizard nice and handy, but he can't possibly have cast those spells last night—not with you, me, and Renée standing right next to him. One of us would have noticed. We have a mystery wizard who is willing to waste power in prodigious amounts in order to get hold of a useless *livre de mémoire*, and a singularly inept burglar who seems to be, in his better moments, a gentleman of sorts. And we have a batch of untrained criminal wizards who, for no reason anyone knows, have suddenly forsaken their independent ways and gone to work for Mannering—except for one, who first gave up or lost her magic and then vanished completely under suspicious circumstances. It doesn't *fit*."

And none of it looks like it's helping to get your magic back. "I could have a talk with Jemmy or Wags," Kim offered, but Mairelon was shaking his head before she even finished speaking.

"No. I'll ask Shoreham to have his people look into it. It's not, strictly speaking, part of the business of the Ministry, but he owes me a favor or two, and I think he'll do it." He eyed Mannering's notes thoughtfully. "I'll take these with me when I visit Shoreham later, if you don't mind. He may have a few more ideas."

"If I don't mind?" Kim said, astonished.

Mairelon gave her a crooked smile. "You're the one who went and got them."

Kim could only nod her assent.

"Meanwhile, I think it would be advisable to make a copy." Mairelon handed her the stack of diagrams. "You do these; I'll see what I can make of the others."

They set to work, side by side at the table. Mindful of the need for accuracy, Kim worked with painstaking care, duplicating even the lines that looked to be accidents or scribbles before she turned the paper face down to go on to the next one. On the third page, she turned the note over and stopped. "Mairelon. This one has writing on the back."

Mairelon looked over. "So it does. Let's see—" He stopped abruptly, frowning at the writing.

"What is it?" Kim said, peering down at it. The writing was, like that of the other notes, nearly illegible, and there were circles and arrows and check marks on top of it that made it even harder to puzzle out.

"It's a list of names," Mairelon said. "French names."

"Not those wizards Mlle. D'Auber was telling us about?" Kim guessed.

"Right the first time." Mairelon said. "But there are only six of them. M. László Karolyi, Mlle. Jeannette Lepain—that one is circled—the Comtesse Eustacie de Beauvoix, the Comte Louis du Franchard—he's circled them, too, and there's a check mark next to the comte's name— Mme. Marie de Cambriol—circled, but no check mark—and the Duchesse Camille Delagardie."

Kim ran quickly through her memory of their conversation with Renée D'Auber. "It's missing Henri d'Armand."

"Yes."

"But what does it *mean?*" Kim said in frustration.

"I don't know." Mairelon looked down at the page, and a muscle by the corner of his mouth spasmed briefly. "But it's the first real evidence we have that Mannering is connected with our bits-and-pieces wizard— the one who was after the de Cambriol book."

And the one that set that trap. Kim scowled at the papers. "Well, it doesn't help much."

"It's something." Still studying the pages intently, Mairelon said, "Let's finish this, and then we'll see what Shoreham has to say."

"We?"

"Yes, of course." Mairelon did not look at her. "He'll want to hear about your visit to Mannering's office, and it will be better if you're there to tell him in person. And there may be . . . other things."

Kim's startled comments died on her lips as she realized belatedly just what "other things" Mairelon was referring to. Spells. If the Earl of Shoreham had anything to recommend, or needed a second wizard to help with any test he wanted to run, someone besides Mairelon would have to be there to do it. And Mairelon would want it to be someone who already knew of his . . . difficulties, which meant either Lady Wendall or Kim.

Feeling more than a little nervous, Kim nodded and returned to her copying. Edward, Earl of Shoreham, wasn't just another toff; he was one of the top men at the government's Ministry of Wizardry, head of a semiclandestine department that was responsible for a great deal of intelligence gathering by both magical and nonmagical methods. He was the one who had persuaded Mairelon to do all of his spying on the French during the last few years of the war. Kim had only met him twice before: once, when he had turned up during the recovery of the Saltash Set, and once a few weeks later, after she and Mairelon had returned to London. Shoreham was, unquestionably, a right knowing one, and though he did not seem to dislike her, he made her uneasy nonetheless.

But when they finished making their copies and arrived at the Ministry of Wizardry with Mannering's original notes, they found that Shoreham was not there. "Gone down to Brighton to meet one of our chaps coming in on the packet," the secretary, an earnest young man, said. "He should be back tomorrow."

"Tell him we'll be by at ten o'clock," Mairelon said.

"He's meeting with the minister then," the secretary replied, checking a book lying open on the desk.

"Eleven, then," Mairelon snapped, and left in more of a temper than Kim could ever recall seeing him in before.

Their visit to the Royal College was slightly less frustrating—Lord Kerring was there, and though he was deeply immersed in some magical project that Kim did not quite understand, he set it aside at once when he heard that Mairelon was in need of help. After hearing their story, he studied the spell affecting Mairelon from several angles, but then shook his head.

"There's nothing I can do about this today. I need an analysis, and from what you say, the standard spell is . . . inadvisable." Lord Kerring scratched his bushy beard. "I'll have to design something that works less invasively than the usual methods."

"How long will it take?" Mairelon said.

"Hard to say," Kerring replied. "I know you're in a hurry, and I don't blame you, but . . . some things, you just can't rush. I'll send you word as soon as I have something feasible, but don't expect it before next week. And it might be longer. It depends on how tricky the interlocks turn out to be."

Mairelon nodded; from the quality of his silence on the ride home, Kim concluded that he had been hoping for a quick solution. When they arrived back at Grosvenor Square, Mrs. Lowe informed them that they had had several visitors in their absence.

"The Marquis of Harsfeld was among them," she said with a significant look at Kim.

"Lord Franton?" Kim said. "He did tell me he was going to call, but I didn't think he meant right away."

"When he discovered that you were from home, he did not stay," Mrs. Lowe said. "I trust that he will have better fortune on his *next* visit."

Mairelon frowned. "Who else did we miss?" he said abruptly.

"Your French friend, Miss D'Auber," Mrs. Lowe replied. "She said that she wished to see how you did. I cannot think where she could have gotten the impression that you were unwell."

"She may have mistaken something I said last night," Mairelon said.

Mrs. Lowe nodded, satisfied. "I told her it must be some misunderstanding."

"Did she say anything else?" Kim asked, hoping to turn the subject before Mrs. Lowe accidentally precipitated a crisis.

"She mentioned that she overheard the Marquis of Harsfeld tell Lady Greythorne that you were even more charming in person than from afar," Mrs. Lowe said. "I am pleased that you managed to make such a good impression last night, though it would have been far better had you been here to receive him when he called today. Oh, and there has apparently been something of a rash of thefts and burglaries lately."

"Really?" Mairelon was suddenly all attention. "Did Renée say who, or when?"

"Someone stole a painting from Mr. Winton's library last week, and Lord Bancroft and his wife lost an urn that had been in the family for several generations, though it was only silver plate. That was Monday. And last night, someone broke in at the George."

"Someone tried to rob a *hotel*?" Kim said incredulously.

"It does seem a bit unusual," Mairelon said.

"It's a mug's game," Kim told him. "People who're putting up at hotels don't cart their silver along with them, and if they've got jewels, they're out wearing them at night. And there's the hotel staff, as well as everybody's servants, so there's at least three times as many people to avoid. Milling a gentry ken is a lot safer, and they're not exactly easy marks."

"Kim," Mrs. Lowe said reprovingly, "you really *must* be more careful about your language. Those . . . cant terms are simply not suitable in polite company."

"I wonder what the cracksman took," Mairelon said.

"Miss D'Auber didn't say," Mrs. Lowe replied stiffly, frowning at him.

"Pity. Kim, I'll want to see you in the library after lunch; we've a good deal of work to do if we're to have that illusion ready for your ball." And with an absent nod, Mairelon escaped up the stairs, leaving Kim with his aunt.

Kim had expected the rest of the day to be quiet, but she was quickly disabused of that notion. Mairelon had not been joking when he said they had a lot of work to do to prepare for the illusion spell, and most of the work was Kim's. Fortunately, Lady Wendell could take over some of Mairelon's part, but there were limits to what she could accomplish from the sidelines without letting it become obvious to everyone that it was she, and not her son, who was assisting Kim with her come-out illusion. The additional parts fell to Kim, and she burned candles late into the evening trying to memorize them all.

Promptly at eleven the next morning, she and Mairelon were at the Ministry of Wizardry once again. The Earl of Shoreham did not keep them waiting long. "I suppose you're here about those French wizards again," he said to Mairelon as they found seats in his office.

"Not directly," Mairelon said. "There have been developments."

"With you, there are always developments," Lord Shoreham said, amused.

"Someone seems to have developed themselves right into my magic, and me out of it," Mairelon said with an unsuccessful attempt at lightness.

"What? Richard, you don't seriously mean—" Lord Shoreham looked at Mairelon, and his amusement vanished, replaced by concern. "You'd better start at the beginning. What has this got to do with your French wizards?"

"If I knew that, I'd be considerably farther along than I am now," Mairelon said testily. "The beginning, so far as I know, was an inept burglar who tried to steal a book from my brother's library. Kim heard him in process, and interrupted before he got what he was after. The book was a *livre de mémoire* written by a French wizard named Marie de Cambriol and rather grandiosely titled *Le Livre de Sept Sorciers*, and so far as I've been able to tell, there's no reason at all why anyone would want to get hold of it.

"Last week someone had another go at it while Kim and Mother and I were at the opera. He used a scrying spell to make certain we were away from home, and then put together a sort of summoning-cum-levitation to bring the book to him. He failed mainly because he didn't have sense enough to find out which side of the house the library was on before he cast his spell; according to my aunt, the book spent half an hour trying to batter through a wall when it could have nipped through one of the windows and been gone."

"Amateur work, then?" Shoreham said.

"Possibly. There was a lot of power behind the spell, but it was very badly balanced; it fell apart almost immediately when I tried to analyze it. I'd guess self-taught, or foreign, or both."

"Ah." Shoreham leaned back in his chair. "Go on."

"The spell reminded Kim of an old . . . acquaintance of hers that lives up by the Charterhouse, a Ma Yanger."

Shoreham nodded. "One of the rookery witches. She's one of the canny ones—we have reason to think she turns an occasional spell for some of the professional thieves, but she's been careful enough that we haven't caught her at it. Most of her trade is minor household-level magic—removing corns, easing aches, the odd love spell. Some of it is the genuine article, but a good deal of it is mere sham."

"From what Kim and I found, she hasn't cast any spells for at least two months, and she's not likely to be doing anything at all for a lot longer than that." Mairelon nodded at Kim. "Tell him."

Startled, Kim hesitated for a moment, and Shoreham gave her an encouraging look. She swallowed and, trying not to feel as if she were betraying her old friends, she explained what Tom had told her about wizards working for Mannering, and then described what she had found at Ma Yanger's.

"Hmph," said Shoreham when she finished. "I'll have to get on to MacArdle; he's supposed to be keeping up on the minor wizards, especially the ones around St. Giles and Smithfield. If he overlooked something like this, we shall have words. Continue."

"Two nights ago, at Lady Greythorne's musicale, our mystery wizard tried his scrying spell again," Mairelon said, and stopped.

"And knowing you, you were ready for him," Shoreham said.

"Not ready enough," Mairelon said. "I had a trace-and-analyze spell infused in a splinter of kindling, all ready to go, and when I felt the scrying spell, I invoked it. But—well, the scrying spell didn't just fracture and fall apart this time; it sucked down my enchantment like quagmire sucking down a horse. And not just the enchantment, either."

"I see." Lord Shoreham looked seriously concerned. "I can't say I've heard of anything like this before, but I'll put some people on it immediately. In the meantime—"

"Kerring's working at the enchantment end of things," Mairelon said. "I spoke to him yesterday."

"Are you sure that's enough?"

"I don't exactly like the thought of everyone knowing that I can't so much as light a fire without flint and tinder," Mairelon said testily. "The fewer people who have the details, the better."

"As you wish." But Shoreham continued to frown, and after a moment he looked at Kim. "It's not really the thing to be asking another wizard's apprentice this, but have you learned Gerard's Refuge yet?"

"No, she hasn't," Mairelon said before Kim could answer. He did not look at all pleased, but Kim could not tell whether he was annoyed with Shoreham, or with her, or with himself.

"What is it?" Kim asked, looking at Mairelon uncertainly.

Mairelon remained silent. Shoreham glanced at him, then said, "It's a minor protective spell, rather like the standard ward but less complex and easier to cast. It doesn't last as long, and it isn't intended to absorb or block magic, the way a ward does."

"Then how can it protect anything?" Kim asked.

"It deflects spells," Shoreham said. "Sort of shoves them to one side where they can go off without doing any harm." He glanced at Mairelon again, then looked back at her. "I think it would be a good idea for you to learn it as soon as possible."

"Teach it to her now," Mairelon said. "I should have thought of that myself." He sat scowling at the front of Shoreham's desk while the earl explained the spell and ran her through casting it several times. It was, as he had promised, quite simple—a single gesture and a word—and it did not take long for her to master it.

When they finished, Shoreham turned to Mairelon. "Now, about those French wizards. I've done some checking since you were last here.

Les Griffonais were of considerable interest to the Ministry in the early years of the French war, even though they had all left France well before the trouble began, so there was more information lying around than I'd expected."

He pulled a sheaf of papers toward him and read from the top of the first page, "M. László Karolyi, Hungarian—close friend of the current Vicomte de Bragelonne. He helped the vicomte escape France during the Terror, in fact. Karolyi was apparently much in sympathy with the aims of the *sans-culottes*, but thoroughly disgusted by the eventual direction their revolution took. He returned to Hungary and has spent most of his time there for the last thirty years, though he has visited England upon occasion—or rather, he has visited those of his French friends who sought sanctuary from the Terror here."

"Lately?"

"No, not since Waterloo," Lord Shoreham said. He turned to the next page. "Mme. Marie de Cambriol—traveled in Italy and Greece after leaving France, then came to England with her husband in 1799. Died of a putrid fever some months later.

"M. Henri d'Armand—also, apparently, inclined to travel after leaving France, but not so successfully. He was on his way to Milan to attend the opening of an opera when his ship sank."

"What?" Mairelon sat up. "D'Armand is dead?"

"And has been for nearly thirty years," Shoreham said. "The accident happened only a month or two after he left France. Is that significant?"

"His name was missing from Mannering's list," Mairelon said. "That may be why."

"The de Cambriol woman is also deceased," Shoreham pointed out, turning over another page. "If I may continue? The Duchesse Camille Delagardie—settled in England with her husband. She has a reputation as both a recluse and an eccentric, though from what I can gather, it's founded mainly on a dislike of making the rounds in Society. She has a small but devoted circle of friends, many of them wizards. Before you ask, yes, she's still alive; I believe she and her husband are somewhere in the North at the moment. They have a little place in Hampstead, when they're in Town."

"Hampstead!" Mairelon said. "Good lord. That's not in Town."

"It apparently does very well for them," Shoreham said. "The Comte Louis du Franchard and the Comtesse Eustacie de Beauvoix—also settled in England, but returned to France last month, possibly to repossess the estates that were confiscated from them during the revolution. Unlike the duchesse and her husband, they socialized rather freely during their twenty-some years here."

"And finally, Mademoiselle Jeannette Lepain—also lived in England for a few years, but in 1801 she married a Russian wizard-prince, one Ivan Durmontov, and moved—"

"Ivan *Durmontov?*" Mairelon interrupted. "Now that *is* interesting."

"So I gather," Lord Shoreham said dryly. "You wouldn't, by chance, care to enlighten me as to why?"

"There's a Prince Alexei Durmontov in London for the Season," Mairelon said, and smiled. "I think perhaps I should have a talk with him. It appears we may have some interests in common."

"Richard—" Lord Shoreham began, and then sighed. "I'd much rather we found out a bit more about him before you go stirring things up. I suppose there's no use telling you to wait?"

"None whatever."

"Very well, then, but for heaven's sake, be careful. If he *does* have anything to do with this . . . this situation—"

"Then I intend to find out what it is as soon as possible," Mairelon said, and his tone was deadly serious. "Anything else, Edward? No? Then we'll be going. Let me know if you find out anything."

"Be sure I will," Lord Shoreham said gravely.

seventeen

As soon as they returned to Grosvenor Square, Mairelon sent Hunch off with a note requesting Prince Durmontov to call at his earliest convenience. Hunch returned an hour later, while Kim and Mairelon were still in the library rehashing Shoreham's comments. He reported that he had left the note, but Prince Durmontov had not been at his lodgings to receive it.

"What?" Mairelon said.

"'E ain't there," Hunch repeated. "The 'otel staff said 'e was upset by the robbery and 'e went off to stay with some friends in the country."

"Upset by the—Good Lord, that's right! He did say he was moving to the George." Mairelon studied Hunch. "He wasn't by chance one of the people who was burgled?"

Hunch nodded. "The 'housemaid says 'is rooms were turned up a rare treat, but 'ooever it was didn't take nothin' valuable."

"That doesn't make sense," Kim said.

"Neither does anything else we've learned," Mairelon said. "Did they take anything at all, Hunch?"

"Some family 'eirloom, she said." Hunch shrugged. "That's why 'e was so cut up about it."

"An heirloom," Mairelon said. "A book, perhaps? That would certainly be convenient—a little *too* convenient, I think. When is the prince returning to London?"

"Nobody knows," Hunch said.

If not for the expression on Mairelon's face, Kim would have been almost thankful to have the visit to the prince put off for a few days.

Between Mairelon, Lady Wendall, and Mrs. Lowe, she was run nearly ragged learning her illusions, helping to check and maintain the protective wards on the house, being fitted for her come-out dress, memorizing what seemed like thousands of instructions for her conduct at the ball, and practicing acceptable social behavior during morning calls, teas, and other social outings.

The attentive Lord Franton added to the number of things that had to be fit into each day. He called several times, and held Kim to her promise to drive with him in Hyde Park two days after the musicale. But though his visits were certainly enjoyable while they lasted, Kim could not help resenting them because of how much more hectic things always were afterward.

Except when Mairelon drilled her in the spells for the illusion, she saw less and less of her guardian as the ball neared. He spent most of his days at the Royal College or at the Ministry of Wizardry, closeted with Kerring or Shoreham. Whatever they discussed, it was plain that they had made no progress regarding the spell that affected Mairelon's magic. Each evening when he returned, he was quieter than he had been the previous day. Lady Wendall developed a small vertical worry line between her eyebrows that deepened whenever she looked in her son's direction. Only Mrs. Lowe seemed unaware that anything was wrong.

The day of the ball, Kim did not see Mairelon at all. She and Lady Wendall were busy most of the morning with preparations for the illusion, drawing diagrams on the ballroom floor with rosewater made in a mirrored bowl, and she spent the afternoon being dressed. After having her hair fussed over, her gown examined and reexamined for creases, and everything from her stockings to her hair ribbon studied and commented on, Kim was nearly ready to scream. Fortunately, the arrival of a charming posy tied up with peach-colored ribbons distracted her well-meaning helpers in the nick of time.

"The very thing!" Lady Wendell said. "Look at the card, Kim, and see who it is from."

"Lord Franton sent it," Kim said after studying it for a moment. She set the card aside, trying not to feel disappointed and wondering why she did.

A second box arrived a few moments later, though it was far too small to hold flowers. "Now, what is this?" Lady Wendall said, frowning slightly.

Kim lifted the lid. Inside, on a small pillow covered in white velvet, lay a gold sunburst the size of her thumbnail, hung on a delicate chain.

It looked a little like the first spell she had ever cast, a small explosion of light recreated in metal, and she was not really surprised to find the card with the single word "Mairelon" scrawled across it.

"Ah," said Lady Wendall, peering over Kim's shoulder. "I'd been wondering—I'm very glad he remembered."

So am I, Kim thought, feeling suddenly much more cheerful.

When all the fussing and fixing-up was done at last, they went down to await their guests. This, too, was a longer and more complicated process than Kim had expected. She and Lady Wendall and Mairelon stood at the head of the stairs receiving the company for over an hour and a half, and the flow of arrivals was so steady that there was no time to pass even a few remarks among themselves. Renée D'Auber came early, and Lord Kerring and his lady wife soon after, but most of the other guests were not well-known to Kim. It was a relief to spy the occasional truly familiar face; even Letitia Tarnower, who had somehow managed to be included in the party from Kirkover House, was almost a welcome sight. For the rest, Kim's part was no more than to smile and curtsey as Lady Wendell presented her to those guests whom she had not previously met. This gave her far too much time to think about the upcoming illusion. By the time the stream of incoming guests began to thin, she had worked herself into a fair case of jitters.

The Marquis of Harsteld was among the last to arrive. He smiled politely as he greeted Lady Wendell, but his eyes strayed to Kim's hands, and his smile warmed noticeably when he saw his flowers attached to her wrist. "I had not dared to hope you would accept my tribute," he said softly when he reached Kim.

"I'm— It was— Thank you," Kim said, and passed him on to Mairelon.

"I notice that Durmontov hasn't shown up yet," Mairelon commented when the marquis had passed out of hearing.

"Renée D'Auber tells me that he does not return to Town until some time next week," Lady Wendell said, and Mairelon frowned. Lady Wendall turned to Kim. "Ten minutes more, and we shall go in. We really cannot delay the dancing any longer than that."

Kim swallowed. Ten minutes, and she would have to perform a spell before several hundred members of the *ton*, with most of whom she had barely a nodding acquaintance. If it were just for Mairelon and Lady Wendall and Renée D'Auber, and maybe Lord Kerring and Lord Shoreham, it wouldn't be so nervewracking.

"The last few minutes before the show are always the worst,"

Mairelon said, as if he knew exactly what she was thinking. "You'll do very well." Kim smiled at him gratefully, then belatedly connected his remark with the performances he had once given in the Hungerford Market. Maybe he *did* know exactly what she had been thinking. The thought that even Mairelon had been nervous before his shows made her feel a little better. Still, it seemed as if far less than ten minutes had gone by when Lady Wendall signaled to Mairelon to take Kim in to the ballroom.

As they entered, the hum of conversation sank to a mere murmur and heads turned to look at them. Kim shivered slightly; she was more used to avoiding attention than accepting it. Almost involuntarily, her free hand rose, seeking reassurance, and touched the gold sunburst that Mairelon had given her.

Mairelon led her to the center of the floor. She hardly heard his introduction; she was suddenly, frantically certain that she did not remember a single word of the illusion spell. *Brevis lux, nox . . . nox . . . What comes after* nox? And then Mairelon drew his arm away and stepped back, and she stood isolated under the eyes of more toffs than she had ever thought to see, let alone draw the attention of.

She took a deep breath, and her self-consciousness receded. Fixing her eyes on a candle sconce on the far wall, she raised her arms and—in a clear, steady voice—began the invocation.

At the end of the first five lines, Mairelon's voice joined hers as if he were supporting and assisting in the spell. This was the trickiest part, for it was Lady Wendall who was really performing the magic. As the primary spellcaster, Kim had to merge the two enchantments into one—a difficult task indeed when she not only could not hear Lady Wendall's voice, but also had Mairelon's to distract her.

Somehow, she managed it all—keeping the timing right, reciting her own part, and building the images in her own mind as she spoke. She knew, as she said the final phrase, that it was going to work, and with a triumphant sense of satisfaction she brought her hands down and together in the gesture that set the spell in motion.

All of the candles went out. The guests gasped, then hushed again as a glowing cloud of white smoke erupted from the bare floor in front of Kim, where she had knelt all morning with the rosewater. From the center of the smoke, a voice called, "Come one, come all! Prepare to be amazed and astonished by the one, the only—Mairelon the Magician!"

With the last words, the smoke dissipated. Where it had been rose the image of a wooden stage, and in the middle of the stage stood

Mairelon as Kim had first seen him, in a black opera cape and top hat, wearing a small, neat mustache. He raised a silver-headed walking stick, and a grubby, dark-haired boy in a ragged jacket jumped out of the darkness onto the stage beside him. The two images held the pose for a long moment while a murmur of surprise rose from the watchers, and then the real Mairelon and Kim stepped forward and took their places beside the images of their former selves. The candles flickered into flame once more, and the illusion faded, leaving only the true Mairelon and Kim in their formal finery.

A scattering of applause broke out. Light-headed with relief and triumph, Kim grinned at Mairelon. Mairelon smiled back at her, bowed, and stepped forward to take her hand as the musicians began the opening dance.

Other couples fell in behind them after the first few bars. Kim let the music lead her feet without paying much conscious attention; after the successful spellcasting, a mere misstep held no terrors for her. Indeed, she felt as if she *could not* put a foot wrong this night.

At the end of the first dance, Mairelon relinquished her to a throng of intrigued gallants and retired to the sidelines. Kim had more than half expected that the illusion, with its reminder of her too-humble origins, would put a damper on her social prospects; instead, it seemed to have significantly increased the number of gentlemen taking an interest in her. Mindful of Lady Wendall's—and Mrs. Lowe's—strictures, she was careful not to agree to more than two dances with any of them, but there were so many that she was on her feet for most of the evening. Several times, she caught sight of Mairelon watching her as she danced, but he did not return to claim a second dance for himself.

Lord Franton presented himself promptly for his first dance, and though he did not press her for another immediately afterward, he seemed always to be nearby when she finished a turn with some other partner. He would make light conversation for a moment or two, and then yield his place to the next gentleman. After a while, Kim began wondering when he would claim his second dance, and whether his attentions would be as assiduous once he had had it.

The dance the marquis chose at last revealed that he was no mean strategist: it was the supper dance, and since Kim had not previously engaged with anyone to take her down to supper, Lord Franton naturally claimed that privilege when the dance ended.

"Now, that is the outside of enough!" said one of the other gentlemen, arriving just too late to put forward his own claim. "It's taking unfair advantage, that's what it is. You'd be justly served, Harry, if my friends were to call upon you in the morning."

"You've no one but yourself to blame," the marquis said, grinning unrepentantly. "If you hadn't been so determined to cut me out for the galliard earlier, you might have secured this last dance yourself."

"If you weren't given to underhanded tactics, I wouldn't have needed to," the other retorted.

Lord Franton only laughed and swept Kim off on his arm.

As they made their way in to dinner, Lord Franton said, "I don't believe I've told you how impressed I was by your introductory illusion."

"I was worried that no one would like it," Kim confessed. Although "not liking it" wasn't quite what she meant. But she couldn't bring herself to tell Lord Franton, Marquis of Harsfeld, that she hadn't been sure about the wisdom of flaunting her past as a street thief in front of a bunch of toffs, no matter what Mairelon and Lady Wendall had said. Judging by people's reactions so far, however, they had been right in advising her not to fret.

"It was . . . unusual," the marquis said in a thoughtful tone. "I assume the details were accurate?"

"We spent a lot of time getting it right," Kim said. "I think climbing roses would have been easier."

The marquis laughed. "So someone told you that that's what the young ladies normally do. This was much more original and memorable, believe me." His face grew serious. "It's a bit like the Cinderella fairy tale for you, isn't it? Except that you've had a magician for a godfather instead of a fairy godmother."

"And my clothes won't turn to rags at midnight," Kim said lightly. "And I don't have to try to dance in glass slippers." *And Cinderella didn't have to be talked into it; she* wanted *to go to the ball.*

"I can't imagine how your magical godfather happened to overlook so many important details," the marquis said, shaking his head in mock sadness. "It seems a shocking oversight."

"He's . . . had a lot on his mind," Kim said.

"At least he has not stinted in the matter of handsome princes," Lord Franton said. "There seem to be any number of candidates eager to apply for the position." He nodded in the direction of the still-faintly-glowering young man who had hoped to take Kim in to supper.

"Well, it's a good thing there are," Kim said, falling in with his bantering tone. "The Prince of Wales is above my touch, and the only other prince I know of is Prince Durmontov. He was invited, but he's away until next week."

"Ah?" Lord Franton gave her a sharp look. "Perhaps that is as well for the rest of us." He did not pursue the matter further, but instead turned the conversation to Mairelon's exploits during the French war. He seemed quite disappointed when Kim professed ignorance of any details.

"You'll have to ask Mairelon about that," Kim told him. "Or Hunch; he was there for a lot of it."

"Hunch?" Lord Franton looked puzzled.

"He's . . ." Kim hesitated, unable to think of a suitable description. "He works for Mairelon."

Lord Franton nodded. "I wanted to join the army, when I was younger," he said a little wistfully. "I even thought about running away and enlisting."

"You did? Why? I mean, why didn't you?"

"Responsibilities. By the time I would have been old enough, I was the heir to the title and there was no getting out of it." He grimaced. "The army is much too risky a place for a future marquis."

"Oh." Kim found it difficult to understand why anyone would want to have off to some foreign country in order to eat short rations and get shot at, but it wouldn't do to say so. Still, it was one thing to join up because you didn't want to see the French marching up High Holborn, and quite another to go off just because you wanted an "adventure." Toffs could be incomprehensible.

Lord Franton seemed to sense her mood, and did not pursue the subject. Instead, he amused her with unexpected comments and stories about the dignified ladies and gentlemen conversing with such elegance around the tables. It made Kim feel much more at ease to learn that the formidable Lord Benton was still known as "Piggy" because he had fallen off his horse into a sty during his second hunt, that the Carringtons kept eight pug dogs at their house in Town and a great many more at their country seat, and that the correct Lady Catherine Abelside had tried to elope with her dancing master two weeks into her first Season.

After dinner, the dancing resumed. The last of the guests did not depart until nearly three in the morning. With evident satisfaction, Lady Wendall pronounced the party a triumph, and sent Kim off to bed, warning her once again to be sure to stay late in bed the following day.

"Casting that illusion was more draining than you will have realized, and with the rest of the evening's excitement, you will be far more tired than you expect," Lady Wendall said.

"I will make your excuses to any callers," Mrs. Lowe put in.

Kim nodded, though receiving callers had never been prominent among her reasons for getting up in the morning, and went up the stairs, her head still whirling with the dizzying idea that she, Kim, was an unqualified social success.

eighteen

Despite Lady Wendall's warning, Kim was amazed to find that it was long after noon the following day by the time she awoke. When she came downstairs, she was further astonished—and a bit dismayed—by the size of the stack of cards and invitations that had accumulated while she slept. Her dismay proved well-founded. When Lady Wendall reviewed them, dealing out the invitations with all the concentration of a cardsharp dealing to a bunch of flats, the pile of engagements to be accepted was enormous.

The remainder of the week passed in a dizzying round of social activity. Kim drove in the park with no less than four gentlemen, including Lord Franton; attended a Venetian breakfast, two balls, three dinner parties, and a card party; and paid and received more calls than she could keep track of. Lord Franton called twice and turned up at dinners, balls, and assemblies with such regularity that Kim suspected he had somehow got hold of her schedule.

She hardly saw Mairelon at all, for though he accompanied Kim and Lady Wendall to a few of the events, he generally excused himself the moment they entered the doors and went off to the card rooms. After the second ball, Kim realized that he only joined them at events where Shoreham or Kerring was likely to be present, and he could speak with them privately. It seemed excessive to her, when Mairelon already spent most of his days in one or another of their offices, but the deepening lines in Mairelon's face prohibited comment.

As far as Kim could tell, there had still been no progress in defeating the spell that had removed Mairelon's magic. She did not like to ask;

refraining from making irritating comments was practically the only thing she could do to help. Two days after her come-out ball, she tentatively brought up, for the second time, the subject of talking to Jemmy and Wags, and was informed that they had dropped out of sight as completely as had Mannering, at least as far as Shoreham's informants were concerned. Privately, Kim was convinced that her chances of locating them were much better than Shoreham's, but with all her social commitments, she did not have an unsupervised moment in which to try, even if she had been willing to break her promise to Mairelon not to do so.

She began to look forward with considerable anticipation to Prince Durmontov's return to the city. At least talking with the prince would give Mairelon something new to do, rather than just sitting around fretting himself to flinders.

Kim was not the only one who had noticed Mairelon's erratic social performance. At Lady Souftmore's rout-party, a week after Kim's come-out, she was accosted by Letitia Tarnower, who paid her several compliments as fulsome as they were insincere and then said, "I cannot help but wonder that your guardian does not accompany you. Shall we see him later in the evening?"

"No," Kim said. "He's working on something."

Letitia raised her eyebrows. "He is very devoted to his work, then?"

"Yes," Kim said. "Excuse me; I think Lady Wendall wants me for something."

She made her escape, but spent the next hour wondering whether she ought not to have made a push to find out more from Miss Tarnower. She felt as if she ought to tell Mairelon about the conversation, but there was so little to tell that when she imagined herself repeating it to him, she felt foolish.

Her preoccupation continued, and after answering Mr. Cromie twice at random and throwing Lord Rencombe into a pother by the unguarded remark that his mother strongly resembled one of the apple women in Covent Garden, Kim decided that she had better get out of the crush and think for a moment.

The throng of guests made escape difficult and privacy all but impossible. Kim checked several of the small rooms along the hall, only to find them filled with card players. She returned to the ballroom, hoping that a corner of the balcony might be empty and quiet.

The glass balcony doors had been blocked off by a China silk screen placed several feet in front of them to prevent drafts. Kim rounded the edge just in time to see Letitia Tarnower step out onto the balcony.

Another encounter with Letitia was the last thing Kim wanted; fortunately, Letitia hadn't seen her. As she moved away from the screen and back into the ballroom, she saw Lord Gideon Starnes coming toward it from the opposite side, scanning the crowd anxiously over his shoulder as if to see whether anyone was following him. He hesitated briefly, then slipped behind the screen. An instant later, Kim saw the tops of the balcony doors open and close, the movement only just visible above the silk screen.

Uneasy curiosity warred briefly with Lady Wendall's instructions on proper behavior. Curiosity won. Kim eased herself behind the screen and pushed the near door open a cautious inch, then backed into the shadows behind the brocade curtains, where she was not likely to be seen from outside, and set herself to listen.

"—can't mean that!" Lord Starnes was saying in low, passionate tones.

"Really, Gideon, don't be absurd," said a light female voice that Kim had no trouble identifying as Letitia Tarnower's. "I most certainly can and do mean it."

"After all your promises, you could not be so heartless!"

"Promises? Stuff! I was seven years old, and you no more than ten. It was children's play, no more."

"I felt it more," Lord Starnes said heavily. "I thought you did, as well."

"No, Gideon, you *haven't* thought," Letitia said. "I do feel something for you, but what of it? You haven't a feather to fly with, and I *won't* spend the rest of my life scrimping and fending off bailiffs the way Mama has."

"If it's only the money—"

"If *you* had spent your life penny-pinching and wearing made-over dresses, you wouldn't say that it was *only* the money," Letitia replied sharply, and for once Kim found herself in sympathy with the other girl. "This is my once chance at something better, and I don't intend to waste it, Gideon."

"But I'll *have* money soon," Lord Starnes protested. "More than enough. If you will only wait . . ."

Letitia gave a tinkling laugh. "What is it this time, a sure thing in the races at Newmarket? Or will you stake your stickpin on the turn of a card, and mend your fortunes with the winnings? And when that doesn't come through, you'll ask me to wait for a cockfight that's certain to pay you a hundred to one, or for the dice to favor you. No. If you have your fortune in hand before I get Humphreys or Merrill up to scratch, you may speak to me about it then, but I won't gamble my future on your luck."

Kim's budding sympathy evaporated. It shouldn't have been a shock to hear Letitia state her intentions toward Mairelon so baldly, not after the way the girl had been behaving, but a shock it was, nonetheless.

"Lord Humphreys," Lord Starnes said with disgust. "He's ten years older than your father!"

"So much the better," Letitia replied. "I won't have to put up with him for long."

"And Merrill. Of all people, why Richard Merrill?"

Kim tensed; she had been wondering that herself. Mairelon didn't seem the kind of person that would attract someone as relentlessly social as Letitia Tarnower.

"He's wealthy, he's well-connected, and he's the sort that will be so preoccupied with his little magical projects that he won't notice or care what his wife does," Letitia answered promptly. "I'd thought of that Russian Prince Durmontov for a while, but he's a bit too wide awake to suit me, and he's the sort everyone watches. Merrill isn't so prominent that the old cats will scrutinize every step his wife takes. That ward of his will have a harder time than she thinks once she's married to Lord Franton."

"Is that settled?" Lord Starnes said, momentarily distracted. "Because I haven't seen him here tonight, and I've got a bet in the book at White's . . ."

"No, it's not settled and he isn't here, but anyone can see which way the wind is blowing," Letitia said. "And everyone can also see you making a cake of yourself every time I'm at a party. I wish you wouldn't."

"But Letitia, I love you!" Lord Starnes said desperately.

"Yes, you've said so often enough," Letitia said. "About once a month for the past three years, ever since I turned fifteen. And you're quite personable, and very amusing when you aren't pouring your heart out at my feet, and I do like you. But one can't live on love and wit, my dear. Find yourself an heiress, and let me be."

"You are entirely heartless."

"No, merely practical. And if you cannot behave yourself in company, I do not wish to see you again. Do I make myself clear, Lord Starnes?"

"Abundantly."

"Then I give you good evening." There was a rustle of skirts and

Kim shrank back into the curtains as the balcony door opened. To her relief, Letitia Tarnower swept out into the ballroom without glancing around. Kim gave her a moment to get clear, then slipped around the far edge of the silk screen. She'd heard all there was to hear, and Lord Starnes would be leaving the balcony, too, in another minute.

Kim's mind was in considerable turmoil. Mairelon had been quite right; Letitia Tarnower was not the widgeon she pretended to be. Indeed, if she had settled on anyone other than Mairelon as a prospective husband, Kim would have been more than a little sympathetic to her position. *If it was anyone but Mairelon.* . . . And *was* everyone expecting the marquis to make an offer of marriage for Kim?

The rest of the evening seemed to drag on forever. Kim was even more distracted and preoccupied than before, until she noticed Lady Souftmore and Mrs. Lowe exchanging significant looks. After that, she exerted herself to pay attention, but though the gentlemen redoubled their efforts to be charming, she was considerably relieved when the time came to leave at last.

When they arrived back at Grosvenor Square, Kim lingered in the hall for a moment to charge the footman not to let Mairelon out of the house next morning until he had spoken with her. She still wasn't sure what she was going to tell him, or what good it might do if she did. *At least maybe it'll distract him some.*

As she reached the top of the first flight of stairs, she saw a gleam of light coming from the half-open library door. Curious, she stepped forward and peered around the door.

The fire had died to embers; the light she had seen came from a single candle, burned down to barely an inch above the socket, which stood near the far end of the library table. Next to the candle stood a cut-glass brandy decanter, over half empty. Slumped in the chair at the end of the table, cradling a glass in both hands, was Mairelon. His dark hair looked as if he had run his hands through it several times, and there were shadows like bruises under his eyes. *He looks as if he hasn't slept in a week*, Kim thought, and unconsciously took another step forward.

The movement attracted Mairelon's attention, and he looked up. He frowned for a moment, as if collecting his thoughts from somewhere very far away, and then said, "Ah, Kim! Come in and toast your good fortune." His voice had an unfamiliar, almost mocking edge to it.

"My good fortune?" Kim stepped into the room and studied Mairelon for a moment. "You're foxed," she said in mild surprise. She'd

never seen Mairelon even a bit on the go before, not for real, though
she'd seen him play the part once or twice.

"I'm not foxed yet," Mairelon said. "The decanter isn't empty.
There's another glass somewhere; sit down and join me."

Uncertainly, Kim pulled up another chair and sat down on his right.
Mairelon blinked owlishly at her. "Don't look so glum," he said, the
mocking edge strong in his voice. "You should be celebrating. Though
I'll grant you, the prospect of congratulating Aunt Agatha on her per-
spicacity might take some of the satisfaction out of it."

"You *are* foxed," Kim said. "What are you on about?"

Mairelon raised his eyebrows. "Dear me, don't you know?"

"No, I don't." Kim clenched both hands in her lap to hold in her
temper.

Mairelon's eyes narrowed and he studied her for a moment; then he
sat back, his mouth twisted in a self-mocking smile. "Ah. Obviously I
was mistaken."

"*Mairelon*," Kim said, exasperated. "You're just as annoying foxed
as you are sober. Mistaken about what? What are you talking about?"

"Lord Franton, Marquis of Harsfeld, visited me earlier today,"
Mairelon said. "He asked my permission to pay his addresses to you."

"He—You mean that Tarnower chit was *right*? He's going to make
me an *offer*?"

"I believe that is what I just said." Mairelon sank down in his chair,
studying his brandy glass. "He seemed to have no doubt about your
answer."

"He wouldn't," Kim said in disgust. "Of all the sapskulled things to
do! I don't want to marry a toff, and certainly not a marquis!"

Abruptly, Mairelon's eyes focused on her with alarming intensity.
"You don't?"

"Well, I don't have anything against marquises in general," Kim said,
considering. "But I don't want to marry Lord Franton."

"Why not?" Mairelon said, still with the same intense focus. "He's
rich, he's titled, he's nearer your age than . . . He's near your age. And
Aunt Agatha was quite right—you couldn't be better established than to
marry a marquis."

Kim shook her head, searching for words. "If all I wanted was money
. . . Lord Franton's nice enough, but . . ."

"You're not still worried about being socially acceptable, are you?"
The edge was back in Mairelon's voice. "Not after the triumphs of the
past week!"

"Triumphs!" Kim snorted. "I'm a novelty, like a performing bear, that's all."

Mairelon's eyes dropped to his glass. In a completely colorless tone, he said, "Lord Franton doesn't seem to think so."

"Lord Franton ain't got no sense," Kim said flatly.

"I didn't think him so utterly senseless as that," Mairelon said, and an odd smile flickered over his lips.

"Well, you ain't got no sense sometimes, neither," Kim retorted. "Thinking I'd get leg-shackled to a marquis just because— If I'd of been that interested in money, I wouldn't of worked so hard to stay out of the stews all those years."

Mairelon blinked, plainly startled. "It's not the same thing at all."

"It ain't?" Kim shook her head and shivered slightly. The brothels of Southwark had been among her worst nightmares since she had first learned of their existence when she was five or six. "Marrying a marquis because he's rich and titled would be more comfortable and more permanent than working Vauxhall or Drury Lane, but I can't see that there's much other difference."

"Ah. I had never considered it in that light." Mairelon raised his glass and drank, then set it too-carefully on the table.

"Jenny Correy didn't marry Tom because he was well off, because he wasn't, then," Kim went on, half to herself. "And a lot of folks said she was throwing herself away on him, when she could have had Barnabas Totten, who's got his own pub, or Henry Miller down at the shipyard. But Jenny and Tom are a lot happier than the ones who picked the best catch. They . . . like each other, and they get on well. Most of the time. More than anybody else I know, anyway."

"I am justly chastened," Mairelon said, sounding more like himself. "Is there, perhaps, some other gentleman among your suitors whose addresses you *would* welcome? The marquis gave me to understand that he knew he was being a bit hasty, but he was desirous of, er, beating the competition to the gate."

"You mean he thinks I'm going to get *more* offers?" Kim said, appalled.

"He doesn't seem to be the only one who thinks so," Mairelon said. "Aunt Agatha mentioned it to me yesterday afternoon. *Is* there anyone, or would you prefer that I turn the lot of them away?"

Kim shook her head. "There isn't anyone."

Except you.

The revelation was so blindingly sudden that the words almost slipped out, and she had to bite her tongue and look away. *And you thought Lord Franton hadn't got any sense*, she castigated herself. But sense had nothing to do with it. She swallowed hard, and tears stung her eyelids. If a beauty like Letitia Tarnower couldn't interest Mairelon, and a brilliant wizard like Renée D'Auber hadn't attracted him in all the years they'd known one another, what chance did she, Kim, have?

"Kim. . . ." There was a long pause, and then Mairelon said in an altered tone, "You know, I believe you are right; I *have* had a little too much of this brandy."

With a lightness she did not feel, Kim replied, "If you hadn't, you wouldn't have been so nattered about Lord Franton. Silly clunch."

"Is that remark meant for me, or for Franton?" Mairelon said. "Never mind. If anyone else wishes to propose to you, I shall send him away, but I'm afraid you'll have to deal with the marquis yourself."

"I don't—" A prickle swept across her shoulder blades, and she stiffened and broke off in midsentence. After a moment, she realized that she had cocked her head as if she were listening for something, which was ridiculous—you couldn't hear magic. "Something just touched the house-ward," she told Mairelon. "It's still up, but—" Another twinge interrupted her. "There it goes again."

"A probing spell?" Mairelon said urgently. "Or a steady pressure?"

"Not steady," Kim answered. "Not really like a probe, either, at least, not like the ones your mother showed me. More like—" she groped for the image, "—like somebody throwing a rock through a window and running away."

"Probably nothing that needs immediate attention, then," Mairelon said. "I hope it didn't wake Mother."

Kim nodded. In the silence that followed, they heard a loud creak from the lower stairway. Immediately, Mairelon leaned forward and pinched out the candle. In the dim glow from the dying embers of the fire, he rose and made his way carefully to the library door, where he flattened himself against the wall. After a moment's thought, Kim also stood. Taking care not to make any noise, she slipped toward the bookshelves behind the door. There was nothing she could do about the pallor of her lilac gown, but at least she would be out of the line of sight of anyone entering the room.

There was another creak, louder and nearer, and then the library door swung wide and a dark figure entered. Mairelon waited until the man had passed him, then kicked the door shut and jumped. The two shapes went down with a thump. Kim snatched up a vase, then hesitated, unable to tell which figure to brain with it.

"I have him," Mairelon's voice said a moment later. "If you'd be good enough to manage the lights, Kim? I'm a bit occupied at the moment.

"*Fiat lux,*" Kim said hastily, and a rather wavery ball of light appeared above the two combatants. She frowned and concentrated more carefully, and the light steadied.

"Well, well," Mairelon said. "Lord Gideon Starnes. To what do we owe the pleasure of this unusual call, my lord?"

nineteen

Lord Starnes stared at Mairelon for a moment, and then all of the tension left his body and he sagged toward the floor. "It *would* be you," he said bitterly, and his words slurred very slightly as he spoke. "I suppose now you'll tell her, and I'll have no chance at all."

"I should be more concerned about my telling the Runners, if I were you," Mairelon said.

"I haven't done anything," Lord Starnes said with as much dignity as he could manage while lying on his back with Mairelon half-kneeling on top of him.

"Breaking into a house is something," Kim pointed out. "Even if you aren't very good at it."

"And especially when it's the second time," Mairelon said.

Lord Starnes jerked. "How did you— It wasn't me!"

"Looby," Kim said. "If we hadn't guessed before, we'd know now." Holding the light spell steady, she crossed to the table and relit the candle, then fetched two more from the candlebox and lit them as well. It looked as if this was going to take awhile, and she wasn't sure how long she could keep the spell going, especially if Lord Starnes was going to start saying things interesting enough to distract her.

"Very good, Kim," Mairelon said when she finished with the candles and let the light spell fade. "Now, Lord Starnes, I should dislike having to summon the Watch or lay information against you in Bow Street— but I shouldn't dislike it enough to keep me from doing it. You had better explain."

"And hurry up, before the rest of the house gets here," Kim advised.

"Oh, that won't be a problem," Mairelon said. "I made it quite clear that I didn't want to be disturbed this evening."

Kim frowned, but she couldn't ask him anything in front of Lord Starnes, even if Starnes was, as he appeared to be, considerably more foxed than Mairelon.

"Letitia will never have me now," Lord Starnes said miserably at that moment, drawing Mairelon's attention back to him.

"Letitia?" Mairelon frowned. "Not the Tarnower chit? What has she got to do with you breaking into Andrew's library?"

"She told him to sheer off, tonight at Lady Souftmore's rout," Kim said. "She's hanging out for a rich husband, and he wouldn't be one."

Mairelon gave her an inquiring look.

"They were talking out on the balcony and I . . . happened to over-hear," Kim said. "I was going to tell you, but we got to discussing other things."

"I can't imagine why you thought I would be interested in Letitia Tarnower's *amours*," Mairelon said. "No doubt you had your reasons."

"That wasn't all they were talking about. I'll tell you later."

"Do you mean that?" Lord Starnes said, raising his head. His voice was suddenly hopeful.

"Of course she means it," Mairelon said.

"No, did you mean what you said about Letitia—Miss Tarnower, that is?"

Mairelon frowned. "Do you know, I was under the impression that *I* was the one who was going to be asking questions and *you* were the one who was going to answer them. I can't think how I made such a mistake. Possibly it has something to do with the brandy."

"What brandy?" Lord Starnes said, bewildered. "I wasn't drinking brandy; I was drinking gin."

No wonder he hadn't noticed the smell on Mairelon's breath. Kim sighed and plopped into the nearest chair. If the two of them kept it up, this would take even longer than she had thought.

"Is that why you broke into my brother's house?" Mairelon said politely. "Because you've been drinking gin?"

"Of course not," Lord Starnes said. "Can't expect to find Blue Ruin in a place like this."

"Why not?" Mairelon said. "The cellars at Osterly House are half full of it, and the Racknetts practically bathe in the stuff. Not to men-tion—"

"Why *did* you come, then?" Kim interrupted before Mairelon ended up enumerating every gentry ken in town at which one could perfectly well expect to find gin in great quantities.

"I came for the book," Lord Starnes said.

"That, we know," Mairelon said. "The question is, why? It isn't good for anything."

"It is the key to a fortune!" Lord Starnes said dramatically, then broke out in a coughing fit. "Could you move your knee?" he asked Mairelon plaintively when he recovered.

"If I move my knee, I won't be able to balance," Mairelon said. "Get up, and we'll sit down at the table and talk in comfort."

"Oh, very well," Lord Starnes said.

They rearranged themselves according to this program, while Kim shifted impatiently in her chair. Then Mairelon looked at Lord Starnes and said, "Now, about this fortune?"

"It was the wizards," Lord Starnes explained. "The Frenchies. There were seven of 'em, and they knew the Terror was coming, so they put all their valuables in a secret vault and locked it with a spell. They each put part of the spell in a book, because they didn't trust each other, y'see, and then they left France. And the vault is still there, with a fortune in it seven times over, because they never went back. But it takes all seven books to get in."

"Fascinating," Mairelon murmured. "And how do you come to know all this?"

"M'grandfather knew one of 'em," Lord Starnes confessed. Having begun, he seemed almost eager to tell his story. "Fellow he met at a concert in Vienna, named d'Armand. They hit it off wonderfully, and d'Armand told him the whole story and gave my grandfather his book for fear of losing it."

"That sounds extremely unlikely," Mairelon said. "Especially since d'Armand was killed very soon after he left France. Have some brandy."

Lord Starnes shrugged as he took the glass Mairelon proffered. "My grandfather had d'Armand's book, and he said that d'Armand must have had a what-you-call-it, a vision that he was going to die, because a week later he drowned. And since grandfather didn't know any of the other Frenchies, and had no idea how to get in touch with them, he didn't do anything."

"That sounds even more unlikely," Mairelon said.

"You never met my grandfather." Lord Starnes sighed. "Lucky man."

"Me, or your grandfather? Never mind. What made you decide to

collect the rest of the books? I assume that is what you have in mind—
collect all seven of the books and claim the fortune."

"Letitia Tarnower," Kim said. "That's what did it. I told you, she's
hanging out for a rich husband."

"I will hear no word against Miss Tarnower," Lord Starnes said
belligerently.

"No one has spoken any," Mairelon reassured him. "About these
books—"

Lord Starnes heaved a sigh. "I would never have thought of it myself.
But Mannering assured me that no one would know, and it would be
the making of both of us."

Kim's eyes widened, and she and Mairelon exchanged glances. "Mannering?" Kim said in a careful tone.

"Yes, he's a cent-per-cent, a moneylender, that I've done business
with," Lord Starnes said. Kim nodded, and helpfully refilled his glass.
Lord Starnes took an absentminded pull and went on, "I gave him
d'Armand's book last year as collateral, along with some other things. I
thought he'd take it because he has a great interest in wizardry, though
I didn't realize at the time that he was one himself."

"He isn't," Kim said before she could stop herself.

"I've seen him work spells myself," Lord Starnes contradicted her.

"When was that?" Mairelon said.

"About a month ago, right after he offered to take me into partner-
ship over this French vault," Lord Starnes answered. His shoulders
sagged. "I didn't realize he wanted a lot of poking and prying and sneaking into people's houses. I thought we'd just quietly buy up the other
books somehow, and then I'd go to France and . . . and . . . collect everything."

"I see." Mairelon rubbed his chin thoughtfully. "And when did you
discover that the business was more complex than you had anticipated?"

"When Mannering sent me to get the first two books," Lord Starnes
said. "I thought—but he gave me a couple of twigs that he'd set spells
in and told me to break into the house. It was some awful place north
of the city—"

"Not Hampstead?" Mairelon said.

"No, but near there, I think," Starnes replied. "It took me forever
to find it, and then when I got inside it was a regular rabbit's warren.
Books everywhere, stacks of them, in the drawing room and the dining
room and even the *bedrooms!* I could only find one of the ones Mannering
wanted. I think they only *had* one—they were the two wizards who were

supposed to be married, you know, and what would they want with one each? Especially when they had all those others. But Mannering was very upset about it."

"Ah, that would be the Comte du Franchard and the Comtesse de Beauvoix," Mairelon said, refilling Starnes's glass once more.

Lord Starnes didn't notice. "Yes, that's right, the comte and comtesse. And then we had to track down the book you have, and I didn't manage to get hold of it, either." Lord Starnes sighed. "Mannering was livid. Said that if I couldn't get him the book, I'd have to make payments on the loan he'd given me! I had to go down to White's and it's a dashed good thing the cards were in my favor that night. Most of it."

"Is that when you lost your ring to Lord Moule?" Mairelon said. "The gold one with the ruby center?"

"Now, how did you know about that?" Lord Starnes said, astonished.

"Magic," Kim told him.

"Oh, of course." Lord Starnes tried to look intelligent. Failing, he took another drink of brandy instead.

"It's obvious how you were planning to, er, acquire the books that were here in England," Mairelon said thoughtfully. "But how were you planning to get hold of the Russian book? And the Hungarian one? Or didn't you know about them?"

"Oh, I knew the books weren't all in England," Lord Starnes said. "That's one of the reasons I never bothered to try for the seven of them myself. But Mannering said he'd arrange for the other two to be brought to London, and Durmontov showed up right on schedule. Whatever it was, it doesn't seem to have worked with the Hungarian, though."

"So Prince Alexei Durmontov is also involved in this interesting scheme of yours?" Mairelon kept his voice carefully neutral.

Lord Starnes looked startled. "No, of course not. If we'd gotten him involved, we'd have to split the money with him. No, no, Mannering tricked him somehow."

"That explains it," Kim said, topping off Lord Starnes's glass again.

"It didn't occur to you, I suppose, that the surviving wizards might want their belongings themselves?" Mairelon said in a deceptively mild tone.

"They've gotten along without them for thirty years," Starnes said sullenly. "If they wanted the treasure back, they should have made some push to get at it. And anyway, they can't get in without d'Armand's book."

Kim shook her head incredulously. "So you and Mannering decided to lighten *six wizards*? Of all the cloth-headed notions! Nobody with any sense tries to crack a frogmaker's ken, let alone six of 'em. It's too chancy."

"I'm a bit of a wizard myself," Lord Starnes said with dignity. "I got past your wards tonight, after all."

"It didn't do you much good, did it?" Kim retorted. "And anyway, you didn't get past them. You set off all the warning spells."

"I was afraid it was three circles, and not two," Lord Starnes muttered, suddenly deflated. "But if I'd gotten the spell right—"

Kim snorted. "It still wouldn't have done you no good. Amateurs! Magic won't help if you can't even put your feet down careful."

Mairelon's mouth twitched in amusement. "Yes, well, no doubt he didn't anticipate running across an expert on the crack lay," he said to Kim.

"Part of the job is looking ahead," Kim said crossly. "He should of known I was here."

"Should have known," Mairelon corrected. He leaned forward, and Kim saw an almost undetectable tension in his shoulders. "I don't suppose you know where Mannering is at the moment?" he asked Lord Starnes in a casual tone.

Lord Starnes shook his head. "He's gotten very . . . strange these last few weeks," he said in a confidential tone. "Flies out at people for no reason, that sort of thing. And then a week and a half ago, he closed his office. I was afraid he'd got hold of the other books without me and gone off to France, but it turned out it was no such thing."

"And how do you know that, if you haven't seen Mannering in a week and a half?" Mairelon said.

"Oh, I've *seen* him. Twice. I just don't know where he is."

Mairelon and Kim looked at him in wordless expectation.

"He sent me a note," Lord Starnes explained. "And then I went down to meet him at some warehouse off the docks. It was a dreadful place, worse than Hampstead. Took my valet half a day to get the smell of fish out of my coat."

"You said you'd seen him twice," Mairelon said, emptying the last of the brandy into Lord Starnes's glass. "Was it the same warehouse both times?"

"No. The second one was even worse." Starnes shuddered in remembrance. "Mannering didn't look well, either. I think his brain is turning. He talked of sending a couple of footpads after that Russian fellow. What's the point in that, when we've already got his copy of the book?"

"Footpads?" Mairelon said thoughtfully. "What a good thing for the prince that he's out of town."

"I've thought a couple of times that I'd be better off out of it," Lord Starnes said. "But there's Letitia. . . ."

"Yes, well, I doubt that Miss Tarnower will look favorably on your suit if you end up in gaol."

Lord Starnes' eyes widened. "I hadn't thought of that. But you know, you're right." He emptied his glass and gazed mournfully into the bottom.

Kim rolled her eyes. Mairelon gave her a stern look and said to Starnes, "You go home and think it over. If you have any more messages from this Mannering fellow, let me know and I'll deal with him. But if you do any more breaking into houses or stealing books—or even merely *trying* to steal them—I'll be down in Bow Street the next morning. Is that clear?"

Lord Starnes was initially disposed to argue, but between them, Kim and Mairelon got him out of the house at last, with the clear understanding that he was not to attempt any more amateur burglaries.

"Do you think he'll remember in the morning?" Kim said as they watched Lord Starnes wobble off down the street.

"He'll have the devil of a head after mixing gin and brandy, but he's not so well to live that he'll forget what happened." Mairelon rubbed his forehead. "Neither am I, though I almost wish I were. The more we find out, the less sense any of it makes. If this keeps up, I'll be ready for Bedlam by the end of the week."

Kim swallowed hard as the memory of Ma Yanger rose unbidden in her mind. "Don't joke about it."

"What? No." Mairelon sighed. "I'm too tired to think straight now; it'll have to wait until morning. Don't run off with one of your swains tomorrow until we've had a chance to talk."

"I won't," Kim told his back as it retreated up the stairs.

twenty

Kim did not get to sleep for a long time; she had too much to think about. She was no more satisfied with Lord Starnes's explanation than Mairelon had been—it left too many things unexplained. How could Mannering have so suddenly become a wizard? Who was the foreign wizard who had left those spells in English on Mannering's desk? And if Mannering was working with a foreigner, which of them had ensorcelled Ma Yanger and Mairelon? And why had they bothered? There seemed to be no connection between the spells and the supposed fortune that Lord Starnes was so eager to obtain, though it was certainly plausible that Mannering would be more than a little interested in the money.

On top of Lord Starnes and Mannering, Kim was concerned about Mairelon. He was taking the loss of his magic even harder than she'd realized, if he'd started drinking nights in the library. But the most disturbing thing of all, to which she kept returning like a tongue probing a sore tooth, was the realization that she had fallen in love with her guardian.

When had it happened? She wasn't quite sure. At their first meeting, she had feared his magic, but that had not lasted more than fifteen or twenty minutes. The often-exasperated fondness that had replaced the fear wasn't love. Nor was the gratitude she felt because he had taken her out of the precarious street life that was all she had known until then, nor the also-often-exasperated respect that she had learned for him as a teacher, nor the equally exasperated friendship that surfaced when they were poking around some problem together. Exasperation, in fact, seemed to be a keynote of her feelings toward Mairelon. Was that how you fell in love with someone, then—by getting exasperated with him?

It had certainly worked with Mairelon, though to the best of her recollection he had never shown any feeling for her except a mild and absentminded affection. Maybe she should try to make him exasperated with her. Kim sighed. Attractive as the idea was, she doubted that it would help any, even if she could manage to do it. Mairelon was harder to annoy than anyone she'd ever known; it was one of the things that made him so exasperating. She smiled fondly, then caught herself. Rolling over, she punched her pillow hard in frustration.

Stupid, stupid, stupid. Even if she could, by some miracle, get Mairelon to reciprocate her sentiments, what good would it be? For all his turns as a marketplace performer, Mairelon was a gentleman born, and she didn't know how to be a toff's wife. She didn't know how to be *anyone's* wife. She barely knew how to be a girl.

I used to be good at ignoring what I wanted, when I knew it was impossible. What happened? But she knew what had happened: she'd spent a year in Mairelon's company, learning wizardry and having dreams come true that she hadn't even known she'd had. And anyway, you couldn't ignore anyone as exasperating as Mairelon.

She buried her head in the pillow. *I am going to sleep. There is no point in thinking about this. I am going to sleep. Now.*

Eventually, she did. But she did not sleep well, and when she went down to breakfast the following morning, Mrs. Lowe commented that she appeared to have been overdoing her social life.

"Yes, you do look a bit hagged," Lady Wendall said. "Perhaps we should not go to Lady Sefton's tonight, after all."

Before Kim could answer, the door opened and Mairelon entered. He looked tired and drawn, and he winced a little at the light from the windows, but his expression was nonetheless more cheerful than she had seen it in several days. "Ah, good, you're up, Kim," he said. "Are you free of engagements this morning? I'd like you to join me on an errand or two."

"Richard," Mrs. Lowe said reprovingly, "we were just commenting that Kim has been doing too much. It would be much better for her to stay home and rest."

"I don't mind," Kim said quickly. If she had to miss something, she'd rather it was a fashionable do at Lady Sefton's than a few hours of Mairelon's company.

"You're sure?" An uncertain, anxious look crossed Mairelon's face.

It was gone in a moment, so quickly that even Lady Wendall did not notice, but Kim frowned. *This has to have something to do with his magic.* "Of course I'm sure," she said.

"That's all right, then," Mairelon said in a tone of mild relief that was altogether at odds with that brief expression of uncertainty. He picked up a plate and then hesitated, eyeing the eggs and sausage with evident doubt.

Mrs. Lowe frowned. "But, Richard—"

"I think it is a very good idea indeed," Lady Wendall interrupted. She had been looking sharply from Mairelon to Kim, but now she gave Mrs. Lowe her full attention. "We have been remiss in allowing Kim to fall behind in her magic lessons; and magic is, after all, a significant part of the good impression she has made. Of course she must go with Richard." She glanced at Mairelon and added sweetly, "And I am sure you will tell me *all* about it when you return."

"Oh, I doubt that there'll be much to tell," Mairelon said. "Errands are generally uneventful, you know."

"Not yours, dear," Lady Wendall replied.

Feeling considerably more cheerful herself, Kim applied herself to her breakfast. Mairelon did not eat much, so they finished at about the same time. "Don't forget your sunshade this time, Kim," Mrs. Lowe advised as they rose to leave.

Kim made a face, but made sure she had it with her as they left the house. Not listening to another one of Mrs. Lowe's thundering scolds was worth the minor inconvenience of carrying a parasol, especially since she could always leave it in the carriage.

"Where are we going?" she asked Mairelon as he handed her into the coach.

"The George," Mairelon said as he settled into the seat opposite. "If Prince Alexei Durmontov is back, they'll be the first to know where he's putting up; he'll have to let them know where to send his mail. And if the prince hasn't returned, someone may have an idea where he's gone. I don't like the sound of those footpads Starnes was talking about last night."

Kim frowned. Then, reluctantly but unable to resist asking, she said, "Why do you want me along for that?"

The coach began to move. Mairelon hesitated, then, with an evident reluctance more than equal to Kim's, said, "I promised Shoreham I wouldn't go anywhere without someone along who can handle protective spells."

"What?" Kim stared. "You mean, that's why you haven't gone any-where unless Shoreham or Kerring was around?"

"Shoreham's worried about another attack," Mairelon said. "I think he's wrong; the only time the house-wards have even been tested was last night, and that turned out to be the congenial Lord Starnes. But that's Shoreham for you."

"And you're counting *me* as a wizard?" Kim said, completely thun-derstruck. She wasn't nearly good enough for something like this; she could barely handle a standard warding spell!

"You've been doing the house-wards for a week and a half," Mairelon said in a low voice. "And Shoreham taught you Gerard's Refuge himself. Besides, I'm not anticipating any trouble."

"That's the problem," Kim grumbled. "You never do."

A reluctant smile tugged at the corners of Mairelon's mouth. "Never? Surely I haven't been *that* consistent."

Kim laughed in spite of herself. "I bet Hunch would agree with me."

"That's taking unfair advantage," Mairelon said.

"What's unfair about it?" Kim demanded.

The coach drew up outside the George, relieving Mairelon of the need to answer. Inside, the concierge informed them that Prince Dur-montov had returned to town late the previous evening. It was a very great pity that they had not arrived a few minutes earlier; he had just that morning been to the George to pick up his letters. No, he had not left very long ago. Where? Probably on some errand. The prince did not discuss his schedule with the staff. Yes, he had had several messages wait-ing; Mr. Merrill's was undoubtedly among them. Well, he really wasn't supposed to talk about the guests' affairs, but since Mr. Merrill was so generous, and the prince was no longer really a guest . . . There had been a note from a lady—no direction, naturally, but quite clearly feminine in origin—and a number of invitations and cards, as well as two or three other personal notes, and a singularly odd missive delivered by a scruffy fellow with a sour disposition, not at all the sort that the George was accustomed to receiving. That one? Yes, now that Mr. Merrill mentioned it, it was after reading that note that the prince had left, and in a bit of a hurry. And he had asked for directions to Gray's Inn, though that was clearly not his destination; no gentleman would—

"Mannering owns a bowsing ken by Gray's Inn," Kim interrupted. "And around there, anyone who saw a couple of wild rogues taking a gentry cove would be careful not to take notice."

"We'll try that, then," Mairelon said. "Come on; if we hurry, we may catch up with him before they do." He tossed the concierge another guinea as they departed. As the carriage rattled over the cobblestones, Mairelon said, "Have you practiced Gerard's Refuge since Shoreham taught you?"

"A couple of times," Kim said warily. "Do you think we'll need it?"

"It's possible," Mairelon said. There was a new tension in his shoulders, and he leaned forward slightly in his seat as if urging the coach onward. "Mannering would be a fool to decoy a wizard without being prepared to deal with magic. And so far as we know, he's not a fool."

And we know how he deals with wizards. Kim shivered. No wonder Mairelon was in a hurry; the thought of another wizard falling prey to the same antimagic spell affecting him would make him wild.

"I don't suppose you'd be willing to stay in the carriage?" Mairelon went on, giving her a sideways look.

"No," Kim said firmly. "If anybody stays, it should be you. I'm just an apprentice; you're a wizard, and if they think you can do magic, they'll go for you first. And after the way we did the illusion at that ball, they have to think you can still do magic."

"That's true," Mairelon said, sounding more cheerful. "I'd forgotten."

Kim blinked. "Then you'll stay here?"

"What! No, of course not. With any luck—"

The carriage stopped abruptly, and they heard Hunch swearing from the coachman's perch. Mairelon opened the door and sprang out without waiting for the steps to be let down. "Cast the Refuge," he said over his shoulder, and ran forward.

Cursing her skirts, Kim struggled out of the carriage and looked around. Hunch was still occupied with the reins, though a groom had jumped down from the back of the coach and was running to take the horses' heads. Mairelon was halfway down a narrow, refuse-choked alley leading directly away from the carriage door. At the far end, two solidly built men with their faces wrapped in mufflers were dragging a third man toward a waiting cart. True to Kim's prediction, the few people in the vicinity were paying no attention whatever to the attack in progress; they seemed far more interested in the presence of a gentleman's coach-and-four in such an unlikely location.

Kim started forward, clutching her sunshade like a club. Then she heard the sharp-edged words of a spell coming from the far end of the alley, and hastily cast the refuge spell that Shoreham had taught her. An instant later, an enormous gout of flame exploded around the combatants, roaring from wall to wall as high as the second row of bricked-up windows, and she felt a magical pressure against her shield. Over the roaring of the flames came a loud, high-pitched whine that hurt the ears even as far back as Kim was standing.

The cart horse shied and bolted, taking the cart with it and leaving the attackers nowhere to take their victim. The attackers themselves lost interest in their erstwhile prey and ran hell-for-leather down the alley toward Kim. One of them slammed full tilt into Mairelon, and both men went down. The other villain continued toward Kim, oblivious to his companion's misfortune.

With great presence of mind, Kim stepped to one side and, as the runner passed her, thrust her sunshade between his feet. He fell headlong, and the force of his movement snapped the shaft of the sunshade in two. Before he could scramble to his feet once more, Kim sat down hard on his upper back, driving the breath out of his body. For the next moment or two, all the bully-boy could do was gasp for air, and by the time he at last managed to refill his lungs, Hunch had come up with them.

"You can get up now," Hunch told her. "I'll 'andle 'im if 'e tries anything."

Kim bounced once, just to make sure the fellow wasn't up to anything, and stood up.

"Get him into the carriage," Mairelon's voice said. Kim looked over her shoulder to find him standing behind her, half-supporting Prince Durmontov. The prince looked rather dazed, but seemed largely unharmed; Mairelon's coat sleeve was torn, his cravat had come half-undone, and he was liberally streaked with mud, but he, too, did not appear to be injured. "The other man got away, and I think there was a driver in that cart; there's no sense hanging around here until their reinforcements arrive."

The flames and the whining noise had stopped some time during Kim's encounter with the man she had captured. Glancing around, she was unsurprised to find the street deserted. Nobody wanted trouble with wizards.

Hunch nodded at Mairelon and hauled their prisoner to his feet. The man's muffler had come undone, and Kim blinked at him in surprise. "Jack Stower!"

"Well, well," Mairelon said. "This *is* going to be interesting. Into the carriage, Kim, Hunch."

Hunch pushed Jack forward without comment, but when they

reached the coach, he frowned. "You ain't a-going to take this 'ere cove in there with you, are you?" he said.

"How else are we going to ask him anything?" Mairelon said. "He won't make any more trouble—not with three wizards keeping an eye on him."

Glowering, but unable to object publicly to this outrageous statement without giving Mairelon's incapacity away, Hunch did as he was told. A little nervously, Kim took the seat in the far corner from Jack; Mairelon helped the prince in opposite her, and slid in beside her himself. As the coach started off, he said, "Now, Mr. Stower, kindly explain your part in this little contretemps."

"I ain't sayin' nothing," Jack said sullenly.

"Very well," said Mairelon affably. "We'll just let Shoreham get it out of you. We're on our way to the Ministry now; I just thought it would save a little time if you talked to us first."

Prince Durmontov raised his head. "Ministry?" he said hazily. "What Ministry?"

"The Ministry of Wizardy," Mairelon said. "It's not far, and we'll take you back to the George after. Or wherever you prefer. You look rather done up."

"That spell is draining." The prince smiled a little wanly. "It is an old one, used in Russia to keep wolves off a sleigh. One use is all that is generally needed, so recovery does not need to be quick. If those men had soon returned, I would have been in . . . difficulty. I am in your debt."

"Spells," Jack said bitterly. "He said you didn't have no spells. Chicken-hearted gooseberry."

Kim felt Mairelon go tense beside her. "Mannering told you that?" "How'd you know it was him?"

"Never you mind. What else did he tell you?"

Jack was disinclined to answer, but by the time they reached the Ministry, Mairelon had pried most of what he knew out of him. It was not much. Mannering had ordered Prince Durmontov brought to the cellar of a pub in Smithfield and left there; he had assured his men that Durmontov would not be capable of using spells against them; they were to pick up their payment from the clerk in Mannering's office the following day. Jack had no idea where Mannering was hiding, only that something had sent him scurrying for cover.

With that unsatisfactory information, they were forced to be content. They turned Jack over to Lord Shoreham, who accepted with equanimity

Mairelon's muddy arrival and even muddier prisoner. Returning to the carriage, they found Prince Durmontov looking much more himself.

"Where now?" Mairelon said. "Back to the George?"

"No, if I may impose a little upon you," Prince Durmontov said. "I am concerned for family friends who may be also of interest to the man behind those—those—"

"Footpads," Kim offered.

"Yes," the prince said. "So I would like to go at once to Hampstead, to warn my friends."

twenty-one

Kim and Mairelon stared at the prince for a long moment. "Hampstead?" Mairelon said at last.

"Yes, to Duc and Duchesse Delagardie," Prince Durmontov replied. "They are only just returned from Edinburgh, and—"

"By all means," Mairelon replied. "And we have a great deal to discuss on the way. How fortunate that it is such a long drive."

The prince blinked, but gave Hunch the direction. Hunch scowled disapprovingly at Mairelon, but climbed back onto the box without comment, and in a few moments they were under way once more.

"How is it that you know the duc and duchesse?" Mairelon asked.

"One of my aunts knew them many years ago in France," Durmontov replied. "It is, in fact, partially on their account that I came to England."

"That would be the former Mademoiselle Jeannette Lepain? One of the seven French wizards once known as *Les Griffonais*?"

"Yes," said the prince, frowning. "How is it you know this?"

"I have had occasion to find out," Mairelon said. "Perhaps it will enlighten you somewhat if I tell you that some years ago, my father purchased a copy of *Le Livre de Sept Sorciers: un livre de mémoire* by one Madame Marie de Cambriol, and that someone has twice tried to make off with it in the past month."

"Three times," Kim corrected.

"I don't think you can count Lord Starnes's little excursion last night," Mairelon said. "His heart really didn't seem to be in it."

"What is this?" the prince said, his frown deepening.

"Wait until we reach the duc and duchesse," Mairelon said. "There's no sense in going over everything twice. Besides, you were about to tell us what your aunt's former associates have to do with your being in England."

Prince Durmontov studied Mairelon for a long moment, then capitulated. "Very well. A little time ago, my aunt received a message of a . . . magical nature. It involved an obscure threat to the Duchesse Delagardie and advised my aunt to bring her *livre de mémoire* to England. Though this message was not entirely clear, it disturbed her greatly. She is, however, deeply involved in an extended study of magic on the Indian subcontinent, and did not wish to break it off at a critical point to make so long a journey, most particularly because she could not be positive that it was necessary."

"Ah. So she sent you instead."

The prince inclined his head. "As you see."

"And since your arrival . . . ?"

"I have been very much confused," Prince Durmontov admitted. "First there seemed to be no threat—the Duchesse Delagardie was not even in London. Then, at Lady Greythorne's musicale, came that scrying spell which sent you hurrying off, and when I returned to my lodgings, someone had gone through my protections and stolen my aunt's book. I felt then that it was urgent to speak with the Duchesse Delagardie, but she had not yet returned. So I went to look for her."

"And found her, I take it," Mairelon murmured.

"She had been visiting a friend in Edinburgh named Lady MacKay, and had broken her return journey in York. She, too, was much puzzled when I told her of my aunt's message, and very troubled that someone had succeeded in removing my protections and stealing her *livre de mémoire*. The spells I had used were, you understand, some of those that the Duchesse Delagardie and my aunt and their friends had invented for their own use, and it would take more than a common wizard to avoid them."

"There is at least one extremely uncommon wizard in this somewhere," Mairelon said grimly. "Go on."

"I have little more to tell," the prince said. "We returned last night from Edinburgh. When I returned to the George this morning to arrange these last few matters, I found a note waiting for me, bidding me to a certain public house to learn more of the matter which brought me to England." He shrugged. "There was also your message. Had I answered it first—But one cannot live in might-have-been."

"No." Mairelon's voice had an undercurrent of irony, and Kim knew he was thinking of his ill-fated attempt to trace the scrying spell at Lady Greythorne's musicale.

There was a brief lull in the conversation; then the prince looked at Mairelon and said, "How is it that you performed such a timely arrival?"

"We hurried," Mairelon said.

Kim choked back a snort of laughter.

"And how did you know that it was necessary to hurry?" the prince asked politely, looking from one to the other.

"We had it from an inept gentleman-burglar late last night," Mairelon said. "He mentioned, somewhat in passing, that you were likely to be set upon. When we reached the George to leave you a warning, and discovered that you had already been and gone . . . well, hurrying seemed like a good idea."

"But why should anyone attack me?" the prince said, frowning.

"If we knew that, we'd be considerably further along than we are," Mairelon replied.

"Maybe Mannering wanted to find out where this Duchesse Delagardie is," Kim suggested.

"Mannering?" said the prince. "Who is—" He broke off as the familiar tingle of magic swept over them. "Ah!" he said, and raised his hands in an arcane gesture.

Kim lunged across the coach and grabbed his wrists, forcing his arms down before the gesture could be completed and ruining whatever concentration the spell required. "No!" she said forcefully.

The prince and Mairelon both stared at her as the tingling receded, the prince with restrained anger, Mairelon with a mixture of alarm and speculation. "Another scrying spell?" Mairelon said tentatively after a moment.

"I don't know," Kim said, sitting back. "Something, anyway. And it's gone now, like the other ones."

"There is some reason why you did not wish this spell traced?" Prince Durmontov said coldly.

Kim looked at Mairelon, who sighed. "We would very much like that spell traced," Mairelon told him. "Unfortunately, tracing it seems to have . . . unpleasant consequences."

"Indeed?" Durmontov looked skeptical but interested. "Yes, I recall that at Lady Greythorne's musicale you took a backlash from the spell. But—"

"It was more than a backlash," Mairelon said harshly. "It was a trap. A particularly nasty one."

The prince raised an eyebrow inquiringly, but Mairelon did not continue. After a considerable pause, Kim said, "He needs to know. If we hadn't been here, and he'd done that trace . . ."

"Yes, yes, all right," Mairelon said testily. He looked at Durmontov. "When my tracing spell connected to the scrying spell at Lady Greythorne's, it got sucked straight into it. Along with everything else."

Durmontov blinked. "Everything else . . . ?"

"I haven't been able to sense a spell-in-process, much less work one of my own, for nearly two weeks," Mairelon said, clipping the words off sharply. His face was stony, defying comment or sympathy.

Prince Durmontov's eyes widened and he sat back heavily against the squabs. "I . . . see." He turned to Kim. "I would appear to be doubly in your debt." He hesitated, looking at Mairelon. "I can see that you do not wish this to be talked of. Nor would I, in your place. But when we reach the duchesse, she must be warned."

"Of course," Mairelon said without enthusiasm.

The conversation died. Kim thought of half a dozen questions she would have liked to ask, but in the face of Mairelon's heavy silence and the prince's contemplative one, she didn't quite dare. She found herself torn between sympathy for Mairelon and annoyance at his behavior. She knew, none better, how difficult it was to reveal a weakness or a vulnerability, even to a friend—but she also knew that if Mairelon hadn't blown the gab, he would have blamed himself for whatever grief the prince came to later on. He knew it himself, but he was sulking like a sweet-stealer with a pain in his tooth.

They reached Hampstead at last, and descended from the coach in front of a small white stone house set well back from the street. A flagstone walk led to the doorway, past short clumps of new-green plants and some kind of thorn-covered vine that was just leafing out. Inside, a housemaid showed them to a small drawing room that looked as if it had been hastily and rather incompletely tidied, and left to fetch her mistress. On closer examination, the air of disorder proved deceptive. The books and papers on the corner tables were arranged neatly between bookends; the silver candleholders gleamed, and the chairs and woodwork shone with beeswax. It was the number and variety of books and furniture that gave the impression of confusion.

A few minutes later, a short, plump, bespectacled woman entered the room. She wore her ginger hair unfashionably long and loose beneath her proper lace cap, and her blue velvet gown, while clearly expensive and in the best of taste, was not in the latest mode. "Good morning, Alexei," she said. "You have brought friends to meet me? But you have had some accident!"

"No accident," said Prince Durmontov. "I was set upon, but thanks to these two, I am not harmed. Allow me to present Miss Kim Merrill and her guardian, Mr. Richard Merrill. This is the Duchesse Camille Delagardie."

"You have no notion how happy I am to make your acquaintance at last," Mairelon said with feeling.

The duchesse's eyes twinkled behind her spectacles. "No? Then you must at once seat yourselves and explain, and I shall have Liza bring in tea. For it is obvious that there is some long explanation to come, and I find that long explanations always go well with tea. It is an English custom of which I thoroughly approve."

They followed this program at once. The account took some time, for, somewhat to Kim's surprise, Mairelon did not play off any of his tricks for avoiding explanation on the duchesse. Instead, he gave her a more detailed version of the story he had told Lord Shoreham, compressed but complete in all the essentials. The duchesse lost her twinkle almost immediately, and listened in thoughtful silence. Her expression grew grave when Mairelon described the trap that had caught him during Lady Greythorne's musicale, but it was not until he reached the previous evening and Lord Gideon Starnes's tale of the treasure vault in France that the duchesse was betrayed into exclamation.

"But that is absurd!" she said. "Or rather— No, go on. I will know the whole of it, before I take my turn."

"There's not much more to tell," Mairelon said. "Starnes mentioned that his compatriot had said something about setting footpads on Prince Durmontov, and we thought it best to warn him. When we got to the George, he'd already been and gone, so we went after him."

"And arrived in a most timely fashion," the prince put in. "I thought it wise to tell you at once, since it seems connected with that peculiar message my Aunt Jeannette received. And then during the ride here came another of these scrying spells, and only Miss Merrill's prompt action kept me from falling into the same trap as Mr. Merrill."

"Very good," the duchesse said, nodding approval at Kim. "I, too, am in your debt. I would not like anything unfortunate to happen to Jeannette's nephew, though he is in general quite capable of taking care of himself."

"And that," said Mairelon, "is all. If you can shed any light on the matter . . ."

"I do not know that I can," the duchesse said slowly. "You see—no, I shall begin at the beginning." She eyed Mairelon apologetically. "It is no great matter, you understand, only that it is a little uncomfortable to admit the follies of one's youth."

"I am all attention," Mairelon said. His tone was polite, but the tension in the set of his shoulders had returned.

The duchesse sighed. "It was twenty-six . . . no, twenty-seven years ago. Things had been growing more and more difficult in France, and it was plain to all of us that some sort of upheaval was soon to come. And it was likewise clear that the nobility and the wizards would have the worst of it. And since the seven of us were all wizards and all French aristocrats—"

"Except for M. Karolyi," the prince put in. "He is Hungarian."

"*Very* Hungarian," the duchesse agreed with a smile. "He is, however, a wizard and a dear friend of the Vicomte de Bragelonne, and as such, we expected that he would fare no better than the rest of us. So the seven of us came together and placed our most precious possessions in a vault— actually, it was a very large room in Marie's cellar. Well, it had to be, with all the books."

"Books?" Mairelon said with interest.

The duchesse nodded. "Marie stored almost her entire magical library, as well as her silver and most of her jewels, and Eustacie had at least as many, and Henri and Jeannette, also. And there was my library, too. We were days hauling it all down. László put in only those things he had with him in France, of course, which was not quite so much. When we finished, the seven of us worked a spell to seal the room completely. It was a very good job, I think. The *sans-culottes* could have burned the house overhead, and the fire would have stopped at the ceiling boards. Not so much as a speck of ash would penetrate."

"That sounds . . . thorough."

"Marie and I were worried about mice getting at the books," the duchesse said placidly. "When one stores such things in a cellar, and there are no cats about, it is a reasonable concern."

"So the treasure vault is real," Mairelon said thoughtfully. "And the seven *livres de mémoire* are the key?"

The duchesse shook her head. "But no! That would have been folly. We did not know, of course, that poor Henri's ship would go down so soon after we left France, but with the times so unsettled we could not be sure that all seven of us would be able to return to open the vault, or even send a key with someone else. And to make the key a book, which is so vulnerable to fire and damp . . . no. That is why I said this Lord Starnes's story was quite absurd."

"Then how *did* you reopen the vault?"

"The key is quite a simple spell, very easy to remember," the duchesse replied. "I don't believe any of us even wrote it down in our *livres de mémoire*. But we never went back to reopen the vault. The Terror . . . was worse than we expected anything to be, and lasted longer, and after that came Bonaparte. By the time he relented somewhat toward wizards, we had all made our lives elsewhere, and we did not feel the risk was worth it." She smiled slightly. "As long as we left everything there, you see, it was quite safe, but it would be easy enough to confiscate it once the spell had been removed. And transporting all those things out of France without attracting attention . . ." She shook her head.

"You mean it's all *still there?*" Kim said. "The silver and the jewels and everything?"

"It is the books I regret most," the duchesse said.

"My aunt, also," said Prince Durmontov, nodding.

Kim blinked at them both in disbelief and shook her head. She saw the corners of Mairelon's mouth twitch in amusement. *Toffs!* she thought. *I'll never understand them.*

"I'm surprised Mme. de Cambriol's husband didn't return, even if none of the rest of you did," Mairelon said. "From what we know, he had a thin time after she died."

"He considered it," the duchesse said. "But he was not himself a wizard; one of us would have had to accompany him to cast the spell to open the vault. He would not ask us to take the risk. Besides, he was always quite certain that his next hand of cards or the next horse race would render the trip unnecessary, and his luck did indeed run well now and then."

"Gamesters often feel so," Mairelon said. "Then as far as you know, the vault is untouched?"

The duchesse nodded. "That is why Louis and Eustacie have returned to France: to open the vault and retrieve our belongings at last. I do not know what we shall do with Henri's and Marie's portions. They have no living relatives I know of."

Mairelon raised a hand to rub his temples. "So we might just as well have given Lord Starnes the de Cambriol book and wished him godspeed that first night," he said bitterly. "He and Mannering are chasing a will-o'-

the-wisp; even if they get hold of all seven books, they won't be able to open the vault in France, and even if they could, they'll find it empty by the time they get there. And none of the rest of this would have happened."

"*If* the treasure is all they want," Kim said.

Mairelon looked at her.

"I never knew Mannering much," Kim went on, "but people said he was a fly cove and right knowing. And anyone can see that that Lord Starnes is as cork-brained as they come, even when he's not bosky. *I* wouldn't tell Starnes anything important, and I'm nothing like as downy as Mannering."

"True." Mairelon's expression brightened briefly, then he shook his head and said in a tired voice, "But in that case, we're no further along than we were before."

The duchesse made a hesitant gesture. "There is one more thing, of a sort. I would not have thought of it, only you said that it was Henri's *livre de mémoire* these people have, and Henri—" She smiled reminiscently and shook her head. "Henri d'Armand was a most unusual person. Things that came easily to the rest of us were most difficult for him, and things most persons find greatly difficult were for him very simple. He was in many ways a brilliant wizard, but he never truly believed that."

"I am afraid I don't understand," Mairelon said.

"I explain very badly," the duchesse told him. She thought for a moment. "A *livre de mémoire* is for writing down things that one is most likely to forget. For most of us, that is the unusual—the word that must be changed for a spell to work *so* and not *so*, the one corner of a diagram that must be circled instead of crossed, the ingredient one always forgets. For Henri, it was otherwise."

"But what else—" Prince Durmontov began, then stopped, frowning.

"Henri remembered changes easily enough," the duchesse said, nodding. "It was the original spell itself he sometimes had difficulty in recalling. So his *livre de mémoire* was full of spells, like a true grimoire, except that most of them did not work correctly because he had not yet worked out the necessary changes. We used to laugh with him about it."

"So d'Armand's *livre de mémoire* looks useful, but isn't quite," Mairelon said thoughtfully. "Do you think that Mannering is after the other books in order to correct the spells in the one he's got?"

"That would be of little use," the prince said. "Without knowing the wizards, he could not know which spells the bits and pieces in the other *livres de mémoire* refer to."

"Bits and pieces." Mairelon's eyes widened. "All his spells are bits and pieces, strung together. . . ."

"This is all very possible," the duchesse said. "But it is still not quite what I wished to say." She hesitated, then went on slowly, "Your description of this . . . this trap, M. Merrill, sounds familiar—very like something that happened once by accident when the seven of us were constructing a new spell. If you do not object, I would like to examine the remnant that you say still affects you. I think perhaps, if I am right, I may be able to offer some suggestions."

"I am at your disposal, Your Grace," Mairelon said instantly. "So long as you are quite certain your examination will not expose you to the same . . . misfortune."

"If it is as I suspect, I can assure you it will not." The duchesse rose and nodded to Kim and the prince. "I trust you will excuse us. My workroom is not large enough for so many. I do not expect that we will be long. M. Merrill? This way."

twenty-two

Kim could not help fidgeting in Mairelon's absence, but he was not gone long. In less than half an hour, he and the duchesse returned. The duchesse looked grave; Mairelon seemed in a state of suppressed excitement. "I will let you know as soon as I am certain," the duchesse said to Mairelon. "I cannot promise anything yet, you understand, but the basis is plainly Henri's spell for sharing *la puissance.* I do not see how this wizard has— But it may be clearer after I check some of my reference books."

"I sincerely hope so, Your Grace," Mairelon said.

"You understand the risk?"

Mairelon's jaw tightened. "Thoroughly. I will . . . consider the matter carefully."

Kim gave him an inquiring look, but neither he nor the Duchesse seemed inclined to explain.

They took their leave soon after. Mairelon spent the journey back to London in a brown study. Prince Durmontov, after one or two unsuccessful attempts to rouse him, beguiled the time by telling Kim about his family in Russia. It was very interesting, and she was almost sorry when they let him off at his new lodgings.

"Prince Durmontov," Mairelon said as the prince climbed out of the coach. "From what the Duchesse Delagardie has said, we may need more than one wizard to . . . remedy the current situation. As you are already somewhat involved—"

"You may depend on me," the prince replied.

Mairelon relapsed into reverie as soon as the coach pulled away, and remained so until they reached Grosvenor Square. There he roused himself to send Hunch off with messages for Lord Kerring, Lord Shoreham, and Renée D'Auber. Kim knew better than to insist on touchy explanations in front of the grooms and footmen, but by the time they entered the house, she was bursting with impatience.

"Is my mother in?" Mairelon demanded of the footman. "Well, when she arrives, tell her I would like to speak with her. I'll be in the library."

"Mairelon," Kim said as they climbed the stairs, "what did that duchesse tell you? And what did she mean about risks?"

"Hmm? Oh, I thought that she'd made that clear." Mairelon turned in at the library door and began scanning the shelves.

Kim followed him in and shut the door behind them. "She maybe made it clear to you, but I wasn't there," she said. "What did she say?"

"The magic-draining enchantment does seem to be based on an early version of a spell the duchesse is familiar with," Mairelon said without looking at Kim. "*Les Griffonais* invented it for their own use, years ago. Unfortunately, that particular spell was flawed to begin with, and the version that's affecting me has some unusual variations."

"The duchesse can still get rid of it though, can't she?"

"Possibly. She suggested casting the spell afresh, properly, and then disassembling it. The odds are good that doing so would take this other enchantment with it." He frowned suddenly and turned. "I have covered that with you, haven't I?"

"It was in that first book you gave me," Kim said. "The one with all the Greek."

"And?"

This is not *the time I'd pick for lessons.* But she could see that Mairelon wouldn't tell her any more until she answered. She thought for a moment, trying to remember what the book had said. "The easiest way to correct a flawed spell is to cast it a second time and do it right. The structure of the new spell is stronger, and . . . and it sort of takes over the one with the mistake in it."

Mairelon smiled suddenly. "Not quite the way Cornelius phrased it, but correct in its essentials. D'Armand's spell was meant to be cast by himself and his six friends, as a way of sharing their magical abilities during major projects. They used it only for short periods; keeping it going for more than a few days was, er, uncomfortable for everyone, and they suspected that long-term maintenance would have . . . unpleasant consequences."

Ma Yanger, Kim thought. "Does that mean that whoever is keeping this spell on you is uncomfortable?"

"I devoutly hope so," Mairelon said. "But according to the duchesse, the early versions of the spell were unstable—they fell apart after a few minutes, or hours at most. Our mystery wizard seems to have found some way of stabilizing the spell without correcting any of the other fundamental flaws." He frowned again. "He also seems to have altered the spell a bit."

"Altered it?" Kim said. "Why would he change the spell and not fix any of it?"

Mairelon shrugged. "The flaws have to do with the way magical power is shared among the seven participants. Our mystery wizard has found a way to use it to strip away power, rather than share it. Possibly he didn't think it necessary to fix the parts he didn't need. But because of the changes he made, we can't be perfectly certain that recasting the spell will work the way it's supposed to."

"Is that what the duchesse meant when she talked about risks?" Kim said, frowning.

"Partly." Mairelon went back to scanning the shelves; after a moment, he pulled out a thick brown book and carried it to the library table.

"What's the other part?" Kim said, her stomach knotting. Mairelon only got like this when he was about to do something dangerously goose-witted—and knew it.

"Other part of what?" Mairelon said.

"The risk."

Mairelon looked at her, then looked away. "There's a distinct possibility that if this doesn't work, I'll lose my magical abilities permanently. You don't have to be concerned about your training," he added hastily. "Kerring will be happy to take you on, if . . . But it's not likely to be necessary."

"The training ain't what I'm nattered about!"

"Isn't what you're upset about," Mairelon corrected, then added in a low voice. "I appreciate your concern."

It ain't just concern! "Mairelon . . ." Kim hesitated. "Is it worth it?"

"It will settle matters, one way or another. And the risk isn't great." But his eyes did not meet hers, and she knew he was not as certain as he pretended. She could also see that he had made up his mind, and, having done so, was not about to change it.

"Of all the buffle-headed things to say!" she said angrily. "Next you'll be telling me that gallivanting around France with the whole army after you wasn't dangerous. Have a little sense!"

Mairelon looked at her and smiled crookedly. "Why should I start now?"

The library door opened and Lady Wendall entered. "You wished to see me, Richard? Good heavens, look at the pair of you! I can see you have a great deal to tell me."

"More than you realize," Mairelon said. "We may have found a way of removing this antimagic spell or whatever it is. It'll take six wizards besides me; I trust you'll be one of them?"

"Of course, dear. Who are the others?"

"Kerring, Shoreham, and Renée, if they agree; Prince Durmontov already has, and the Duchesse Delagardie will be directing the spellcasting. We'll need to clear out the ballroom; the library isn't large enough for the floor diagrams."

"Very well," Lady Wendall said, stripping off her gloves. "But you appear to be leaving out a good deal, and you *did* promise to tell me all about it when you returned."

"Did I?" Mairelon said. "Well, I suppose it is only fair."

As Lady Wendall and Mairelon settled in to talk, Kim stole quietly out of the library, her emotions in turmoil. Mairelon's choices for the other six wizards to cast the spell that would—they hoped—return his magic to him were logical ones; all six were either trusted friends, like Kerring and Shoreham, or wizards already involved in the matter, like the duchesse and Prince Durmontov, or both. But though she knew it made no sense for him to include a mere apprentice in the spellworking, she could not help feeling hurt and left out because there was no place for her.

She did not have much time to indulge in hurt feelings; less than half an hour later, Lord Franton arrived and requested the favor of a private word with her. Kim swallowed hard when the message was brought to her; in the excitement of the morning, she had forgotten— or allowed herself to forget—that she could expect a visit from him. *Well, at least I'll get it over with.*

Lord Franton was waiting for her in the drawing room. He looked up and smiled as she entered. Kim swallowed again, and he must have seen something in her expression, for his smile became uncertain at the edges. "Miss Merrill—"

"Mairelon told me—I mean, I—" Kim's face grew warm and she stuttered to a stop, unable to think of a way to phrase what she wanted to say. She should have just let him speak, instead of trying to refuse him before he'd even begun.

The marquis looked at her. His eyebrows flew up and his expression stiffened slightly. "Am I to understand that you are aware of my intentions, but are not willing to entertain my offer?"

"That's it," Kim said with relief.

There was a pause. "May I inquire as to the reason?"

Kim hesitated, searching for a way of expressing her difficulties that would be neither insulting nor wounding. "We'd both end up being miserable. I'm no wife for a gentry cove."

"Is it your background, then?" Lord Franton smiled and shook his head. "That need not worry you. You're a wizard now; what you were before does not matter to me."

"Yes, it does," Kim said softly. "Because part of the time you're sorry about it, and part of the time you think it makes me interesting, and part of the time you ignore it. But you never *forget* it." Mairelon was the only toff who truly didn't care that she'd been a street thief . . . but she'd best not think of him just now.

"I do not—" Lord Franton cut off his automatic denial before it was well-launched. He considered for a moment, his lips pressed tightly together, then looked at Kim once more. "I think I see what you are getting at," he said with reluctance.

"You never really forget it," Kim repeated. "And I don't think you ever would."

"I could try," he offered tentatively. "That is, if your sentiments are such that you would reconsider . . . ?"

Kim could only shake her head wordlessly.

"I see," Lord Franton said after a moment. "I . . . honor your frankness, and I wish you well. Give you good day."

He bowed and left. Kim stood staring at the door for a long time afterward, wondering why she did not feel more relieved and hoping she had not just made the biggest mistake of her life.

By evening, preparations for the spell to disenchant Mairelon were well underway and Kim felt more excluded than ever. A message from the duchesse arrived late in the day, and was apparently very promising, for it set off another round of notes and letters to the proposed participants. Mairelon spent the remainder of the evening shut up with his books, and the following morning conferring with his mother; then Renée D'Auber and Prince Durmontov arrived, and the four of them went into the ball-room to prepare for the casting ritual.

Under other circumstances, the activity would have been fascinating, for Kim had not previously seen a major ritual spellcasting requiring several wizards. All of the participants, however, were too occupied with learning the parts required of them, and with making certain that every aspect of the spell was precise to a fault, to explain anything to Kim. Nor could she bring herself to distract any of them with questions—not when Mairelon's magic depended on their getting everything exactly right.

So she ran whatever mysterious errands anyone thought to ask of her, supplied the wizards in the ballroom with new grapes, sour wine, and powdered pearls on request, and concealed her fears as best she could. Lord Kerring and Lord Shoreham turned up shortly after the preparations had begun and went instantly to join the others, leaving only the duchesse still unaccounted-for.

Mrs. Lowe was somewhat disturbed to learn that callers other than the participating wizards were to be denied, but after expressing her opinion of the imprudence of such a move and of the folly of suddenly determining to perform a major spellcasting at the height of the Season, she retired to her rooms and did not reappear. Consequently, it was Kim, waiting impatiently in the drawing room for the duchesse to arrive, who heard the commotion from the front hall. Slightly puzzled, she hurried out into the hallway and down the stairs.

"Don't go gammoning me!" a young voice said belligerently as she made her way downward. "I come for the frogmaker. I got a message, and I ain't givin' it to nobody else. So you just hop to it and tell him so, see?"

"Mr. Merrill is not at home to callers," the butler said with the air of someone repeating himself.

"That's nothing to me," the belligerent young voice said. "I got a message for that Kim, and I'll see him straight and no bobbery."

"I'm Kim," said Kim, coming around the last turn. "What do you—Matt!"

The dark-haired youth who had somehow insinuated his way into the front hall turned and gaped at her. "Garn!" he said after a moment. "I knew you was a frogmaker, but—" His Adam's apple bobbed as he swallowed hard and shook his head. "Well, I'm scunnered, that's all," he announced.

"You said you have a message for me?" Kim said sedately, imitating as best she could Lady Wendall's calm, matter-of-fact responses to startling announcements and events. Tom Correy's nephew could think what he liked; she owed him no explanations. Tom would be another matter.

"Tom needs to see you, right away," Matt said, confirming her misgivings. Well, she'd known she was going to have to face Tom sooner or later and tell him the truth about her sex; she just hadn't expected it to be this soon.

"Tell him I'll come by this evening," she said. They'd have finished reworking the spell on Mairelon by then, and they'd know the results. One way, or another.

"*No*," Matt said with considerable force. "Right now! You got to come back with me."

Kim frowned. "Something's happened?"

"Yes–no— You just got to come," Matt said desperately. "Tom'll explain."

"Oh?" Kim's eyes narrowed. Matt was Jack Stower's nephew, as well as Tom Correy's. But Jack was safe in Shoreham's hands, and had been since yesterday morning. Still . . . "How do I know Tom sent you?"

"He said to tell you to mind when the rattling cove took you for a mumper, and the old fussock rang a peal over him to get you off."

Kim nodded, satisfied. No one but Tom and Mother Tibb knew about that incident, and Mother Tibb was dead.

"You'll come?" Matt said anxiously.

"Let me think a minute," Kim said. There was nothing for her to do here but fret; running off to see Tom would at least occupy her while the spellcasting went forward. It felt like abandoning Mairelon—but she couldn't help him, and if she *could* help Tom, shouldn't she do it? She'd known Tom Correy longer, and she owed him a good deal. "I'll be back in a minute," she told Matt, and ran upstairs to the ballroom.

The wizards had finished the preliminaries, and were standing in a clump near the door. In the center of the ballroom floor, two overlapping triangles had been drawn by carefully spreading wet rowan-ash in straight lines, forming a six-pointed star. A small table had been placed just outside each point to hold the various items the wizards would need for their parts in the spellcasting.

"We'll begin as soon as the duchesse arrives and checks everything over," Mairelon was saying as Kim entered. "It shouldn't be— Kim! Has the Duchesse Delagardie come?"

"Not yet," Kim said. "They'll bring her up as soon as she gets here, though. I got to go down to see Tom Correy; something's happened."

Mairelon frowned. "You're sure—no, of course you are. But . . . Now?" He glanced at the windows, alight with the afternoon sun.

Kim shrugged. "Tom's got to find out I'm a girl sometime."

"All right. But take Hunch."

Kim nodded, swallowing a small lump of disappointment. She had, she realized, been hoping he would tell her to stay. Well, that was Mairelon for you. She hurried back toward the stairs, and nearly ran into Mrs. Lowe.

"Kim! Really, you must not race about like that."

"Sorry," Kim said, intent on getting past her.

Mrs. Lowe grasped Kim's arm and gave it a gentle shake. "Whatever is your hurry?"

"I'm going out," Kim said. "Excuse me, I have to go."

"Without your abigail?" Mrs. Lowe said, maintaining her grip on Kim's arm.

"It's . . . wizard business; Mairelon knows all about it." At least, he knew as much as she did. "And I'm taking Hunch."

Mrs. Lowe considered. "Hunch is no doubt very useful, in his way, but it is hardly proper for you to wander about the city in his company, even if it is on *wizard business.*" She sniffed. "I shall come with you myself."

"No! I mean, I don't think—"

"I was under the impression you were in a hurry," Mrs. Lowe said. "Shall we go?"

"It isn't anywhere proper," Kim said. "You won't like it."

"I had already formed that conclusion," Mrs. Lowe replied. "I may also add that I am neither blind, nor deaf, nor foolish, and if you think I am unaware that something is very wrong and has been for some time, you are very much mistaken."

Kim could only stare at her in consternation.

"It is not my place to pry into matters which my nephew plainly does not wish to confide in me," Mrs. Lowe went on. "I can, however, make sure that his ward does nothing disgraceful while he is otherwise occupied. And I intend to do so."

"It isn't disgraceful. And I told you, he knows about it already."

"Richard," said Mrs. Lowe austerely, "is frequently oblivious to the social niceties." She paused. "Should you wish to continue this discussion, I suggest we do so in the carriage. That is, if you are in fact in so much of a hurry as you at first appeared."

"Oh, I am," Kim muttered, and started down the stairs, wondering what Tom would make of this.

twenty-three

Matt was eloquent in his disapproval of Mrs. Lowe's presence; fortunately, he expressed himself in terms utterly unintelligible to her. He was somewhat mollified when he realized that they were to travel in a bang-up gentry coach. Mrs. Lowe ignored him. Hunch, on seeing the oddly assorted group, blinked and began chewing on his mustache. Kim felt entirely in sympathy with him.

As they drove off, they passed the Duchesse Delagardie pulling up in a landau. *That means they'll be starting the counterspell soon,* Kim thought, and shivered. Such a complex spell would take considerable time to cast, but even so, everything would probably be finished by the time she returned. *One way or another.*

Possibly because he was feeling the same anxiety as Kim regarding Mairelon's welfare, Hunch not only took the most direct route to Tom's but also drove the horses rather faster than was either wise or required. Matt was much impressed, and said so at some length until Kim advised him to stubble it. Somewhat sulkily, he did so.

When they pulled up outside Tom's shop at last, Kim descended and hurried inside without waiting for Mrs. Lowe or Matt. Tom was sorting through a pile of old clothes on one of the tables, but he looked up when he heard the door. His eyes widened in startlement, and he said, " 'Morning, miss. Anything I can do for you?"

"You're the one that sent Matt to get me," Kim said, half enjoying his bafflement, half fearing his reaction when he finally realized who she was.

"*I* sent—" Tom stared at her and his jaw dropped. *"Kim?"*

402   *MAGIC AND MALICE*

"Matt said you wanted to see me right away," Kim said nervously. "And I didn't think I'd pass for a boy in daylight, and I thought it was time I told you anyway, and— What was it you wanted?"

"Kim." Tom's astonished expression slowly gave way to something very like horror. "I never knew. I wouldn't of done it if—I mean, I thought—I—you—"

"What's the matter?" Kim said, frowning. "Why'd you want to see me?"

"He didn't," said a deep voice from behind Tom. "I did." The owner of the voice moved out of the shadows as he spoke. He was not much taller than Kim, but broad and square and as solidly built as the cargo-handlers on the London docks. His clothes, however, proclaimed him no dockworker; they were the neat and well-tailored wear of a respectable businessman who might be expected, on occasion, to deal with members of the *ton*. Though "respectable" was not the usual term employed to describe the sort of business Kim knew he engaged in.

"Mannering!" she said in disgust, and looked at Tom reproachfully. She was more annoyed than frightened, even when a second man with the look of a bully hector about him joined Mannering. She was considerably nearer the door than they were, and the carriage was no more than two feet beyond that; if anything looked like trouble, she could pike off in a twinkling long before it came near.

"I'm sorry, Kim," Tom said. "But he—I wouldn't of done it if I'd known you—I'm sorry."

Kim shook her head. Tom's betrayal had surprised her, but only a little. Kim knew well enough the pressure that someone like Mannering could apply to compel cooperation, and the sort of loyalty that could stand up under such an assault was a rare commodity. Or at least, rare in the rookeries, tenements, and stews; she was quite sure that no threat could have persuaded Mairelon to bend to Mannering's schemes.

"Hold your tongue!" Mannering said to Tom. "Your young friend and I have business."

"Indeed?" said Mrs. Lowe from behind Kim. "Then I suggest you execute it so that we may be on our way. This is *not* the sort of establishment at which I wish to linger."

"What? Who's this?" Mannering demanded.

"I do not desire to be presented to this individual," Mrs. Lowe informed Kim. "You will oblige me by not doing so."

Kim nodded and looked at Mannering. Swallowing seven or eight questions that she wanted to ask immediately, she settled for a cautious, "What is it you want?"

"This is *private* business," Mannering said with a significant look first at Tom, then at Mrs. Lowe.

With evident reluctance, and a worried look at Kim, Tom vanished through the rear door. Mannering jerked his head at his henchman and said, "Watch him."

The henchman started to follow Tom out, then hesitated, eyeing Kim. Mannering scowled. "I said, watch the togs-man," he repeated. "I can deal with a couple of women myself."

The henchman nodded and left at last. Mannering looked pointedly at Mrs. Lowe. Mrs. Lowe, however, was unmoved. "I told you, this business is private," Mannering said pointedly after a moment.

"I am not in the least hard of hearing," Mrs. Lowe replied. "However, if you think that I propose to leave my nephew's ward alone with a person such as yourself, you are quite mistaken."

"Madam," said Mannering in a threatening tone, "I am a wizard!"

"What has that to do with the matter?" Mrs. Lowe returned imperturbably. "The social niceties, as I have repeatedly pointed out, must be observed." She paused. "You will not, I hope, pretend to offer either of us a mischief—not in broad daylight with two grooms and a coachman just outside."

Mannering looked from Kim to Mrs. Lowe, plainly off balance.

"If you have something to say to me, you'd better say it," Kim told him.

"And you had best say it quickly," Mrs. Lowe said. "Perhaps I should also mention that before I came in, I sent that singularly impenetrable young man—the one who brought your message—in search of a constable. While he did not impress me as being particularly reliable as a general matter, I think that in this instance he can be depended upon to fulfill his commission."

"You're lying!"

"Care to wager on it?" Kim said. Though it wasn't likely to do much actual good; in this part of town, Matt could be hours finding anyone. "Pay or play; I got business elsewhere."

"This is more important," Mannering said, still eyeing Mrs. Lowe doubtfully.

Frowning slightly, Kim glanced at Mrs. Lowe herself. Mairelon's aunt stood in front of the grimy windows of Tom's shop, looking enormously proper, entirely sure of herself, and totally out of place. Kim blinked, then suppressed a grin. *Mannering's dealt with gentry before, but I'll wager he's never dealt with one who didn't want to borrow money—and for sure he's never had to face a respectable lady before. No wonder he's nattered.* Anything that made Mannering uncomfortable was a good notion as far as Kim was concerned; she looked back at Mannering and said, "What's so important? That de Cambriol book?"

"You've got it," Mannering said, leaning forward. His eyes glittered, and he seemed to have suddenly forgotten Mrs. Lowe's presence entirely. "My clerk said you showed it to him. I'll pay a round sum for it."

"How much?" Kim said, hoping Mrs. Lowe would have sense enough to keep her comments and opinions, whatever they were, to herself. If she could get him talking . . .

Mannering stepped forward. "How does fifty pounds sound?" he said in a voice just above a whisper.

Kim's eyebrows flew up. Fifty pounds was an undreamed-of fortune, by the standards of her old life. Coming from a usurer accustomed to dealing with the gentry, however, it was nothing short of an insult. "I ain't no gull," she said scornfully. "Mairelon gives me more than that for pin-money. Make a serious offer, or I'm leaving."

"I'm serious." Mannering stepped forward again, and Kim felt a twinge of fear. "Oh, I'm very serious. You have no idea how serious I am. Give me that book!"

"I think not," Mrs. Lowe put in calmly. "Kim, am I correct in guessing that this . . . person is responsible for that outrageous disruption in the library two weeks ago?"

Kim turned a little to answer, and took the opportunity to put a little more space between herself and Mannering. She was still well out of his reach, but a little caution never hurt anybody. "He was behind it," she told Mrs. Lowe.

Mrs. Lowe's head moved a fraction of an inch, shifting her attention to Mannering. Mannering fell back a step. Mrs. Lowe continued to study him for a moment; finally, she said in tones of icy reproof, "I take leave to tell you, sir, that you are unprincipled, presumptuous, and criminally self-serving; moreover, I must assume from your behavior that you lack both manners and wit into the bargain."

Mannering stared at Mrs. Lowe as if he could not believe his ears. Kim wondered whether he had ever before had his character so thoroughly cut up in quite such a formal and cold-blooded manner; somehow, she doubted it. "Wit?" he said in a strangled voice. "You think I lack wit?"

"It is the obvious conclusion," Mrs. Lowe said. "For even if one sets aside the illegal aspects of pilfering a book from my nephew's library, a more poorly conceived and badly executed endeavor than your attempt would be difficult to imagine. Nor has my opinion of your civility or intelligence been improved by your actions since our arrival today."

"I am a genius!" Mannering's eyes widened in passion and he raised a beefy fist for emphasis.

Mrs. Lowe was unimpressed. "I have seen no sign of it."

"I am a wizard!"

"So is my nephew," Mrs. Lowe said. "And while I do not by any means consider him unintelligent, he is certainly no genius."

"Ah, but he was born a wizard," Mannering said. "I made myself a wizard! No one else has ever done that."

"Indeed?" Mrs. Lowe said in tones of polite disbelief.

Mannering flung his arms out and gave an unintelligible roar. Magic exploded into the shop with such force that Kim's skin stung. The pile of clothes in front of her shivered and rose into the air. It hovered for a moment, then began to spin. Tattered shirts, worn breeches, several mufflers, and a jacket with a hole in the left elbow went flying in all directions. Kim dodged one of the shirts and two mufflers, keeping her eyes on Mannering all the while. She hadn't really believed, until this minute, that Mannering could be a wizard.

As suddenly as it had begun, the spell stopped. The flying clothes plowed into walls with the last of their momentum and slid down into limp heaps. "There, you see?" Mannering said.

"That is precisely the sort of display I was referring to earlier," Mrs. Lowe said. "You would have made a more favorable impression had you chosen to *reduce* the mess in this room, rather than to increase it."

"How *did* you make yourself a wizard?" Kim put in quickly, before Mannering took a notion to blow the whole shop up just to prove his genius to Mrs. Lowe.

"You'd like to know that, wouldn't you?" Mannering said. "You and your toff friends don't want anyone doing real magic but you. That's why you won't give me the book, isn't it?"

Kim blinked, startled by this leap of logic. "We haven't agreed on a price yet," she pointed out cautiously.

"Hang the price! I want the book. Now."

"What, you think I'm a flat?" Kim shook her head and snorted. "I don't cart it around with me everywhere I go. What do you want it for, anyways?"

Mannering smiled. In a calm, too-reasonable voice, he said, "Why, to make it hold on steady-like."

"To make *what* hold on?"

"The spell." Mannering rocked forward on the balls of his feet. "It keeps wobbling," he said in a confidential tone. "And it takes more magic to straighten it out every time. I have to keep finding new magic to keep it from collapsing. If I had the right book, I wouldn't have to work so hard to keep them in line."

A chill ran up Kim's spine; she wasn't quite sure what Mannering was getting at, but she was positive that she wasn't going to like it one bit once she figured it out. And she didn't like his erratic behavior. Still, his mercurial changes of mood had kept him talking so far; if he continued, she might find out something useful. "Keep who in line?"

"My wizards," Mannering said. "Some of them used to be your friends. You used to like Wags, didn't you? And Bright Bess, I know you got on with her. You don't want them to end up like that Yanger woman, do you?"

The image of Ma's slack-jawed, drooling face rose in Kim's mind. Kim's stomach tightened. "What did you do to Ma Yanger?"

"I didn't do anything," Mannering said, still in the same much-too-reasonable voice. "Not really. She could even have had her magic back, if she'd been willing to go along like the rest of them. Some of her magic, anyway. It was your toff friends who destroyed her, and now you're going to do the same to the others."

"Gammon!" Kim said. "I ain't doing nothing."

"I believe that in this instance, doing nothing is indubitably the wisest course," Mrs. Lowe commented. "I must deplore your manner of expression, however, no matter how appropriate it may be under these circumstances."

Mannering turned on her in sudden fury. "Interfering harpy! If you were a wizard, I'd do you like Yanger!"

"So you *were* behind it!" Kim said.

"No, I told you, it was your toff friends," Mannering said, abruptly reasonable once more. "They unbalanced the spell, and . . ." He shrugged.

Kim frowned. "You still aren't making sense." She was beginning to think he never would. *One thing at a time.* "What has this got to do with the de Cambriol book?"

"It has the rest of the spell in it," Mannering said. "It has to, or they wouldn't be trying so hard to keep me from getting it." He rocked back on his heels. "The comte's book only had a few words, and the Russian's was no help at all."

"The rest of the spell that lets wizards share their power?" Kim guessed.

"You know it!" Mannering rocked forward, eyes glittering feverishly. "You've read the de Cambriol book, haven't you?"

"I've heard talk," Kim said cautiously. "Is that how you made yourself a wizard—by getting somebody to share his power with you?"

"Of course. He didn't know I wouldn't have to give it back as long as I kept the spell going."

"Kept it going?" Kim stared, then shook her head, remembering what Mairelon had told her. "You gudgeon! That spell was never meant to last more than a day or two!"

In the doorway, Mrs. Lowe pursed her lips and gave Kim a reproving glance, but said nothing.

"That's what they want you to think," Mannering said, and smiled slyly. "I've kept it up for months now. It just takes adding another wizard's power now and then, to keep up the level of magic in the spell."

"You cast the whole spell again every couple of weeks?" Kim said, thinking of the elaborate preparations in the ballroom at Grosvenor Square.

"No, of course not!" Mannering said. "Just the last bit, that links a wizard in with the main spell. I thought of that myself," he added with pride. "And I don't even have to do that very often, because the spell absorbs the magic whenever someone attacks me."

Not just when someone attacks, Kim thought. Mairelon's spell had been intended just to trace Mannering's scrying spell, but all his magic had been swallowed up by this . . . this enchantment of Mannering's. The thought made her feel ill.

"It's getting harder to keep it balanced, though," Mannering went on. "I need more power, but if I get too much at once it starts to burn out the spell. That's what did for Ma Yanger—when those wizard friends of yours attacked me just for looking at them at that opera, it was too much for my sharing-spell to handle all at once."

Mairelon's first tracing spell, Kim thought, feeling even sicker than before. They'd found Ma the day after the incident with the flying book, and they'd known she couldn't have been incapacitated for very long, but they'd never connected the two.

"The wobble hurt everybody else in the link, too," Mannering went on, "but it burned the Yanger woman's mind out completely." He laughed suddenly, a harsh, half-mad sound. "Serves her right for being so uncooperative."

"Uncooperative?"

"She wouldn't work for me," Mannering said in the pouting tone of a child complaining that he had been denied a sweet. "I'd have let her have a little magic, if she had agreed, but she wouldn't." He frowned and added fretfully, "The spell's been unbalanced ever since. I thought it would settle after I added that Russian's magic, but it's worse than ever. I'm going to need a new wizard soon. I suppose I'll have to take Starnes after all, but I wanted to have everything steadied down before I started on wizards with real training."

And in another minute or two, it might occur to him that he had a wizard right in front of him who was barely started on her "real training," and therefore much safer to steal magic from than Lord Starnes was likely to be. Surreptitiously, behind a fold of her skirt, Kim made the one-handed gesture Shoreham had shown her and murmured the activating word of the spell in a voice too low for Mannering to hear. If he had all the skills of a real wizard, and not just the borrowed power, he'd feel the refuge spell go up, but by then it would be too late for him to stop it. From what Shoreham had said . . .

Mannering's head jerked back as if he had been struck. "What are you doing?" he demanded. "You're trying to trick me, like those others, like that Russian. Well, I'll stop that! *I hold yours, to me thy power comes!*"

The air crackled with the power of Mannering's final words, and Kim felt his spell strike her shield. The force behind the blow was enormous; had the shield been meant to withstand it, force for force and power for power, Kim knew it would have failed. But Gerard's Refuge didn't block or absorb or resist attacks—it "sort of shoves them to one side where they can go off without doing any harm," Shoreham had said. Mannering's spell slid sideways and whizzed invisibly past Kim's ear.

Kim stared at him in shock. "You cast that spell in *English!*"

"Of course! I am an English wizard," Mannering said proudly. His expression changed. "You— How are you keeping your magic? I should have it by now!" He raised his hands. "*I hold yours, to me—*"

"That is *quite* enough of that!" Mrs. Lowe said, and stepped in front of Kim.

"*—your power comes!*" Mannering finished. Kim flinched, but Mrs. Lowe did not seem to feel a thing as the spell hit her. Mannering, however, groaned and clutched his head.

"What did you do?" Kim asked, staring at Mannering.

"Nothing whatever. Nothing was all that was necessary." Mrs. Lowe gave a small, wintry smile. "While I did not entirely comprehend what this . . . person was saying, it seemed clear from his remarks that whatever spell he was casting was meant to affect another wizard's magical powers. As I am no wizard and have no such abilities, the spell could not affect me. I presume it recoiled on him, and though I understand that spell recoils can be quite painful, I must say that I think he deserves it."

Kim found herself heartily in agreement with this sentiment. "How did you guess it would work that way?"

"My dear Kim, I have not spent years as a member of a family rife with wizards without learning some of the basic principles involved in magic! One need not have the ability in order to understand the theory, after all." With a brisk nod, she resumed her place in the outer doorway, watching Mannering.

Mannering looked up, panting, and took a deep breath. "You're keeping me from your magic. How are you keeping me from getting your magic? That Russian taught you, didn't he?"

"Prince Durmontov?" Kim said.

"I got his magic, all of it, but he still cast a spell at my men when they went to bring him here. How could he do that?"

So Mannering didn't know which wizard's magic he'd stolen on the night of the musicale. Well, she certainly wasn't going to straighten him out. "Why did you want to talk to the prince?" Kim asked.

"He's got training," Mannering said patiently. "I'd have given him back a bit of his magic, just like all the others, in exchange for his help holding the spell together."

"If you think anyone would help you under such circumstances, you have even less intelligence than I had given you credit for," Mrs. Lowe commented. "Why should he help you keep hold of his power?"

"He wouldn't want to end up like the Yanger woman, would he? That's what will happen if the spell breaks apart. They all know it, too, all my wizards." Mannering frowned. "But I forgot; he still has magic. Maybe he wouldn't end up a Bedlamite like the rest of them."

But it wasn't Prince Durmontov's magic that Mannering had stolen; it was Mairelon's. And from the sound of it, Mannering's spell had worked exactly the same way on Mairelon as it had on the lesser wizards whose power he had stolen. *Which means that if Mannering's spell breaks apart or goes unstable, Mairelon's likely to end up just as witless as Ma Yanger did.* Kim swallowed hard, hoping her face didn't show what she was thinking. "If you're having trouble keeping the spell stable, why don't you just let it go and start over?" she suggested in what she hoped was a casual tone.

"I can't do that," Mannering said patiently. "If I let it go, I won't be a wizard any more, and none of them would ever let me try again. And they'd all be angry, and if I wasn't a wizard anymore, how could I protect myself? No, what I need is—" Mannering stopped abruptly, and his eyes widened in terror. In a voice that was almost a squeak he said, "What are you doing? Stop—stop it!"

"Stop what?" Kim said, frowning.

"You can't—you don't want this!" Mannering said in tones of desperation. "You won't just destroy me; you'll destroy every wizard in the link!"

No! Mairelon's in the link! thought Kim, and suddenly realized what was happening. The wizards in Grosvenor Square had started recasting the power-sharing spell, and Mannering could feel the beginnings of it because he was linked to Mairelon's magic. Her eyes widened as she remembered her conversation with Mairelon. The duchesse and Lord Kerring and the others thought that Mairelon had been stripped of his magic; they didn't realize that he was somehow part of Mannering's linkage. When they brought Mairelon into their newly cast spell, they'd be bringing in Mannering's entire network of spell-linked wizards as well— and they wouldn't be expecting it. The duchesse's spell was supposed to be the final, unflawed version of the one Mannering had cast, and therefore able to absorb and overpower it, but the duchesse's spell was designed for only seven wizards, not a dozen or more. And on top of that—"Did you cast that power-sharing spell in English, too?" Kim demanded urgently.

"I cast all my spells in English," Mannering said with dignity. "I am an English wizard. I had the others use English, too; I'm not such a flat as to let someone cast a spell on me when I can't understand what he's saying."

"You are a blithering idiot," Kim snarled. *Casting a spell in a foreign language keeps power from spilling into it uncontrollably.* And uncontrolled power was unpredictable; it could make spells stronger, but it also could change their effects. Her own experiment with working magic in English was still vividly clear in her memory; she could practically see the spots dance in front of her eyes. If Mannering had persuaded one of the untrained wizards from the rookery to cast d'Armand's already-flawed power-sharing spell—and to cast it in English—then it was no wonder the spell didn't behave anything like the way it was supposed to.

Kim stared blindly at Mannering, thinking furiously. What would happen when the duchesse's spell linked the magic of six fully trained wizards to Mairelon . . . and through Mairelon, to Mannering's warped version of the same power-sharing spell? More than likely, the two spells would merge, flooding Mannering's network with power. And if absorbing Mairelon's spell had been enough to destroy Ma Yanger's mind, the unexpected addition of six wizards' worth of magic at once would probably burn out the mind of every wizard in the link, just as Mannering claimed. Jemmy and Wags and Bright Bess would turn into vacant-eyed, mindless husks . . . and so would Mairelon.

On top of that, the duchesse and Lady Wendall and Lord Shoreham and the others who were trying to help Mairelon would also be linked into Mannering's network as soon as the spells merged. At best, they would probably lose their magic to his twisted version of the power-sharing spell; at worst, their minds might be burned out as well. Who could tell what effect the uncontrolled power in Mannering's spell might have?

"We got to get back and stop them!" Kim gasped, and started for the door.

"No!" Mannering said, darting forward and grabbing at her left arm. "You have to stay— You have to give me— You have to tell me—"

Kim let his grasp swing her around. As she turned in to face him, she brought her free arm up hard and fast. The heel of her open palm connected cleanly with the bottom of Mannering's chin, snapping his head up and back. He let go of her and staggered backward, off-balance. His head hit the jamb of the rear door, and he went down in a dazed heap.

"Get Hunch!" Kim said over her shoulder to Mrs. Lowe, and started forward. They would have to take Mannering with them; left to himself, there was no knowing what he'd do or whether they'd be able to find him again. And if the duchesse and Kerring and Shoreham had Mannering himself to interrogate, they might be able to figure out a safe way of removing his spell from Mairelon. *If* they got back to Grosvenor Square before the current spellcasting was finished . . .

"Not just yet, I think," Mrs. Lowe murmured. Stepping forward, she jabbed Mannering with the point of her sunshade. Mannering yelped and fell sideways. Mrs. Lowe picked up the thick wooden shaft he had been lying on and barred the rear door.

A moment later, the door rattled as if someone were trying to enter. "Mr. Mannering?" said a muffled voice. "Is everything all right?"

Mannering was shaking his head and trying to rise; Kim knocked him back against the door jamb once more with a well-placed kick. "Get Hunch," she repeated.

Mrs. Lowe pursed her lips disapprovingly, crossed to the outer door, and vanished outside.

I got to get Mairelon to teach me some spells for this kind of thing, Kim thought as she grabbed a linen shirt from the nearest pile of clothes. Keeping a wary eye on Mannering, she yanked at the tough fabric.

The outer door opened again and Hunch and one of the grooms entered. "Now what 'ave you gotten into?" Hunch growled.

"Mr. Mannering?" The barred door rattled again.

"We got to get back to Grosvenor Square as fast as we can, or it's all up with Mairelon," Kim told Hunch, ripping a strip from the shirt as she spoke. "The bully-boy in back don't matter, but we got to take this cove with—" she nodded at Mannering "—and he's a weird sort of frogmaker. If we tie his hands and gag him—"

"I know 'ow to 'andle 'is kind," Hunch said. "I've 'ad to do it for Master Richard a time or two." His hands were busy with the linen strips as he spoke, and in a few seconds he had Mannering expertly bound and gagged. With the groom's help, they loaded him into the coach.

As she climbed in beside Mannering and Mrs. Lowe, Kim heard loud thumping noises from the interior of the shop; apparently Mannering's henchman was trying to break down the door instead of going out the back way and nipping around to the front entrance. She spared a fleeting thought to wonder how much trouble Mannering's bully-boy would make for Tom once he finally got into the front room and found Mannering gone. Well, it was Tom's problem, and with luck Matt would have gotten back with a constable by then. She leaned out the coach window. "Spring 'em," she said to Hunch.

twenty-four

The trip back to Grosvenor Square seemed to take forever, though Hunch urged the horses to a speed far greater than was really safe on the crowded streets. Mrs. Lowe sat stiff as a poker beside Kim, radiating disapproval but not saying anything. Mannering had recovered from his daze and alternated between glaring balefully at Kim over his gag and making terrified whimpering noises. On the whole, Kim preferred the glares; as long as he was sane enough to glare, she knew that the wizards in Grosvenor Square hadn't completed their spell.

It's a complicated spell, it'll take a long time. But would it take long enough? The picture of Mairelon turned empty-eyed, grunting, and helpless haunted her. *Faster,* she thought at the horses. *Hurry faster.*

At last they pulled up in front of the door. Kim was out of the coach almost before it stopped moving, and banging the knocker long before any of the grooms reached the door. When it opened at last, an interminable time later, she darted past the startled footman and ran up the stairs to the ballroom. As she tore down the hall, she heard a muffled feminine voice rising toward a climax, but she couldn't tell whether it was Lady Wendall's or the duchesse's. The duchesse was supposed to be last. . . . She flung herself through the ballroom door.

The air inside the ballroom was heavy with power; the sharp, glittering structure of the spell nearly complete. The Duchesse Delagardie stood in one of the triangular points of the star that Kim had watched the wizards preparing. Lady Wendall, Lord Shoreham, Lord Kerring, Renée D'Auber, and Prince Durmontov occupied the other points, and

Mairelon himself stood in the center of the star. The duchesse had her back to the door, and her arms were raised in the final invocation.

Kim hesitated. To interrupt now would shatter the spell, and the enormous power that had already been poured into it would recoil on the wizards, doing nearly as much damage as Mannering's spell would. To let them continue would destroy Mairelon's mind as soon as he was linked into the duchesse's spell, not to mention the minds of the other wizards whose magic Mannering had taken, and quite possibly the six spellcasters themselves into the bargain. As soon as Mairelon was linked to the duchesse's spell . . . but if the duchesse linked her spell to *someone else*, instead of Mairelon . . .

Without pausing to think further, Kim picked up her skirts once more and ran forward. Mairelon saw her and took a half-step to meet her, then stopped, plainly realizing that to move any farther he would have to step outside the star. Renée and Lord Shoreham saw her next and frowned; then the other wizards—all but the duchesse. As Kim reached the edge of the star, she realized that the duchesse had closed her eyes to speak the closing words, and a tiny corner of Kim's mind sighed in relief. At least she wouldn't accidentally distract the duchesse and cause the spell to shatter.

Kim made an urgent shooing motion at Mairelon and pointed emphatically to the floor outside the star. *If only he doesn't take a notion to get stubborn* . . . Mairelon hesitated and glanced at the duchesse; he knew, even better than Kim did, the possible consequences of miscasting a major enchantment. Frantically, Kim gestured again for him to move.

On the far side of the diagram, Shoreham frowned and shook his head, but Mairelon's gaze was fixed on Kim's face, and he didn't notice Shoreham's gesture. *Move, move, get out of the star!* And finally, his eyes alight with questions, Mairelon nodded and stepped sideways out of the diagram. As he did, Kim stepped into it, taking his place.

Mairelon turned, an expression of horrified comprehension dawning on his face. He reached for Kim, but he was an instant too late. The duchesse spoke the final syllable and brought her arms down in a decisive movement, finishing the spell.

Power crashed down on Kim, filling her to bursting and beyond, burning through her mind. *Is this what it felt like to Ma Yanger?* The room went dark and she felt herself away. Far away, a babble of voices broke out, but the only one she could decipher was Mairelon's: "Duchesse! The counterspell, quickly!"

Three words blazed across Kim's mind like lightning bolts across a darkened summer sky, and then the storm of uncontrollable power passed. Almost gratefully, she started to collapse. Arms caught her as she fell; she struggled mindlessly until she heard Mairelon's voice by her ear and realized the arms were his. Then she relaxed into unconsciousness.

Her insensibility could not have lasted more than a moment or two, for the first thing she noticed when she began to recover was Mairelon's almost panic-stricken voice in her ears: "Kim! Kim?"

"Mairelon?" she said hazily through a pounding headache. "Oh, good, it worked."

"Thank God!" he said, and kissed her.

Kissing Mairelon was much nicer than she had ever dared to imagine, despite the headache. After much too short a time, he pulled away. "Kim, I—"

"I see you have decided to take my advice after all, Richard," Lady Wendall's amused voice said from somewhere above and behind him. "Marrying your ward is *exactly* the sort of usual scandal I had in mind; I wonder it didn't occur to me before."

"However, it is quite unnecessary for him to add to the talk by kissing her in public," Mrs. Lowe put in. "If he *must* indulge in vulgar behavior, it would be far better done after the notice of his engagement has appeared in the *Gazette*. And in private."

Mairelon looked up, plainly startled, and Kim's heart sank. Then his face went stiff, and her heart sank even further. "It was a momentary aberration, Aunt," he said in a colorless voice. "It won't happen again."

"I should like to think not," Mrs. Lowe said. "It is, perhaps, too much to hope that once you are married you will settle down, but Kim appears to have had at least a little success in keeping you out of trouble. Which is more than can be said for anyone else."

"You don't understand," Mairelon said dully. "Kim doesn't want to marry a toff."

Was that *what was bothering him?* "Well, of all the bacon-brained, sapskulled, squirish, buffle-headed nodcocks!" Kim said with as much indignation as she could muster. "I was talking about the *marquis*, not about *you!*"

Mairelon's eyes kindled. "Then you would?"

"You've whiddled it," Kim informed him.

As he kissed her again, she heard Mrs. Lowe murmur, "Mind your language, Kim," and Shoreham say in an amused tone, "Yes, Your Grace, I believe that was an affirmative answer."

"I'll send the notice to the *Gazette* tomorrow," Mairelon said when he finally came up for air. "No, today. Where's Hunch?"

Kim, feeling rather light-headed, leaned back on Mairelon's shoulder and looked around. Lady Wendall and Renée D'Auber were watching them with expressions that could only be described as smug; Prince Durmontov looked mildly bemused; the Duchesse Delagardie was smiling like a gleeful pixy; and the Lords Shoreham and Kerring were exchanging glances of enormous amusement. No one seemed to be either surprised of disapproving, not even Mrs. Lowe.

"In a minute, dear," Lady Wendall said to Mairelon. "And now that *that* is settled, perhaps you will let Kim explain the necessity for this interesting interruption. I confess, I do not understand it at all."

"Mannering!" Kim said. She tried to struggle to a sitting position, but gave up when her head began to swim. Apparently, the light-headedness hadn't just been an effect of kissing Mairelon. "He ain't piked off, has he?"

"Mannering?" Lord Shoreham frowned. "You don't mean to say you've located the confounded fellow! Where is he?"

"I believe he is currently on the lower stairs," Mrs. Lowe said. "Richard's man has him in charge, and I expect they will arrive momentarily."

"Aunt Agatha, you amaze me," Mairelon said. "How did you come to be, er, involved?"

"If you will assist Kim to one of the sofas, where she may be more comfortable, I am sure she will explain everything," Mrs. Lowe replied.

Mairelon promptly picked Kim up and carried her to the nearest seat. She did not protest; the headache was beginning to recede, but she still felt shaky and weak. Mairelon took the seat next to her so that he could put his arm around her, and she leaned gratefully into his shoulder. Lord Shoreham, Lord Kerring, and Prince Durmontov pulled up chairs for themselves and the ladies, and they all sat down and looked at Kim expectantly.

"Um," said Kim, trying to decide where to begin.

The doors at the far end opened and Hunch entered, dragging the still-bound-and-gagged Mannering. "Now what?" Lord Shoreham said.

"This 'ere is that Mannering fellow you been a-wanting," Hunch said, looking at Mairelon. "Kim says 'e's some kind of wizard. Where do you want me to put 'im?"

"The far corner will do nicely for the time being, Hunch," Lady Wendall said. "And perhaps you would remain to keep an eye on him for a few minutes? Thank you."

"Mannering." Lord Shoreham shook his head and looked back at Kim. "Where did you find him? And how?"

"I didn't," Kim said. "He found me. He got Tom Correy to send Matt with a message, and—"

"That message was from Mannering?" Mairelon's arm tightened around Kim.

Kim nodded. "He wanted me to nobble the de Cambriol book for him—at least, that's what he started with."

"Wait a minute," Lord Kerring said. "Who is this Mannering person? Yes, yes, I know he's tied up in the corner, but what does he have to do with this interruption? That's what I want to know."

"He's a moneylender, and he's the one behind the magic-draining spell on Mairelon," Kim said. "Only it isn't really a magic-draining spell; it's that one for sharing power, and he's kept it up for months."

"*C'est impossible!*" the duchesse exclaimed.

Renée D'Auber tilted her head to one side. "I think, me, that it will be altogether better if Mademoiselle Kim begins with the beginning and goes on without the interruptions. Or we will very likely still be sitting here tomorrow morning." Beside her, the prince nodded emphatically.

Shoreham laughed. "You are quite right, Mlle. D'Auber. Miss Merrill, if you would proceed?"

"I think it starts with Mannering and Lord Starnes," Kim said after considering for a moment. Taking a deep breath, she plunged into the story: how Starnes had offered Henri d'Armand's *livre de mémoire* to Mannering as part of his collateral for a loan; how Mannering must have found the power-sharing spell and persuaded one of the rookery hedge-wizards to cast it in English; how he had kept the spell going by continually adding new wizards to the linkage.

"Only he must have been running out of wizards," Kim said. "There aren't many real magicians in St. Giles or Covent Gardens. He'd have to find some new wizards to steal power from, or figure out some other way to keep the spell stable. That's why he was trying to steal the rest of the memory books—he thought one of them would tell him how to make the spell permanent."

"Why didn't he just release—oh, of course," Lord Shoreham said. "The rookery wizards would have torn him limb from limb the minute they got their magic back, if he'd tried to release the spell and start over."

Kim nodded. "And without the power-sharing spell, he isn't a wizard at all. He *couldn't* start over."

"And how did you come to learn all this?" Lord Shoreham asked mildly.

"He told me a lot of it himself." As rapidly as she could, Kim laid out the particulars of her visit with Mannering, and the conclusions she had drawn from his ramblings and boasts and threats. It took longer than she had expected, but eventually she finished.

"You took a terrible chance, taking Richard's place in the spell like that," Lady Wendall said. "Without preparation, and barely a year into your apprenticeship—the possible consequences don't bear thinking of."

"Well, it worked," Kim said practically as Mairelon's arm tightened around her once again. "And there wasn't time for anything else." She looked at Mairelon. "I'm just glad you didn't give me any real argument about getting out of the diagram."

Mairelon shrugged. "You'd obviously found out something new, and equally obviously thought it was urgent enough to interrupt. I trusted your judgment—though I might not have if I'd known you intended to take my place in the star!"

"Just as well you didn't, then," Kim said gruffly. Nobody had ever trusted her like that before . . . but then, Mairelon wasn't like anybody else.

"It certainly is," Lord Shoreham agreed. "We owe you rather a lot, Miss Merrill."

Kim's face grew hot, and she shook her head, unable to find words.

"Yes, of course," Lord Kerring said. "But now let's have a look at this Mannering fellow. I confess to a certain curiosity, after all the trouble he's caused." From the expression on his face, Lord Kerring expected his curiosity to be satisfied, one way or another, and he didn't much care what happened to Mannering in the process.

"Yes," said Renée. "That seems to me a most excellent idea."

But when the gag was removed from Mannering's mouth, it quickly became clear that he was wandering mentally in some other realm, where he ruled all wizards with an absolute power and even the King asked for his advice and help. After several fruitless efforts to get something sensible out of him, it was agreed that Lord Kerring and Lord Shoreham would convey him to the Royal College of Wizards, where Lord Shoreham could see that he was properly guarded while Lord Kerring and the duchesse studied the spell that linked him to Mairelon and the other wizards, in hopes of finding a way to undo it.

For the next two days, Mairelon paced the floor, waiting for news. Only the duchesse's strict instruction that he was not to interrupt—and the determined efforts of Lady Wendall and Kim—kept him at home. On the third day, Lord Kerring arrived without warning and carried Mairelon off, leaving Kim to be the one pacing and fretting.

But when Mairelon returned two hours later, it was plain from his expression that the duchesse and Kerring had succeeded in their efforts to return his magic, even before he bounded up the stairs and swung Kim off her feet in his exuberance.

"Put me down!" Kim said, grinning in spite of herself. "You want to break both our necks?"

"Nonsense!" Mairelon said, but he set her on her feet.

"I take it everything worked fine?" Kim asked, just to make him say it straight out.

"Perfectly," Mairelon assured her, and to prove it, he muttered a rapid phrase and made a string of bobbing fairy lights appear and circle their heads briefly.

"Good!" Kim said. She hesitated, then added, "What about Jemmy and Wags and the others? Are they going to be . . . all right, too?"

Mairelon's expression sobered. "Probably, but it will be a tricky business seeing to it. Kerring's been comparing Mannering's spell to a pile of jackstraws; they have to take it apart in exactly the right order, or the whole thing will collapse and damage everyone involved."

"How much time do they have to do the taking apart?"

"No more than a few weeks; if it isn't done by then, the spell will get so unstable that it will collapse anyway." Mairelon's expression was grim. "Shoreham is trying to round up as many of the rookery magicians as possible—dismantling the spell will be quicker and easier if they are present, and we don't want any more like Ma Yanger if we can help it."

Kim nodded soberly. Shoreham's men had found Ma the day before, in a back room at one of Mannering's warehouses. After a careful examination, all of the wizards had agreed that returning her magic to her would do nothing to restore her mind, nor were there other methods that might help her. Shoreham had set one of his men to arranging for her care; the costs would come out of Mannering's property.

"Shoreham will be by later this evening to see you," Mairelon added, studying his hands with an innocent air.

"To see me?" Kim looked at him suspiciously. "What for?"

"I believe he wants to offer you a job, of sorts."

"What sorts?"

"Much the same as the one I've been doing from time to time," Mairelon replied. "He, er, admires your initiative. And this is the second time you've gotten mixed up in some of his doings; I believe he'd be more comfortable if it were official."

Kim snorted. "That business with the Saltash Set was your doings, not Shoreham's, and so was this."

"Yes, well, Shoreham doesn't see it that way. But you needn't agree, if you'd rather not."

Kim paused, considering. "It sounds a lot more interesting than balls and teas and morning calls." Another thought struck her, and she looked at Mairelon. "Am I done with those, now that we're engaged?"

"The Season's only half over," Mairelon said. "But I suppose that if you'd really rather not—"

"Good!" Kim said emphatically. "Let's go tell your mother, quick, before she finishes that note she's writing to Renée D'Auber about going shopping tomorrow."

Mairelon looked suddenly wary. "I, er, believe she has something else in mind."

"No, she said I needed more gowns." Kim shook her head. "I have a wardrobe full of gowns already; what do I need more for?"

Mairelon pursed his lips and said nothing.

"Mairelon . . ."

"Well," he said in an apologetic tone, though his eyes were dancing, "we *are* getting married, you know."

"Oh, Lord," Kim said, appalled. "Bride-clothes! I'll be stuck at the dressmaker's *forever!*"

"Better you than me," said her unsympathetic bridegroom, and offered her his arm to escort her down to dinner.